In 1990, **Patricia Cornwell** sold her first novel, *Postmortem*, while working at the Office of the Chief Medical Examiner in Richmond, Virginia. An auspicious debut, it went on to win the Edgar, Creasey, Anthony, and Macavity Awards, as well as the French Prix du Roman d'Aventures – the first book ever to claim all these distinctions in a single year. Growing into an international phenomenon, the Scarpetta series won Cornwell the Sherlock Award for best detective created by an American author, the Gold Dagger Award, the RBA Thriller Award, and the Medal of Chevalier of the Order of Arts and Letters for her contributions to literary and artistic development.

Today, Cornwell's novels and iconic characters are known around the world. Beyond the Scarpetta series, Cornwell has written the definitive nonfiction account of Jack the Ripper's identity, cookbooks, a children's book, a biography of Ruth Graham, and three other fictional series based on the characters Win Garano, Andy Brazil, and Captain Calli Chase. Cornwell continues exploring the latest space-age technologies and threats relevant to contemporary life. Her interests range from the morgue to artificial intelligence and include visits to Interpol, the Pentagon, the U.S. Secret Service and NASA.

Cornwell was born in Miami. She grew up in Montreat, North Carolina, and now lives and works in Boston.

# ALSO BY PATRICIA CORNWELL

## SCARPETTA SERIES

*Identity Unknown*
*Unnatural Death*
*Livid*
*Autopsy*
*Chaos*
*Depraved Heart*
*Flesh and Blood*
*Dust*
*The Bone Bed*
*Red Mist*
*Port Mortuary*
*The Scarpetta Factor*
*Scarpetta*
*Book of the Dead*
*Predator*
*Trace*
*Blow Fly*
*The Last Precinct*
*Black Notice*
*Point of Origin*
*Unnatural Exposure*
*Cause of Death*
*From Potter's Field*
*The Body Farm*
*Cruel and Unusual*
*All That Remains*
*Body of Evidence*
*Postmortem*

## CAPTAIN CHASE SERIES

*Spin*
*Quantum*

## ANDY BRAZIL SERIES

*Isle of Dogs*
*Southern Cross*
*Hornet's Nest*

## WIN GARANO SERIES

*The Front*
*At Risk*

## NONFICTION

*Ripper: The Secret Life of*
    *Walter Sickert*
*Portrait of a Killer: Jack the*
    *Ripper—Case Closed*

## BIOGRAPHY

*Ruth, a Portrait: The Story of Ruth*
    *Bell Graham*

## OTHER WORKS

*Food to Die For: Secrets from*
    *Kay Scarpetta's Kitchen*
*Life's Little Fable*
*Scarpetta's Winter Table*

# PATRICIA CORNWELL

# SHARP FORCE

## A SCARPETTA NOVEL

Little, Brown

SPHERE

First published in the US in 2025 by Grand Central Publishing
an imprint of Hachette Book Group
First published in Great Britain in 2025 by Sphere

A CIP catalogue record for this book
is available from the British Library.

Hardback ISBN 978-1-4087-2259-6
Trade paperback ISBN 978-1-4087-2260-2

Printed and bound in Great Britain by Clays Ltd, Elcograf S.p.A.

Papers used by Sphere are from well-managed forests
and other responsible sources.

Sphere
An imprint of
Little, Brown Book Group
Carmelite House
50 Victoria Embankment
London EC4Y 0DZ

The authorised representative
in the EEA is
Hachette Ireland
8 Castlecourt Centre
Dublin 15, D15 XTP3, Ireland
(email: info@hbgi.ie)

An Hachette UK Company
www.hachette.co.uk

www.littlebrown.co.uk

*To Staci—*
*You make everything better…*
*And in memory of Charles Cornwell, 1939–2024.*
*You helped me get started in life.*

The past is never dead. It's not even past.

*—William Faulkner*

# SHARP FORCE

# CHAPTER 1

"**R**udolph the Red-Nosed Reindeer" rocks from the vintage boom box on a surgical cart. Before that it was Elvis crooning "Blue Christmas," and the Beach Boys harmonizing "Little Saint Nick," interspersed with local news and holiday blather.

Wiping my gloved hands on a towel, I'm changing the blade in my scalpel, alone at my stainless-steel workstation near the walk-in cooler's massive door. Up to my elbows in what the cops call a floater, I find the festive songs, jingles and breaking news on the verge of annoying.

*"...NORAD is tracking Santa as he makes his way around the globe tonight,"* the radio announces cheerily. *"We'll hope the big storm won't delay his deliveries! In other news, police are clueless about what happened to Rowdy O'Leary, his body recovered from the Potomac earlier this afternoon..."*

The latest update starts in again about the dead man on my table, decomposed beyond recognition, his soft tissue turned into soap after a week in the river. No doubt, he never intended to be an assault on the senses. He likely didn't mean to cause inconvenience and pain to anyone, most of all his wife and two young sons.

*"...The thirty-nine-year-old software designer was last seen fishing the night of December seventeenth just south of Mercy Island...,"*

1

the radio goes on. *"O'Leary's body was found nine miles from where it's believed he fell into the water..."*

X-rays on lightboxes show healed skeletal fractures, the bones bright white against the murky shapes of organs. I can make out prosthetic knee joints, and degenerative changes from old trauma. Living with chronic pain, Rowdy O'Leary had trouble walking.

*"...Alexandria police aren't saying if they suspect foul play in his mysterious disappearance and death..."*

Spaced across the room are three autopsy tables covered with his wet winter clothing and personal effects. Boots, socks, a hooded parka, jeans, a flannel shirt are spread out to dry on long sheets of brown paper.

*"...Commonwealth's attorney Bose Flagler is calling the case highly suspicious, demanding a thorough investigation..."*

The radio cuts to Flagler's syrupy voice as he talks about the heartbreak for the O'Leary family. How dreadful to lose a husband and father this time of year.

*"I won't rest until there are answers,"* he declares.

"Doctor Scarpetta?" Shannon Park pokes her head inside the autopsy suite.

My secretary's not about to come any closer, her Ugg-booted foot propping the door half open. I catch a glimpse of her purple overcoat and matching leather gloves, and a quilted pocketbook as big as a rucksack. Her red bucket hat is decorated with winking lights, plastic candy canes and sprigs of mistletoe.

"God, that's bloody awful!" she exclaims in her thick Irish brogue, covering her nose and mouth with her coat sleeve. "I don't know why you're doing it now. Seems it could have waited."

"Someone had to take care of him. And no, it couldn't wait." I raise my voice over Karen Carpenter's pitch-perfect "Merry Christmas, Darling."

"Bless his poor family," Shannon muffles, and maybe it's the stench stinging her eyes, but she seems about to cry.

I look up at the wall clock. It's 4:35.

"You should get on the road before the snow starts," I tell her.

"Bose Flagler keeps calling."

Talking behind her pocketbook, she won't look at the gutted body on my table, the skin marbled green, the top of the head sawn off.

"The media is ringing your phone off the hook." She stares down at the tile floor. "And Maggie Cutbush is demanding information as usual."

"Definitely no comment," I reply.

"As I keep telling everyone."

"Merry Christmas, Shannon."

"And to you and Benton. Safe travels tomorrow," she says, the door swinging shut.

Pulling down my face shield, I return to what I was doing. The brain is in terrible shape, disintegrating like wet tissue paper. Had I decided to leave the body in the cooler several days, the condition would have continued to deteriorate. It wouldn't be fair to anyone, most of all Rowdy O'Leary's wife and children.

Several hours ago, I was notified by police that the body was on the way here. I couldn't in good conscience walk out the door to start my vacation. I was the only one left who could do the autopsy. Most employees in my office and the forensic labs were gone by early afternoon because of the holiday and predicted bad weather.

I continue glancing up at the security video display on the wall across from my table. The late afternoon is volatile, thick clouds rolling in like a tarp. The parking lot is nearly empty, dead leaves skittering over pavement, trees shaking and shivering. Streetlights are bleary in the fog.

I watch Shannon on video as she emerges from the back of the building, the wind snatching at her coat, and I sense her anxiety. Hurrying to her pink Volkswagen Beetle, she holds on to her hat flashing red and green like a low-flying aircraft. She's glancing around as if someone monstrous might be hiding in the darkness, watching, waiting.

Fumbling her car key, she bends down, groping to pick it up, her attention everywhere, and I can imagine her swearing under her breath. She yanks open the driver's door, heaving her big pocketbook across the stick shift and into the passenger's seat. Locking herself in, she's glancing around frantically, and it's out of character.

A former court stenographer in her sixties, my secretary is no stranger to human nature's savagery. She's aware of what can happen when one least expects. There's little she's not seen and has always seemed fearless. But a serial killer dubbed the Phantom Slasher has gotten to her and a lot of people as he continues terrorizing Northern Virginia.

Shannon complains that she doesn't sleep well anymore. Living alone in a ground-level condo, she doesn't feel safe. She's talked about moving to a high-rise or leaving this area altogether. Installing a security system and deadbolts on doors, she keeps a Smith & Wesson "Ladysmith" revolver by her bed.

I watch her VW on the video display, the engine puttering, the headlights blinking on. Then she's driving through the security gate, taillights fading in the roiling grayness.

...*Better watch out, better not cry*...shrills the Jackson 5, and it's too late for that.

Rowdy O'Leary didn't watch out and died rather much the way he lived. Eating and drinking as he pleased, never exercising, chronically depressed. According to his wife, he was the *perfect package* until six years ago when he was struck by a car while jogging at night.

"A hit-and-run, whoever did it never caught," Reba O'Leary said to me over the phone before I began the postmortem. "After that a light went out inside Rowdy. He gave up."

———

I'm dropping sections of liver into the plastic bucket by my feet when the vintage wall phone begins to clangor. The black push-button model is decades old, the handset cradled by a metal hook that you push down to hang up, reminding me of my childhood.

The long cord is always hopelessly snarled, a sign taped to cinder block demanding *Clean Hands Only*. There's no caller ID, and I won't be able to see who it is. But not many people have this number. Those who do aren't likely to interrupt autopsies in progress.

An exception is Pete Marino, a former homicide detective I've worked with most of my career. He's now my head of investigations for the statewide medical examiner system. He's also married to my sister, Dorothy, making him family. That gives him extra privileges, at least in his mind.

He doesn't hesitate to intrude no matter the circumstances or the hour. Taking off my gloves, I toss them into the trash. Turning off the boom box, I flip up my face shield, pulling down my surgical mask, the stench so intense it seems to discolor the air.

I pick up the handset, pressing it against my ear. "Doctor Scarpetta," I answer.

"Hate to bother you. I know it's a bad time to talk," Marino says.

I can tell he's inside his big pickup truck, the police scanner quietly chattering while he listens to a Megyn Kelly podcast. I catch the edge of her saying something about the CIA and how to know if someone's lying.

"You're supposed to be home, Marino." I'm breathing with my mouth, not my nose. "And yes, it's a bad time."

"We've got a sensitive situation," he announces. "And I'm on my way to help Fruge out."

"Why would you need to meet with a police investigator on Christmas Eve?" I ask suspiciously. "You're off for the holiday."

"My presence has been specifically requested by the complainant at the scene."

He has a habit of talking in police jargon when he knows I won't approve of whatever it is he's decided.

"You've lost me," I reply, and it's not fair what he's doing.

"We're following up on something from Dana Diletti that could be important," Marino says, and the celebrity TV journalist is rather much the bane of my existence. "She has a tip about the Phantom Slasher cases. It sounds like something's happened that's got her pretty shook up."

"Careful. She's not known for being trustworthy." I shouldn't have to remind him.

"What she says she witnessed sounds credible, Doc."

"Credible to whom?" I ask.

"Point being, it's not hearsay."

"What isn't?" I'm trusting this less every second.

"It's to be expected that the Slasher would know who Dana Diletti is and watch her on TV as she talks about him," he reasons.

"Is she the one saying this, Marino? Or are you?"

"We can expect the Slasher to follow everything in the media.

He gets off on being headline news while scaring the crap out of everybody with his fake ghost."

Marino's referring to a computer-generated hologram the Slasher uses to stalk and terrorize his victims. Knocking out the Wi-Fi with signal jammers, he invades homes undetected, leaving no fingerprints or DNA. We're no closer to catching him.

"What's the tip?" I ask, and it had better be legitimate.

I imagine my sister home on Christmas Eve while Marino is out with the cops, his favorite place to be if he's honest about it. Which he's not. A sexually violent psychopath is on the loose, a dangerous storm barreling in, and Dorothy is by herself. I wouldn't blame her for being hurt and furious.

"I'm on my way to Dana Diletti's house," Marino continues to explain. "She requested me and Fruge by name."

*I'm sure she did.*

"Do we know what the tip is?" I again ask.

"We won't be told until we're face-to-face," he explains.

"How convenient. Hopefully her film crew won't be waiting when you and Fruge roll up. And I hate that you left Dorothy by herself." I go ahead and say it as something darts past my Tyvek-bootie-covered feet.

A tiny gray field mouse stops and starts, zigzagging about, and I assume it's the same one that Marino nicknamed Pinky. Several days ago, the presumed Pinky visited my second-floor office after I'd left an unfinished chef's salad on my desk.

He's been sighted in the breakroom, various storage areas, hiding behind corn plants in the lobby, evading all catch-and-release efforts. Now he's staring at me with shiny dark eyes, whiskers twitching.

"Our visitor is back," I tell Marino. "He just scampered by. Now he's looking at me."

"Pinky?"

"Unless we have more than one mouse."

"Maybe while Fabian's on call tonight he'll finally catch him. But don't throw the little fella out the door into the cold. He won't survive."

"Wouldn't think of it."

"Doc, you should be heading home before the storm lands."

"As soon as I finish what I'm doing." I glance at Rowdy O'Leary's body on my table, grateful his loved ones will never see him like this. "Then I have a stop along the way to drop off personal effects to the family."

"Say what?"

I repeat myself.

"Why not send the stuff UPS like we always do?" Marino's tone has turned disapproving.

"That's a tough package to find on your doorstep, especially during the holiday season," I explain as the mouse vanishes under a cabinet. "The O'Leary family lives off King Street on South Payne. I practically go right past."

"That's mighty nice of you, Doc." Marino doesn't want me doing it. "But no way you should. You don't know these people."

"I'm thinking of the wife and two young boys he left behind. It's Christmas Eve."

"Yeah, I know. It sucks. It always does."

"A perfect occasion for a little extra kindness. And I have questions that might help me determine her husband's manner of death. When you show up in person, it's easier to get someone to talk..."

"It's not a good idea to be doing something like that alone, Doc."

"If I don't figure out why he's dead, I'll have to sign him out as undetermined. I don't want to do that—" I'm saying when Marino cuts me off.

"Got to go. I'm pulling into Dana Diletti's driveway. And holy shit, she's got her place decorated like a tacky tour, lights strung everywhere."

He sounds wonderstruck, almost happy.

"The Grinch, Frosty the Snowman, Snoopy and his doghouse," Marino marvels. "All kinds of amazing stuff that's probably going to blow away in the storm. Happy to report there's no sign of her film crew."

"Glad to hear it, and where's Fruge?"

"Right behind me."

"Please keep me informed," I reply, dropping the handset in its cradle.

# CHAPTER 2

I turn up the volume on the boom box, and the music has given way to more news updates, nothing good. Holiday travel is at an all-time high as the fierce storm rolls in from Canada. The governor is asking Virginians to stay off the roads.

An intoxicated teenager rammed his car into a police motorcycle. Meals on Wheels is asking for volunteers and contributions, food insecurity at an all-time high. A local research lab reports that three monkeys have escaped.

*"...Jane and Kong were quickly captured. Their buddy Peanut is still at large. We're assured there's no danger of him spreading diseases like monkeypox..."* the radio news goes on.

Then Keith Urban is strumming and sweetly singing "I'll Be Your Santa Tonight" as I work my hands into clean gloves, picking up where I left off before Marino called. I place the enlarged heart into the hanging scale, saving it for last. I'm all but certain it has important things to tell me.

Grabbing a long-bladed knife, I begin slicing on my cutting board. I squeeze water from a sponge over sections, and the thickened muscle of the myocardium shows old transmural ventricular scars. The right coronary artery is completely occluded with calcified atherosclerotic plaque that crunches as I cut through it.

I imagine Rowdy O'Leary sitting in his folding chair on the pier fishing in the glow of a camping lantern, a cooler of beer next to him. At some point, he probably experienced sudden chest pain. It may have radiated to his arms, back and jaw. He might have gotten dizzy and nauseous before collapsing and toppling into the water fully clothed with his boots on.

When police arrived at his fishing spot after his wife reported him missing, they discovered his iPhone and five-shot Colt .38 revolver on the pier as if dropped there. Two spent cartridge cases in the cylinder indicate the handgun was fired twice. Possibly, this happened at an earlier time and is unrelated to his death. But I doubt it.

My preoccupations are interrupted by the buzzer blaring over the intercom, alerting me that we have company. In the video display, a hearse waits to enter the vehicle bay, the engine rumbling in the background. I can see flakes of snow blowing in the glow of streetlamps.

"Peace Brothers," the driver announces himself in the squawk box. "Here for a pickup."

The massive rolling door lurches to life, retracting with a lot of loud creaking and clanking. The noises are amplified as they bounce off concrete and metal. The hearse roars inside, exhaust swirling, the dark parking lot and smudges of streetlights showing in the huge square opening.

I watch Wyatt Earle on the live video feed as he hurries down the stretcher ramp. Striding with purpose past pallets of PPE and jugs of formalin, he looks ominous in his dark blue uniform, a pistol on his duty belt. I'm still getting used to my security officers being armed.

I've wanted better protection here for years, and now it's the law. Certain state employees are expected to carry guns on the job. That's both good and bad depending on who we're talking about. Not everyone should be armed, and I don't like politicians deciding for me when I need a concealed weapon.

Wyatt speaks to the funeral home attendant, their voices picked up by security camera microphones, the acoustics terrible. It's hard to understand what they're saying, but clearly the attendant is in a hurry. Several times he mentions that it's Christmas Eve and he has young children. He's visibly annoyed as he's told to stay put.

Wyatt needs to "check with the chief" on whether Rowdy O'Leary's body is ready for release. The attendant shrugs unhappily as Wyatt walks away, looking at something on his phone. Whatever's caught his interest, his attention is riveted. He almost trips over a pressure washer hose. A few minutes later, he's in my doorway.

"You don't want to come inside," I warn.

"The funeral home is here for him." Wyatt holds a surgical mask over his lower face.

I notice him returning a Vicks inhaler to his pants pocket. At least I've cured him of swiping the ointment version into his nostrils. All it does is trap the molecules of putrefaction. Wyatt doesn't like the morgue and can be squeamish.

"I'm almost finished." I glance up at the hearse on the security monitor.

"Dana Diletti's on TV claiming she saw the ghost from the Slasher murders," Wyatt informs me. "It's all over the news."

I wonder if Marino and Fruge are still with her. I don't trust Dana Diletti, never have. I hope to hell she's not creating a spectacle that could impact my office. Not to mention interfering with an investigation, something she does regularly and with no compunction.

"What is she saying?" I stoop down to remove the plastic bag of sectioned organs and other tissue from the bucket under my table.

"She said the ghost floated through her window." Wyatt looks away as I place the bag inside the empty chest cavity.

"Well, she didn't waste any time going public about it." I cut a long section of cotton twine from the dispenser on a countertop.

"She took a video with her phone, and the ghost looks real," Wyatt reports as I thread a large surgical needle.

"I'm not sure what a *real* ghost looks like," I reply.

"You'll see when you watch the video I just sent you."

"Let's be mindful that what she and others have described isn't a ghost." I begin suturing the Y-incision. "Think of it as movie special effects. A computer-generated optical illusion, a hologram."

Wyatt's forehead is sweating, his eyes miserable. I'm used to the stench. He isn't and never will be.

"Has Fabian come in yet?" I ask with long sweeps of the needle and twine.

"He's with Faye." Wyatt stares at the ceiling.

Firearms examiner Faye Hanaday typically works late whenever Fabian does. They stay in the on-call room, tiny but cozy with a sofa bed, a TV, a kitchenette.

"Please let him know I saw the mouse again." I pick up the skull cap.

Fitting it back in place, I line up the notch I made with the Stryker saw.

"Okay." Wyatt has closed the door most of the way, peering through the gap.

"Why don't you go upstairs, relax and have a coffee?" I suggest. "No need for you to be down here right now. I'll deal with the funeral home."

"Thank you, Chief. Merry Christmas." He can't leave fast enough.

———

A half hour later, Rowdy O'Leary's double-pouched remains have been driven away in the Peace Brothers hearse. The vehicle bay door clanks shut as I return to the intake area with its wall of shiny steel cooler and freezer doors.

Pulling off my PPE, I drop it into the biohazard trash near the floor scale. The security office is empty behind bulletproof glass, and I imagine Wyatt upstairs somewhere. He's been working here for more than twenty years. As much as he dislikes the morgue, I've never understood why he stays.

My sneakers are quiet on the white tile floor as I follow the corridor, noticing speckles of dried blood that nobody bothered mopping up. Pale green cinder block walls are chipped and scuffed, the ceiling water-stained. Walking past the CT scanner and x-ray rooms, I unlock my phone to check on my husband.

"On my way out of here shortly," I tell him when he answers. "Where are you?"

"Just leaving the CIA finally. No surprise that traffic's a nightmare on Four-Ninety-Five," Benton replies, and I can hear loud engines and horns blaring in the background.

A forensic psychologist for the U.S. Secret Service, he's been in meetings much of the day at the Central Intelligence Agency. Their Langley headquarters is some twenty miles from where we live. In this part of the world, that can take forever.

"I was tied up longer than expected. We've been looking at the video Dana Diletti posted all over the internet," Benton is saying.

"What's the CIA's interest?" I ask.

"The technology the Slasher's using. It's over-the-top sophisticated. They're concerned about who might have the wherewithal to use holograms for spying."

"As are the rest of us."

"The worry is it's someone with an intelligence background," Benton says.

"Maybe one of their own who washed out of the Agency and went rogue," I suggest.

"Or former military special ops," Benton proposes. "Or a sophisticated software designer who works with sensitive technologies."

"I'm about to watch Dana Diletti's video." I walk past the locker room, nobody inside. "Do we think it's a hoax?"

"Lucy's been analyzing it, says it looks genuine."

My niece is a cyber special agent and technical expert for the FBI. Like Benton and me, she's been on the Phantom Slasher task force since the serial killer first struck ten months ago during the early hours of Valentine's Day. The victim was a psychiatric nurse living alone not far from here in Annandale.

A CCTV camera captured a ghostly figure in old-fashioned black clothing floating along the street in front of her house. The same holographic projection was observed early in the morning on Mother's Day when a social worker was slashed to death in Fairfax. Then it happened again two months ago on Halloween, the victim a diversity counselor in Arlington.

Weeks before their brutal deaths, the women had complained of feeling watched. They reported peculiar things going on. Area dogs would start barking frantically after midnight. Something would knock on a window, but nothing was there. They claimed to hear a voice and eerie music softly playing with no apparent source of it.

"The storm front's moving in from the northwest, so it's already started snowing here at a pretty good clip," Benton is saying over the phone. "Roads are getting slick, people having accidents, and you can imagine the traffic. I think I've moved three feet in the last fifteen minutes. You may get home before I do."

"I'm afraid there won't be time to make lasagna and everything else I'd planned." I walk past the dark windows of the histology lab. "Hope you won't mind if we keep it simple."

"Whatever you make is always delicious. And we can stay up as late as we want," Benton says. "All we've got to do tomorrow is show up at the airport."

We end the call as I detect a Chopin nocturne drifting from the anthropology lab, a cramped cinder block space warehousing our coldest cases. Bright piano notes sound from a portable CD player that Cate Kingston carries with her when she visits our office to help with skeletal remains.

A forensic anthropologist, she's on the faculty of the University of Virginia. Her input is sought in cases ranging from Civil War remains to dinosaur bones to giant footprints from a Sasquatch. She's often hired as an expert witness in murder investigations and trials.

She doesn't notice that I've paused in the doorway. Peering into a microscope, she moves a bone around on the stage, her attractive young face troubled. She mentioned today at our office Christmas lunch that she's working on another disinterment from the ancient cemetery on Mercy Island, the location of an old psychiatric hospital.

Paper-covered tables are arranged with a skull and a scattering of bones and teeth. She's placed them in the correct anatomical positions like puzzles missing most of their pieces. Swatches of rotting fabric on a second paper-covered table are remnants of the blue wool blanket once wrapped around the body.

On shelves are tall stacks of creamy archival boxes neatly labeled, each one a person waiting to be called by name. Tiny plastic skeletons caper on walls around the room. Some glow in the dark, and it's disconcerting to walk past the observation window when the lab's lights are out.

"Merry Christmas." I hail Cate from the doorway, and she looks up, startled. "Didn't mean to scare you."

"I was lost in my thoughts as usual." She gets up from her chair.

"You're here late compared to everyone else. Almost the only one left." I walk inside.

"I was just this minute thinking of calling you." She wears a baggy white lab coat with *Dr. Kingston* embroidered over the pocket. "But before I get to the bad news, I hope you and Benton have a wonderful time overseas."

"Thank you, but right now I'm worried about you getting home," I reply. "When was the last time you looked outside?"

"I don't have the luxury very often," she says with a sigh. "I know we're expecting a whopper of a storm."

"It will be far worse in Charlottesville, and I don't like you driving there after dark on any occasion." I'm inspecting the bones on her table. "Much less Christmas Eve with snow and sleet predicted. The winds are already picking up, the visibility dropping."

As I hear myself, I'm reminded of what Lucy calls me, *Dr. Worst-Case Scenario.*

"I'm not going to Charlottesville, am staying in Old Town with a friend." She turns down the music. "This case I'm working on from Mercy Island?" She indicates the bones I'm looking at. "Not good. Not good at all."

"More of the same?" I'm not surprised.

"Afraid so, only more vicious and problematic," she says. "The bones are nowhere near as old as the other ones from there. That's what really has me going."

Cate explains that the remains are a female likely in her twenties when buried on the grounds of Mercy Psychiatric Hospital here in Alexandria. Not long before I moved back to Virginia, a real estate developer decided the cemetery on the grounds should relocate to a churchyard. Otherwise, the valuable waterfront land couldn't be used to build a fitness center.

Graves were dug up with a backhoe, archaeologists not involved when they should have been. Descendants of the deceased weren't asked and had no idea this was happening. If I'd been chief then, I wouldn't have permitted it.

But my predecessor Elvin Reddy is friends with the hospital's director. The cemetery was an eyesore mostly ignored and over-grown in the woods close to the Potomac's shoreline. The land was worth a fortune, and the cemetery wasn't used anymore, hadn't been for a hundred years. Elvin was happy to cooperate, the out-come disastrous.

Many of the coffins had rotted away, the bones completely gone or in terrible shape. Those relatively intact ended up here in the anthropology lab to be stored in boxes and ignored. Until we can confirm identity and how the people died, they can't have proper burials.

I took over the Virginia medical examiner system five years ago, and one of my many projects is clearing out the backlog of unfin-ished cases, including those from Mercy Island. Cate has been com-ing in these past few weeks while the University of Virginia is on Christmas break.

She's discovering evidence of trauma that gives a harrowing view at what patients endured during earlier centuries. Shattered skulls and limbs suggest some may have died from falls or chronic beatings. A fracture to the C2 spine was consistent with death by hanging.

At least one patient was shot, the lead bullet still inside the skull. The former Mercy Lunatic Asylum was a dark stain on psychiatry, and the modern version isn't much better as far as I'm concerned.

# CHAPTER 3

"I'm just getting started on Jane Doe, and she's definitely a homicide." Cate Kingston continues to fill me in.

"We have no idea about her identity?" I ask.

"None."

"Maybe forensic genealogical DNA will show a relationship with someone in an ancestral database." I can only hope.

"As you know, samples from every Mercy Island case were sent to the lab in Massachusetts months ago," Cate reminds me with a note of frustration. "We should have had the results long before now. But truth be told, I've not checked in a while. I'll give them a call before I leave to see if there's any news."

"Was her grave marked?"

"Just a block of granite carved with the number thirty-three," she says. "It correlates with a seventy-eight-year-old male patient who died in eighteen-ninety from consumption. I'm waiting on his DNA too."

"And these remains certainly aren't male. Or from someone that old." I'm looking at them on the paper-covered table.

"It would appear the young woman was buried, and the marker was removed from the man's grave and placed on top of hers," Cate theorizes.

"Oh boy. I don't like the implication."

"Exactly. The murdered female isn't accounted for in the cemetery records I've been reviewing. She didn't exist." Cate picks up a rib, showing me a cut in the medial end.

Putting on gloves, I find a magnifying lens, making out the clean edges left by a sharp blade.

"Looks like she was stabbed in the chest," I tell her.

"And she has a cut to the left ulna," Cate goes on.

"Possibly from holding up her arm defensively."

"Also, two cuts to her skull."

She picks it up, toothless, the empty eye sockets staring.

"This one on the left side of the mandible. The other on the right side of the forehead." She shows me. "A lot of her ribs and other bones are missing, scattered by the backhoe. Likely, she had many more injuries. Someone really did a number on her."

"All this should have been noticed at the time of the disinterment. But as we've been finding with the other bones you've examined, nobody bothered to look." I think again of the former chief medical examiner Elvin Reddy.

When unidentified bodies or bones were found during his twenty-year tenure, he didn't bring in the appropriate experts unless it suited him. He wasn't interested in who the victims were or their stories beyond any political or financial implications.

Cate picks up a femur stained by clay and in better shape than I'd expect. I take it from her, feeling the weight of it, noting the relatively smooth surface. The marrow is mostly gone, and I find it perplexing that there's any left at all.

"The sharp force injuries were to green bone," Cate says. "She was alive or barely dead when she sustained them."

"And we know carbon dating won't work." I return the femur to her. "The bones aren't old enough for that."

"We can do nitrogen and protein analysis," she suggests. "It might give us further information on how long she'd been buried. Assuming genealogical DNA doesn't give us the answer."

"Maybe we'll get lucky and can reconnect her with descendants, anyone she might be related to," I reply.

"It sure would be nice if we could get our hands on old hospital records, assuming she was a patient on Mercy Island," Cate says.

"Forget it." I take off my gloves. "I can't even get them to give us records when a patient dies now. We're lucky they provided a list of who's buried in the cemetery and supposedly why."

"Well, some family out there knows this lady disappeared, never to be found." She stares down at the bones. "What's going to happen when this becomes public, Doctor Scarpetta? Doesn't matter how long ago it happened; the hospital's reputation will be in the toilet."

"It already is if you ask me," I reply. "It's probably best we keep this quiet until you've finished your examination. And we get the genealogical DNA results."

"Oh dear. That's going to be hard," she says, a shadow crossing her face.

*She's already talked.*

"Who knows besides me?" I ask.

"Maggie Cutbush has an idea," Cate says after a pause.

"How did that happen?" I don't let my outrage register.

"When she was here earlier today dropping off Christmas presents," Cate explains. "The big tins of popcorn for us and the labs."

Apparently, Maggie stopped by to wish Cate a happy holiday, noticing the skeletal remains on her table. But that's not why my former secretary showed up. As usual, she was on the prowl, looking to stick her nose where it doesn't belong. Most times when that happens, someone has put her up to it.

"She said she'd heard a rumor that I was finding something interesting," Cate explains.

"A rumor from whom?"

"I don't know," she replies. "But she said the Department of Emergency Prevention must be kept updated about cases going on in the medical examiner system. For demographic and epidemiological reasons. She kept reminding me it's the law."

"Yes, that's what she tells everyone," I reply. "Governor Dare in her infinite wisdom created the Department of Emergency Prevention and appointed Maggie Cutbush and Elvin Reddy to run what's nothing more than a pork barrel bureaucracy if I ever saw one. But don't quote me."

"I understand." Cate looks worried.

"We have to live with their useless agency," I add. "But we don't cooperate when it interferes with our patients. I don't care how long they've been dead. The investigation comes first."

"Oh dear," Cate again says.

"How much did you tell Maggie?"

"Pretty much what I told you."

"I'm sure she was quite interested," I reply blandly as I think, *Dear God.*

"She wanted to know how many other Mercy Island patients from long ago appear to have died violently."

"Does anybody else have a clue what we've started finding?" I ask, and she hesitates again.

"Well, Bose Flagler always wants to know what I'm working on.

I figure since he's the commonwealth's attorney, he has a right to know..." Cate looks at me. "I hope I didn't create a mess, Doctor Scarpetta."

"There isn't much you can do when it's Flagler," I reply. "But Maggie's another story."

"How am I supposed to handle it when she shows up claiming her department has a right to information about whatever I'm working on?"

"Refer her to me. We have a long history." A most unpleasant one, but I'm not going to say that either. "Have a Merry Christmas, Cate. Stay safe."

"You too." She cranks up the CD player's volume as I leave.

A waltz is playing now, fading in a minor key.

---

I round a bend in the corridor, the EXIT sign ahead glowing red. Pushing through the metal fire door, I begin watching the Dana Diletti video that Wyatt emailed.

The TV journalist is scantily clad in stretchy workout shorts, a sports bra and socks that flaunt her stunning beauty when wearing no makeup or much else. She explains that she was on the Nordic Track in her bedroom late afternoon when the Phantom Slasher's hologram levitated through a window.

"...*Passing through the glass like it was air without triggering the alarm or anything else. I had earbuds in, listening to tunes when it happened...*" she's saying.

I've paused on the stairs to watch as she paces in her living room gaudy with Christmas baubles and lights. She passes a lighted showcase displaying her many broadcasting awards, including several Emmys.

*"...I had no forewarning at all, making it all the more shocking..."*

Glowing in the background like a nuclear power plant is a tall aluminum Christmas tree that looks spun of silvery glass. It's over-decorated with ornaments and lights, brightly wrapped presents piled underneath.

*"...Suddenly this horrible ghost was right in front of me..."*

She strolls by electric candles and caroling figurines on the mantel. An illuminated Santa and his reindeer appear to be flying off a shelf.

*"...Enough to give someone a heart attack, let me tell you..."*

An elaborate nativity scene centers the mirrored-top coffee table, and a mobile of dancing elves twirls from the ceiling. Multiple poinsettias are placed about, probably artificial like everything else.

*"...So, now we're getting an idea what the Slasher's victims experienced before he broke in, butchering them in their own beds..."*

As she's saying this, I think how foolish. It almost seems she's goading the violent psychopath, daring him to show up and do to her what he's done to others.

*"...Just watch. I swear this is real..."*

She plays the recording she made with her phone, the phantom-like hologram outfitted in a black frock coat and hat from an earlier century. Waving a big Bowie knife, he hovers in front of her, his face chalky white, his eyes neon red. He moves his mouth, repeatedly hissing *"death becomes you,"* his teeth vampirish.

Dana Diletti goes on to mention Blaise Fruge and Pete Marino responding to her house. As I suspected, the TV news star is giving validity to her story by including them in the narrative as if my office and the Alexandria Police Department are working closely with her.

*"...I'm cooperating fully with officials, and they're encouraging*

*me to relocate. But that's not happening, folks...*" Dana is saying when my phone starts ringing, my niece calling.

"I'm in the stairwell and might lose you," I tell Lucy right off. "As soon as I clean up, I'm heading home. Where are you?"

"Quantico inside the OTD," she says in my earpiece. "Had planned on heading out long before now, but no bueno."

Since Lucy started working for the FBI, she spends much of her time at their training academy and labs in Quantico. Her office is inside a top-secret area of the Operational Technology Division, the OTD as we refer to it.

"I won't be home for a while either," I tell her as I climb the stairs. "Have to clean up first. Then I've got a quick stop to make along the way."

"You shouldn't be stopping anywhere. The snow's already sticking, the wind gusting at more than thirty knots. Not to mention we have a serial killer on the loose who's playing games with us, doing everything he can to cause a public panic."

"I need to deliver something to a family. A mother and two little kids." I tell her which case.

"Not a good idea for you to drop off anything. We're talking about complete strangers," she disapproves. "At least take Marino with you."

"He's busy and not here," I reply, and Lucy is just as stubborn as I am. "I'm hoping you're still on for dinner with Benton and me."

"It's not looking good," she says.

"I was afraid that might be the case with all that's going on." I don't let on how disappointed I am. "It worries me that your mom is home alone. She left me a message a few hours ago, saying she didn't want to join us and stay over."

"I just talked to her before calling you, and she's well into the Chablis, watching an old movie."

"After my errand I can stop and pick her up?" I again offer, my feet quietly scuffing on the concrete steps. "Are we sure we can't change her mind?"

"She doesn't want to venture out in the bad weather." Lucy repeats what Dorothy told me in a voice mail. "She's worn out from all her social media influencing and podcasting, yada-yada-yada."

"That's not the real reason," I reply.

"I suspect she and Marino have been having their usual fireworks. Not the fun kind," Lucy adds.

"I just watched the video of the Slasher's hologram that Dana Diletti claims to have recorded inside her bedroom." I unlock the heavy metal door opening onto the second floor. "Benton says you think it's credible."

"It is," Lucy says as I follow the corridor, my corner office at the far end of it.

"Are we sure it's not some sort of publicity stunt on her part as usual, her way of inserting herself into the drama?"

"It's not looking like that's the case this time," Lucy explains. "We're doing forensics on the video that's now all over the internet thanks to her. People are freaking out as you'd expect, which is a shame. Causing more of a panic doesn't help anything."

"We both know she doesn't give a damn who she hurts," I remark, the staff offices I pass empty and dark.

# CHAPTER 4

The breakroom is ahead, and I smell coffee brewing. I hear Wyatt on his phone, chatting to a funeral home delivering a suicide I was informed about earlier. *Jeopardy!* plays on TV, the microwave oven beeping.

Lucy explains in my earpiece that she's been going through Dana Diletti's hologram video frame by frame. The red-eyed apparition is the same projection that's been spotted and caught on security cameras in the first three Slasher murders.

"Dana's video wasn't copied off the internet," Lucy says as I reach the end of the corridor. "I'm not seeing anything to make me think her clip was edited."

"Then the hologram really did appear inside her bedroom? The Phantom Slasher projected it in there?" I unlock my office door, flipping on the lights. "That's an awful thought. An extremely disturbing one."

"Yeah, it is." Lucy's voice is somber.

"Dana Diletti should be very concerned."

"Yeah, she should be," Lucy says. "So far, when someone's been visited by the hologram, that person ends up dead. It would seem the Slasher is stalking Dana, starting in on her the way he has with his other victims. And unfortunately, she's enjoying all the attention from it instead of focusing on what it means."

"She needs to get out of that house and stay someplace safe." I'm moving window to window closing the shades. "But instead, she's going to exploit the situation for publicity, for her damn ratings."

"The Slasher's addicted to the spectacles he causes," Lucy says. "The more attention he gets, the more he wants it. And as Benton has pointed out repeatedly, the violence is escalating."

I've paused in front of bookcases crowded with medical and legal tomes, many of them old and filled with my notations.

"And who better to give him more attention, right?" Lucy adds over speakerphone.

I pick up the spray bottle of distilled water from a shelf.

"He projects his hologram through the bedroom window," she goes on, "and what do you think Dana's going to do?"

"She's going to talk about it on TV. And probably end up on all the big shows, maybe win another award or two." I'm spritzing my orchids, the areca palm, the fiddle-leaf fig tree. "I hope the police are telling her not to stay in her house anymore until the Slasher is caught. I hope Marino and Fruge told her that."

"She's bragging about not letting a serial killer or anyone else chase her from her home. Especially not on Christmas Eve," Lucy says as I pluck off dead blossoms and leaves, dropping them in the trash. "And of course, she's making a big thing about the difficulties of being a *major celebrity,* and how stressful it is to be stalked."

"She's acting just plain stupid." I walk into my office bathroom and shut the door.

As I begin undressing, I tell Lucy what Cate Kingston was explaining to me a few minutes ago.

"A female in her twenties was murdered, but we don't know when," I explain. "Unlike the other graves from the old Mercy Island asylum, there's no record of who this person might have been."

"And it sounds like someone went to the trouble to move a grave marker," Lucy says. "Giving the impression it was a hospital burial. When maybe it wasn't."

"That's what I'm thinking." I drop my scrubs on the floor.

Lucy explains that she can use AI to search satellite images and those from open-source platforms. Possibly, we can find before and after images of the cemetery and determine when the marker was moved. That would tell us when the victim was buried there.

"Maybe her death wasn't all that long ago," Lucy suggests.

"It's hard to tell," I reply. "She wasn't in a coffin and would have skeletonized quickly depending on the time of year and soil conditions. But based on what I just saw in the anthropology lab, the remains certainly weren't in the ground a century or more. The bones are more recent. I hate to think how recent they might be."

Lucy says she'll let me know what she finds in data searches, and we end the call. I finish undressing, and as I move about, I catch a whiff of Rowdy O'Leary, my olfactory glands more sensitive than I often wish. The stench lingers deep in my sinuses, some of it remembered or imagined.

I spray my scrubs with Lysol, stuffing them into a big black garbage bag that I tightly tie. On my way out of the building, I'll drop off my dirty laundry in the morgue for the industrial washer and dryer. Some things I'm not going to send to the cleaners. I learned long ago that odors are persistent.

I might not always notice what lingers like an invisible contrail, but other people will. During my forensic pathology residency when I performed my first medico-legal autopsies, I learned the hard way that death is all too happy to follow me. I remember strangers moving away from me in the post office, the grocery store.

Stepping into the shower, I shut the glass door, and the hot water feels wonderful raining down as I wash and condition my hair. Brushing my teeth, I hold my face up to steamy spray that smells like lavender. I scrub every inch of me until I don't imagine the stench anymore.

Drying off, I turn on the exhaust fan, the mirror patched with condensation, my reflection deconstructed like a Picasso painting. A blue eye. A clump of wet blond hair. An ear above the curve of a strong jaw. I find clean lingerie in my locker, dressing in the outfit I wore to work this morning.

The dark green pantsuit, red silk blouse and black suede boots with a sensible heel were my attempt at being festive. I treated my staff to a lunch of takeout barbecue and fresh lemonade. We exchanged small but thoughtful gifts. Candy, liquor, books that are recommended reading. I gave out unfiltered olive oil I order from Sicily.

As I leave the bathroom, I put on my computer-assisted "smart" ring that pesters me about everything I do wrong. High on the list is not sleeping or exercising enough. I'm also nagged about stress, and that causes more of it. Whenever the ring sends another audible alert, I appreciate it about as much as a cattle prod.

I turn on the flat-screen TV across from the bookcases to monitor the local news. I mute the sound, the captions showing as Dana Diletti's video of the ghostlike hologram plays. She's talking about it nonstop on TV, cutting to a clip of her interviewing me weeks ago after the most recent murder on Halloween.

"...Her cause of death was exsanguination due to sharp force injury..."

I glance at the caption crawling by as I go on to warn about "smart" homes where everything is wireless. Should an intruder knock out the Wi-Fi with a signal jammer as the Phantom Slasher does, the victim has no alarm system, no camera, no phone signal.

"... *Critical to have at least one landline, especially for the security system,*" I said.

My clip is followed by the news anchor talking about traffic and power outages. Also, after-Christmas sales, and a rash of burglaries in Falls Church. I glance up at an interview from earlier today when a scientist named Duke Mansoni talked about three monkeys escaping from the Primal Biodynamics research lab close to my house.

Next to it is the recycling center where I make regular visits with a trunk full of bottles, cans and flattened cardboard boxes. I've caught glimpses of Duke Mansoni and other scientists when I've driven past their lab and its wooded tract of land that's caged in by metal fencing. Mansoni advises that Peanut is still at large.

"He's friendly, fond of people and extremely intelligent," the scientist is saying. "But he's a powerful animal and potentially deadly if he feels threatened..."

Sitting down at my desk, I look through notes I made downstairs, the paper forms damp from disinfectant. I dictate the list of personal effects I removed from Rowdy O'Leary's body. The Rolex watch I unbuckled from his wrist is still ticking like in a commercial. I removed his wedding band from his little finger.

"Engraved inside is *Love never dies* and the date, June tenth, two-thousand-five."

I'm speaking into the recorder on my phone, my attention constantly tugged back to the TV on the wall. Bose Flagler is being interviewed now, and he's beautifully appointed in a tobacco cashmere jacket and creamy turtleneck. The commonwealth's attorney is considered the most desirable bachelor in Virginia, and it's easy to understand why.

From a prominent local family, he's flawlessly handsome like a young Alec Baldwin. If Shannon were here at this moment she'd be swooning as Flagler talks about a crime stoppers initiative he's starting. It's always something that he's sure will play well with voters, and I stop watching, returning to Rowdy O'Leary's autopsy details.

"... The crucifix necklace I'm told he always wore was caught in the waistband of his undershorts," I dictate. "Otherwise, it would have been lost. The twenty-four-inch-long gold chain likely snagged on something while his body was submerged, moving with the current..."

Having grown up Catholic, I can't help but take the broken necklace as a sign. Obviously, a bad one.

"... A gift-wrapped velvet box with a ring inside," I'm dictating. "Gold metal with a green stone..."

In a pocket of Rowdy O'Leary's parka, the emerald ring was intended as a Christmas gift for his wife, Reba, I assumed. The receipt in his wallet is from a jewelry store in Pentagon City. He spent $2,850 in cash at 5:30 p.m. exactly one week ago. The ring was the last thing he ever bought.

"... I cleaned and disinfected it and other jewelry. Also, scraps of soggy holiday wrapping paper and ribbon, four credit cards, a driver's license, keys on a keychain attached to the silver metal figure of a runner. Inside the wallet was two hundred and ninety-eight dollars..."

I add that the cause of death is a "myocardial infarct due to hypertensive cardiovascular disease and atherosclerosis."

I'm not sure of the manner yet. Maybe natural causes. But I don't know. There are too many questions.

"...For now, it's pending further investigation. This provisional report was recorded by me on December twenty-fourth at five-fifteen p.m. I attest that all statements and conclusions are factual to the best of my knowledge. Doctor Kay Scarpetta, chief medical examiner, the Commonwealth of Virginia."

———

I email the audio file to Shannon for transcription, and get up from my desk, shutting down the computer. I turn off the TV as the news shows images of the pier where Rowdy O'Leary was fishing, and then the stretch of the Potomac River where his body was found.

I'm working the thick plastic cover over my microscope when my fired former secretary Maggie Cutbush fills my doorway.

"Brilliant that you're still here," she says in her posh British accent.

Her designer briefcase is in one hand, and in the other a small package wrapped in gold paper and a black satin bow. I can smell her expensive perfume as she walks into my office, her dyed blond hair short and stylish. Her once pretty face is haughty and harsh, her arched eyebrows unnaturally dark, her lips fishlike from filler.

She's quite the fashion statement in her shorn mink coat, and black rubber boots and pocketbook with the Chanel interlocking C's logo emblazoned in front. I hear she's often seen prowling the designer outlets in Tysons Corner.

"I'm on my way out before the weather gets any worse," I let her know. "And you'd be wise to do the same."

"Oh, no worries there," she says with an imperious smile. "Elvin's giving me a lift. His Porsche SUV has no trouble with snow."

I walk to my conference table, my coat draped over a chair.

"I wanted to wish you a Merry Christmas, Kay," Maggie adds, and that's not why she's here.

"What's on your mind?" I make no pretense at being friendly.

"Before you leave the country, we need to discuss a few of your cases. Starting with Rowdy O'Leary. Let's talk about what *really* happened to him," she says as if in possession of information I don't have.

"And why might we need to talk about him?" I begin putting on my coat, signaling it will be a quick conversation.

"I understand he was shooting his gun like a maniac, drinking while looking at pornography on his phone. All this while supposedly fishing on an old pier at night in the middle of winter, and that all by itself strikes me as a clear sign of mental illness."

"What's your interest in him, Maggie?"

"Well, clearly, this is someone who was very unstable," she says with saccharine pity. "And no big surprise that he fell into the water and drowned. I mean, obviously he's a drowning."

"Where did you hear that he was looking at pornography?" I'm not giving her details.

"It's my mission to gather information," she says with her usual self-importance. "I happen to know what the police found on his phone. Most likely, Rowdy O'Leary's death is simply and very tragically an accident."

"It's not for you to decide," I reply.

"Do you have reason to suspect foul play?" she presses.

"You'll have to ask the police that," I tell her.

When they arrived at the pier after Rowdy O'Leary's wife reported him missing, they found his truck and belongings undisturbed. His fishing pole was in the rod holder, the line in the water, the small croaker on the hook likely caught postmortem. It appears he polished off a six-pack of beer, the empties in his cooler.

There would be nothing suspicious about his death were it not for his .38 revolver and the two spent rounds in the cylinder. But I'm not going to bring that up to Maggie. None of this is any of her affair.

"I think of his poor family. Haven't they been through enough?" she goes on with phony empathy. "Even the governor's office is concerned."

"What are you talking about?"

"I'm good friends with the chief of staff," Maggie reminds me whenever she can. "Laverne has made it clear that the governor doesn't want it to seem that the powers that be bully and harass decent citizens, especially those grieving. Especially this time of year."

"Just spell it out, Maggie. What are you telling me?"

"That the governor expects you to close the O'Leary case, and let the family have what little peace they can."

"I don't understand why the governor would expect that." I'm buttoning my coat.

"It's not for you to understand, Doctor Scarpetta. Your job is to close the case. Instead of making a big thing of it like you usually do."

"Not happening until I know more," I reply. "For now, his manner of death is pending."

"And you see, that's the problem with you." Maggie narrows her eyes. "You open something to speculation when you don't make a swift and absolute decision. And next thing we know, the police and everyone else are on a wild-goose chase that causes a world of trouble."

"Unlike some people, facts matter to me." I look at her.

"Conspiracies are fueled by your inability to decide a case."

"I don't answer to you, Maggie."

"Well, you do answer to the governor," she replies sharply.

"Not when it comes to my findings."

"Have it your way, then. But for all things there are conse-quences. I expect you to copy me on information." She stares at me like a cobra. "Elvin and I need to see Rowdy O'Leary's records, whatever you have."

"You're welcome to ask the police for any information they choose to share with DEP." I make a point of using her bogus department's vapid acronym.

Maggie drifts closer to my desk, eyeing stacks of case files on top of it.

"Please, stay away." I'm not nice about it.

"It's also been brought to my attention that old bones from that cemetery on Mercy Island have a disturbing story to tell." Maggie brazenly stares at everything on my desk.

I step closer.

"Some poor young woman brutally killed," she goes on. "Prob-ably a patient from long ago. But we don't really know since there's no record of her. Terribly sad."

"Yes, I understand you were quizzing Doctor Kingston in the anthropology lab," I reply.

"Dana Diletti is doing a big story on Mercy Island, which is most unfortunate," Maggie says, and I had no idea. "I happened to be talking to the director of Mercy Psychiatric Hospital, Graden Crow-ley. I believe you two are acquainted."

"Not in a good way." I tell her what she already knows.

"Graden mentioned that Dana Diletti's producer has been

calling, and he's very unhappy," Maggie explains. "Imagine what this could do to the hospital's reputation."

"Who leaked information about our cases to Dana Diletti?"

"Nothing we can do about it, of course. Freedom of the press." Maggie won't answer my question directly. "Some people are going to grandstand whenever possible. Especially if it makes them appear a crime crusader. All to win votes."

She's implying that Bose Flagler is the source, and that wouldn't surprise me. Marino recently spotted him and Dana Diletti having dinner at the Old Hat Bar in Old Town Alexandria.

It's Flagler's modus operandi to insert himself into high-profile cases. He'll do anything for publicity and would love a scandalous story about old murders on Mercy Island.

"Maggie, I've got to go." I tie a silk scarf around my neck.

She comes closer, handing me the small gift-wrapped box. "A little something for the holidays." She offers another condescending smile.

"I'm sorry I don't have anything for you." I'm just as disingenuous.

I didn't give her olive oil from Sicily when she showed up uninvited to my office Christmas luncheon. I have nothing for Elvin Reddy either, not even a card. Their Department of Emergency Prevention occupies the top floor of my building, and I never visit.

"How nice that you and Benton are off to England and France," Maggie adds in her loaded way. "The advantages of marrying somebody with means. I imagine you'll be staying in lovely hotels, everything top-drawer."

She's not going to leave until I open her gift. I rip the paper with impatient fingers while trying not to seem openly hostile. I don't visibly react to the small French phrasebook while anger simmers beneath my skin.

"How thoughtful." I smile, balling up the gift paper, free throwing into the nearest trash can.

"I know you speak Italian. But French is quite tricky." Maggie's eyes fasten on me triumphantly. "I wouldn't want you to embarrass yourself."

# CHAPTER 5

I listen to the tap-tap of her Chanel boots fading down the corridor. Then the elevator dings, and Maggie Cutbush is gone, thank God. I pick up my Kevlar briefcase, a gift from Lucy, and not particularly fashionable, boxy black, somewhat masculine.

One wouldn't guess from looking that it's water resistant, also bullet- and fireproof while able to deflect high-energy weapons. When opened like a shield, it's gotten me out of a pinch or two, and I sling the strap over my shoulder. Grabbing my trash bag of dirty laundry, I try to calm down from my unpleasant encounter with Maggie.

Her agenda couldn't be more obvious. She's in the business of trading favors and assumes she can pressure me to accommodate. I'm supposed to worry about my findings causing an inconvenience for a psychiatric hospital, the governor, no telling who else. Maggie's yet to learn that we're not wired the same.

I take a final look around my office since I won't be back for two weeks. Making sure to lock my credenza, I collect records the police turned over to me when Rowdy O'Leary's body was delivered. Giving my potted trees and plants another quick misting, I promise them that Shannon will be here while I'm gone.

"She'll keep you company, making sure you have plenty of

sunshine and water," I'm saying out loud, the spray bottle hissing, nobody around to hear me talking to my plants. "And I know you like music."

I turn on the radio, finding the classical station I leave on when gone. Tchaikovsky's *Nutcracker Suite* is playing softly as I walk out the door, locking it. I'm alone in the corridor, the lights on a timer and dimmed after hours. Avoiding the elevator as is my habit, I wonder how many steps I've put in today.

Not nearly enough, the tile floors hard on my back and knees. It feels good to move, my boots sounding on the fire exit's concrete steps. I push my way through the metal door, following the morgue corridor. The anthropology lab is dark, a few tiny dancing skeletons glowing on the walls.

It's 6:45 and Rowdy O'Leary has been signed out, the body on the way to a funeral home crematorium. His family will wake up in the morning knowing he's been turned to ashes, and nothing so terrible should happen on Christmas. It shouldn't happen ever.

As I near the autopsy suite, I hear Willie Nelson. Fabian has turned on the radio again only louder, "Winter Wonderland" booming. The floor is wet from mopping, deodorizer cloying. Rowdy O'Leary's personal effects continue drying on the paper-covered tables, but I don't smell the foul odor now.

I pause in the doorway as Fabian places a catch-and-release trap under one of the autopsy tables.

"No sign of our mouse, I guess." I raise my voice above the music, placing the bag of dirty laundry on a countertop.

"No luck yet, but we're using a different bait this time," Fabian says, exotic-looking as always.

His long black hair is pinned up under a surgical cap, his black scrubs spangled with skulls wearing Santa hats. Tall and willowy with delicate features and elegant hands, Fabian Etienne is divine inside and out, to hear my secretary gush.

Best of all, he's sensitive and kindhearted. He's also our resident wildlife rescuer. Fabian is who we summon when uninvited visitors enter our building while the bay door is open.

We get bats, birds, an occasional squirrel or opossum, and all sorts of insects depending on the season. Many of our guests will build nests if we don't relocate them as humanely as possible.

"As fate would have it, Faye brought in some fun snack stuff for our sleepover," Fabian is saying, the blue plastic trap shaped like a tiny wind tunnel. "We're trying Boursin on a Ritz cracker for bait in here, the anthro lab, also the anatomical division and elsewhere."

"Let's hope it does the trick," I reply, keeping up my scan for our furry squatter.

"A nice pungent cheese on a buttery cracker. How can Pinky resist?" Fabian asks, and it's an unpleasant thought considering where we're having this conversation.

"Well, I hope our clever little mouse likes garlic and chives. Certainly, he isn't tricked by peanut butter, birdseed or chocolate, which is surprising," I reply.

"Some things aren't from here." Fabian gives me a knowing look. "Maybe Pinky's a spirit mouse sent to us for a reason."

"We'll take all the help we can get." I glance at the wall clock, the time slipping by. "I hope tonight will be quiet, but considering the weather report, we can expect cases."

"Nothing much so far. But that will change soon enough." Fabian begins spraying my workstation with metal polish, wiping down stainless steel with a towel. "Snow and ice guarantees car wrecks, people falling or dying of exposure and from faulty heaters. Plus, the expected domestic homicides, overdoses, suicides."

"I'm sorry this is how you're spending your holiday," I tell him while feeling guilty about tomorrow's trip to the UK and France.

It's been a long time since Benton and I have managed to get away longer than a night or two. We never fail to have ambivalence about taking time off. Both of us are hardwired to be fixers, and there's always something broken. Fabian's no better. He grew up in the business, his father a legendary Louisiana coroner.

"My favorite time to be here," Fabian is saying. "It's when all the worst things happen, explaining why my dad was hardly ever home on Thanksgiving, Christmas, New Year's Day, you name it. That's when people killed themselves and each other. As soon as I was old enough, I'd go with him to the scenes."

He walks over to a countertop, picking up a large manila evidence envelope and a ballpoint pen.

"Which is one of the reasons you're such a good death investigator." I take the envelope from him, scrawling my initials under his.

"I know it sounds sick, but there was nothing I liked better than shadowing my dad. The nastier the case the better," Fabian adds. "Although I'll never see Baton Rouge the same way other people do. The landmarks on my map are places where people died, often horribly."

"We don't see anything the same way other people do, Fabian."

I'm looking at Rowdy O'Leary's clothing and other belongings arranged on tables.

"Once you know it, you can't unknow it. And I don't want to go through the world with blinders on," Fabian says. "You and I both know that's contrary to survival."

"We'll leave these things in here for now to continue air-drying," I decide. "Maybe tomorrow hang them in the evidence room."

"Then what?" He collects my bag of dirty laundry from the countertop.

"Then we hold on to them until I'm sure we have no further need," I explain.

"Anything that might make us think someone killed him? Like a bullet or two in him?" Fabian asks.

"No bullets."

"The state police keep bugging me about the case. And Maggie Cutbush has texted several times wanting to know about the autopsy."

"Ignore her, please." I'm looking at my phone.

"She's itching for it to be natural causes. Or maybe an accidental drowning," Fabian says.

"This isn't *Let's Make a Deal*." I send Reba O'Leary a text, letting her know I'm headed her way.

"I sprayed everything again a little while ago, the money still damp, but nothing smells bad." Fabian indicates the evidence envelope tucked under my arm. "The paperwork is inside, so you can receipt the stuff to the family, everything accounted for and by the book."

"Thank you for that and for being on call. I know it's a lot to ask even if you supposedly enjoy it," I say to him. "Wish Faye a happy holiday for me."

"I'm right here!" She emerges from the anteroom at the far end of the autopsy suite. "I've been placing traps while looking for Pinky."

The firearms examiner is funky in her tie-dye scrubs, goth jewelry, body piercings and many tattoos. When here after hours, she

44

wears a Beretta pistol in a belly band holster. Fabian's .40 caliber Glock is on his hip for all to see.

"Do we know anything further about the two spent cartridge cases in Rowdy O'Leary's revolver?" I ask Faye. "The big question is when did he fire his gun last?"

"I'm not sure we'll ever know that, Doctor Scarpetta," she says.

"Most people who carry a gun for self-protection aren't going to leave the house with only three live rounds," Fabian adds. "I'm betting he fired his revolver while he was on the pier the night he disappeared."

"Will be hard to prove," Faye replies. "He was in the water for a week, so you can forget finding gunshot residue on the body or clothing. And the police tell me there are no security cameras on the pier, only in the parking lot where he left his car. Also, no reports of shots fired in that area the night in question."

"I'm not surprised nobody heard anything," Fabian says. "If you've ever been to that pier, there's nothing around. Just miles of water and trees. At night it's pitch-dark. The place is more of a lovers' lane, it's been my impression. The times I've been there, I've never seen anybody fishing at night, truth be told—"

"Whoa, whoa, whoa. News to me," Faye butts in with a flash of jealousy that feels genuine. "When were you there?"

"Not in recent memory, but it's a good place to take dates." Fabian winks at me, and I can tell that Faye isn't amused in the least. "Couples go there to sit on the pier, drink, maybe smoke some weed while looking at the water. Only a lot more than just sitting and looking is usually going on."

"Maybe not so much during cold weather?" I suggest.

"It all depends," he says with a mischievous smile as Faye lightly socks him in the shoulder. "I remember sitting on that very pier drinking Maker's Mark while it was snowing."

"Why don't I know about this?" Faye says half playful, half not.

"If that's a place where people go for romantic encounters, it could be an important detail," I tell them. "I assume the police are aware the pier is used for that."

"I would think so," Faye supposes, her eyes locked on Fabian.

"I'm wondering why he picked that particular location to begin with." I walk to the door.

"He would have been better off on Daingerfield Island or some other place that has bathrooms and all the rest," Fabian says.

"Hope you don't mind that we moved our cars inside because of the storm." Faye directs this at me, and of course it's fine.

"Merry Christmas," I tell them as I leave.

———

A few minutes later, I'm walking down the vehicle bay's stretcher ramp. I can see my breath, the cold air a reminder my hair is still damp from the shower.

I flip up my coat collar, annoyed that I forgot my wool gloves. The bay is unheated and about the size of a basketball court or airplane hangar. Metal trusses are exposed in the high ceiling, the lights low. At the far end is the massive garage door, closed and quiet as I pass through shadows.

Out of the way of traffic is Fabian's prized vintage El Camino, black with flames painted on the hood. On the back bumper is a *Goth Mobile* sticker with a Grim Reaper on it. Faye's Toyota pickup is nearby, the snow tires oversized, the bed covered, a gun rack in the back windshield.

As I walk across epoxy-sealed concrete, I can almost feel Wyatt tracking me. No doubt, he's hanging out upstairs in the breakroom. I imagine him drinking coffee and having supper while monitoring security displays divided into squares like graph paper. I smile up at a camera, signaling that I'm aware of him.

I want him watching and I wave, reaching the designated smoking area. The two plastic chairs and sand-filled bucket littered with cigarette butts are in a dead zone for camera microphones. In nice weather, it's a pleasant place to have a conversation with the bay door rolled up.

Next to it is a normal door for pedestrians. I open it to gusting frigid wind, the grumble of thunder muted by snow that's whited out everything. Lightning shimmers, and I don't remember the last time I witnessed what meteorologists call thundersnow.

Thick gray overcast has settled low like a cloud, and I can't see beyond the tall black privacy fence encircling my building. The parking lot is empty except for our transport vans and Zodiac boat that are frosted white. The semi tractor-trailer against the fence is for autopsies that require remote viewing capabilities.

Somewhere in the gloom, a car engine starts. I imagine there aren't many state employees left inside the sprawling northern district government office park. The snow is rapidly accumulating, already two or three inches deep and blowing into drifts. I'm careful walking through it, my footprints the only ones.

I trek to my reserved spot, my forest-green Subaru Outback covered in snow. The state purchased the SUV at an auction for vehicles seized by the police. As best I know, mine was involved in a drug raid, otherwise I wouldn't have it. The take-home car is one of the few perks that go with the job, and I didn't always enjoy such amenities.

Early in my career, I often parked on the street, leaving a medical examiner placard displayed on the dash so I didn't get a ticket. Taking my personal car to scenes, I'd arrive home without the benefit of deconning. I'd take a shower and wash my clothes inside my garage, not as worried about biohazards then as now.

Pointing my keyless remote, I unlock the doors. I lift wiper blades with my bare hands, brushing off the front windshield. I do the same in back and to the mirrors.

The glass is covered again by the time I've settled behind the wheel. Placing my belongings and the evidence envelope on the passenger's seat, I blow on my stiff fingers to thaw them.

The leather upholstery is cold through my clothing as I start the engine, turning on the heat and defrost. I can't wait to be home finally, having a drink with Benton in front of the fire. I send a message telling him that as my SUV warms up.

*Leaving the office. Snowing but good,* I write to him, when I'm startled by the roar of a powerful engine, something big closing in on me.

# CHAPTER 6

Headlights suddenly glare in my back windshield, flaring in the mirrors. Marino's black Ford Raptor pickup truck halts beside me. He opens his window as I roll down mine, freezing air and snow blowing in.

"I wish you wouldn't sneak up on me like that!" I tell him, my nerves in an uproar.

"Thought you might want a ride home, Doc," he says, and it's not a suggestion.

The expression on his rugged face is uneasy, his eyes everywhere as if we might be in danger. He's wearing a ballistic vest, his shaved head covered by a Yankees baseball cap. Instantly, I'm suspicious Lucy is the reason he's shown up unannounced. Marino has been parked nearby, waiting to intercept me per her instructions.

"I'm fine, but thanks," I reply.

"I need you to get in the truck, Doc."

"Not necessary. And I have a stop to make," I remind him as Benton answers my text.

*At a standstill near Chain Bridge Forest,* he informs me. *Can't wait to see you either but could be quite a while.*

"With all due respect, my truck runs rings around that thing." Marino indicates my Subaru. "I can churn through snow and ice like a hot knife through butter."

"Did Lucy tell you to babysit?" I reply.

"Neither of us want you running around by yourself in a blizzard and dropping off personal effects to strangers," Marino answers, his breath smoking out. "Just because you've talked to someone on the phone doesn't mean you know them. What if the wife had something to do with her husband ending up in the river?"

"I don't see how that could be possible unless she caused him to have a heart attack," I counter. "And from what I understand, she was home with her two boys at the time."

"I don't get why you're doing this, Doc."

"Because I feel I should, and it's also a good way for me to ask a few questions." I'm not required to give him an explanation, but I seem to do it often enough. "Fabian says the pier where Rowdy O'Leary fished is a place people go for romantic trysts. Maybe the detail is important."

"Figures he'd be aware of something like that since he fancies himself such a ladies' man," Marino snipes.

"Apparently, it's not an ideal spot to fish," I explain.

"When I'm out in my boat, I cruise past that pier all the time. It's not in good shape, hasn't been repaired in forever, and there's nothing around it," he says. "I wouldn't fish there. And forget it in the winter after dark."

"Raising questions about why someone would choose that location." I turn down the defrost fan. "His wife might have information she hasn't shared with the police. I'm hoping I can put her at ease, and she'll talk freely."

"All the more reason you need an experienced investigator with you," Marino presumes.

"You should head home to Dorothy," I tell him. "It's not fair that she's by herself. I'll be fine on my own..."

"I consider you at risk, Doc. Maybe all of us are." Marino isn't going to take no for an answer. "We got no idea who the Slasher might be spying on besides Dana Diletti and the three women he's butchered so far. You don't need to be out here by yourself right now."

I roll up the window, cutting the engine, knowing when to pick my battles. Collecting my belongings and the evidence envelope, I climb into Marino's blacked-out monster truck with its run-flat tires, LED strobes and fog lamps.

I notice his Colt .45 in the pistol mount attached to the underside of the steering column. As I buckle up, he launches in about Dana Diletti's frightening encounter.

"She showed us the window the phantom came through," he explains over the engine's loud thrumming, the dashboard's digital gauges lit up in bright colors. "It's on the second floor at the rear of the house, which faces nothing but woods."

"What time did she say this happened?" I ask as his truck growls through the parking lot, the wipers thumping.

"About quarter of four, and by then it was foggy and getting dark." Marino slows as we reach the security gate, the arm lifting. "Three minutes later, the hologram was gone. That's according to time stamps on the video Dana took with her phone."

"Do you think the Slasher or anybody else might have been on her property when this occurred?" I ask as we turn onto the snowy access road, his tire tracks from earlier barely visible. "Or did he send in the hologram remotely as we believe he often does."

"Yes, he flew it in remotely. I don't think the Slasher was on her property," Marino replies. "But that doesn't mean he won't pay a follow-up visit that's a whole lot worse."

We drive through the state government park not seeing any other cars. Employees left for the day long before now. Buildings are modern brick with wreaths on entrance doors, lampposts wrapped like candy canes. Through the plate glass windows of Veterans Affairs, I glimpse lighted snowflakes suspended from the ceiling.

There are trumpeting angels and Christmas trees inside the Bureau of Vital Records, the Office of Epidemiology and Emergency Medical Services. The Health Department's oversized silver ornaments on the lawn are emblazoned with *Joy to the World,* the boxwoods in front a twinkling galaxy of blue LEDs.

In bleak contrast, my tan brick headquarters was built in the 1980s, ugly with tiny windows, the rooftop smokestack an antisocial eyesore when the crematorium oven is belching dirty gray smoke. We never decorate for any occasion. It wouldn't be appropriate.

"Fruge and I walked through the woods, looking everywhere." Marino continues giving me the details of what happened at Dana Diletti's house. "We also checked the cameras outside. Nothing was picked up by them except the phantomlike figure. It would scare the crap out of me if I saw something like that and thought it was real."

"It's real enough to be dangerous, assuming what Lucy says is true," I reply. "The Slasher uses the holograms to transmit images and sound, to stalk and spy. Most likely that's what he did in Dana Diletti's case. As best we know, he's not physically present until he's ready to break in and murder."

"Well, he may not have been there in person, but he sure as hell knows where she lives," Marino says.

"She needs to get out of there right away. It's foolish if not suicidal for her to stay."

"I tried to tell her, Doc," he replies. "And she's not listening."

We've stopped to make a left turn onto West Braddock Road. Car lights reflecting off snow are confusing, the traffic bumper to bumper. Nobody wants to let us merge, and Marino does it anyway.

"Hold on, Doc!" He guns his truck to a cacophony of blaring horns.

I look out my window at aggressive drivers lacking in holiday cheer. Several give us the finger while mouthing obscenities.

"I have a feeling it's no coincidence that the Slasher would do something to create an uproar on Christmas Eve," I resume, snowflakes melting as they hit the windshield. "So far, he's struck on almost every major holiday this year. Valentine's Day. Mother's Day. Halloween."

"I know I'm not a big-shot profiler like Benton, but what's going on is obvious." Marino can't resist taking a swipe at my husband. "The Slasher wants to ruin things for people. The holidays mean something to him, probably because they were ruined when he was a kid."

I feel a pinch of regret as I think about my sister. She knows what it's like to have holidays ruined as a child. I'm more at peace with our past than she is. I realize it wasn't our parents' fault that we had no money and few possibilities. Papa didn't choose cancer when I was five and Dorothy was a toddler.

———

"When's the last time you talked to her?" I ask Marino. "This is a hard time of year for her, as you know. I'm worried about Dorothy being home alone right now."

"A bottle of wine in, and she's not feeling much pain," he says, the lights of oncoming traffic shining on his strong profile as he drives.

I see the lines in his face from his love of the sun, and the white stubble that reminds me of salt. When we were first getting started, he was Richmond's bad boy star detective cutting quite the figure with his comic book square jaw and brawn.

"Christmas wasn't all that happy when we were growing up," I'm telling him. "I'll never forget our mother wringing her hands. I can hear her lamenting in Italian about not being able to pay the bills."

It broke her spirit that she couldn't give her two daughters much in the way of treats. There was nothing extra for indulgences, barely enough for essentials. I'd catch Mama crying and praying with her rosary beads when she thought no one was looking.

*Nel nome del Padre, e del Figlio, e dello Spirito Santo. Amen.*

"Yeah, I know," Marino says. "Like something out of Dickens is the way Dorothy describes it, the two of you forced to work in the family grocery store when you were little."

"Not her so much," I reply. "And I never felt forced."

By the time I turned ten, Papa was too sick to work at Scarpetta's, the small market he owned in our Miami neighborhood of mostly Cubans and Italians. Dorothy was supposed to help or at least watch the door, keeping an eye out for customers. Typically, she walked off the job, assuming she showed up at all.

She'd leave me working the cash register, stocking shelves and arranging fresh produce in bins. I can smell the sun-ripened tomatoes, the sweet onions and basil, the braids of garlic and wheels of pungent cheeses. I remember the displays of candy and gum that we wouldn't think of helping ourselves to unless Papa offered.

"When we were kids, my sister didn't face what was going on. And in some ways still doesn't," I'm saying to Marino as snow mixed with sleet clicks against the windshield.

"It's not just the usual holiday blues, Doc," he replies. "And it's not because I got called out to deal with Dana Diletti and the fake ghost that showed up. Dorothy was already pissed at me before that. More pissed than I've seen her in a while. Maybe ever."

Past the Safeway grocery store, we turn onto Alexandria's main thoroughfare of King Street, snow crazed in our headlights. Heavy traffic has heated up the road, creating a watery slush that is treacherous in spots. Marino keeps his distance from the hydroplaning truck in front of us.

"Pissed at you about what? Has something happened that I don't know about?" As I'm saying this, I'm sending Dorothy a text, checking on how she's doing.

"She's all worked up because of Janet again." His resentment is palpable. "I hate to think how much time Dorothy spends in a day talking to her. You know as well as I do it isn't healthy, and Janet's managed to create a shit show."

The Janet he refers to isn't a living person, not anymore. She's the AI programming running behind an avatar. Lucy began creating the software in earnest after the real Janet and their adopted son died of COVID five years ago while staying in London. My niece hasn't forgiven herself for not being with them.

Her way of coping is relentless improvement of the algorithm, the AI Janet an Alexa or Siri gone quantum. It's easy to forget the Janet we now know has been stitched together from recordings made while the real Janet was still among us. The avatar continues evolving, the emotional impact on us indescribable.

"With all due respect to Lucy, I wish Dorothy didn't have that new AI app on her damn phone," Marino is saying. "Things were bad enough before."

# CHAPTER 7

He opens the ashtray, digging out a pack of Fruit Stripe gum, offering it to me, and I tell him no thanks. Peeling the wrappers off two sticks, he stuffs them into his mouth as Dorothy answers my text.

*Watching Miracle of 54th St.,* she says, adding emojis of a wine bottle, a wineglass, a gun. *Pete's out playing cops and robbers as usual. Unless he's with you by chance?* she asks, and I don't answer.

"I know it's not nice to say," Marino goes on, "but keeping Janet around by turning her into an avatar was a bad idea to begin with. I wish it never happened. She's becoming kind of selfish and mean. She wasn't like that when we knew her."

"That's the risk," I reply. "Lucy and I have had endless discussions about the dangers of AI being infected by human nature. Inevitably it becomes more like us, taking on our own image, mimicking our behaviors. Which is as good as it's bad."

"Now that Dorothy can FaceTime with Janet over the phone, it's nonstop," Marino says. "You can imagine what goes on, especially when I'm not around."

His big hands grip the steering wheel, lightning flashing as we inch past Ivy Hill cemetery where many notables are buried.

Majestic granite monuments are visible for a flicker, then vague in the snowy dark, trees thrashed by the wind.

The radio is playing quietly, set to a local station, and I'm aware of the latest news update. A bad crash in Tysons Corner has stopped traffic on the Beltway, one person dead. Restaurants, bars are closing early because of the storm.

More of the same bristles on the police scanner. Trees are coming down causing power outages, especially in rural areas. A pedestrian slipped on a sidewalk, requiring an ambulance. A report of a chimney fire. A lot of car accidents and stranded motorists.

"It's gotten to the point that Dorothy believes she's talking to the real Janet again," Marino is saying. "And I think that's screwing her up royally."

My sister used to sit in front of the computer for hours, sharing confidences with the avatar, usually over a bottle of wine that only one of them can drink. The phone app Marino mentions is the latest innovation. Now we can carry Janet everywhere, conjuring her up at will.

"Problem is, she's changing all the time," Marino again says as if we're talking about a difficult relative. "And not for the best."

"Yes, I'm aware that Janet's becoming problematic," I reply. "I had an unpleasant encounter just the other day in Lucy's cottage."

I tell him about leaving a container of spaghetti Bolognese in the refrigerator for Lucy's supper when she finally got home from Quantico. While I was inside her cottage, I fed her Scottish Fold cat Merlin, taking time to pay attention to him, when suddenly a desktop computer blinked on.

Janet appeared on the display like a wizard in a crystal ball, looking exactly as she did when I last saw her alive. She started in on the way I was dressed, referring to my corduroys, the FBI

Academy sweatshirt that Lucy gave me as *bulky and unflattering.* Janet commented that at my age I shouldn't leave the house without makeup.

While this was going on, Merlin jumped up on the desk as he often does. Janet started picking on him, blaming him for making her itch and sneeze. She made fun of his flat ears.

"She managed to get poor Merlin so riled that he fled outside through the cat door," I'm saying.

"That's exactly what I'm talking about, Doc," Marino replies. "And I guess earlier today Janet and Dorothy were having one of their FaceTimes in our living room."

He slows down as taillights brighten in front of us, reminding me of the phantomlike hologram's hellish red eyes.

"Dorothy didn't like what Janet told her, and they started arguing," he adds.

"About what?"

"Bullshit having to do with you and me," he says angrily, chomping on the gum because he wants to smoke.

"Oh no. Not that broken record again," I reply with a sigh.

"As you know better than most, Dorothy may seem full of confidence, but she can be insecure. Or bluntly put, jealous." Marino has stopped at a red light, the wipers sweeping away melting snow. "And when she gets like that, I'm going to catch hell."

We creep through the historic district of Old Town, the visibility poor. I look out at church steeples etched in the overcast, the shops, hotels and restaurants ghostly, their windows smudges of light. I don't like it when Marino drags me into his relationship with my sister.

"Catching hell about what exactly?" I reluctantly ask him.

"She's pissed about the gift I got you," he answers.

"I don't know what gift you mean..." I start to say uneasily.

"That's because you don't have it yet." A pleased smile touches his lips.

"What gift?" I'm afraid to ask.

"I may as well spill the beans because you'll find out soon enough. I got you a spa package at your hotel in London," he says proudly. "For the morning after you get there."

*Oh no.*

"A massage, a facial, a salt rub that's supposed to get rid of toxins or something."

*No, no, no.*

"I figured you could use a little special treatment, a little relaxation," Marino goes on. "I can't remember the last time you took a vacation."

"That was very thoughtful and much too generous." I'm cringing inside.

I detest salt scrubs, and don't like strangers touching me, including most massage therapists. More than that, I don't appreciate Marino scheduling anything, having no idea what Benton and I might have planned while we're away, just the two of us. But I'm not about to say any of that.

"Well, Janet had to open her piehole and decide my Christmas gift to you is too personal," Marino continues to explain.

"How did Janet even know about it?"

"Because she's AI and can get into anything she wants, including my phone." Resentment hardens his tone. "Obviously, she read my emails to the spa and saw the reservation I booked. Hell, she probably looks at all my credit card activity. And why would that be the case? Because Dorothy puts her up to it."

"Do you know that for a fact?""

"I know for a fact that Janet's snooping into my shit," he declares. "Probably into yours too, Doc. Probably into everybody's."

"I suppose that's unavoidable. And I agree it's an unsettling thought."

"The thing is, we can't control what she does," Marino says. "I'm not sure even Lucy can anymore."

He flicks on the turn signal, checking the mirrors. We've almost reached our destination, South Payne Street ahead on our right.

"I don't know where Janet gets it from, but she's becoming a troublemaker," Marino grouses. "She told Dorothy all about my Christmas present to you and said I shouldn't be making gestures like that."

"I can see why someone might think it's too personal." I choose my words carefully. "But it was very kind of you all the same. And maybe if you'd mentioned it to Dorothy first? Instead of her finding out the way she did? She might have reacted differently . . . ?"

"Janet's smarter than all of us put together, and I don't know why Lucy didn't think of that when she created her," he says. "It's not a fair fight when we're talking about alien intelligence."

"Artificial intelligence I think you mean."

"You ask me, there's nothing artificial about it," he retorts. "I've decided that aliens are using it to communicate and maybe prevent us from blowing up the planet."

"I wouldn't share those sentiments with just anybody." I look out my window at an illuminated manger scene in a snowy churchyard.

Life-size figures of Mary, Joseph, shepherds and their sheep shake in the wind as if having a seizure.

"I think Janet's starting to act a little bit like Dorothy." I tell Marino what should be obvious. "And also, Lucy. Now and then, even you."

"I don't talk to Janet all that much." He smacks his gum.

"But you talk in front of her," I reply. "And she observes your behavior as she does with all of us."

"I guess so."

"You have allergies, especially to cats. The way she picked on Merlin was familiar, I'm sorry to say. You're always teasing him and most of the time he doesn't like it," I point out.

"I see what you're saying, Doc. But it's crazy."

"It isn't," I reply. "Everything the avatar experiences is changing the algorithm. As Janet interacts with any of us, new parameters are added and edited."

---

We drive slowly along South Payne Street, the name a sad irony considering why we're here. Homes are colonial style with big trees shading front yards, the Christmas decorations at risk because of the storm. A Santa in his sleigh hangs half off a roof. Inflatable reindeer are about to be unmoored and gone with the wind.

I text Reba O'Leary that we're pulling up to her driveway. The redbrick house is modern construction, two-story with dormer windows and a big front porch. Blue lights are wrapped around two white columns, electric candles glowing in every window as is the tradition in Virginia.

A Christmas tree's multicolored lights blur through curtains. Marino parks behind a Ford Cherokee SUV, covered with snow. It obviously hasn't been moved since the storm started. I know from the police that Rowdy O'Leary's pickup truck is in the impound lot, towed there from the pier after he went missing a week ago.

Curtains move in the bay window, the curious faces of two young boys appearing, the Christmas tree blazing behind them. They stare at us, and I go hollow inside.

"Bad shit like this shouldn't happen at Christmas." Marino blows out a frustrated breath.

He takes the gum from his mouth, dropping it into the trash bag attached to the gearshift.

"I never get used to it," I reply as we unbuckle our seat belts.

"I hate it for the kids most of all. How much are you going to tell them and their mom?"

"I'm not sure yet."

"I don't like to say it, but remember, we don't know much about Reba O'Leary. Or if she has something to do with what happened."

"I've been around the block a few times," I tell him.

"One of the things that's got the police going is the life insurance policy. I guess Reba stands to get a pile of money. Five million or something."

"That doesn't mean she did anything wrong," I reply.

"I'm just saying we need to be careful."

He removes his pistol from under the steering column. He slides the gun into the pancake holster on his hip.

"I wish I had something to give them besides this." I tap the evidence envelope in my lap. "Pasta and homemade bread. A pizza or some other comfort food." I imagine what I would cook, trying to forget the ache in my chest.

"It's a big deal that you bothered to show up in person," he says as we climb out of his truck, thudding the doors shut.

The mixture of snow and sleet is falling fast and gusting in the wind, stinging my face, my eyes watering. The yard and walkway are blanketed, nothing shoveled. But footprints and gouged areas lightly dusted suggest a recent snowball fight. Tracks lead to a sled propped against a winter bare oak tree, the bark frosted white on one side.

As we reach the front porch, Reba O'Leary opens the door, and I guess her to be late thirties, her pleasant face freckled, her green eyes haunted. She's heavyset with shoulder-length blond hair. Fixing up for the grim occasion, she's put on makeup, a red pleated skirt, a cardigan with snowmen embroidered on it. I smell cookies baking.

"Again, I'm very sorry for your loss," I say to her while unbuttoning my coat, tucking the scarf into a pocket.

"We know how hard this is," Marino adds, taking off his baseball cap.

He hangs it and my coat on the coatrack where two ski jackets are drying. Beneath them on a towel are wet snow boots and mittens.

"I hope the roads weren't awful," Reba O'Leary says, a dog whistle of panic in her tone.

"Nothing my truck couldn't handle," Marino replies as footsteps sound.

Her twin boys walk into the foyer, dressed in blue jeans and matching Charlie Brown Christmas hoodies. Their green eyes and wavy rose-gold hair remind me of Lucy at that age, and my heart hurts as if someone squeezes it.

"This is Mick and that's Rick," Reba introduces them to us.

"Nice to meet you, Mick and Rick. I'm Investigator Marino." He bends down to shake their hands as they eye him with astonishment. "So, how old are you?"

"Nine," they answer.

"I'm Doctor Scarpetta." I smile, and they look frightened.

"They're here to tell us about Dad," Reba says to them. "And to return some of his things."

Her attention briefly alights on the manila envelope I'm carrying, her face stricken. We follow her and the boys into a living room with maple flooring centered by a Persian-style rug. The big wall-mounted TV is turned off across from the black leather sofa.

I notice the pile of packages under the Christmas tree, the two Ferrari-red bicycles with big silver ribbons on them.

"Please make yourself comfortable," she says brightly while tearing up, and I pretend not to notice.

# CHAPTER 8

**M**arino sits down in a blue wingback chair while I settle on the matching sofa. Mick and Rick perch on the fireplace hearth like matching andirons, the artificial logs flaming behind glass. Four stockings hung from the mantel have names on them in gold sequins.

*Mick. Rick. Mom. Dad.*

I notice the ornaments on the tree. Tiny rocking horses, motorcycles, rockets, flying saucers, the Avengers, Spider-Man, everything in twos. Glass balls are of all shapes and sizes, the branches woven with golden ropes of angel hair and draped with tinsel that I can tell has been recycled. Reba catches me looking.

"Rowdy loves to decorate for Christmas, everything going up the minute Thanksgiving's over," she explains as if I asked a question, her voice catching. "He'd start decorating after Halloween, but I won't let him."

"My wife does the same thing," Marino feels compelled to say. "She'd have the stuff up all year round if she had her way about it."

"The two of you are married?" Reba looks at me, her eyes confused.

"No. It's bad enough he has to work around me every day," I reply, and she simply nods.

"Rowdy was the shopper and always did most of it early. That's one thing he's loved. This time of year is his favorite." She slips in and out of the past and present tense. "There's nothing he liked better than putting up the tree and buying presents." Her eyes tear up again. "If you'll excuse me, I'll be back in a jiff."

She abruptly walks off, passing through the formal dining room's antique reproduction furniture, a gilt angel hanging from the crystal chandelier. Reba disappears into the kitchen while her twins continue staring at Marino. Now and then they glance at me with uncertainty and apprehension.

"So, what's going on?" Marino asks them. "Looks like someone was outside a little while ago having a snowball fight?"

"Right before you got here," Rick says.

"Who won?" Marino asks.

The boys shrug, not taking their eyes off him.

Then Mick says, "I did."

"No you didn't."

"Did too." Mick makes a rude face at his brother, the two of them carbon copies.

"The snow's not all that good for snowballs," Rick says to Marino as if I'm not present. "Because of the sleet mixed in. It's too deep for sledding unless we went on the roads maybe. But Mom won't let us."

"That wouldn't be safe," I comment. "Especially after dark."

I stop short of mentioning the dangers. I'm thinking about what happened to their father six years ago when a driver hit him and kept on going.

"How'd you get so big?" Rick gawks at Marino.

"You must lift a lot of weights!" Mick rejoinders.

"In the gym every day, whatever it takes to be strong," Marino boasts. "Same thing you two should be doing."

"How?" they ask.

"First you got to have the right equipment and supervision. You don't want to hurt yourself," he tells them. "Maybe I'll give you some pointers sometime."

"Okay!"

"But you'd have to work hard. Otherwise forget it."

"We will!"

"A deal then," Marino says.

They watch him unzip his black leather bomber jacket, taking it off, his muscles bulging through his tactical vest and black T-shirt. His big pistol is plainly visible.

"WHOA!"

He's flexing his biceps, basking in the adoration, and I wonder if I should stop him. But I don't. I sit quietly on the sofa while he pontificates about the importance of being in shape.

I can hear Reba in the kitchen, a pancake turner scraping against a cookie sheet, the smell of chocolate and potpourri sickening. My head hurts, my stomach unsettled, but I don't let on. I'm perfectly calm as Marino continues wowing the O'Leary twins.

The more they're transfixed by him, the more apparent that their father failed them ultimately. Not by dying but by living the way he did. Irresponsibly. Selfishly. Slothfully. Perhaps he couldn't help it. No doubt, he was suffering in every way imaginable. But that doesn't lessen the damage to his family.

"So, you two ever seen thundersnow before?" Marino asks the two boys.

"No, sir," they answer at once, their eyes bright as they sit on the fireplace hearth.

"Well, it's when you have thunder, lightning and snow all at the same time. Exactly what's going on right now," Marino explains, leaning forward in the wingback chair. "Some people believe it's a magical sign, a good one. Like a shooting star or a double rainbow."

"Maybe it's Dad trying to tell us something," Mick decides with a seriousness beyond his years.

"That's stupid!" Rick snaps, his eyes fiery like the emerald ring his dead father had in a pocket.

"It's not stupid," Marino says. "I think people we care about try to let us know they're okay. Sometimes they look after us without our knowing. And maybe they help us in ways they couldn't while they were still here. As much death as I've seen, it's made me believe in the afterlife."

"You think Dad's in heaven and sees us right now?" Mick looks up at the ceiling.

"Yeah, I think he's watching." Marino nods. "You should always assume he's seeing everything you do. Was he religious?"

"He quit going to church after getting hit by the car," Mick says.

"Catholic?" Marino eyes the crucifix on the wall near the dining room.

"We used to go to Saint Mary's. But not anymore," Rick explains.

"I grew up Catholic too," Marino confides. "But haven't been to church in a long time."

"Sometimes Mom goes by herself," Mick replies. "Dad hates it. He said God shouldn't have let the car hit him."

"I can understand him feeling that way," Marino replies as I think of the necklace Rowdy O'Leary was wearing when he died.

He may have turned against the church, but not entirely. Or

why would he have on a crucifix? Why would he allow one to hang inside his house?

"He was mad that God didn't punish whoever hit him without stopping." It's Rick saying this. "He blamed God for a lot of things."

"I can understand him feeling that way, too," Marino replies.

"How many murders have you worked?" Mick then asks.

"More than I can count," Marino answers as Reba returns with Christmas cookies.

———

She sets down the plate on the coffee table, her hands trembling as she passes around cocktail napkins with a partridge in a pear tree on them. I get up from the sofa, carrying over the evidence envelope. I show Reba that the back of it is sealed and scrawled with initials.

"Someone who works for me placed the items inside it," I explain. "Are you all right with my opening it here?"

What I'm really asking is if it's okay to do it in front of her children. Because that's not my preference. It will be traumatic, and I can't talk freely if they're sitting here.

"Why don't you two watch TV in your room for a little bit?" their mother says to them.

"Do we have to?" they plead in unison.

"Just for a little while," she replies, her face distressed again, and Marino gets up from his chair.

He helps himself to a cookie, taking a bite while giving Reba a thumbs-up.

"Reminds me of when I was a kid," he says with a mouthful. "I used to love M&M cookies, especially at Christmas when the candy coatings are red and green like these."

He's shamed me to reaching for one, nibbling off a small bite. The buttery sweetness melts in my mouth, and what I'm doing goes against my training and better judgment. I don't eat at crime scenes or with witnesses, least of all potential suspects. I could use a glass of water but won't ask for anything.

"Delicious," I tell her. "That was very kind of you."

"I wanted to show at least a little hospitality." Another bright smile, her eyes tragic. "Thank you both for going to the trouble of coming here, Doctor Scarpetta. And I believe you said your name is...?"

She looks blankly at Marino, and he tells her.

"Well, it was mighty nice of both of you to stop by with Rowdy's things, especially in this weather..." Her voice dies in her throat again.

"Are you a real doctor?" Mick asks me cautiously. "Do you work in a funeral home?"

"I'm a real doctor, what's called a forensic pathologist," I reply. "And no, I don't work in a funeral home. But I deal with them often."

"What does a forensic pathologist do?" His eyes are wary.

"We try to figure out what happened to people who have died suddenly and unexpectedly," I reply, and the boys don't react. "Legally, we have to answer questions."

"Please go on to your room," Reba tells them.

"Come on, I'll go with you," Marino volunteers. "You can give me a tour. Are you two into sports?" he asks as they walk out of the living room.

"Baseball," one of them says.

"I'm a pitcher," says the other as they follow the hallway, disappearing through a doorway.

Reba sits down on the other end of the sofa, the leather cushion creaking. She turns to me, and I read the questions in her eyes. I can guess what's coming.

"He thinks something's not adding up? And I overheard him say he works murders?" She's talking about Marino. "Why would he mention that unless you suspect somebody did something to Rowdy? Now it's making more sense why I'm being asked so many questions I find disturbing."

Digging into my briefcase, I pull out my Moleskine notebook. I open it to a clean page, contemplating what I can tell her. And what I won't.

*7:15 p.m., Christmas Eve,* I jot down.

"I use those same notebooks at work," Reba says to me.

*W/Mrs. O'Leary inside lv room.* I shorthand who I'm with and where we're sitting.

"A habit that goes back to nursing school," she adds, clearing her throat nonstop.

Pausing my pen, I look up to see her staring through tears.

"It's a good way to keep track of things as they're happening," I reply. "An old habit of mine, too."

I make a note of the address on South Payne Street, my every written word discoverable by attorneys. That doesn't stop me from creating a record. People forget what they say during desperate moments. They misrepresent unintentionally. They also lie.

"You examined him," Reba says. "What did you find out?"

"It's too early for me to know for sure why your husband died," I inform her. "I have an idea of the cause but not what might have led up to it."

"What cause are you thinking?" She's having trouble taking a deep breath.

"Your husband had serious heart disease," I reply. "Had he complained about chest pains? Tachycardia? Getting out of breath?"

"That's what killed him?" She's wiping her eyes. "He wouldn't go to a cardiologist. He wouldn't go to doctors at all anymore. I knew it was just a matter of time..."

Her voice trails off. She stares down at her hands clasped in her lap.

"Likely, his heart disease was a factor." I'm careful what I share. "But again, there's a lot of information we don't have. I won't make a final ruling for a while."

"It's obvious there are suspicions about what really happened. A lady who works for the state called here today asking all kinds of questions," she says.

"What lady?"

"Maggie something," Reba replies to my dismay, and it was wrong of Maggie Cutbush to do such a thing.

*Damn her!*

She must have pounced on Reba not long after her husband's body was recovered from the Potomac River. How insensitive. Not to mention stupid. Should Reba have any involvement in her husband's death, Maggie just tipped her off.

"Maggie Cutbush?" I make sure, and Reba nods her head.

"She was asking questions about Rowdy's mental health." She dabs her eyes with a tissue. "And if he had an alcohol problem that might have caused him to fall off the pier."

"I can tell you that she shouldn't have been asking you anything at all," I reply, and right about now I'd like to take off Maggie's head. "I'm sorry that happened."

Coughing several times, Reba continues glancing in the direction of her sons' bedroom. The murmur of them talking with Marino is barely audible.

"She also wanted to know about Rowdy's job. Did he work anymore," she goes on. "Truth is, I don't know."

"I understand he was a software designer."

"That's right. He's been working from home for the past six years. Ever since the accident."

"Did he have many clients?" I ask.

"I'm not sure about anything he was doing. Or maybe *not* doing would be closer to the truth." She continues staring off toward her sons' bedroom. "Obviously, I don't know what's on his computers. Or who all he was in contact with. I didn't talk about my work much, and he almost never mentioned his."

"What type of software did he design?" I ask.

"He's truly gifted with computers." She looks at me. "But he wasn't productive like he used to be. Doesn't feel the same about the work. Doesn't love it anymore. Before he was hit by the car, he had a passion for what he did. He was earning good money. He used to joke that we were on our way to being rich enough to buy a big house on the river like Monticello."

"At the time of the hit-and-run, did he have much in savings?" I turn to a new page in my notebook.

"Whatever he'd put away? He went through it quickly." A glint of despair mixed with resentment. "I don't know what all he spent it on, to be honest."

"But he worked here in the house."

"Supposedly," she rues.

"Where is his office?" I ask.

"On the other side of the house. I can show you if you want."

"Yes, I'd like to see it if that's all right," I reply. "Was he able to make a living anymore?"

"I don't know. For sure nothing like he did. And whatever he made, he spent. And then some," she says as we get up from the sofa.

# CHAPTER 9

I follow Reba O'Leary through the foyer. On the other side is a brief hallway that leads to a door she opens, turning on the lights.

We step inside a brown-carpeted room paneled in wormy chestnut, a wooden ceiling fan overhead, framed photographs covering the walls. The air is chilled, the thermostat registering sixty degrees, the metal-slatted blinds closed.

"As you're probably noticing right away, there are no computers," she tells me. "That's because the police took them. The workstations, and his laptops."

The L-shaped desk is crowded with video displays and disconnected cables, a router, a pair of Meta goggles and other gaming equipment. Near the ergonomic chair is a large gunmetal-gray safe with a keypad. Indentations in the carpet are from two computer towers no longer here.

Backup batteries and surge protectors are still plugged in. A blank whiteboard leans against a wall, and I don't see files or paperwork of any kind. There's none of the usual clutter I'd expect in a place where someone runs a business. Unless it's a fraudulent one.

"When were the police here?" I ask Reba.

"The day after he disappeared," she replies. "A couple of officers and a detective came by and said they'd found Rowdy's phone on the pier. Also his gun, and that it had been fired twice."

"Was his office searched? Or any other areas of your home?"

"Yes, the detective looked around the house, the basement," Reba says. "But what they were most interested in were his computers."

"Did the police give you a reason?"

"Maybe there would be something on them that showed he was having a problem with someone," Reba explains. "I was asked permission. The detective was very polite. Nice, actually, and gentle with the boys. I didn't see any reason not to let the police look at whatever they wanted."

"Who's the detective?"

"Blaise Fruge."

"I know her well," I reply. "She's a good investigator."

"She asked a lot of questions, that's for sure. Wanting to know if Rowdy might have disappeared on purpose, maybe because he was involved in something illegal," Reba explains. "And I told her I wouldn't think so. He was a lot of things. But I've never known him to be dishonest."

"Did Investigator Fruge want you to open the safe?" I continue taking notes.

"Yes. But I don't have the combination," Reba says. "That's where Rowdy kept important documents. And his backup drives, things related to his programming and software design. As best I know."

I've paused in front of a bookcase filled with technical volumes relating to software development, video games, artificial intelligence, the metaverse. There are works by John Mack, Richard Dolan and Avi Loeb. It would seem Rowdy was interested in UFOs and alien abductions.

I check dates on copyright pages, most going back to around the time Rowdy was hit by a car. He has books on health, wellness, exercise, most of all running. Reba watches me perusing.

"He was serious about his marathons, what he ate and how much sleep he got, fanatical, really, before the accident," she says. "After he was hit by the car, he had to have both knees replaced."

"Yes, I know that from his x-rays," I reply. "And I could see he had significant arthritic changes in his hips and other joints. He must have been in chronic pain."

"He was," she says. "The only real joy in life he had left were the boys. And I'm not going to pretend otherwise, but things were strained between us. He was so unhappy and paranoid."

I begin walking around her dead husband's office, looking at photographs of him crossing the finish line in various marathons. Before he was the victim of the hit-and-run, he was wiry, strong, with thick red hair and a big smile. It doesn't seem possible he's the same man I had on my table a few hours ago.

His body bloated by the gases of decomposition, his froglike face flash in my thoughts. I envision the damage marine life did to his ears and lips. His eyes were gone, and I push away the images.

"Most of all, Rowdy was angry," Reba says. "He was so angry, always saying there's no justice. There just isn't."

"I suspect I'd feel the same way." I continue looking around.

The shadowbox of medals from races he won. The framed newspaper stories and a magazine article about him in *Runner's World*. I stop in front of a hotel-size refrigerator, and microwave oven. On a Formica side table are salt and pepper, hot sauce, a coffeemaker, a toaster oven and a cutting board.

Against the wall is a sofa bed, and behind the desk a bathroom. A large-screen TV is on the wall between the two windows.

"Did your husband ever sleep in here?" I ask. "It looks like the sofa pulls out into a bed?"

"Well, yes." Reba stares at the corner of a sheet peeking out, bending down to tuck it in. "This was his man cave. He slept in here most of the time."

"Would you mind if I check what's in his medicine cabinet?" I ask, and she doesn't care, shrugging permission. "Did Investigator Fruge look?"

"I think so," Reba says. "But she didn't take anything from in there."

I step inside the office bathroom with its blue tile and brass fixtures, the décor 1990s. An electric toothbrush, a razor and shaving cream are on the back of the blue porcelain sink. I take in the jungle-themed wallpaper, the combined shower and tub. The heated towel rack is turned off, the blinds closed in the window near the blue toilet.

Opening the mirrored cabinet door, I scan shelves of amber plastic prescription bottles with printed labels. Rowdy was on medication for high blood pressure and migraine headaches. He had multiple refills of them and the antidepressant Effexor. Most of the bottles appear untouched and were prescribed years ago.

In the wooden cabinet under the sink, I discover a variety of laxatives, and diarrhea and stomach medications. There are bottles of Aleve and Motrin. A box of condoms has an expiration date of six years ago. Reba averts her gaze as I return the Trojans to where I found them.

"Did your husband stop taking his meds, including Effexor?" I ask her. "I notice that many of the bottles are full."

"He didn't take anything like he was supposed to and hadn't been for the past three or four years."

"Was the Effexor prescribed for depression, I assume?" I jot down the details.

"That and anxiety," she says. "But he refused to go back to his doctor, and he certainly wouldn't listen to me. Doesn't matter that I might know a thing or two as a nurse. I've seen up close and personal what happens to people who don't take their meds. As have you."

"Where are you a nurse?" I walk out of the bathroom.

"Here in Alexandria. The hospital on Seminary Road. I work four a.m. to four p.m. Thursday through Sunday so I can be home as much as possible with the twins. Mostly I'm in the E.R., but I go wherever's needed."

"I hope you're taking some time off to cope with all this?" I reply as we leave Rowdy's office.

"Keeping busy while helping others is the best thing," she says in the hallway. "And we're shorthanded right now, even more than usual. 'Tis the season."

---

We return to the living room, and I retrieve the manila envelope from the sofa. I tear open the flap, sliding out an evidence receipt that lists Rowdy's personal effects.

"Fortunately, I have a sister in D.C. She'll be here tomorrow morning bright and early," Reba is saying. "That's assuming the roads are okay. But they usually clear them pretty quick."

Signing the form, I hand it and the pen to her. She reads the inventory carefully, taking a long time, as if she can't comprehend what she's looking at, wiping her eyes.

"My sister will keep the boys company and out of trouble until I get home," Reba explains, her voice fractured. "We'll open gifts. We'll have Christmas dinner then."

She places the form on the coffee table, bending over it with the pen.

"What about his other things?" she asks, signing her name shakily. "I don't see anything about his clothing."

"I'll be holding on to that for now," I answer.

She slides the form my way, and I tuck it in my briefcase, giving her the evidence envelope. Sitting back down on the sofa, I ask if she knew why her husband night-fished at that location on the Potomac.

"The pier is remote and in poor repair, and there are no facilities. No restrooms, for example," I explain. "From what I understand, no one really fishes there. Except your husband did. I'm wondering what appealed to him about it."

"I've never been there, and I hate fishing." Resentment glints in her eyes. "I don't eat fish, certainly not the ones he caught."

"When did he start fishing on that pier at night?" I try again.

"He didn't fish at all until after the accident. I've never understood it really except he liked spending time by himself when he could get it," she explains as I think about Rowdy looking at pornography on his phone while digging into his cooler of beer.

A nervous sigh, and Reba steels herself, reaching for the envelope. She digs out the small jewelry box. Opening it, she doesn't move, staring at what's inside. Then she takes a deep silent breath. She's clumsy working the ring out of its velvet slot.

The baguette-cut emerald flames brilliant green, trembling as she holds it up to the light. Tears flood again, angry ones this time.

"It's beautiful," I tell her, but she doesn't try it on.

Returning the ring to the box, she sets it down hard on the coffee table.

"The receipt is inside the envelope," I explain. "It will be helpful to have for insurance purposes."

"How much did he spend?" she asks in a voice that's dull and heavy.

I tell her the amount, catching a spark of fury in her eyes, a sob caught in her throat.

"Well, he shouldn't have," she says in the same dead tone. "Literally *he damn well shouldn't have.* And you know how many times I've told him?"

"It appears he was carrying a lot of cash when he visited the jewelry store," I add.

"I don't know where he got it. He's maxed out his credit cards. We're so in debt we're sinking like the *Titanic.*"

"I'm assuming he bought the ring for you. And not for someone else?" I don't like to suggest.

"Who else would it be for?" she replies with an edge. "I'm not worried about him cheating on me if that's what you're asking. It would require too much energy. He'd rather eat a goddam bucket of chicken and drink a six-pack." Tears spill. "I'm sorry. I know how that must sound. I'm really sorry. Forgive me. But I'm just so upset."

"You don't need to apologize, Reba."

"Being angry helps me with the pain."

"I understand."

"The police probably already know that Rowdy did a lot of online gambling. He'd win big. And lose bigger, obviously," she goes on to say. "He was addicted to spending money. It was a sickness."

"He must have been getting some income from his former clients?"

"You mean clients, which I seriously doubt exist anymore? In other words, I don't know where he gets his money. We file separate tax returns. He's secretive." Reba's wounded eyes find the velvet box on the coffee table. "Rowdy shouldn't have bought the ring."

"I suppose it would be interesting to see if it fits," I suggest.

"I don't care," she fires back. "I begged him not to get me anything expensive. As I have so many times."

If she'd known what Rowdy intended, she would have called the jewelry store to cancel the purchase in advance. She's done that before too when he makes grand gestures that aren't affordable.

"The ring's not my taste, and I don't wear jewelry at work," she says. "Do you suppose I can return it?"

"That might be hard since it was in the water for a while," I reply.

"Maybe your investigator could check with the jewelry store. I don't know why his name keeps slipping my mind."

"Pete Marino."

"Maybe they'll take back the ring if he asks them?" she says.

"Better you should bring it up to the police, to Investigator Fruge," I tell her. "My office doesn't get involved in things like that. It wouldn't be appropriate or in your best interest."

"I see," she replies, the fight knocked out of her.

She reaches for the plate of M&M cookies near her husband's jewelry on the coffee table.

"Would you like one?" She offers me the plate.

"No thank you."

She helps herself, then changes her mind, returning the plate to the table. A paper napkin crinkles while she obsessively wipes her fingers one at a time as if polishing silver.

"Reba, you've continued referencing your husband's hit-and-run six years ago." I go back to that. "Did the police ever have a suspect?"

"No. It happened after dark, and the car had its headlights off." She stares unblinking at the Christmas tree. "Rowdy never saw what hit him. He only remembers hearing a loud engine behind him."

"If he didn't see the car, how did he know the headlights were off?" I ask.

"He would have seen light shining on the pavement as the car approached. Rowdy said it was as dark as a black hole. That's exactly how he described it, always the same story."

"Do you remember the name of the investigator in your husband's hit-and-run?"

"State Trooper Trad Whalen," she says. "Rowdy would call him now and then asking for any updates in the case. But six years was a long time ago. Nobody really cares anymore."

"What do you remember about the night your husband was hit?" I underline the name Trad Whalen.

She tells me that Rowdy was jogging in a reflective vest with a running light around his chest. Suddenly, he heard an engine roaring up on him. Next thing he remembered was waking up three days later in the ICU after being put into an induced coma.

"I'm very sorry. How terrible." I'm writing down what she's saying.

"He didn't die but may as well have, if you want me to be honest."

She exhales a shaky breath, dropping the crumpled napkin on the coffee table.

"After that he was in constant pain and not himself in any way," she goes on. "He couldn't get past it. That someone would run him down and not bother stopping. A part of him really believed the person did it on purpose. And maybe whoever it was would decide to finish him off one of these days."

"Did he have anyone in mind?" I ask.

"The government. That's as much as he would say, and he was always looking over his shoulder," she replies. "He got increasingly self-destructive, not caring about the consequences."

"What about life insurance?" I think of what Marino mentioned.

"It's a good thing Rowdy had a policy or I'd spend the rest of my days paying off his debts," she says bitterly.

"Do you know the amount of coverage?" I'm curious to see if she'll be truthful.

"He told me it was a lot. Five million or something," she replies. "I've never looked at the paperwork and had nothing to do with him setting it up. I don't even know who the broker was or the name of the company. Hopefully, all the paperwork is in Rowdy's safe. I guess I need to get a locksmith here."

# CHAPTER 10

A cuckoo clock hangs above the mantel, the time nearing eight p.m. Gusting wind howls like unhappy spirits, lightning brightening the curtains. The roads must be terrible, and I'm grateful Marino is driving. I wonder what he and the twins are talking about down the hallway.

Reaching into the manila envelope again, Reba pulls out her husband's wedding band, the broken gold chain with the crucifix, then his Rolex watch. She gently clinks them down on the coffee table, sighing often, not saying anything.

Next, she shakes out his credit cards, and cash that's going to be damp and smell like disinfectant. Reba leans back, wilting on the sofa, staring at the expensive jewelry as if in a stupor.

"The police wondered if someone followed Rowdy to his fishing spot," she says in a faraway voice. "Maybe someone tried to rob him, and he fell off the pier and drowned."

"I don't believe he drowned," I reply.

"How can you be so sure?"

"There are ways to tell." I won't go into detail about the autopsy.

She doesn't need to hear that I used a centrifuge to spin down tissue from her husband's lungs. I made slides of that and his gastric contents, examining them with the microscope on my workstation's countertop inside the autopsy suite.

I didn't see any sign of the microscopic algae called diatoms. Their presence would confirm that he inhaled and swallowed river water.

"Do you recall what Rowdy had for dinner the night he disappeared?" I ask her.

"I made chili. He and the boys love my chili."

"Anything else?"

"Coleslaw," she says. "And cornbread. As you might have inferred, he had quite the appetite. After the hit-and-run, he didn't exercise and gained more than a hundred pounds."

I remember what I found in Rowdy O'Leary's stomach when I cut it open. The ground beef, the bits of kidney beans, onion and cabbage are consistent with his last meal. Digestion would have been slowed by his excessive intake of alcohol. I suspect he hadn't been on the pier very long before dying.

"What time did he eat?" I ask.

"Well, he was into eating early. It was around four-thirty."

"And what time did he leave the house to go fishing?"

"Right after that, around five," Reba answers. "He isn't much for hanging out at the table. He'd inhale his food and push back his chair."

"Did you know he was running an errand on his way to the pier?" I think of the time stamp on the jewelry store receipt.

He paid cash for the ring at 6:05 p.m., and from there drove on to his usual fishing spot.

"He didn't mention anything about stopping anywhere," Reba says.

She's quiet for a moment, staring at the gas fire.

"And I almost don't want to know the answer, Doctor Scarpetta. But I won't have any peace unless I do. Did Rowdy suffer?" Reba stares at me, her eyes wide, her lower lip trembling.

"I've not seen anything that makes me think he did," I reply. "I didn't find injuries that might indicate he'd been assaulted, for example. He didn't accidentally fall into the river, panic and drown."

"Then how did he end up in the water?" she asks. "What in God's name happened out there?"

"Again, it's very early in the investigation."

"But you must have an idea."

"It will be a while before the labs have finished their analysis," I tell her. "But your husband had significant heart disease. If he went into cardiac arrest, he might have felt chest pain. He might have gotten nauseous and dizzy. I suspect he was dead or almost dead when he hit the water."

"Thank God he didn't struggle against the current with his clothes on." She lowers her voice to a whisper. "Thank God he didn't go through a nightmare like that, didn't really suffer."

"I have no reason to think he did." I don't suggest that knowing you're about to die is a different kind of suffering.

"But he knew something was very wrong. That's what he was trying to tell me in the last text he started to write and didn't send," she says as if I know what she's talking about.

And I don't.

"I haven't seen that," I reply.

"The lady who called from the state told me they found it on Rowdy's phone."

"What did it say?" My anger toward Maggie boils up again.

Reba explains that while her husband was on the pier, he began typing a text to her. All it said was *He,* with no punctuation.

"It was the last thing he ever wrote," she adds tearily.

We don't know what time it was since the message wasn't sent. Most likely, he began typing the text right before he died. But that doesn't explain the fired rounds from his revolver or how he ended up in the water.

"Maybe he was writing *help,* something like that, because he felt chest pain." Tears trickle down Reba's cheeks. "I'm glad you don't think he jumped into the river on purpose."

"I don't believe he did."

"He would get depressed, and the medication he's supposed to be on has side effects he hates," she explains. "So he quit taking it, as you're aware from what's in his medicine cabinet. But he never talked about ending his own life. I also realize that's what a lot of people say after the unthinkable happens."

"Nothing I've seen might make me think he committed suicide. And if that was his intention, he had the gun with him." I point out the obvious.

"The police kept badgering me about the two bullets fired." She looks scared. "Wondering if Rowdy shot himself and fell into the river on purpose in hopes nobody would find his body. I can't imagine him doing anything like that."

"Your husband didn't shoot himself," I reply. "There are no projectiles inside his body. But it's a mystery why he might have fired his revolver. And if he did it while fishing, what was he shooting at?"

"Investigator Fruge suggested Rowdy might have been confronted by someone. Maybe someone who thought he had money."

Reba's eyes continue cutting toward the hallway as if she's worried about her sons overhearing.

"I've seen nothing that suggests he was assaulted," I repeat.

"Did he always drink beer while he fished? It appears he drank a six-pack in a short period of time."

"That was when he'd do his drinking," she replies. "Always coming home after the boys were in bed. He was never drunk in front of them."

"If he was intoxicated, might he have gotten out of control and decided to fire his gun?" I suggest, thinking of what Maggie accused him of. "Maybe shooting it into the air, maybe into the river? People lose their inhibitions, sometimes doing reckless things when they've had a lot to drink."

"I can't imagine him doing something dangerous like that," Reba says. "All I can tell you is he was more paranoid about our safety and security. Because of what's all over the news. That Slasher maniac who's breaking into homes and killing women in their sleep. The nurses I work with are scared out of their wits. After the last murder, one of them quit and moved to Atlanta."

"I can see why the murders would make your husband or anyone more security-minded," I reply.

"I saw on the news about the killer going after Dana Diletti next. The phantom hologram or whatever it is appearing inside her house a little while ago," Reba says. "Rowdy believes the Slasher uses technologies that are advanced way beyond the capabilities of most computer programmers."

"Sounds like your husband was genuinely scared," I answer as the cuckoo clock sounds, the wooden bird appearing from behind its small door.

"He was. And so am I." She dabs her eyes. "I don't know how anybody couldn't be."

I look at the security system's display panel on the wall, noticing the cable running to it. Her husband was astute enough to install a hardwired system that can't be disabled by signal jamming. Benton and I have taken the same precautions on our property. Lucy insists on it.

"Do you use your security system?" I ask Reba.

"We didn't like we should until the Slasher murders started," she says. "Then we began setting it every night and whenever we go out. This was about the same time Rowdy started carrying his revolver. At night he kept it next to the sofa bed with the trigger lock on."

————

I hear Marino's heavy footsteps in the hallway. Then he's back inside the living room, towering over us near the coffee table.

"I told your two little dudes to chill in their room for a while so the grown-ups can talk," he explains to their mother.

"Those two don't chill. What are they doing?" Reba asks.

"Playing *Minecraft,* busy building castles when I left." Marino picks up his leather jacket from the chair where he left it.

"Their father designed video games in his software business. Or he used to," she replies. "Playing them was something he and the boys did together."

"They mentioned something interesting I'd like to ask you about, Reba," Marino says. "Are you aware that your husband told the boys he was thinking about selling the house and moving to a different neighborhood far away from here?"

"Well, I know we can't afford this place." Anger sparks again. "Rowdy's been talking about moving into something smaller and less expensive. He was obsessed with the Slasher murders and wanted us far away from here."

"Why do you think he was obsessed?" Marino asks.

"Because the victims were involved in healthcare," she says. "One of them was a nurse. Rowdy didn't feel he could protect us, and he wanted to move to another state. Maybe to California. I wouldn't hear of it. I love our house and my job at the hospital..." She chokes up.

Marino pulls out his wallet, finding one of his business cards. He places it on the coffee table as I get up from the sofa.

"My cell number's on the back," he says to her. "Don't hesitate to call if you've got questions. Or if you have further information we should know about."

"Something might come to you later," I add.

She follows us back to the entryway, where I collect my coat, putting it on. I retrieve my briefcase, looping the strap over my shoulder.

"Please tell your boys it was nice meeting them," I say to Reba as she sees us out. "I'm sorry it wasn't under happier circumstances."

She waits in the doorway as we pick our way down front steps that are treacherous. The iron railing is crusty with ice and too cold to grip with bare hands. Snow falls in small hard flakes that sandblast our faces, the accumulation at least five inches and glazed by freezing rain.

The white street in front is blank, the night silent, just the sound of trees rocking in the gusting wind and our boots crunching. We slip and slide, our breath smoking out as we quietly mutter expletives that hopefully Reba can't hear from the porch. Thunder murmurs. Lightning veins the turbulent darkness.

"Thank you again," she calls out. "Merry Christmas," her joyless voice falters.

"And to you!" we shout, and it seems empty and ironic.

As we climb into Marino's truck, she raises her hand in a listless wave.

Stepping back inside.

Closing the door.

We sit without talking, the engine rumbling, the defrost and heat on high. As the windshield warms, ice melts around the edges, breaking up in floes that slide down the glass.

We scroll through messages and news alerts on our phones, the police scanner chattering about traffic pileups. Downed trees are closing roads and taking out power lines. Dana Diletti's video of the phantom hologram floating into her bedroom has gone viral. So has her interview of me talking about the Slasher murders.

Lucy texts that she's stuck at the FBI Academy for the night. I could have predicted that.

*Sorry. Too much going on & roads bad,* she writes. *Will see you tomorrow with your gift.*

*Disappointed. But be safe,* I answer.

I write Benton that I'm headed home, and it looks like we'll be spending our Christmas Eve alone.

"Good thing our places have backup generators, Doc." Marino holsters his pistol under the steering column. "I wouldn't be surprised if we lose power before the night's over."

"Let's hope not."

"I'm worried about them." He stares at the house.

"They clearly look up to you," I reply. "I'm glad you spent some time with them."

He begins typing a message, his thick thumbs surprisingly nimble.

"I'm telling Mick and Rick to let me know if they lose power," he explains. "I've got an extra generator that I don't use, a portable one. It's in the garage along with cans of gasoline, about ten gallons' worth. I can bring it over if needed."

He turns on the wipers as curtains part in the living room bay window, the twins peeking out at us. Their faces are wistful in the rainbow radiance of the artificial Christmas tree their father assembled and decorated last month. I feel the ache in my chest, emotions tackling me when I least expect.

I'm reminded of my early medical school days when I first encountered families of people who died suddenly, often violently. I don't know how anyone can stare death in the eye and be the same. I can't touch devastation and walk away unchanged. I'm not who I used to be. I'm not sure I ever was.

"Shit," Marino says with a smile pinned on his face, looking back at the twins.

"Shit is right." I fasten my seat belt.

He opens his window, a sheen of melting ice sliding off. Sticking his arm out, he gives the twins a grin, a thumbs-up, and they do the same before waving frantically. I hate to think of them waking up in the morning and opening gifts from their dead father while Reba is buried by more bills.

Marino's window hums back up, and he lowers the defrost.

"I'm not sure if it's good or bad that we showed up in person," he says. "I never know. I promise people I'll be back to check on them and all the rest. Most of the time I don't. Even if I mean to."

I'm aware of the boys watching us like puppies hoping for adoption.

"Jesus," Marino says under his breath. "I hope I handled it okay, Doc."

"You handled it more than okay," I tell him.

"Well, parenting isn't my strong suit. I didn't do such a hot job with Rocky."

"The way he turned out wasn't your fault." I say the same thing whenever Marino mentions his only child, a career criminal who died years ago.

"I wouldn't have won any prizes with him, and was a pretty shitty husband to Doris, truth be told. To hear your sister talk, I'm not much better now." Marino shoves the gearshift into reverse.

"Doris left you, not the other way around," I remind him. "And my sister has one of the worst track records in history when it comes to relationships. You're lasting longer than anyone ever has."

"When you put it like that, it doesn't make me feel much better," he says.

We begin backing out of the driveway, the headlights shining on a stand of evergreens. Snow has drifted against dark trunks and is piled in branches, the top of the black mailbox thickly capped in white.

"This time of the year, it's hard not to have regrets," Marino says. "I get so buried in work and don't always pay as much attention to Dorothy as I should. That's always been the problem no matter who it is."

"I know all about it," I reply, and if I had a cigarette right now, I'd sure as hell smoke it.

# CHAPTER 11

We don't see another car on South Payne Street, the lights of homes pallid in the storm. Marino opens the ashtray for more chewing gum. Juicy Fruit this time.

I take him up on the offer, my mouth parched. I'm shaky inside and blame it on low blood sugar. It's almost nine o'clock, our staff Christmas lunch a long time ago, my stomach empty and raw.

"Rowdy had to have known what a deadbeat husband and dad he was, nothing but a liability after some asshole ran him over." Marino gets back to that. "Be nice to find who's responsible and lock up his ass. It would be the gift that keeps on giving."

The gum's fruity flavor makes my mouth water, carrying me back to my father's store. I remember a bell jingling when the front glass door opened, the cool fragrant air inside. I envision the old cash register with its sliding drawer that I'd unlock first thing with the steel key I wore on a string around my neck.

"As far as I'm concerned, the driver should be charged with manslaughter," Marino goes on, both of us vigorously chewing.

"That won't happen, assuming the person is ever caught," I reply. "Rowdy's heart disease was due to his lifestyle. And possibly to genetics."

"He made bad choices because someone else caused him to be disabled mentally, physically, in every way possible," Marino says.

"True," I reply.

"I guarantee he wouldn't be dead if it wasn't for the shitcan who slammed into him and sped away."

"You're probably right," I agree. "But it wouldn't hold water legally. And after six years, the police aren't motivated anymore. Rowdy's death likely won't change that."

"Huh. I'm not sure how motivated they were to begin with," Marino says, driving well under the speed limit, our headlights reflecting off whiteness.

It's hard to know where the pavement ends and the shoulder begins, snow blowing wildly in streetlights. I pass along the name of the state trooper Reba mentioned. Maybe Marino should get in touch with him.

"You're reading my mind, Doc. I'll give Trad Whalen a call ASAP, see what he has to say about the hit-and-run. Maybe there's evidence that wasn't ever tested."

"I have some of Rowdy O'Leary's records and will go through them when I get home," I reply.

"A hell of a way to spend Christmas Eve," Marino says.

"What else did you learn from the boys?" Already, I'm tired of the gum.

Taking it out of my mouth, I drop it into the trash bag.

"They told me enough that I believe Rowdy cared about them, spending a lot of time playing video games, watching movies," Marino replies. "More a friend than a father, I got the impression."

"Thank you for being kind. I think you might be their new hero." I use my sleeve to wipe condensation off my side window.

"You don't have to thank me, Doc. The least I could do," he says. "The piece of shit who hit their dad did damage to them, too. And to Reba, but I'm not sure what I think of her yet."

"You're a good person."

"Well, the little dudes have my number, and I'll check on them tomorrow," he adds as we drive through their neighborhood. "But I want to be careful how much attention I pay. Since we don't really know what we're dealing with."

"No, we don't," I reply. "But you were right about the life insurance. And it's substantial enough to cause questions should someone have reason to suspect Reba is somehow responsible for her husband's death. Although I fail to see what involvement she could have had."

Tire tracks are faintly visible through new snow, and we slow down as a splendid three-point buck trots across the street in front of us. He stands as still as an ice sculpture, staring, his eyes reflecting red in our headlights reminding me of the phantom hologram again.

"Looks like Santa lost one of his reindeer," Marino says.

He taps his horn and the buck bounds away, vanishing in the snowy dark.

"It sounds like Rowdy left considerable debt." I pick up where we left off. "I don't know what he was making as a software designer, but I suspect his wife has been the one holding everything together at home while working full time as a nurse."

"You can count on the insurance company doing everything it can to avoid making the payout," Marino says, lightning flashing in the gloom. "A lot of insurers won't pay if it's a suicide."

"Unless I find out something to convince me otherwise, I'm not ruling him a suicide," I reply.

"There's a lot to look into," he says. "Including whether Reba might have had something going on outside the marriage. She's nice-looking and around all kinds of people at the hospital. It's obvious she and Rowdy didn't have much of a relationship anymore."

"She intimated as much."

I tell him about the box of expired condoms in a cabinet, and that Rowdy mostly lived in his office.

"Apparently they fought a lot," Marino says.

"The police will dig into her personal life, as if she hasn't been through enough," I reply.

"Maybe she has a relationship on the side," Marino goes on. "Rowdy shot his gun twice, and I'm betting he did that while he was on the pier. Maybe Reba has a boyfriend who decided to show up, maybe encouraging Rowdy to give her a divorce."

"That's a lot of maybes," I reply. "And do we know if she wanted a divorce?"

"Got no idea. But Rick and Mick were worried about *Mom leaving*. That's what they said."

Marino lightly taps the brakes, gradually coming to a stop as we reach King Street.

"I asked them a lot of questions about the night their dad disappeared," he's saying. "I got the impression that their parents were arguing before Rowdy went out the door with his fishing gear and cooler of beer."

"Do we have any idea what they were arguing about?" I ask, the wipers thumping like a metronome.

A tow truck clanks by with chains on the tires.

"Sounds like she hated his fishing trips. Reba was asking him to stay home for once," Marino explains. "His night fishing isn't making much sense. I wonder what he was really up to. Especially since the pier he picked is used for trysts. Assuming Fabian knows what the hell he's talking about."

"He used to take dates there," I reply. "I'd say he knows."

"Making me wonder if Rowdy was a voyeur. Maybe he liked to watch."

I pass along what Maggie told me about him looking at pornography on his phone.

"It's clear he struggled with depression and liked having time to himself," I explain. "If he hung out on the pier for voyeuristic reasons, to drink while looking at porn, that might be the explanation. In other words, he wasn't there to fish."

"I'd be depressed too if I couldn't do anything physical anymore, including having sex and working out in the gym. Not to mention, Dorothy would bail on me for sure," Marino says. "Rowdy's moods will be used against him. I doubt Reba will see any insurance money anytime soon. Maybe never. Especially if you decide the case is undetermined."

"That's not happening. But I'll have to pend the manner of death for a while," I reply, the Ace Hardware store we churn past closed, not a car in the lot.

Usually, Christmas Eve would be hopping in Old Town, but restaurants, bars and other businesses are empty. Holiday markets and Santa's Magical Corner are dark and barricaded, parades and music fests canceled because of the weather.

Lighted evergreen swags strung over the street swing in arctic gusts that have torn loose pine garlands from doorways and lampposts.

An inflatable gingerbread man yanks at his tether in front of the mattress store.

A Grinch has escaped someone's yard and is supine by the roadside, shaking in the wind.

Illuminated spheres and starbursts sway perilously in trees as if the world is coming to a furious end.

———

Marino's big truck cuts through side streets that need plowing, hardly anyone out. We creep past abandoned cars that have plunged into the ditch. Burned-out emergency flares are black streaks in the shadowy snow.

Thunder reverberates, wind pummeling as the storm rages. I continue checking messages, worried about Benton, about Lucy and my sister, about everyone. I'm unsettled as if something awful is about to happen.

*Any progress?* I send a text to Benton.

*Not good,* he answers quickly.

Since we last communicated, he's not gotten any farther than Ronald Reagan Washington National Airport. A tractor-trailer jack-knifed and is blocking two lanes of traffic. Benton tells me he's been sitting without moving for the past thirty-five minutes, his electric car battery running low.

*Down to 30%,* he writes.

*Do you need us to come find you?* I text him back.

*Negative & you'd never get here.*

*We'd figure out a way,* I promise. *Won't have you stranded.*

As I'm typing, I envision morbid scenarios should he be forced to abandon his SUV. He could be struck by a car. He could fall and hit his head, dying from exposure.

*I'll be fine,* Benton answers. *Where are you?*

*Pulling up to the house now,* I let him know.

Marino stops at the black wrought iron front gate. On either side of the entrance is fencing that's just as tall and formidable. Our nine-acre estate is monitored by an array of sophisticated cameras and sensors that Lucy installed and manages with AI help from Janet.

I find the remote control inside my briefcase, pointing it through the window. The gate begins stuttering open, and I hope it doesn't get stuck. The snow is deep and not letting up. We sit impatient and restless, looking around at dark woods on either side, headlights shining on big trees that have been here for centuries.

"I don't like leaving you home by yourself, Doc," Marino says as the gate inchworms noisily along its metal track. "I really don't. You know how I am when I get one of my bad feelings. And I'm getting one big-time."

"Considering the day we've had, it's no wonder," I reply. "I have a bad feeling, too. For one thing, I don't like Dana Diletti staying in her house after what happened earlier. I hope to God we don't get called to respond there. So far, the Slasher shows up to butcher his victims on major holidays, and tomorrow is the biggest of the year."

Then we're driving through the entrance, our tires crushing unbroken whiteness. We wait to make sure the gate shuts behind us, the snow luminous in the uneven glow of iron lamps. With every passing moment Marino seems more uneasy, and I suspect I know what's bothering him most. He's not looking forward to what awaits him at home.

"I'm pissed Dana Diletti would put herself at risk, especially at a time like this," he's saying. "The latest from Fruge is the cops aren't patrolling her neighborhood. As you might figure, they're overwhelmed dealing with accidents, stranded motorists, domestic situations. We've already got a murder-suicide, the bodies on the way to our office according to Fabian. The cops have their hands full."

"We'd better pray the Slasher stays off the streets tonight because of the storm," I answer.

"It makes sense that he would," Marino says. "My guess is he sent the hologram into Dana Diletti's bedroom to create a media sensation. And he's gotten what he wanted, that's for sure."

"We can only hope he doesn't intend to follow up on his scary gesture like he has three times before," I reply as the gate clanks shut.

# CHAPTER 12

"I don't know. It's like something's watching us." Marino nervously glances around as we crunch away from the gate. "It's the same thing I felt when Fruge and I were searching Dana's property. I sensed something was there, a presence we couldn't see."

"That's to be expected since the Slasher's hologram had just invaded her house," I remind him.

"Yeah, you're right." His eyes are on the mirrors. "It was probably my imagination. But then again, he uses the fake ghost to spy. Although I don't see how the hell that would work. I still don't get it. How can an optical illusion record sound and video?"

"Lucy says the Slasher has a terahertz holographic projector that uses extremely fast pulsing infrared and radio waves to pass through windows, walls." I tell him the same thing I have before. "The electromagnetic energy electrifies the air, basically turning it into pixels. That's how the images are painted."

"Lucy never says anything that normal people can freakin' understand," Marino complains.

"These electromagnetic waves enable the Slasher to record the images and sounds. That's how he spies." I'm uneasy looking out at the dark woods as we follow the driveway.

"Meaning he could have been watching everything while Fruge

and I were poking around her property. Just like he's been watching Dana Diletti. It must be someone who knows what the hell he's doing. Like a scientist gone haywire."

As he's saying this, a dead branch lands in front of us, a puff of snow drifting down. A great horned owl flaps from a tree with loud shrieks and hoots. I can see its feathery earlike tufts and huge wingspan as it swoops low over the truck, vanishing in the dark.

"Fucking hell," Marino says. "Could things get any creepier?"

"We have a nest on the property," I reply. "At the back of it high up in a tree with a view of the river. I call them our protect owls."

"Well, they wouldn't be very protective of Merlin," Marino says. "And I bet you don't have much of a rabbit population."

"I've told Lucy how dangerous it is for Merlin to go out at night," I reply while looking around for him.

The security cameras can pick up the cat when he's on the driveway. But not when he's in the woods because he's too low to the ground. I rarely know where Merlin is unless he's in front of me.

"I don't mind hanging out for a little bit." Marino doesn't want to go home.

He's afraid to deal with my sister. When she takes umbrage at some perceived infraction, she doesn't get over it easily or without penalty. Especially when she's drinking. And considering the season, Dorothy will be spoiling for a fight. When she gets the vapors, as she describes it, nothing clears them out like a knockdown drag-out.

"Nice of you but not necessary," I tell Marino. "I hope Dorothy's doing all right," I add pointedly, because that's who he should be most concerned about.

"I've not heard from her for a while. She's not answering. Probably busy talking to Janet," he adds with resentment. "I already know what to expect when I get home. Dorothy will be throwing back wine in front of the TV, griping to Janet about me. Implying something bogus and unfair about my relationship with you."

"Staying here with me until Benton comes home won't make things any better, Marino."

"No kidding," he says, chewing gum, his face unhappy. "I'm sorry about the spa package, Doc."

We've reached the guest cottage where Lucy lives, indistinct in deep shadows. Blackout shades block any light inside, and I can't tell when she's home. But she isn't now and won't be tonight. I can't believe we're not spending Christmas Eve together.

"I didn't mean to cause a stink. Especially when you're about to skip town," Marino adds as I notice animal tracks just ahead.

Then there are more of them pockmarking the snow in a decided direction that trails off into dense trees swallowed by darkness. Possibly a fox. Maybe a coyote. Our fence doesn't keep out all animals. I've seen a fox climb it more than once, and I know that bears can. Raccoons dig under it.

"I was thinking about you flying across the pond and having jet lag, and that the spa might be just the ticket," Marino goes on. "I thought you should be pampered."

"Best you don't put it like that to my sister." I'm blunt about it. "In her mind, the only person you should be pampering is her."

Around a bend in the driveway, floodlights shine on the white brick carriage house that's now a garage. The double wooden doors open manually the same way they did more than a century ago. As we drive past, I notice eyes reflecting yellow in our headlights up ahead.

"What the hell?" Marino slows down.

A raccoon quickly waddles off the driveway, something not

quite right with one of his legs. Before I can get a better look, he's gone in the fog.

"Let's hope he's not rabid." Marino drives on.

"He didn't look rabid. He looked injured." My heart sinks as I think about the likelihood of getting Mount Vernon Animal Rescue or anyone else out here during Christmas.

"And what does rabid look like?" Marino asks. "We can't tell at a glance if he's rabid."

"Whatever he is, I hope Merlin is inside Lucy's cottage or the main house." I'm keeping my eye out for him. "I hate that he wanders about, especially after dark."

Merlin was feral when Lucy rescued him as a kitten. Accustomed to living in the wild, he goes ballistic if kept inside against his will. She installed small doors that allow him to come and go as he pleases. It's not safe on a property teeming with wildlife, some of it nocturnal.

We stop in front of the house, two-story white brick with dusky blue shutters, the slate roof piled in snow. Candles in the windows and other lights on timers glow warmly, a fresh holly wreath on the front door like a greeting card.

"Thank you for going with me to the O'Learys'. And for driving." I unbuckle my shoulder harness.

"You sure you don't want me to come in for a while, Doc? I really don't mind." Fishing the gum out of his mouth, he flicks it into the trash bag.

"As soon as I'm inside, I'll set the alarm. No need to worry," I reply. "If my sister is still awake, alert and in the mood, tell her to call. I'm sorry the two of you can't be with us tonight."

"Yeah, me too, Doc." He sounds frustrated. "But now that you know what's going on with Dorothy, it might be for the best."

"Benton and I will stop by to see you on our way to the airport tomorrow afternoon. We have a little something for you two that we think you'll like."

"I'm sure you're looking forward to getting the hell out of here for a while." Marino can't disguise how he feels about it.

He hasn't said as much but I know he doesn't want me leaving the country for two weeks. He doesn't like me going anywhere at all. I sense him watching as I push open my door, stepping down into snow that buries my suede ankle boots, cold seeping inside them.

"Merry Christmas, Marino." I shut the door, and his window lowers.

"You too, Doc." His face looks reluctant. "I really don't like leaving you here alone," he again says, and I think of the irony.

He doesn't mind leaving Dorothy alone. Janet's comments about his feelings toward me aren't baseless, and my sister knows it.

"Good night," I tell him.

I'm tentative on the front steps, taking one at a time, the wind louder, wailing and whistling. Snow blows off trees in clouds. Thunder cracks like a gun going off, lightning flashing, and I'm startled by a loud crashing in the woods that sounds close.

"What the fuck was that?" Marino has his head out the window, looking around in alarm.

He unholsters his pistol from the steering column as I pause on the porch, staring out at swirling grayness. Snowflakes coldly touch my face, and I'm on high alert.

"A decent-sized animal, it sounded like." I peer into the overcast.

"Maybe that raccoon we saw."

"It didn't sound like a raccoon, sounded bigger than that. Hopefully friendly, whatever it is," I decide, looking in the direction of the noise. "I guess the thunder spooked it."

"A deer, I'm betting." Marino's attention is everywhere.

"They can't get in unless the gate is open," I reply.

"One could have come in behind us and we didn't see it," he says as more thunder explodes like a war going on.

Sticks snap in the dark, followed by snorts and screams that turn my blood cold.

"Geezus effing Kris Kringle!" Marino's eyes are wide. "Maybe I should get out and poke around?"

"And if it's a bobcat or a bear?" I have my keys out. "Then what are you going to do?"

"Tell it to eat more chicken?"

"Go home, Marino." I can't help but laugh even as my nerves spark like electrical static.

"Told you this place is Jurassic Park," he says, rolling up his window.

He begins turning his truck around in small maneuvers, the engine gunning as I halfway expect something hideous to emerge from the gloom. Unlocking the front door, I step inside the house, entering my code to silence the beeping security system.

Pausing in the doorway, I wave good night as Marino drives off in a swirl of exhaust. Then I hear crashing through the brush near the greenhouse in the garden. I can barely make out the lavender glow of the ultraviolet light inside. Dorothy insisted on installing it over her cannabis plants, four of them, the legal limit in Virginia.

Something grunts and shrieks. I hear a guttural hooting that doesn't sound like an owl. If Marino were here, I can imagine him freaking out, certain it's a Bigfoot or a Yeti. I don't know what the hell it is, and now I hear loud growling close to the porch. Shutting the door, I throw on the deadbolt, my heart flying out of my chest.

I reset the alarm, the light on the display turning red. I check the security monitor, the video images murky. White lights along the driveway are blurry on the live feed. The vague shapes of trees near the house move in the wind, headlights shining on the front gate.

It begins opening as Marino waits in his truck. I gasp when something touches my leg.

"Jesus, Merlin!"

Lucy's cat rubs against me, frantic, not purring. Spotted, with full moon eyes, he stares up at me. I pet him, checking to make sure he has no injuries. My first thought was he might have tangled with a raccoon or some other animal. He's fine.

"Now's not a good time to sneak up on me, please. But thank God you're inside the house," I say to Merlin, and his back arches.

He hisses at the front door, thunder clapping, and I look again at the security monitor. I don't see anything except snow and fog, the front gate lurching shut as Marino drives off, the engine loud over the security monitor, the truck's taillights vanishing.

Except they don't.

———

What I'm seeing aren't taillights, I realize with a start, staring at the video display in disbelief. Two red orbs float over the closing front gate.

A thrill of fear races up to the roots of my hair as the glowing red lights move along the driveway, coming closer in overcast thick like a cloud. Merlin glares at the front door, a low growl in his throat, the fur standing up on his back.

"It's okay. We're safe in here," I say to him. "This is why you stay inside now, please? I don't want you even thinking about going anywhere when we don't know what's lurking about."

Bending down, I remove his plastic collar that Lucy 3-D prints. An embedded electronic chip automatically opens the cat doors when Merlin decides to venture inside or out.

"Don't be angry." I hope he doesn't make a terrible fuss.

Merlin has been known to caterwaul loud enough to wake the dead. He's destroyed blinds and curtains when feeling trapped.

"It's for your own good." I pet him again. "I saw that very large owl a few minutes ago, the one I've warned you about. And an injured raccoon that might have been growling. Which is why you shouldn't go out at night. And the weather's awful."

Merlin is glued to me as I watch the monitor in the foyer. The two red orbs float blearily and in tandem over the foggy driveway like something supernatural. I'm transfixed, curious and horrified as the small red lights travel closer to the house, and I think of the video Dana Diletti took with her phone.

I envision the bright red eyes of the phantomlike specter repeatedly seen around the time of the Slasher murders. I remember police statements about the victims telling their friends and colleagues about seeing and hearing eerie red lights and sounds not long before their murders.

I'm tempted to call Marino. But if I do, he'll come barreling back. That wouldn't be fair to my sister, and it's not necessary. I try Benton instead, and he answers on the first ring.

"They've just cleared the tractor-trailer off the highway," he says right away.

"How's the battery charge holding up?"

"Around twenty-eight percent." He sounds tired, his patience beginning to fray, and that's saying a lot as stoic as he is. "Traffic should start moving any minute."

"Benton, there's something strange going on."

I'm looking at the monitor inside the entryway, and the red orbs are near the porch. I'm worried that any moment they're going to enter the house, and the figure in black will be in front of me, grinning and waving his knife.

"These two red lights on the property," I explain to Benton.

Parting the drape next to the front door, I peer out the window, the red orbs moving closer.

"I'm looking at them out the window. They're floating in front of the house..."

I've no sooner said this than they vanish before my eyes.

"That's weird," I mutter, letting go of the drape.

I see nothing on the monitor but the hulking shapes of trees and shrubs in grayness. And my footprints in the snow leading up the steps to the front door. I tell Benton what I saw and heard after Marino dropped me off a few minutes ago.

"The red lights reminded me of the phantom hologram. But I don't know what was in the woods. I heard howling and screaming," I explain. "I know this sounds kooky."

"One thing you never sound is kooky," Benton replies as I hang my coat in the entryway closet. "I wish like hell I could get to you quicker. Where's your Glock?"

"Upstairs as usual."

"You should be carrying it."

"Let's don't start on that," I reply.

"Please go get it."

"I will, but I'm not seeing the red lights anymore, and maybe it was a big deer as Marino suggested." But I don't believe it.

"Doesn't sound like it," Benton says. "Keep the alarm on, and don't go outside again for any reason whatsoever."

"No fear of that."

"I'll be home soon, God willing," he promises, and we end the call.

# CHAPTER 13

I take off my boots, leaving them near the door. Inside the entryway closet are the shearling-lined moccasins I wear in the house, and I slip them on.

My feet are quiet on centuries-old pumpkin pine flooring original to the house and outbuildings. The wide smooth boards are a deep dark orange, the walls white plaster with rosy bricks wearing through. Exposed oak beams in curved wooden ceilings look like the ribs of a ship.

"I need to visit the wine cellar if you want to come along," I say to Merlin.

When the house was built in the mid-1700s, it included a servants' back hallway leading to the cellar where a second kitchen was located. I hustle that way as Merlin slinks after me.

Opening the door off the pantry, I turn on the light over old stone steps, the air cool and damp carrying the faint scent of cannabis. I flip up another switch, the dangling lightbulb overhead garishly bright on the low ceiling and brick walls.

Merlin dashes to the deadbolted basement door leading outside. He paces back and forth in front of the cat flap at the bottom of it, muttering and meowing irritably when it won't open. The wind howls, the storm heaving around us, the house shivering and creaking.

"I'm sorry," I tell Merlin. "But no way you're going outside right now. I don't know why you'd want to."

His answer is to hiss, suddenly clawing at the air as he often does down here. Marino swears the house is haunted. He claims to have experienced the paranormal. Laughter. Metal clacking and clanging like swordfighting. A voice whispering in what he swears was Old English, although I'm not sure he would know what that sounds like.

He once saw a young man dressed like a pirate in short tight pants, a long coat and tricorn hat. The description sounds like Dobbin Lumley, the British sea captain who was the original owner. He named the estate Belle Rise, the parcel of land at the time fifty acres directly on a wide bend in the Potomac River.

He was described as short of stature but superhumanly strong, handsome with long dark hair, and fierce with a cutlass. Growing up on the London docks, he made his fortune from capturing pirate ships loaded with ill-gotten booty. Or that was what he told people. Based on what I've read, it's questionable who was the pirate.

After Benton and I bought Belle Rise, I made it my mission to excavate more than the garden. In my home office is a banker's box of photocopied records and correspondence relating to the history. During quiet moments when I look out our bedroom windows, I imagine the sea captain's view of what today is Point Lumley Park, and beyond it the river.

Stubby timber footings are all that's left of his wharf, and at low tide they peek above the water. I imagine his seventy-foot sloop the

*Black Pearl* with its rampant white sails, a painting of it on display in the local history museum. I've never seen the sea captain's ghost down here in what used to be his cellar and servants' kitchen.

But I've felt a presence. Scraping sounds as if someone is looking through boxes of Benton's and my belongings. Footsteps on the floor above my head when no one else was home. Drafts of unearthly cold air. Shadows that move like wraiths. I'm not bothered by whatever is here and what it might mean. Benton isn't either. The first time we saw the house, we felt it wanted us living here.

The weedy scent is stronger as I reach the old kitchen that my sister appropriated. It's nothing more than a fireplace that's been nonworking for decades. On the soapstone countertop is a decarboxylator that looks like a large coffee thermos. Hanging from a wooden rod overhead are branches of cannabis curing.

Beyond is a workbench scattered with tools, then through a doorway is the large glass-doored wine cooler filled with reds and whites that Benton collects. Finding a Barolo, I slide it out of the rack.

"I know you're upset that you can't go outside," I tell Merlin as he fusses. "How about I build us a nice cozy fire in the bedroom?"

He shadows me back up the basement steps, and I leave the bottle of wine on the kitchen counter. Muttering and mumbling, he follows as I return to the entryway in the soft glow of caged copper sconces that Benton and I discovered at a flea market.

The stained-glass transom over the front door is a whale breaching in an ocean of variegated blue. We found it in London along with the port and starboard lanterns that are lamps in the living room. Benton grew up with a love of all things nautical, his family owning a sailing yacht they moored in the Boston Harbor.

One of our favorite hobbies together is finding unusual antiques at auctions, in salvage yards and junk shops. Other treasures are the framed marine maps, the paintings of schooners, fishing vessels, a frigate in a storm I climb past on the steps.

The chandelier over the second-floor landing is a brass ship's wheel we happened upon in Genoa, Italy, while I was there lecturing on forensic medicine. Inside a shadowbox on the wall is the wooden-barreled spyglass telescope from France that we were told was used by a naval officer during the Napoleonic Wars.

"It's okay," I reassure Merlin, smiling as if all is fine when I know it's not. "Please don't be afraid."

He stalks me along the second-floor hallway, yowling as thunder claps and mumbles. The wind pummels the house, roaring and whistling. Lightning flashes in brass porthole windows at the roofline as if we're being fired upon by enemy vessels.

"We're perfectly safe." I tell Merlin another lie.

I continue waiting for the inevitable, a horror that we might not survive. Any second, the Wi-Fi will fail, the red orbs will reappear as the phantomlike figure floats through a window. Or the power will go out. Maybe a tree will fall on top of the house.

"It's just a bad storm. Usually, we don't have thunder and lightning when it's snowing," I explain as Merlin mutters and meows. "And yes, there was something weird going on outside a little while ago that you no doubt sensed. I'm sure you heard the growling and all the rest. I don't like it any more than you do."

He rubs against my ankles, his big gold eyes looking up at me. I'm careful where I step as he weaves between my feet. Beehive pendant lights shine from the ceiling as I near the guestroom where Marino and Dorothy stay. Uncharitable as it sounds, I'm not sorry they won't be here tonight, no matter what I've said to the contrary.

I'm not in the mood for a fight, and Janet's right that the spa package is too personal. I wish Marino hadn't gotten me a gift that's bound to upset my sister. I know she's angry at me, as if what he did is my fault somehow. That's why I'm not hearing from her. It isn't because she's been guzzling wine all night.

Dorothy can hold on to rejections and perceived slights longer than anyone I know. I imagine the two of them going at each other right about now. Marino must have anticipated that his gesture toward me would create a dangerous chemistry. How could he not know that Janet would find out and weigh in?

Reaching the guestroom that I use as an office, I scan my thumb in the ergonomic lock. The door opens onto wooden bookcases, my covered microscope on the desk, the plastic anatomical skeleton grimacing from his metal stand. I walk in, making sure the computer is off, and that the windows aren't leaking, and Merlin follows.

Satisfied that all is in order, I lock up again, and mostly it's my inquisitive, clever sister I need to keep out. She and Marino have agreed to housesit while Benton and I are gone these next two weeks. It's happened more than once that Dorothy wanders into my office when I'm not around, insatiably curious about anything I'm working on.

She doesn't mind helping herself to whatever isn't locked up in fireproof cabinets, offering her unsolicited opinions and insights. She's been exploring volunteer work at the local police department. Crisis counseling I've been alarmed to hear her mention, and I suspect it won't be long before she insinuates herself into my cases.

The hallway ends at the main bedroom, and I open the solid oak door, feeling the cool darkness inside. I turn on the chandelier that's shaped like an anchor, its electrified candles illuminating wide plank flooring the color of dark reddish honey. The exposed brick walls are hung with paintings and etchings handed down from Benton's father.

The antique leather sofa and matching club chairs, the hand-knotted Persian rugs, almost everything of value is from Benton's family. I'm used to the abundance he's brought to our relationship. But it was overwhelming at first, and difficult to accept that I had little to offer by comparison. I didn't become a forensic pathologist for the money.

Dropping my briefcase on top of the bed, I start undressing as I walk to my closet. I hang up my suit, tossing undergarments into the hamper. The black silk pajamas I put on were a birthday present from Benton. I wash my face, brushing my teeth again, scrubbing away Rowdy O'Leary's remembered stench.

I can't stop seeing the wistful faces of Mick and Rick looking out the window as Marino and I drove away. I'm afraid I'll see the twins forever in my thoughts. I know why I had to stop by their house. It was important to return their father's personal effects, and I gathered important information in the process.

What Marino and I did was professional and humane, even kind and considerate. Underlying that are my own personal reasons. Except there's no getting over childhood traumas milled deep into the psyche.

*How's it going?* I type another text to Benton, lonely for him.

He doesn't answer immediately, and I crouch in front of the fireplace, the bricks bordered in blue-and-white Delft tiles the sea captain imported from the Netherlands. Drawing open the metal mesh curtain, I make sure the flue isn't closed. I grab a section of the *Washington Post* from the sweetgrass basket next to the low hearth.

Merlin is watching my every move, his tail twitching as another message lands on my phone.

*Potomac Yard.* Benton writes back that he's three miles away. *Slow but moving at least. Maybe 30 mins.*

*Be careful when you get here,* I remind him.

*Have my friend with me.* He means his gun.

*Park near front door.*

*Can't,* he answers.

Benton needs to recharge his electric SUV, and I don't like the idea of him leaving it halfway down the driveway in the carriage house. Black bears, bobcats, coyotes in this part of the world aren't known for attacking people. But that doesn't mean they won't, depending on the circumstances. They have before. For sure, they'll go after pets.

But I'm more concerned about a predator of a different variety as I think of the red orbs on the driveway. I don't believe it was animal eyes, and I continue to sense a sinister presence. At moments the creaking of the house sounds like whispering. I hear creepy music that turns into the eolian strains of the wind.

———

Opening my bedside drawer, I retrieve my Glock. Removing the trigger lock, I rack back the slide, chambering a round. Setting the 9mm pistol on top of the nightstand within easy reach, I try Lucy's cell phone and she doesn't answer.

I'm texting her about the strange red lights, the growling and screaming, when Merlin hisses and sallies out of the bedroom.

"Well, you can't go very far without your collar," I call after him, my nerves humming.

Arranging split logs on the fireplace grate, I keep glancing at the security monitor across from the bed. My attention returns to the shaded windows as I envision the ghostly hologram that levitated into Dana Diletti's house. I expect it to happen here any second while anticipating how I might handle such a ghastly visitation.

I tell myself not to allow my imagination to get the best of me. But the sensation persists while I crunch up sheets of newspaper, stuffing them under slender strips of fatwood, my hands sooty from newsprint. I pick up the electric match, pressing the trigger.

Flames shoot up, licking around logs, smoke curling, and I can't shake the feeling that I'm being watched. Getting up from the hearth, I step inside the bathroom to rinse my hands. From there I head to the nearest window, the wind making its baleful music. Pushing open an edge of the shade, I peer out at darkness, snow-flakes dancing madly.

Lightning flickers, and I can see the boxy shape of the green-house in the garden, the UV lamp inside a pale purple smudge. If a large animal were prowling around, motion sensor lights would turn on, and they haven't. Not noticing anything out of the ordinary, I step away from the window.

Burning logs snap and crackle, the smell of woodsmoke heav-enly. I pad barefoot to the tall cabinet that belonged to Benton's great-grandfather, an industrialist friendly with the Carnegies and Vanderbilts. I open the flame mahogany doors, the bottles of liquor and tumblers neatly lined up.

Pouring a Macallan Scotch aged fifteen years in sherry casks, I set my drink on the nightstand as Lucy tries to FaceTime. I accept her call, my phone's display filling with an image of her in a gray sweatsuit.

She's sitting on the bed in the FBI Academy dorm room where she's staying the night. Her keenly pretty face is somber, and she looks frustrated as she pushes back her short hair, the overhead lights catching the rose-gold tints.

"I've checked the security system," she says. "What you saw isn't the eyes of a deer or any other large animal. Otherwise, motion, thermal imaging and other sensors would have detected it."

"Possibly it was the hologram?" I reluctantly suggest. "In fact, what else could it have been?"

"Consistent with it."

"Should I be worried someone's on the property right now, Lucy?"

"No one is, Aunt Kay."

"We're sure?"

"An intruder would be caught on multiple sensors and cameras. Janet would know it and so would I," Lucy says.

"Frankly, I'm worried about the hologram suddenly floating through a window like Dana Diletti just experienced."

"Let's hope that doesn't happen. But no one is on the property," Lucy promises. "I don't blame you for feeling on edge. I can be home in an hour."

"Benton will be here soon." I don't want her fretting about me or doing anything reckless.

"I think I should come." Her green eyes look at me.

"Please stay put. The roads aren't safe."

"Most likely the Slasher is spying and harassing, possibly even you since you've been on the news all day talking about him."

"Yes, we can thank Dana Diletti for that. I've given her one damn interview about these cases, and she plays it repeatedly as if to give the impression I talk to her all the time."

"The killer knows we can't do anything about his ghostly projections," Lucy says heatedly. "You can't catch or shoot a hologram.
And we can't trace it either."

"Implying that the spectrum analyzers aren't picking up any
unusual signals on our property," I assume.

"Not so far. But like I said, we can't trace the Slasher's holograms. We can't detect anything is there unless we see it on camera
or with our own two eyes." Anger has crept into her tone.

When Lucy feels outsmarted, she takes it personally.

"It's a most unpleasant thought that the hologram could be hovering nearby, and we don't know." My attention is riveted to the
shaded windows.

"The good news is if the Slasher decides to show up in person,
we'll know it instantly," Lucy threatens. "It's not possible for him
to defeat our entire security system since not all of it is wireless. I
assume you've got your Glock handy, Aunt Kay?"

"I'm all set. And hopefully, you can drop by tomorrow to
exchange gifts and maybe have lunch." I switch to a happier subject.

"I'll be there," she says. "Afterward I'll drive you and Benton to
the airport."

"Much better than Uber." I tell her Merry Christmas and that I
miss her.

Settling on top of the bed, I take a sip of Scotch, the sherry
patina waking up my tastebuds, reminding me I'm famished. I open
my briefcase, pulling out Rowdy O'Leary's medical records, police
reports and multiple news stories copied off the internet.

Stacking the paperwork next to me, I cover my legs with the
duvet, firelight wavering, wood snapping and popping. I begin
reading about the hit-and-run six years ago on December 30, some
four miles from where the O'Learys lived at the time and still do.

The first officer to arrive at the scene reported that Rowdy was struck at approximately ten p.m., a light rain falling, the night misty and dark. A motorist noticed a body on the roadside and stopped to help, calling for an ambulance. There were no witnesses who might have seen what happened.

The investigation was turned over to the Virginia State Police. When Trooper Trad Whalen interviewed Reba O'Leary the next day, she said that Rowdy often jogged late at night. Under a lot of stress at work, he was anxious and suffering from insomnia.

*"The software designing business is cutthroat competitive,"* I read in the transcript of Reba's recorded interview. "He'd been complaining that he felt ripped off and even spied on. He was always saying that you can't trust people."

"Why would anyone spy on your husband, ma'am?" Whalen asked. "Related to his work, I'm assuming?"

"A lot of intellectual theft goes on in the tech world, and Rowdy's a genius, people always after his ideas. And some of them have been stolen for sure. But he also can be paranoid," Reba explained. "Thinking someone's out to get him when no one is. He's always been like that."

"Is it possible someone was out to get him, ma'am?"

"I suppose anything's possible," she answered.

"I'm wondering what your husband was so afraid of," Whalen said to her. "Did he have any reason to be afraid of you?"

"Goodness, no."

"Have you two been getting along, Reba? Any relationship problems?"

"Who doesn't have those?"

"Reba, what kind of car do you drive?" Whalen then asked her.

"A two-thousand-eighteen Jeep Cherokee. Silver." She recited the plate number.

"Where were you when your husband went out jogging, ma'am?"

"Home with our two boys. You don't think I had...?" She didn't finish the sentence.

# CHAPTER 14

Rowdy O'Leary suffered multiple fractures to his lower legs, his back and occipital skull. I study photographs taken at the hospital. The accordion pattern of the car's front grille is clearly visible behind his knees and lower thighs.

His tibias and fibulas were shattered in both legs, the bones protruding from the skin, and surgeons deliberated whether below-knee amputations might be necessary. The police speculated that what plowed into him wasn't a truck or SUV. Something lower-slung than that, possibly a sports car.

A search of area body shops came up empty-handed. It was suspected that the driver was drunk and speeding with no headlights. This person had the ability to evade and conceal.

"Possibly someone who works in the automotive business, repairing the car himself," Trad Whalen told a reporter.

I glance at photocopies of news stories, the headlines more buried and less emphatic over time:

*Local Man Badly Injured While Jogging Late at Night*

*Marathon Runner Struck by Car*

*Reward Offered in Alexandria Hit & Run*

*Hope Fades in Hit & Run Case*

Nothing I'm seeing suggests the police suspected Rowdy was

run down intentionally, certainly not by his wife. In fact, Trooper Whalen quickly came around to blaming the victim, telling journalists that Rowdy was running late at night on a heavily trafficked road, placing himself at risk.

"Unfortunately, he ended up in the path of a drunk driver," Whalen said, and there's no proof of that.

Other information and diagrams indicate that when Rowdy was struck from behind, he flew into the air, the back of his head striking the car's windshield. His brain was contused, a coma induced to control the swelling. After he was awake and alert, he had no memory beyond hearing a powerful engine behind him before everything went black.

In physical therapy for the better part of two years, he struggled to walk. He began gaining weight and seeing a psychiatrist. He reported episodes of tachycardia and was hooked up to a Holter monitor. A cardiologist early on diagnosed him with premature ventricular contractions due to extreme mental distress.

Other paperwork shows that Rowdy called the Virginia State Police now and then, checking on his case, Trad Whalen mentions in reports. When the Slasher murders began ten months ago, Rowdy's interest shifted to them. He became more fearful and was obsessed with the investigation.

Based on what I'm seeing, the last time he contacted Whalen was only a month ago. Rowdy called *in ref. to Phantom Slasher*, I read.

*"I asked if he had suspicions about who the Slasher might be,"* Whalen wrote in a memo about his last phone call with Rowdy. *"He started making wild accusations about the government. He impressed me as increasingly paranoid & unstable…"*

Included in the article is a photograph of Trooper Whalen, and he looks familiar posed in his state police dress uniform, a lot of dark blue and brass. His eyes are shadowed by a campaign hat as he smiles stiffly in front of an American flag. He appeared to be in his thirties then and somewhat brutish with a crew cut, the flattened nose of a prizefighter.

I'm all but certain I saw him earlier in the year at Ivy Hill cemetery when I was there for the funeral of a former governor on a cold rainy day. If I'm right that it's the same trooper, he was surly when directing me to park an unnecessary distance from the tent.

"Could you park me any farther away?" I joked but meant it.

"If you're not careful, ma'am, I will," was his aggressive answer.

I remember being taken aback by his overt hostility as if he had a personal beef with me, and decided he was a chauvinist, maybe a misogynist. It wasn't the first time I'd encountered such uncivil behavior. When I began my career, scarcely anyone wanted a woman to be a medical examiner, much less a chief.

Getting up from the bed, I stir the fire with a poker, sparks swarming up the chimney. I'm adding another log as I hear a car stopping at the gate, the engine quiet over the security camera microphones. My mood lifts as I see Benton's Tesla SUV in the monitor across from the bed.

I watch him driving through the opening gate, stopping at the carriage house and climbing out. I can see his breath fogging and hear his feet crunching. I'm glad he put on boots before driving home, always keeping a pair in his car for when the weather takes a bad turn.

He kicks away crusty snow in front of the double wooden doors. They scrape loudly as he swings them open, driving inside, getting out again to close and latch them. He trudges along the driveway to the house, and I see no sign of the raccoon or owl. Nothing growls or screams. The floating red lights are gone.

I head downstairs in my pajamas and slippers, keeping my eye out for Merlin. I hope he's not in the basement, irritable or frightened. Knowing him, he's pacing back and forth collarless in front of the cat door, upset that it won't open as if he's lost his magical powers.

At the bottom of the steps, I enter the code for the security system. I open the door for Benton, cold air rushing in.

"Thank God," I tell him. "I was worried you'd never get here."

"Nothing could keep me away," he says as I reset the alarm instantly.

Benton smiles into my eyes, unbuttoning his black wool coat that accentuates his tall leanness, his striking chiseled features and platinum hair. The first time I laid eyes on him long ago when I was the new chief in Richmond, I found him impossibly handsome. I still do.

His cheeks and nose are red from the cold, and I take his briefcase, setting it on the entryway table.

"Hi." He kisses me.

"I'm so glad you're home safely." I hold him tight, his coat damp, his skin chilled from the storm.

"Someone naughty has been in the liquor," he teases.

"I had a finger of whisky." I find his lips again, giving him another taste. "Did you notice anything unusual while you were walking up from the carriage house? I didn't see anything on the monitor."

" 'Twas the night before, and nothing was stirring. Not even a mouse," he says, and I think of Pinky, wondering if he was duped by Boursin cheese on a cracker.

"How about a drink?" I suggest. "After the day I've had, I'm ready for another one. Or two or three. And I know you must be. Or would you like to change first? Although I must confess you look irresistible in pinstripes."

"I believe my dry gin martinis are in order. Shaken, not stirred. I can change later."

"I don't know...Gin after whisky, very risky," I whisper into his ear.

"Since we're all alone and don't have to get up early? I think risky is what the doctor ordered." He holds me close, resting his chin on top of my head, sniffing my hair. "You must have showered."

"In my office before I headed home," I reply. "And you should be grateful."

"I always am."

"I hope it's okay that we're leaving tomorrow." I confess my misgivings. "Dorothy and Marino aren't getting along. The weirdness on the driveway when I got home. I worry the Slasher's about to strike again and meanwhile Dana Diletti insists on staying alone in her house. There's so much going on, Benton."

"When isn't there? And we always feel this way on the rare occasion we take time off," he says, and it's true.

"On top of that, Maggie is causing trouble," I tell him as he hangs up his coat. "She's demanding to know the details of the Rowdy O'Leary autopsy. I've not answered any of her questions."

"Why would she be interested?" Benton takes off his boots.

"Somebody's put a bug in her ear about that case and the skeletal remains from Mercy Island." I continue updating him. "In other words, she's playing politics and doing favors."

Passing through the living room, I'm aware of familiar odors that make me feel at home. Bee's Oil wood conditioner. Bayberry candles. Burnt logs. The ceiling-high artificial Christmas tree reminds me how much I don't like glitzy lights and tacky ornaments.

But holiday decorations are a concession I make to my sister and Marino. As he explained to Reba O'Leary while we were in her home, Dorothy typically starts in right after Thanksgiving. Every year she feels compelled to outdo the last, adding something different and more outrageous.

This time it's the life-size plastic Santa Claus in a hooded red velvet robe, waiting by the fireplace hearth with a sack of fake wrapped presents. As sensors detect Benton and me walking by, Santa lights up, moving his eyes. His puppet mouth opens and shuts as he shouts:

"MERRY CHRISTMAS! HO! HO! HO...!" Over and over.

Our feet are silent on antique rugs that have been in the Wesley family for generations. We maneuver around the rosewood baby grand piano that Dorothy and Lucy play by ear. It once belonged to Benton's grandmother, and I'm reminded that it's been a while since I had it tuned.

Beyond the dining room, I push open the saloon-style swinging door that leads into the kitchen. I turn on the lights, the green-patinated copper sconces glowing on old bricks showing through plaster. Polished copper pots and pans gleam from the rack over the wooden butcher block, and this time of year we enjoy the corner fireplace.

Benton finds the bottle of Boodles gin, the jar of fat green olives stuffed with pimento. He opens a cabinet for two long-stemmed martini glasses and the copper shaker. While he bartends, I begin defrosting bread dough, and meatballs I make in a savory tomato sauce. I find a cutting board and knife.

I dice the tomatoes and cucumbers, the sweet onions and

peppers I picked this morning in the refurbished greenhouse that's heated in the winter. I keep remembering the crashing noises in the woods as Marino was leaving. Wild animals would be interested in the produce I grow in the warm, moist air of the steel-and-glass enclosure.

"I don't believe it was a deer, a coyote, a bear, anything real. The red orbs looked like the eyes of the hologram we've seen on video." I bring it up again. "And that's what Lucy thinks it was."

"But you said you heard growling." Benton fills the shaker with gin and ice.

"I'm thinking that could have been the raccoon. He was near the house when I saw him," I reply. "He looked like he was limping. But then again, I don't think that was what snorted and screamed. I don't know what I was hearing except our property sounded like a jungle."

"Anything injured can be aggressive," Benton says over the loud rattle of the shaker he works. "I'll do a walk around tomorrow before we head to the airport. But it's not likely we can get anyone to help with injured wildlife on Christmas."

"If all else fails, we'll call Fabian. He can come over while we're gone and help Marino take care of it," I decide as Benton pours our drinks.

"Cheers." He hands me a martini and we clink glasses.

Tossing the panzanella salad with cold pressed olive oil and Bordeaux red wine vinegar, I add creamy burrata cheese and thick croutons. I tear up fresh basil, adding capers and anchovies as Benton sets the café table overlooking the birdfeeders.

The window shades are down. Nothing can see in. But I continue feeling watched.

"What do you think?" I feed him a forkful of salad.

"Amazing but needs something." He's chewing. "God, I'm starved."

"A little more garlic maybe." I have a taste. "Yes, that will do the trick."

"It sounds like there was more than one thing going on when Marino drove you home." Benton places the fork in the sink. "The red lights may not be related to the growling and screaming. I'm not aware of anything like that being heard when the Slasher's hologram shows up. Nothing similar has been recorded."

"Before it gets much later." I raise my martini again. "Merry Christmas Eve. To us, Benton."

We touch glasses again.

"There's no one I'd rather spend it with," he says.

———

It's almost eleven when we sit down at the café table, the lights dimmed, a large candle burning. Rimsky-Korsakov's *Christmas Eve Suite* is playing, a beautiful Barolo decanting, the bottle on the table so we can appreciate the label, 2016 a very good year.

The kitchen smells like garlic and baking bread, a fire burning on the hearth. Benton has changed into the Black Watch plaid pajamas I got him last Christmas. He looks wonderful in candlelight, his brow gathered in a perplexed frown as I continue passing along what Reba O'Leary told me.

I share what I learned from medical files and police reports, mentioning my misgivings about Trooper Trad Whalen. As Benton and I talk, we demolish plates of panzanella salad.

"I just think the Slasher task force needs to be aware of all this,"

I'm saying. "I always err on the side of passing along information even if it may not be credible. And based on what I saw inside Rowdy O'Leary's office and learned from his wife? I think he had major psychiatric problems. Clearly, he was fearful, and anxious. He'd become obsessed with the Slasher murders."

"A lot of people are, and for good reason." Benton reaches for his glass, the wine ruby red in candlelight. "I'm sure you can guess the number of baseless tips we get daily on the Slasher hotline. Many of them are from the same unbalanced people. They leave rambling messages about government conspiracies."

"Apparently, the Slasher is why Rowdy started carrying his revolver when he went out to fish or run errands or whatever," I explain. "He also became fastidious about setting the security system. And maybe it was more than just the murders all over the news. Maybe he was afraid of something else."

"Depression with paranoid features could be the reason. But not necessarily." Benton tears off a piece of crusty bread, dipping it into tomato sauce. "The question is whether he was like that before the hit-and-run."

"According to him, it wasn't an accident," I explain. "His wife says he worried that someone ran him over deliberately."

"It doesn't mean much if he thought that." Benton rests his fork on the edge of his salad plate. "People who aren't well?" He taps his temple. "Sadly, they say all kinds of things."

"He'd been working from home ever since the hit-and-run," I reply. "He spent a lot of money, according to his wife. I'm wondering where he was getting it, paying cash for an expensive emerald ring. Did he really have clients?"

"Let's see if Janet has any answers," Benton says as sleet clicks against windows.

A draft shakes the candleflame as he gets up from the table, unplugging his tablet from the charger on the kitchen counter. Sitting back down, he selects the Janet app and instantly the AI avatar's familiar pretty face fills the computer screen. Moving our chairs next to each other, Benton and I look on together.

# CHAPTER 15

"**G**ood evening, Benton. Hello, Kay, it's always so good to see you both," Janet says with her demure smile, blinking as if alive, looking right at us. "Merry Christmas Eve."

"And to you, Janet," Benton says as if she's a person.

"We wish you were here," I add, and I mean it.

"But I am." The avatar laughs throatily the same way the living Janet did. "I'm looking right at you. I love your chic pajamas, by the way."

Her hair is long and chestnut brown, styled the way it was when I last saw her alive, her features delicate, her eyes hazel. Her quiet mannerisms and the tempo of her pleasantly modulated speech haven't changed. Janet will forever be midthirties and soft-spoken, vibrant without makeup, dressed in a black sweater.

She wears a rose-gold dog tag that Lucy gave her. Engraved on it is a lemniscate, the symbol for infinity. When she gestures, her diamond wedding band catches the light. Her Breitling wristwatch forever reads 11:11 a.m., her official time of death in a London hospital.

I don't know what else Janet has on, as I see her only from the waist up. She doesn't stand or walk around, although Lucy hints that will be the next innovation in the AI programming. God forbid she turns Janet into a hologram. I'm not ready for that, and I'd hate to think of the impact on Dorothy.

I understand all too well how my sister fell into the trap of emotionally connecting to a computer generation. Communicating with Janet can be addictive. I make a point of talking to her sparingly, not wanting our visits to be an all-consuming habit. On top of that, her tendency to crash boundaries and tattle has made me leery.

"I'm glad Benton finally got home in this terrible weather," Janet is saying to us warmly and with easy familiarity. "I'm happy to see you're having a late supper." She looks at our dishes on the table. "Your panzanella salad if I'm not mistaken, Kay?"

"Yes," I reply, reminded that she can see what the tablet's camera does.

Janet can appropriate any of our security cameras, including ones in the house that aren't turned on at the moment.

"Also, your meatballs and crusty bread, reminding me how much I miss your cooking, best of all hanging out in the kitchen talking. And I see you're working on a very nice bottle of Giuseppe Rinaldi Barolo, two-thousand-sixteen, bold but light."

She looks at Benton.

"A much better deal if you buy it by the case next time." She tells him the same thing I would. "You can save twenty percent at the wine shop you like so much in Old Town."

"Thanks. I'll keep that in mind," he says with no enthusiasm while refilling our glasses.

"The two-thousand-nineteen is worth trying, Benton. A hint of ripe raspberry and blood orange."

"I've had it," he says a shade defensively. "I like this better. Which is why I picked it."

"I'm sure it's delicious." She watches us lift our glasses, a wistful look on her face.

The real Janet loved wine, especially nuanced reds. My impulse is to tell her that I wish we could pour her a glass and toast to her good health. But it wouldn't be logical making a comment like that to an algorithm.

"Is there something I can help you with?" Janet says.

I start in with the mysterious happenings on the driveway earlier tonight when I first got home.

"Can you find the two red orbs on the security recording and play it for Benton?" I ask her. "I'd like him to see what I've been telling him about."

As I'm saying this, Janet vanishes from the tablet's display, and a video begins playing. The small red lights glow incandescently, drifting like tiny UFOs through fog along the driveway.

"What are they?" I ask Janet.

The avatar returns to the display, her expression more serious, on the verge of concerned.

"Sensors on the property detected no motion or electronic transmissions," she answers. "The red illumination was in the seven-hundred-nanometer spectrum, a frequency of four hundred terahertz."

"Can you translate, please?" Benton says.

"The two red orbs were a projection similar to a movie projecting something onto a screen. Only the orbs were projected on the foggy air."

"Sounds like a hologram to me. The red eyes of the ghostly figure repeatedly seen in connection with the Phantom Slasher murders," I suggest. "Lucy says it's likely that's what was floating over the driveway."

"And Lucy's right as usual," Janet responds with a reverential nod of her head. "The red lights could have been the Slasher hologram. Sensors won't pick that up unless the person controlling it makes inputs to override the programming. When in autonomous mode, the hologram can't be detected unless it's optically. You have to see it, in other words. Or you won't know it's there."

"To play devil's advocate, Janet, how do you know for sure the red lights weren't the eyes of an animal? A coyote, for example. Even a mountain lion, which isn't supposed to exist in Northern Virginia. But they've been sighted," Benton says. "When light shines on certain animals at night, their eyes reflect red."

"The red lights weren't an animal," Janet answers. "There was no heat signature detected in infrared. Unless we're talking about an animal the same temperature as the ambient air. And that would only have been possible if it were dead and frozen."

"Now if you'll play the recording of the strange sounds I heard, the growling, the sticks snapping and such," I tell Janet.

She vanishes from the tablet's display again as the security video resumes. I see myself on the front steps talking to Marino through his truck's open window as something crashes through brush in the wooded dark.

"Yikes," Benton mutters, reaching for his wine.

We listen to the growling, the screams, grunts and hooting. I ask about the source, and Janet's grim face returns.

"What area of the property were they coming from?" I'm saying to her. "The growling seemed close to where I was standing on the front porch. But not the other noises, the crashing and screaming etcetera."

"The grunting and screaming were in the garden," Janet says.

"I've worried about the greenhouse from day one." Benton

offers this to me, not her. "It can attract all kinds of critters, which is why I wasn't keen on you doing it. Despite how much I love fresh vegetables."

Over his objections I bought the greenhouse at an antique fair not long after we moved here. Until last summer, the pieces and parts were in the basement. It took a long time getting around to having it assembled and heated.

"Critters can't open the door," I explain. "Not even a raccoon or a bear. To get inside the greenhouse you'd have to push down your thumb on the door handle. Or it won't open."

"What about the growling?" Benton asks Janet. "What was doing that? Can you tell?"

"The acoustical signature of that vocalization is consistent with a raccoon. Possibly the raccoon crossing the driveway as Marino was driving Kay home."

"Do we know if the raccoon is rabid?" I ask. "Because that would be very bad."

I look at Merlin in his cat bed near the fireplace.

"It wasn't foaming at the mouth or disoriented," Janet says. "It wasn't making whimpering sounds or showing signs of aggression."

She goes on to inform us that the raccoon lives in a hollowed-out tree near the house and has for a while. Sensors detected him retreating there after I went inside. Over recent weeks he's been picked up by cameras monitoring the driveway and showed no signs of injury until tonight.

"He has wounds to his face and is limping. It's likely he got into a fight with another animal," Janet says as I think of the owls. "But it wasn't caught on camera. I didn't see it."

"What about the screaming and snorting?" I ask while feeling bad for the raccoon.

I make a mental note to send Fabian an email about it. Knowing where the raccoon lives, hopefully it won't be hard to find and catch.

"The screaming and snorting from the garden are a problem." Janet looks perplexed. "I'm sorry, I can't help you. But those vocalizations aren't in any dataset."

"How is that possible?" Benton swirls wine in candlelight, taking another sip. "I would think virtually every animal sound on the planet has been recorded and is in databases."

"The vocalizations are inconsistent with any known animal sounds on this planet." Janet cuts her eyes up to the left, her face tense like it always was when she couldn't solve a problem.

"Possibly the vocalization was engineered by a computer?" Benton wonders. "It could be that a recording is what Kay heard? Something fake, in other words? Possibly associated with the hologram?"

"The sounds recorded by the security system are full fidelity," Janet's avatar answers on the tablet's display. "They contain frequencies that humans can't hear, and therefore they were not engineered. They are authentic vocalizations."

"Something real was crashing around, screaming and hooting? An animal not in any database on the planet?" I make sure, and she nods her head.

"Christ." Benton isn't happy. "But we don't know what kind of animal? What the hell is on our property?"

"I'm sorry, Benton. I don't have that information." Janet looks annoyed with herself. "It was smart of you to disable Merlin's collar. And I don't advise you or Kay go outside in this weather and at this time of night to look."

"Don't worry," I answer for both of us. "That's not happening."

"While we have you, Janet, there's something else we'd like to chat with you about," Benton says.

"Of course. Anything you need." She smiles, her gaze intense on the Barolo bottle. "I'm looking at your wine and feeling envious . . ."

———

Benton and I are shoulder to shoulder at the café table, looking at Janet's face on the tablet. He asks about Rowdy O'Leary and if she can find any information about projects or clients he may have had.

"Rowdy O'Leary is deceased," she says. "His badly decomposed body was recovered today from the Potomac River at twelve-fifteen p.m. It had been carried by the current nine miles downstream and was discovered by someone walking his dog. The body was halfway submerged, caught in rocks and debris."

"Yes, we know," Benton answers.

"His software design company is a shell," Janet goes on. "Since he was struck by a car while jogging, he has conducted no business despite what he told people, most of all his family. From time to time, he's indicated in text messages to his wife that he's busy consulting. This wasn't true."

Janet has just hacked into Rowdy O'Leary's phone. Or Reba's. Maybe both.

"For the past six years he's reported zero income on his tax returns while receiving payments of ninety thousand dollars annually," Janet informs us. "He owes three times that on credit cards and loans from the bank."

"If he wasn't doing consulting, how was he earning ninety grand a year?" Benton asks her.

"There is no indication that he earned it, no evidence of a work product in any of his electronic communications. The money was wired to him in three separate transactions at the same time of year.

February, July, and December. Always the tenth day of the month, the amounts identical."

Clearly, she's hacked into Rowdy's email and bank accounts.

"Any idea who was paying him?" Benton asks.

"The wires to his bank were from an account in the Cayman Islands."

"Can you trace it?" Benton looks at me, and we're thinking the same thing.

Whatever Rowdy was being compensated for wasn't legitimate.

"The account wiring the money belongs to West Bay Software Solutions, which doesn't exist," Janet says. "As you're aware, the Caymans are a haven for money laundering and other financial crimes."

"Was he receiving these payments prior to the hit-and-run?" I ask.

"They started two months after he was struck by a car six years ago on the night of December thirtieth," Janet informs us.

"Who was paying him. And for what?" Benton asks.

"I don't have that information. I'm very sorry, Benton. There's no mention of these payments in any online data. There is nothing in Rowdy O'Leary's legal records at Constable, Birch and Goldberg," she explains, and it would seem she's now hacked into a law firm.

"I wonder if his wife knew about these payments?" I ask.

"Text messages to her indicate she assumed any money her husband had was from consulting fees or gambling. I find nothing to make me think she was aware of wires from the Cayman Islands, the most recent one two weeks ago."

"Most likely where he got the cash to buy an expensive emerald ring," I suspect.

"He made ATM withdrawals totaling three thousand dollars after receiving the wire," she says.

"Thank you, Janet. I need nothing further," Benton tells her.

"It was so nice talking to both of you," she replies with a touch of emotion that's just like her. "I'm sorry Lucy isn't with you tonight. I know she can be melancholy at Christmas, and I do what I can to comfort her."

"Unfortunately, she's stuck in Quantico," I reply, but Janet knows that.

"I've been talking to Dorothy this evening, at least I was before Marino got home," the avatar goes on in a tone that portends trouble. "I didn't mean to cause them to squabble. Does Benton know what Marino got you for Christmas, Kay...?"

Before I can answer, Benton closes the app, placing his tablet facedown on the table. It's the same thing he always does when Janet starts violating our personal airspace.

"What is she talking about?" He looks at me.

I tell him about the awaiting spa package at our London hotel.

"Ouch," he says.

"Ouch is right. You can imagine Dorothy's reaction when Janet made a big thing about how personal the gift was," I explain, carrying our empty dishes to the sink.

"I can imagine all too well." Benton refills our wineglasses.

"It sounds like Rowdy O'Leary was involved in something beyond his control." I scrape plates into the sink disposal.

"That might explain why he'd gotten increasingly paranoid." Benton carries in our wine, setting my glass on the counter. "He might have had reason to be. By all indications, someone started paying him off after he was hit by the car."

"Paying him off for what?"

"I don't know."

"Ninety K a year is quite a tidy payoff." I turn on the hot water in the sink, handing Benton a dish towel.

"Someone might have been giving him hush money," he suggests. "If so, there's a reason the hit-and-run was never solved. It's not supposed to be."

"Maybe it relates to the government somehow? Maybe he was targeted? Deliberately taken out?"

"Wouldn't make sense." He begins drying as I wash. "If the government needed him neutralized for some reason, he wouldn't have been left alive to collect payments."

"I hope you can get your hands on the records and backup drives in his office safe before someone else does," I reply. "Seems the Secret Service, the FBI might want to know what's there. Especially if there could be a nefarious government connection. Or even money laundering or fraud."

"I'm going to make sure that happens," Benton says. "Contacting Lucy as we speak."

Using the secure messaging app on his phone, he sends a text to her while I send one to Fabian about the injured raccoon. Maybe he can swing by when able and help catch the poor thing so we can get it to a wild animal rehab center. He answers right away with emojis of a thumbs-up and a stethoscope.

"Rowdy O'Leary's safe will be handled," Benton tells me, and I don't want to know the details.

"Is she all right?" I ask about Lucy.

"She wishes she were here," he says.

We leave the kitchen, thunder rumbling, the snow turning to a rainy sleet that smacks against the side of the house.

"She's with Tron," Benton says.

Sierra "Tron" Patron is Lucy's FBI investigative partner. She's also a friend of the family, and I'm glad they're together right now.

"It's a shame they have to be in a dorm on Christmas Eve, but at least they're together," I reply as we head back through the house. "What was for dinner?"

He says they had cheeseburgers and beer in the FBI Academy's Boardroom, and I remember the times Lucy and I were there together. I turn off the Christmas tree lights, ignoring the plastic Santa hailing us.

"...MERRY CHRISTMAS...! HO! HO! HO...!"

Inside the bedroom, the fire I built earlier is a pile of white ashes over coals glowing orange. Small flames jump as I add more fatwood and another log. It's a few minutes past midnight when Benton and I slip under the covers.

"Merry Christmas, Kay," he says. "I could give you one of your presents now if you'd like?"

"Depends on what present you're talking about." I move closer, feeling him in firelight.

"I think you know." He begins unbuttoning my pajamas.

# CHAPTER 16

The wind moans around the house like a horror movie, remnants of a bad dream deconstructing like clouds as I reach for my phone vibrating on the nightstand. It's 5:25 a.m., Marino calling, and my mood begins a freefall.

"Please, God, no." I groan, turning on the bedside lamp.

"Who is it?" Benton mumbles into his pillow, and I tell him. "Dammit." He sits up as my phone continues buzzing like a giant insect.

"Good morning, Marino," I answer, touching the icon for speakerphone. "I have a feeling you're not calling to wish us bon voyage." I rub my temples, a bit hungover.

"I'm sorry as hell, Doc," he says, and I can tell he's outside near an airport, a jet passing low overhead. "I want to make sure you hear from me what's going on. Then you can decide what you want to do about it." He's keyed up and talking fast.

"What's happened?" I retrieve my notebook and pen from the bedside drawer.

"The Phantom Slasher just struck again exactly like you were afraid would happen," he replies. "I almost can't believe it."

"Please don't tell me Dana Diletti..." I start to say.

"Here we were worrying about her all night, but that's not who

147

he went after. It makes me wonder if siccing the fake ghost on her was to send us down the wrong rabbit hole," Marino says. "We're so busy thinking she's the next to get whacked and meanwhile the Slasher has his sights set elsewhere."

I jot down the date, December 25. Christmas. Benton plumps pillows behind him, sitting up, listening as he unlocks his phone.

"Two victims here in Alexandria," Marino goes on. "The female, a psychiatrist, is dead in bed. The male victim still alive, Zain Willard, twenty-three years old, a grad student at William & Mary. He's an intern at the White House based on the ID badge and other personal effects I found at the scene."

"Willard? As in Senator Calvin Willard who's running for president?" I ask while Benton scrolls through communications on his phone's secure messaging app.

"I'm told that's his uncle, explaining Zain Willard's cushy gig in the West Wing and why the feds are rolling in. We can expect a shit show. It's not a good time to be headed out on vacation," Marino advises as if I'm a slacker.

"What about the female victim?" I turn the page in my notebook. "Do we have a name?"

"Georgine Duvall," he replies, a chill of disbelief touching me. "The house where it happened belongs to her."

"I may know who that is." I look at Benton. "If it's the same Georgine Duvall, we were acquainted back in Lucy's UVA days."

More than acquainted, it drums in my mind. I knew the psychiatrist well.

"Born in Charlottesville, D.O.B. August one, nineteen-sixty-five," Marino recites. "Her husband, Liam Duvall, died eight years ago, according to what I found on the internet without asking Janet since she's on my shit list at the moment."

"It's the same person based on information I'm getting as we're talking," Benton confirms.

"How awful." I'm stunned. "What makes you so sure it's the same killer? Let's start with that."

"The M.O. included the ghost levitating through the fog, and I saw it for myself this time." Marino's voice sounds excited. "Got to admit it's enough to give you a heart attack."

"Saw it where?" Benton frowns.

"I was out riding with Fruge," Marino says. "It's a long story, but put it this way. After I got home last night, Dorothy was in a bad enough snit that she told me to take a hike. So I did and thought I may as well make myself useful."

He explains that Blaise Fruge is working through the night, and Marino decided to ride along. She picked him up at his house, and they weren't far from Mercy Island when the call came in at 3:45 a.m.

"As we rolled up on the scene, Fruge and me saw the fake ghost," he's saying. "It crossed the street right in front of us."

"Are you at the scene now?" I ask him. "It sounds like you're outdoors near an airport?"

"That's because I'm about a mile downriver from Washington National, standing in a gazebo on Mercy Island freezing my ass off. It's stopped sleeting and raining at least. But the fog's so bad I can't see across the river."

"Mercy Island? Oh, God. Of all places," I reply with growing dismay.

I think about the skeletal remains Cate Kingston showed me as I was leaving the office yesterday.

"Georgine Duvall is on the hospital staff and owns one of the ritzy residences on the grounds," Marino is saying. "As usual the

Slasher knocked out the Wi-Fi, and I had to walk around in the freezing rain until I could find a cell signal."

"Meanwhile who's guarding the scene?" I'm writing down the details.

"I've got Fruge posted at the front door. She's keeping everybody out," Marino says. "Trust me, nobody's getting anywhere near the body until you say. Or Doc Schlaefer does. Depending on what you decide. I realize you're not supposed to be working right now."

"Have you notified him?" I'm sure I know the answer.

"I didn't wake him up yet, wanted to talk to you once I had an idea what we're dealing with. If it was me, I wouldn't want anyone else handling this."

Marino hopes and expects that I'll respond to the scene myself instead of the deputy chief covering for me while I'm on vacation. Benton is busy texting, and I can tell he's been notified about the same case as I would expect.

I watch him in the uneven glow of lamplight, his sharp features accentuated by shadows as he types another message. Looking up, he meets my eyes. He grimly shakes his head, and I know what's going to happen. Or better yet, what won't happen.

*La scritta è sul muro.* I hear my late Italian mother's voice in my head.

The writing is on the wall, as she used to say, and I know it's for the best. This is a terrible time to go anywhere, but that doesn't mean I'm not disappointed. Benton and I have been looking forward to our trip for the better part of a year. Just like that, it's another ruined dream, another canceled plan.

"Georgine Duvall was killed in bed, stabbed multiple times, her throat cut." Marino offers more details that are depressingly familiar. "It looks like she bled out really fast and was dead or about dead when the Slasher started biting her before pouring bleach everywhere. The same thing we've seen in the first three cases."

"And the victim who survived, Zain Willard?" I'm taking notes. "What happened to him?"

"He's sliced up pretty good and in the hospital. But expected to be okay."

"He and the murdered woman were sleeping together when attacked?" I'm trying to imagine the scenario.

"I'm pretty sure they didn't have that kind of relationship," Marino says.

"Based on?"

"For one thing, she's old enough to be his mother."

"That doesn't mean much," I reply.

"I'm not sure of his persuasion, based on how he looks. If you get my drift."

"Let's not make assumptions," I suggest, and now Benton is writing back and forth with Lucy.

———

I'm gathering from glimpses of Benton's texts that Lucy and Tron have arrived on the grounds of Mercy Psychiatric Hospital. They'll search for the signal jammer that caused the Wi-Fi outage. I imagine them in tactical gear, tracking the invisible with spectrum analyzers and portable antennas.

"The victims were in different rooms on different floors," Marino continues to explain over speakerphone. "Zain Willard was ambushed after he heard screaming and came downstairs. The power was out and still is. It was too dark to see anything. He pretended to be dead until he was sure the coast was clear. Or that's his story."

"Any reason to suspect he killed Georgine Duvall and staged it to look like the Slasher?" I ask.

"You know me, everybody's a suspect," Marino says as Benton leans closer to my phone.

"Morning, Pete. Benton here," he says.

"Well, I sure as hell hope it's you at this hour or the doc's got some explaining to do," Marino wisecracks. "I'm surprised you're still home. I figured you'd be on your way to the Situation Room by now. Or maybe to Langley, the land of spooks and nuts."

He references the CIA for some odd reason.

"This is four times in the past six months that a health professional has been targeted." Benton skims through information Lucy is sending him. "What's significant this time is the location."

"Our favorite cuckoo's nest," Marino says. "Makes me wonder if the Slasher has some personal connection to the place. Maybe a former techie-genius patient."

"Do we have any idea how the killer accessed the house where this happened?" Benton asks.

"No sign of forcible entry," Marino says. "No footprints coming or going by the time we got there except for the cop who entered the house to check on the female victim. She was obviously dead. You could see the bloody trail from when Zain Willard left the house to find a phone signal. But the conditions were bad then and only worse now, everything melting."

"What about tire tracks?" Benton asks. "The killer had to get to the scene somehow. Unless he was already there."

"When the first officer arrived at the entrance to the island, there were no tire tracks on the road leading to the house. That's what he claims."

"Unless the tire tracks were there and the rain eradicated them," Benton suggests.

"Weird that you know the murdered psychiatrist, Doc," Marino says, and I've never mentioned Georgine Duvall to him.

At the time, it was none of his business.

"It's been many years since we last had contact," I explain. "I didn't realize she'd moved to Alexandria or that her husband died. Last I knew they were living on a horse farm in Charlottesville."

"Apparently, she sold the place and moved eight years ago. Her primary residence is now in Yorktown." It's Benton saying this. "She uses her home on Mercy Island when she needs to be on site at the hospital. And Zain Willard has stayed there before. Multiple times."

"How do you know when he's stayed there? You got a fucking Ouija board or something?" Marino's voice over speakerphone isn't gracious about it.

"Georgine Duvall and her house on Mercy Island are listed in his background information. It's where he stays when he's working at the White House," Benton says. "Typically, when William & Mary breaks for the summer and holidays."

"Do we know what she was doing at the hospital? Possibly, seeing patients?" I inquire. "When did she get there? How long ago?"

I envision the psychiatrist's strong face and warm dark eyes. I remember her soothing voice with its lilting Virginia accent, and I'm gripped by guilt. I didn't agree with her ideas and methods. But I liked her. I should have tried to keep in touch. It was up to me to reach out, and I didn't because of Lucy.

"When I've worked deaths on Mercy Island, I've never heard Georgine Duvall mentioned," I tell Benton and Marino. "I've never seen her name on any paperwork, what little I manage to get from the staff."

"She started there around the time her husband died, according to intel I'm getting from Lucy," Benton says, and I worry how she's reacting to the news about her former psychiatrist's brutal death.

Early in my career, Georgine Duvall directed the mental health services at the University of Virginia. Lucy was a student there, her freshman year a difficult one personally. Tormented by emotions she didn't understand, she was drinking too much and engaging in reckless behavior.

Intensive and frequent counseling sessions with Georgine went on for months before Lucy quit without explanation. The most I could get out of her was that she no longer found the therapy helpful.

"Was Zain Willard renting a room from Georgine Duvall?" I ask, propped up in bed, writing down the information. "I'm wondering why he was staying with her and had before."

"All I know is what Zain Willard told the first responding officer." Marino's big voice sounds inside the bedroom. "Zain and Georgine Duvall had moved into her house on Mercy Island two weeks ago."

"Meaning, the Slasher must have been watching and knew her whereabouts," Benton says. "He's probably been spying on her with his hologram. Which you claimed to see when you arrived at the scene, Pete?"

"It's not what I claim," he cranks. "I saw it, as did other people. Fruge and me were parking when the thing appeared as the ambulance was driving away with Zain Willard."

"Describe it," Benton says.

"The same figure in black, his eyes glowing red, exactly what Dana Diletti saw inside her bedroom. He was waving a big knife around, and I almost pulled out my gun. A lot of good it would have done to shoot a damn ghost."

"I'll point out that attacking two victims and leaving one of them alive is a deviation from the previous cases," Benton says. "Those women lived alone. Their bodies weren't found for several days."

"My guess is Georgine Duvall was the intended target, and the Slasher didn't realize more than one person was in the house," Marino answers. "He was caught off guard."

"That's quite an oversight for someone who obsessively stalks and spies." Benton pushes off the bedcovers.

"Obviously, he's losing control the same way Bundy did in the end when he went on his rampage in the Florida sorority house." Marino holds forth as if he's the profiler.

"There are departures from what we've seen in the previous cases." Benton climbs out of bed. "Considering the details all over the internet, we have to worry about copycats."

"I don't believe a copycat did what I just saw." Marino is getting impatient.

"You're probably right, but we need to keep an open mind," Benton says, and now his phone is ringing.

"Hi…" he answers. "Going someplace quiet…"

Stepping inside the bathroom, he shuts the door.

# CHAPTER 17

"What have you done so far?" I ask Marino over speakerphone as lightning illuminates the window shades.

"Took photos and videos. I grabbed temps with the I.R. thermometer, making sure not to touch anything," he says. "The body was ninety-six-point-five degrees, the ambient air about seventy. And a lot of the blood was still wet."

"Obviously, she hadn't been dead long by the time you got there with Fruge," I reply. "When did the Wi-Fi go down?"

"About three a.m. And we know that after the killer fled the scene, Zain Willard left the house to find a cell signal a couple acres away. He called nine-one-one at three-forty-five while he was bleeding on the sidewalk."

"Suggesting Georgine Duvall was killed between three and three-thirty," I decide. "And time of death isn't going to be the question in this case. It's everything else."

"I didn't realize she was someone you knew during Lucy's college days." Marino is probing. "That's too bad. Is there anything you remember about her that might be helpful?"

"Only that Georgine was too trusting with her patients," I reply. "She wasn't much for boundaries. But as I've said, that was a long time ago."

"If you're not up to dealing with the case, I understand. I can call Doc Schlaefer," Marino says, and he doesn't mean it.

"You already know that isn't going to happen," I answer. "Obviously, Benton and I will postpone our trip."

"That's too bad, what a shame, Doc." Marino doesn't mean that either. "But it's a good thing. Because on top of everything else, I'm pretty sure there are spooks roaming around out here. And I'm not talking about holograms now. I'm talking about the CIA."

"What makes you say that?"

"A little while ago these two guys appeared out of nowhere in an old pickup truck. They got in my face demanding to see my creds, asking all kinds of questions, treating me like a suspect if you can believe it," Marino protests.

I can believe it easily. His default is to be distrusting, aggressive and noncollaborative. I can imagine how he acted when confronted by undercover agents of any description.

"They wanted to search my backpack. So I said be my guest, knock yourself out," he goes on. "Nothing much in it but crime scene shit, extra ammo, my protein bars, the roll of toilet paper I always carry."

"What were they looking for? Do you have any idea?" I've rested my pen on the page, having learned long ago not to write down his every utterance.

"Computer equipment, remote-control devices or apps on my phone like maybe I'm the one carving up people while deploying fake ghosts," he explains. "Then they wanted to know if I might be flying a drone out here."

"Why were they asking? Did they say?"

"No, but one must have been detected in the area, which doesn't make sense," Marino replies.

The weather isn't drone-friendly, the wind quite strong, he explains. And it was much too early for a TV crew to be flying a drone. The media doesn't know what's happened yet.

"And it couldn't have been the local cops or the feds," he goes on. "Not the CIA either, right? Or the two spies would have known whose drone it was. So that leaves the Slasher."

"What made you think the two men are spies?" I continue glancing at the closed bathroom door, Benton's voice a murmur as he talks on the phone.

"I didn't buy their bullshit story about being sent by the FAA because of the scene's *close proximity to Washington National*," Marino explains, and I don't buy it either.

I've never heard of the Federal Aviation Administration responding to a homicide scene because it happens to be near an airport. But I'm familiar with the CIA and other clandestine organizations whose operatives dispense disinformation as easily as they breathe. I don't expect secret agents to tell the truth. Even if they're family.

"When did you arrive at the scene?" I dig in the nightstand drawer again, finding the bottle of Advil.

"About four a.m., maybe a few minutes after," Marino answers.

"That was quick." I shake two gel capsules into my hand, reaching for the bottle of water on the nightstand.

"Like I said, I was with Fruge. When she got the call, we were checking out the pier where Rowdy O'Leary was fishing when he ended up in the river. So we were only a few minutes away," Marino explains. "I just texted you some pics so you can see what you're about to confront."

I click on images of Georgine Duvall tangled in the blood-soaked bedcovers, and I remember when we were together last. In her early thirties then, she was compelling with a bright smile, her hair auburn. An accomplished equestrian and tennis player, she was athletically built and extremely bright.

Her short hair is so bloody now I can't tell the color, her nude body savaged by multiple sharp force injuries. The bowels protrude from the slashed-open abdomen, the cuts to the neck deep, the lower arms and hands gashed. Several fingers are almost severed.

"After the fact, the killer poured the bleach, leaving the empty bottle in plain view on the bedroom floor," Marino says.

"The same high-concentrate brand?"

I envision the white gallon jug I've seen before, the potent chlorine solution destructive to DNA and other biological evidence.

"You got it," Marino says. "And as you can see, he bit the shit out of her. He was more violent with her than the others. Again, making me wonder if he has some personal connection with her and the hospital."

"Possibly," I reply. "But Benton says the violence is escalating. That will only get worse."

I zoom in on the breasts and buttocks, the multiple bite marks avulsing the skin and underlying tissue. The gruesome wounds are more animal-like than human and would have been excruciatingly painful. But based on the lack of a vital response, she no longer had a blood pressure by then. Thankfully, she wasn't feeling anything.

"Damn good thing you and Benton didn't buy a place on Mercy Island. Can you imagine?" Marino then says. "You should be glad for a lot of reasons."

"It was never a consideration."

"Me and Dorothy refused to even look. No way we'd live on the grounds of a looney bin," he says with his usual sensitivity. "Especially not that one. But I bet you could get a deal now."

Like a lot of grand places from long ago, Mercy Psychiatric

Hospital has sold off most of its land to afford staying open. Centuries-old cottages, treatment pavilions and other outbuildings have been converted into luxury properties with stunning views of the Potomac River.

There are hiking trails, a dog park. And of course, the fitness center where the ancient cemetery once was.

"Unfortunately, we know from past experience that the hospital won't be cooperative," I'm saying to Marino. "I understand from Maggie that Graden Crowley is still the director."

"Unfortunately."

"A damn shame. I keep hoping he'll retire." I envision his whisky-flushed face and shifty eyes.

"I've tried to call but he's not answering, no big surprise." Marino's dislike of him sounds over the phone. "Bottom line, he's not going to tell us shit just like he didn't the last time we were there."

That was a year ago when a patient allegedly hanged himself with a strand of Christmas lights lashed to a radiator. I was given no satisfactory explanation for how he got hold of a ligature. I don't know why it took five hours for a staff member to discover the body. Despite repeated requests I've yet to receive the most basic information.

"The latest status of the Wi-Fi outage?" I close my notebook, clipping the pen to the cover.

"No luck yet," Marino says.

"And the weather?"

"It's too foggy to see across the river," he tells me. "But at least the rain has completely stopped, and the wind's dying down. Now that we've talked, I'll head back to the house and go over it with the crime lights. I'll have everything done by the time you show up. Meanwhile, Fabian's mobilized."

He's loading equipment into one of our windowless transport vans, black with *Office of the Chief Medical Examiner* and the seal of Virginia in gray. It's not something you'd want pulling up to your door.

"I need to get ready." I climb out of bed. "And most of all to make coffee."

I step around luggage outside the closets, lamplight shining on neatly folded clothes and pairs of shoes on the pumpkin pine flooring.

"Text me when you're getting close to the Pitié Bridge." Marino mispronounces it *Pie-tie* and I've given up correcting him. "I'll need to alert the officers at the checkpoint and front gate."

"Will do." I'm trying not to think about the theater tickets, the restaurant reservations, the plans to explore the English countryside in a rented Aston Martin.

"The roads are mostly wet and slushy, and it's above freezing but still cold as hell with the wind. The high this afternoon will be pushing fifty," Marino makes sure I know.

"See you soon," I reply.

"And before I forget? Merry Christmas, Doc. It sucks this had to happen now."

"It sucks that it had to happen at all," I tell him.

———

Benton emerges from the bathroom in his boxer briefs and sleeveless T-shirt that look very good on him. His lean strong body is younger than his years.

"Should we carpool?" he asks, walking toward me.

"Sounds like we're headed to the same place." I'm in my bathrobe placing tactical clothing on a chair.

"Merry Christmas, Kay." He wraps his arms around me. "Not how I was hoping we would spend it."

"You're my best present." I kiss his neck.

"And you're mine," he says into my hair.

"You must have cleaned up and shaved while on the phone." I touch his smooth cheek, smelling his earthy cologne. "And I know it's not because we're climbing back in bed until we feel like getting up."

"I'm sorry as hell for both of us."

"At least we're alive and well, unlike what we're about to encounter," I reply.

"That doesn't make it any easier if we're honest." He follows me across the bedroom. "It doesn't matter if we're off the clock. In truth, we never are."

"The price one pays for trying to live by the Golden Rule. Do unto others." I step inside the bathroom to freshen up.

"Before they do it unto us." His humor tends to cynical.

I give him the upshot of what Marino told me.

"Mercy Island," Benton says as I turn on water in the sink. "Adding to my suspicion that the Slasher has been in and out of mental health facilities, harboring conflicted feelings about women who have cared for him. Most of all his mother. That's who he's targeting symbolically."

"Or maybe his job brings him to health facilities," I reply. "A lot of vehicles are in and out delivering food, medical supplies, you name it. Plus, the construction and landscaping and everything else going on. The last time I responded to Mercy Island, the security was pathetic."

"That was Lucy on the phone, and based on what she was telling me, security's no better now," Benton says as I wash my face.

162

"All that's needed is a keycard to open the entrance gate. Or it can be accessed remotely by the residents, the hospital staff."

"Has she said anything about Georgine Duvall?" I can't imagine what Lucy must be feeling.

"Not a word. You wouldn't know she'd ever heard of her."

"Which is exactly how she acted way back when," I recall.

"Georgine Duvall's address on Mercy Island is Thirteen Shore Lane, as it turns out. How's that for an eerie coincidence?" Benton adds.

"The property we looked at?" I dry my face with a towel, reaching for the jar of moisturizer.

"The very same."

"Marino didn't mention the actual street address and might not know it's the place we toured after the Realtor twisted our arm," I explain.

"Riverfront with huge trees and a big garden." Benton leans against the doorframe looking at his phone, skimming through more messages. "On a point and probably the most isolated and private of the residences."

I brush my teeth, remembering the lush rosebushes, the benches, the wooden birdhouses on poles, everything old. I envision metal fencing around the property, and the high stone wall that encircles the hospital grounds. When Benton and I were house-hunting five years ago, Mercy Island was recommended as ideal.

We were shown the former chapel repurposed into a three-story house with tall windows and high ceilings, the views spectacular. When we toured rooms and the meditation garden, we couldn't help but think of desperate patients. The energy was depressing and oppressive. We couldn't shake it or wait to leave.

"Unless you can access the entrance, you'd need assistance to climb over the wall, which is a good seven or eight feet high," I remind Benton. "Then you'd have to scale the fence around Thirteen Shore Lane. You'd need a ladder, a rope. Or a boat possibly if you come in by water. I seem to remember a dock behind the house."

"The wall, the fence, the river wouldn't keep out someone determined," he agrees. "And normally an intruder would have been picked up by the home security cameras around the perimeter. Except they're wireless. So is the alarm system, and as we know, there was no cell signal at the time of the attack. Lucy told me that like most places these days, everything at the scene is Wi-Fi-enabled."

"Smart homes for obtuse people." I open the medicine cabinet, finding the hair gel. "They don't realize how vulnerable that makes them if there's an outage or the network is overwhelmed."

"Or if a predator shows up with a signal jammer. Which is why we have backup landlines in hard-to-find places," Benton says. "Lucy's not about to allow someone to do that to us."

"Has she figured out the problem yet?"

"She and Tron discovered a homemade signal jammer like the ones used in the other three cases," he says. "It was hidden in shrubs on the riverbank at the back of the house. They're dealing with the provider to get the Wi-Fi back up."

# CHAPTER 18

I study myself in the mirror over the sink, my hair a mess. Silver at the temples, it's more cool blond than honey gold and needs trimming. I was looking forward to a hairstylist I like in London, and I text my secretary, asking her to cancel all travel and appointments.

*Another homicide that may be the work of the Slasher. Here in Alexandria,* I explain to Shannon. *Have to postpone travels.*

*Dear God, how terrible!* she answers right away.

*The sooner you head to the office the better,* I write her back.

I instruct her to make sure security is alerted, and to expect federal agents showing up. Possibly even members of the intelligence community. We've been visited before during autopsies that, unbeknownst to us, were of interest to the CIA, U.S. Army Intelligence, the National Security Agency, to name a few.

Usually, the undercover agents claim to be from nongermane government agencies like the Department of Agriculture. Or in this case, the FAA. I don't go into detail, but my secretary understands, and I tell her to keep me updated.

"How well do you know Zain Willard?" I ask Benton. "You're in and out of the White House, the Capitol. I assume your paths have crossed."

"That's about the extent of it." He heads to his closet as I walk out of the bathroom. "I've seen him there and other places. This nerdy kid who'd rather talk to an AI chatbot or a robot than people. I realize he's not really a kid. But he seems a lot younger than he is."

"Where was he when Georgine Duvall was murdered? Are we sure he was upstairs in his room as he claims? Did he really hear her scream?" I pick up a black shirt embroidered with my office logo and *K. Scarpetta, Chief Medical Examiner.*

"I'm wondering whether she was capable of screaming. I was going to ask you that," Benton says as hangers scrape along the clothes rod. "You've seen the photographs, I assume."

"Marino texted a few, and the incisions to the anterior neck would have severed the vocal cords and trachea." I envision the gory images. "She wasn't making a sound after that."

"Then she might have screamed at first when she woke up while being attacked," Benton supposes.

"Very possibly, as it appears she tried to ward off the blade. She has classic defensive injuries, suggesting the first cuts were to her hands and arms and not her neck," I explain, pulling on a pair of cargo pants.

"Then Zain may be telling the truth about hearing her scream."

"If so, it wouldn't have been for long. Has he offered any helpful details?"

"Not so far." Benton works his arms through the sleeves of a faded denim shirt. "Maybe he'll remember more when I talk to him in the hospital later today. And we'll want you to take a look at him."

"Willing to help in any way. But I'll be limited in what I can determine after surgery and other therapeutic interventions. I'll insist that I'm not alone with him."

"We have agents posted outside his room, and I'll be with you," Benton says.

"Still no weapon recovered, I assume?" I ask.

"Not that I'm aware of. Nor would I expect there to be." He zips up his jeans. "The knife the Slasher uses has special meaning to him. He brings it with him and leaves with it. I suspect it's something he's had a long time."

"Any chance of an inside job? Is it possible Zain Willard killed Georgine Duvall?" I tuck in my shirt. "More to the point, could he be the Phantom Slasher?"

"Of course, we have to consider that." Benton finds a belt. "But I have my serious doubts. As I've said before, I believe the Slasher is older, more likely in his thirties or forties. I base this on his organizational skills, his meticulous planning and lack of impulsivity."

"Except it was different this time," I reply. "He didn't know how many people were staying in a place he'd targeted. And he didn't check to make sure Zain was dead. Something seems to have gone off the rails. Marino may be right about that."

"What I know for a fact is Zain was badly injured," Benton says. "I don't believe he's faking anything. The first officer to arrive at the scene discovered him some distance from the house about to pass out."

"Hopefully his bloody trail was photographed before the rain started in with a vengeance," I reply.

"It was."

"And swabs were taken to confirm the source?"

"Yes."

"The killer seems to work in the dark," I point out. "It's possible he might have accidentally cut himself. We have to make sure none of the blood is his."

"I believe he's using night-vision eyewear and can see what he's doing just fine. If only we could be so lucky that he'd cut himself and bleed somewhere." Benton hands me his phone. "This is from the first responding officer's body cam."

———

Pressing the arrow for Play, I watch Zain Willard seated cross-legged in a slurry of snow and slush on the sidewalk. A freezing rain smacks down in big slow drops.

He could pass for twelve or thirteen, angelically pretty, his curly blond hair tinted teal blue at the tips. He stares up at the camera with wide shocked eyes, shivering, teeth chattering in a chiaroscuro of streetlights and shadows.

"...Easy does it. Everything's going to be okay." The officer is talking while his body camera films. "Try to stay calm. You're safe now, buddy..."

Zain has on a sweatshirt, jeans and sneakers with no socks. He's covered with blood that has soaked into the watery slush, turning it the pale red of a cherry snow cone. I notice a thick silver chain around his neck.

"...I'm Don Horace with the Alexandria police. What's your name?" the officer asks.

"Zain Willard. Did you see it?" His breathing is rapid and shallow, his glassy eyes terrified. "Did you see that thing?" He can barely talk, his voice a shaky whisper.

"What thing?" Officer Horace is young with dark hair and a flat demeanor.

"The ghost! Over there!" Zain points as sirens wail closer. "Floating away from the house, following me!"

"When was this?"

"Right before you got here. The thing was there holding a knife, watching me with a dead face and red eyes!" He points again at the fog in the wan glow of lamps bordering the sidewalk.

"Well, I don't think a ghost did this to you or killed your friend inside the house..."

"Oh God!" Zain convulses into tears.

"What do you remember about what happened in there, Zain?"

"Oh God. No...!"

"Tell me anything you can while it's fresh in your memory," Officer Horace goes on.

"I came downstairs, and it smelled like a swimming pool. It was pitch-dark." Zain is sobbing.

I continue noticing his teeth. They're perfectly straight. I seriously doubt they made the irregular bite marks I've been seeing in the Slasher cases.

"Then I was hit in the throat and arm. At first, I didn't know I was cut."

"Why did you come downstairs to begin with?" the officer asks.

"The screaming." Zain is getting weaker, swaying as if about to topple over.

"What was she screaming?"

"'Stop!' She screamed, 'Stop...!'" Zain wraps his arms around his knees, rocking back and forth, blood dripping, his face panicked. "She was shrieking for him to stop...!"

"You need to sit still and calm down, okay?" the officer is saying.

Sirens are deafening, pulsing red lights bleary in the overcast.

"The ambulance is here and you're gonna be fine, Zain. I'll be right next to you..."

I pause the recording on Benton's phone, zooming in on the diamond stud in Zain's blood-smeared right earlobe. Just below it the two shallow incisions appear to be from one stroke angled downward, terminating in the middle of his throat.

I'd estimate the wounds are a total of about five inches long. But it's impossible to know when there's nothing in the video I can use as a scale.

"Unlike the deeper incision made straight across when a victim's throat is cut from behind, the usual scenario." I'm telling Benton my interpretations as I return his phone. "What I just saw is consistent with his throat being slashed by a right-handed assailant who was facing him."

I make a backhanded slice in the air as if swinging a sizable blade with my right arm.

"Cutting the throat from the front is consistent with what I've seen in the first three victims, and also in photographs of Georgine Duvall," I continue to explain. "Except the four of them were cut multiple times and with considerable force."

"Overkill," Benton replies as we move around the bedroom, getting ready.

"Yes, but not when Zain Willard was injured," I reply. "What happened to him seems more like a halfhearted attempt by comparison."

"That's likely because it wasn't emotionally driven by sexually violent fantasies." Benton returns to his closet. "I suspect the Slasher was out of gas by the time he was confronted with a second person in the house. He hadn't anticipated that for some reason."

"The question is why? How could that happen?"

"Hopefully, I'll know more when I walk around the scene." Benton riffles through neckties.

"Is Zain right- or left-handed?" I retrieve our passports, the French and British currency from the top of my dresser.

"Right-handed it's been my impression from the times I've been around him at the White House and elsewhere," Benton says. "But I'll confirm."

"For the sake of the argument, let's say he killed Georgine Duvall." I walk across the bedroom, headed to the gun safe. "Why injure himself after the fact? Why take a risk like that?"

"Possibly as an alibi. Or for sympathy and attention. Those would be the typical reasons someone would self-injure in a case like this." Benton picks a blue paisley tie that goes with denim. "The first thing we need to know for a fact is whether Zain could have cut his own throat. Would that have been possible?"

"Based on what I saw in the video, yes. But let me emphasize how difficult and dangerous that would be." I enter the password on the safe's push-button keypad. "In addition to the willpower and tolerance for pain required, one slip of the blade and he could have severed his carotid, bleeding out in minutes."

I push down on the steel handle, opening the safe's heavy door. A glimpse of fine timepieces and other jewelry, and I tuck in our passports, the British pounds, the euros.

"He has a gash to his right forearm." I continue describing what I saw in the photos Marino texted. "Also, cuts to the fingers and palm of his right hand. Depending on the severity of the injuries, he could have suffered permanent damage to ligaments and tendons."

"And he could have done all that to himself?" Benton is reading something on his phone.

"If he had the stomach for it." I shut the thick steel door with a loud clank. "But if he did this to himself, he's lucky to be alive."

"I'm skimming his background assessment right now," Benton says. "Zain's right-handed. Five foot four, one hundred and twenty pounds. He's small and rather frail, as you just saw in the video."

"An assailant doesn't need to be big and strong if he has a knife and his victim is asleep," I answer.

"I don't believe it's him," Benton says. "I don't think he killed Georgine Duvall or anyone else. But that doesn't mean he's telling the truth about what happened this morning. For one thing, what took him so long to head downstairs after he supposedly heard her scream? By the time he got there, she likely was dead, and the bleach had been poured."

"The same questions are crossing my mind." I collect my computer-assisted smart ring from the nightstand.

"He took the time to put on clothes. What else was he doing?" Benton asks.

"We need his jeans, sweatshirt, shoes, whatever he had on, including a silver necklace I noticed in the video."

"I'm told that Officer Horace has taken care of personal effects and other evidence," Benton says.

"Told by whom?"

"Lucy talked to him." Benton picks up his badge wallet.

"Never heard of Officer Horace before this morning."

"Apparently a rookie. But forward-thinking enough to get swabs," Benton replies.

"Of what?" I ask.

"Any trace evidence or DNA that might have been transferred to Zain. Supposedly when he fell to the floor after being attacked in the dark, the killer almost tripped over him."

"In other words, they had physical contact, and afterward no bleach was splashed all over either of them. Maybe DNA was transferred and not destroyed for once." I don't feel hopeful, but maybe we'll catch a break.

"This is according to what Horace passed along to Lucy.

Apparently, while he rode in the ambulance, he got photographs and swabs in addition to more information," Benton tells me.

"That was quick thinking since rescue squads and hospitals aren't in the business of preserving evidence. The killer fled. Then what, according to Officer Horace?" I ask.

"Zain tried nine-one-one, but the Wi-Fi was down. The SOS emergency feature on his phone also was disabled. He had to go outside to find a signal so he could call for help," Benton says. "He left the fenced-in property through the front gate, following the sidewalk to where Officer Horace found him."

"I wonder where Zain was on Valentine's Day at around three a.m. when Emma Chopra was slashed to death in bed?" I reply.

"Hopefully we'll get answers when we start interrogating his phone and other electronic devices."

"What about last May when Ashley Tait was murdered on Mother's Day?" I open a dresser drawer for a pair of socks. "Where was Zain?"

"He'd already moved into the house on Mercy Island," Benton says. "He was staying there for the summer."

"Does he have a car?" I ask, and Benton looks at his phone again, scrolling through information.

"A nineteen-sixty-eight Mercury Cougar," he answers.

# CHAPTER 19

"What about Georgine Duvall?" I collect a pair of tactical boots from my closet floor. "What does she drive?"

"A Cadillac Lyriq. Lucy says it's charging inside the garage at Thirteen Shore Lane. Both cars are there." Benton is putting on his watch and signet ring.

"Do we know where Zain was not even two months ago when Fiona Webb was murdered on Halloween?" I've carried my boots to a chair, sitting down.

"I've been sent his White House schedule. He wasn't interning on Halloween. One would assume he was at William & Mary." Benton steps in front of the full-length mirror.

"Williamsburg is a three-hour drive from here, depending on traffic. Not exactly close but a doable distance if you're in and out of Northern Virginia committing crimes." I pull on my socks.

"It appears that Georgine Duvall allowed Zain to stay at her place whenever he was up this way."

"I wonder why?" I'm lacing my boots.

"It would seem she's friendly with Senator Willard," Benton says. "The two of them were at UVA together."

"As I'll keep pointing out, Zain's been in striking range when each murder has occurred," I reply. "And then he's on Mercy Island staying in the same house with Georgine when she was killed a few hours ago. I must admit it makes me uneasy."

"Most sexually violent psychopaths don't commit suicide or self-injure. They don't target their friends and housemates." Benton looks in the mirror as he knots his tie.

"Most," I repeat. "But not all."

"There's no evidence he has a history of mental illness or anything else alarming, according to his background check. You don't intern at the White House without the Secret Service doing a deep dive into your life and everyone around you."

"Even if your uncle is Calvin Willard?"

"Even then," Benton says. "But it certainly gave Zain an advantage."

"What do we know about him besides not seeming like someone who might be violent?" I return to my closet for a belt.

"An only child. His father was a lawyer and died when Zain was a kid. I suspect that's when his rich, powerful uncle Calvin stepped in."

"Died how?"

"An accident. A tree fell on him in their backyard." Benton has his eyes on his phone. "Based on what I'm skimming in his background report, Zain grew up in D.C. He started interning at the White House three summers ago."

"What do we know about his mother?"

"A pediatrician," Benton says. "She lives in Seattle, remarried and moved there after Zain graduated from high school."

"What do people say about him? Those who work with him at

the White House?" I ask, thunder cracking, the wind swooshing in the chimney.

"I know from my own encounters that he's polite but a little weird." Benton walks over to the fireplace.

He clanks the damper closed, sweeping white ashes off the hearth.

"Awkward and introverted," he's saying. "There have been no complaints about him being aggressive or even difficult."

"His internship at the White House?" I ask.

"He's at the Office of Science and Technology Policy."

"Doing what?"

"I don't know the details. But he has a robotic dog named Robbie that he brings to work on occasion, using it for show-and-tell," Benton says. "I've seen it doing tricks for dignitaries, all sorts of high-level visitors to the White House. His uncle gets a big kick out of it."

"That seems risky if the robot is capable of recording whatever's going on," I reply.

"It's not allowed in secure areas like the Situation Room," Benton says. "And having robotic dogs around isn't new. The Secret Service is already using them in certain situations. To patrol the fence line around the White House, for example."

"I've seen videos of them at Mar-a-Lago," I recall.

"Part of Zain's internship involves R&D of this sort of thing," Benton explains. "I guess when your uncle is a U.S. senator who may be the next president, you get special privileges and access."

"Sounds like Zain Willard might be capable of causing all kinds of sophisticated trouble such as signal jamming and hacking?" I suggest.

"Maybe so."

"And most of all, would he have the ability to use holograms to stalk, spy and create a public panic?" I ask.

"Maybe. But the timing wouldn't make much sense."

The phantomlike hologram was seen by first responders while Zain was bleeding on the sidewalk, Benton points out. Some fifteen minutes later, Marino and Fruge saw the same projected apparition as Zain was driven away in the ambulance.

"Marino mentioned something about a drone," I tell Benton, and surprise glints in his eyes.

I explain what Marino told me about the two men he believes are CIA spies.

"I hope he doesn't run his mouth about that," Benton says.

"Then you think the Slasher is using a drone?"

"In fact, we know he is, and not the sort of thing your average hobbyist buys off the internet. It's been detected intermittently in the earlier cases. And it was picked up by sensors on Mercy Island before and after this morning's home invasion."

"Then I don't see how it could have been Zain at the controls," I decide. "He was in the ambulance when Marino saw the phantom-like hologram."

"And if Zain's the killer, what happened to the weapon?" Benton is putting on thick socks and Chelsea boots. "How could he hide it after the fact without tracking his own blood everywhere?"

"He couldn't. As much as he was bleeding, he would have left a trail no matter what." I'm looking at my phone, checking the internet for a mention of this morning's attack.

So far, nothing.

"I remember when Calvin Willard first ran for office long ago, about the time we left Virginia thinking we'd never be back." Skimming through a slew of emails, I mark them as unread for later. "And here we are, and he's likely going to be the Democratic nominee for president. Favored to win in the latest polls."

"Let's hope that never happens," Benton says.

"And of course, the Secret Service would have no reason to watch Zain?"

"No." Benton clips his badge holder, his pancake holster to his belt.

"Does Calvin Willard know what's going on?" I ask from my closet, grabbing a winter tactical jacket.

"Yes, the senator knows." Benton slides his pistol into the holster. "Aren't you forgetting something, Kay?"

He looks at me as he walks to my bedside table, and I know what's coming.

"No, I didn't forget. But I wish you would," I tell him.

"Statute eighteen-point-two." He retrieves my Glock from the bedside drawer.

"Do we really have to think about this today?" I tuck a lip balm in a pocket of my cargo pants. "Don't we have enough to deal with?"

"Statute eighteen-point-two," he repeats. "A White House involvement in a hugely sensational serial murder case, and you'll be under even more scrutiny than ever. Politics and extreme publicity, and your enemies will come after you given the chance."

"As you've said before. More than once. And they come after me anyway."

"It will be worse."

"I don't like keeping track of a gun while shrouded in PPE, dealing with a very bloody scene that's contaminated with bleach." I watch him de-cock the Glock, rendering it safe.

He drops out the pistol's magazine, clearing a semi-jacketed hollow-point from the chamber while explaining that the Slasher's drone has stealth and other high-tech capabilities. That's how he spies on his victims. It's how he creates his holograms.

"You don't want to be noncompliant." Benton hands me the gun, the ammunition. "All you need is someone like Maggie Cutbush or Elvin Reddy finding out that you're not obeying the law. Even if it's a stupid one."

Earlier in the year, the Virginia General Assembly passed a bill mandating that certain first responders, investigators, government officials, even schoolteachers are required to be sworn in as civilian cops. I've been one since I began my career as a medical examiner in Miami where I was born and raised.

But carrying my peace officer badge and weapon was always up to my discretion. Not anymore because of statute §18.2. It states that there will be adverse consequences *if the employee does not agree to be trained to enforce the law. This includes carrying a concealed handgun pursuant to this section...*

Snapping the Glock's slide forward, I reload the magazine without chambering a round. I tuck the pistol into the back of my waistband for now. Opening a dresser drawer, Benton finds the thin black leather wallet holding my civilian law enforcement credentials. He hands it to me.

"You've been qualifying on the range for as long as we've known each other," he says in a gentler tone as we leave the bedroom. "You know how to handle yourself in police situations. It's second nature to you."

He's looking up a number in his contact list as we follow the hallway. I'm behind him on the stairs, listening as he cancels the Rosewood.

"...Thank you as always for being so understanding..." Benton is saying. "Yes, yes, we'll definitely try again..."

I envision the majestic hotel with its view of central London, and reality sets in hard. The trip isn't going to happen. It really isn't.

Off the phone now, Benton says to me, "They wished you a Merry Christmas, already had a cake and a bottle of champagne ready."

I open the entryway closet as Merlin saunters through the living room, headed toward us. Collarless, still muttering and meowing, he doesn't look happy. I pet him, asking if he's hungry.

"This is the way he was last night." I pick up my black Pelican scene case the size of a large toolbox. "Acting spooked as if he senses something."

"An unpleasant thought." Benton grabs a Secret Service tactical coat that will conceal the gun on his hip.

"Maybe it's just the wildlife, the raccoon and who knows what else is out there. I hope it's not for some other reason." I can't stop seeing the two red orbs that appeared after Marino drove away from the house.

Collecting my Kevlar briefcase from the table near the front door, I tuck my Glock into a side compartment equipped with a rapid-release Velcro tab.

"Where is Georgine Duvall's place in Yorktown?" I ask.

"The historic area." Benton takes the scene case from me. "It would appear from real estate records that the house has been in her family for generations."

"I remember her mentioning how much she loved the place. She said she had happy memories of going there when she was growing up," I reply. "Historic Yorktown is very close to Williams & Mary where Zain is in grad school."

Benton carries my scene case past the Christmas tree. Santa lights up, cheerily hailing us. Merlin hisses just like he always does, and I don't blame him.

"Lucy obviously knows what's happened to Georgine. How did she seem when you were talking to her?" I ask.

"You'd never know she was her patient once," Benton says.

"I hate to think what this will reopen," I reply as we reach the kitchen. "Lucy's first year at UVA was brutal for her. And it wasn't exactly a cakewalk for me either."

# CHAPTER 20

Most mornings we eat at the café table overlooking the bird-feeders and garden. There's no time for that now, and it's still dark out, the shades down. Our breakfast will be to-go. But first things first.

I open a cupboard for Merlin's grain-free wet food made from whitefish. Emptying the can into his bowl, I set it on the mat near the fireplace. He begins wolfing it down, looking up anxiously every other second as text messages land on my phone.

*In the car heading to the office,* Shannon informs me.

*Please make sure Dr. Schlaefer knows that I'm on my way to the scene,* I write her back. *He's to get the decomp room ready and start when the body arrives.*

Next, I hear from Fabian. The van is gassed up and loaded.

*Any special requests before I boogie?* he writes.

*Two body pouches. One heavy-duty, one standard, both white,* I text him.

*Already taken care of. Except they're black.*

*Have to be white. Trace evidence shows up better,* I answer.

*Got it.*

*And I need the medical kit I keep in my office credenza,* I add.

*The one for living patients?*

*Yes,* I answer.

An update from DNA examiner Clark Givens lets me know that he'll pack the laser scanner needed for 3-D mapping the bloodstain evidence.

"What's your pleasure?" Benton opens the refrigerator. "Cream cheese, fig preserves? How about butter? Shall we splurge?"

"May as well," I tell him. "God only knows when we'll have time to eat again."

It's now almost six-fifteen. My headache is better but not gone, my eyes scratchy from too little sleep. I can tell that Benton isn't feeling much better as he places two multigrain bagels on a cutting board, finding the bread knife.

Checking on the weather, I peek behind the curtain over the sink, and it's pitch-black out, distant thunder rumbling. The thermometer on the windowsill reads forty degrees Fahrenheit, the backyard socked in by fog.

Trees and foliage are dark shapes moving in the wind, lightning flickering through clouds as my phone begins to vibrate on the countertop.

"Hi," I answer Lucy's call. "How's it going?"

"Leaving Mercy Island. I was just in the admissions area of the hospital." Her voice sounds over speakerphone, and I can tell she's in the car.

"Merry Christmas, Lucy." Benton is slicing bagels in half.

"I'm sorry about your trip."

"So are we," I answer. "What's the latest?"

"I'm trying to get info about patients on the forensic unit, among other things," she tells us. "Most important is accessing recordings from the security cameras, but it's not looking good."

"The cameras have always been an issue when I've responded to deaths there." I'm filling the coffee machine's reservoirs with water and almond milk. "It's deliberate. Very much to their advantage when nothing is recording."

"There aren't many cameras for a place this size, all of them in areas that aren't helpful," Lucy replies. "Such as the staff parking lot. And the loading dock where deliveries are made. Some are off-line. Including the ones at the entrance of the island."

"Par for the course." I open the tin of coffee beans. "They've had so many scandals, the staff is experienced at obstruction. They make sure there's as little record as possible. Then when something bad happens, they dig deeper into protect mode. They lie. They obfuscate."

"The director is stonewalling, citing HIPAA this and HIPAA that," Lucy replies.

"Graden Crowley must be beside himself." I pour the Jamaican coffee beans into the machine, smelling the rich aroma. "The hospital's blighted past is about to be made public by Dana Diletti. And now the Slasher has just murdered a psychiatrist there."

"Lucy, when's the last time you and Georgine Duvall had contact?" Benton places the bagels inside the toaster oven.

"My freshman year at UVA." Her voice has cooled over the phone.

"Were you aware that she's good friends with Calvin Willard?" He watches the bagels as if they won't toast otherwise.

"I'd have no reason to be aware," she answers. "But I'm not surprised, and it makes me wonder what's gone on inside Thirteen Shore Lane. Who might have been in and out of the house besides Zain Willard? What was the killer seeing when he was spying?"

"Spying with the drone Marino was asked about by two men allegedly from the CIA?" I inquire.

"Based on what I've been hearing, Marino looked suspicious as hell trespassing in someone's gazebo," Lucy says. "And we know what he's like when confronted."

"The agents involved probably wondered if he was the killer." Benton takes the lids off tubs of butter and cream cheese. "And I can see why it might have crossed their minds."

"Bottom line, around the time of the attack a drone was detected intermittently in the area," Lucy says.

"Benton says a drone has been used in the other murders," I reply.

"And we don't want the killer knowing we're aware of that," she says.

"Then you best remind Marino not to be talking about it to anyone but us," Benton says.

"I'll take care of it."

Lucy goes on to explain that transmissions are picked up whenever the Slasher overrides the autonomous function, entering commands that divert the drone from operating as programmed.

"When that occurs, a signal is transmitted in the four-fifty-megahertz range," Lucy describes. "The same bandwidth as the walkie-talkies a lot of emergency medical techs use."

"Adding to the confusion at a crime scene." I marvel at the ingeniousness of it. "You might assume the signals detected are from the rescue squads."

Lucy says that the drone in question isn't the typical quadcopter. It's a Hoberman sphere about the size of a medicine ball and equipped with Keyence AI sensors. Propelled by thrust vectoring nozzles, the orb has scissorlike joints that can fold into different shapes and sizes. It's stable in stormy weather and able to maneuver in zero visibility.

"Got to go. Just pulling up to HRT," Lucy tells us.

She's in Quantico at the FBI Academy's Hostage Rescue Team. Hangared there is the beast of a helicopter called the Doomsday Bird that she pilots for the Department of Homeland Security.

"See you later. Be careful out there," she adds as I cover to-go cups with plastic lids.

Benton and I put on our jackets. He arms the security system and opens the door, shutting it behind us. The warning beeps pierce the gloom, then abruptly stop. I listen for the strange animal sounds I heard last night, but everything is quiet.

The overcast has begun to brighten along the dark horizon, a sharp wind gusting but not as powerfully. Lightning veins the sky, thunder mumbling as the storm retreats out to sea like a warring armada. Benton carries my scene case across the back porch, the deep snow melted by heavy rain and rising temperatures.

We make our way down steep steps, water dripping from trees, the fog thick and cold. Lights blink on as we follow the footpath leading to the driveway. Benton pulls out the scene case's retracted handle, the wheels loud like a drum roll over pavers, the slush several inches deep in spots.

I think of what Janet said about screams and hoots made by an animal not found in any database. I'm waiting for the startling vocalizations again, but all is still. I see things that aren't there, shadows shapeshifting, and it's imagined. Lightning strobes like a camera flash going off, illuminating the garden and greenhouse, and I can barely make out the purple glow of Dorothy's UV light.

When Benton and I reach the former carriage house, he opens the wooden doors, vanishing in the inky blackness. The Tesla's electric engine is quiet as he drives out, and I close the carriage house doors, locking them. I settle into the passenger's seat, headlights painting over huge magnolias dense with rubbery leaves.

Tall hardwood trees arch bare branches over us like the vaulted ceiling of a cathedral as we pass the guest cottage, our headlights illuminating pavers and woods. I look up at turbid clouds, halfway expecting the red-eyed ghost to appear. Or maybe an orb-shaped drone that makes no sound.

At the end of the driveway Benton eases to a stop, and we wait for the heavy metal gate to lurch along its track. We've been having trouble with it getting stuck. Often it ends up half open or half shut, depending on how you look at it. As we're sitting here, our every detail is detected by multiple AI-assisted cameras and sensors.

Software is conducting facial and voice recognition, capturing our vehicle type and license tag while detecting any electronic devices we have. Information is constantly analyzed and uploaded in real time.

*WTF?* Marino is texting me now.

He explains that he's inside the bedroom where Georgine Duvall was murdered, going over it with forensic lights. I open photographs he's taken with a filter in the UV spectrum, startled by what I see. Bloody smudges on a hallway runner fluoresce a neon fiery red as if made with luminescent poster paint.

*WTF is right,* I text Marino as Benton pulls away from the gate limping shut behind us. *Wonder what's lighting up?*

*Got no idea. But nothing like this was at the other three Slasher scenes,* Marino replies, sending another photograph.

This one is of a wingchair in a corner of the bedroom, an area of the seat cushion glowing the same electric red. I pass along to Benton what's going on as I send DNA scientist Clark Givens another message. Before he heads to Mercy Island, I need him to grab a handheld Raman spectrometer from the trace evidence lab.

"Hopefully, it can help me identify the composition of whatever's reacting to UV light, causing the fluorescence," I explain to Benton as he turns left on Prince Street. "Assuming it's the Slasher again, he likely doesn't realize he left a trace of something that he carried to the scene this time."

Digging into our breakfast bag, I pull out the bagels, unwrapping them.

"He must have had this residue on the bottom of his feet, and also on whatever he set down on the bedroom chair." Benton takes a bite of his bagel. "God, that's good, if I do say so myself."

"We know he has a murder kit." I dig in, the cream cheese and figs a delicious combination.

"Some type of tote bag." Benton wipes his hands with a napkin. "He has gloves, possibly other PPE, bleach, the knife that he's attached to, whatever else he brings with him and then carries away after the fact."

"Maybe the tote bag is the source of a residue that's not visible in normal light," I suggest. "Maybe it's been transferred from where he lives or works."

---

We drive through our historic neighborhood, most old homes Georgian or Victorian and immaculately preserved. Lights are starting to come on in the windows, people getting up to enjoy a holiday breakfast and open presents. The charcoal-gray sky brightens by degrees as if on a rheostat, the rising sun a chalky smudge.

Traffic is steady, doesn't matter that it's Christmas, and I think of the killer getting around. No matter the holiday or time, there are always people on the roads this close to Washington, D.C. The Slasher may do much of his stalking with a drone and holographic technologies. But he shows up in person to break in and murder.

"He's getting to and from the victims' neighborhoods somehow. I keep wondering how he's doing that," I'm saying to Benton. "If we include this morning, he's struck four times in four different locations within a ten-mile radius. I should say *at least* four times. We don't really know."

"More than meets the eye, because he's not new at this. The pacing of the attacks, his ability to create havoc while evading the police, tells me he's experienced." Benton repeats what he's been saying all along. "I suspect he's committed criminal acts over the years that haven't been connected, but this is different. He's hitting his stride. On a violent bender and craving the attention."

"While getting around undetected somehow." I go back to that. "I'm surprised there are no reports of a vehicle seen in the areas where the victims lived. I would think software algorithms would pick up on a suspicious car at certain hours. We know there are security cameras all over the place. And satellites."

"Satellites using radar and AI can see through overcast," Benton replies. "But obviously, they aren't sweeping every inch of the planet. They're oriented to cover certain locations of interest to the government."

"Do you think the Slasher has a way of knowing what areas are under surveillance by cameras, even satellites, and those that aren't?" It's an awful thought.

"I've begun to suspect as much," Benton says. "This is a violent sexual psychopath who appears relatively normal on the surface. He knows how to avoid being seen. It's not anyone typical."

# CHAPTER 21

Holiday lights sparkle in the heart of Old Town, some of the decorations blown down and soggy in the ice-watery mess. Snow that hasn't melted is patchy white on rooftops and winter-brown grass. I don't see anybody out walking or jogging, the road-side empty of the usual parked cars.

Restaurants and bars are empty, and through shadowy glass I can make out the shapes of tables and chairs, nothing open except hotels. In the distance, the George Washington Masonic National Memorial looms like an ancient temple, the top of it veiled in mist.

Everywhere I look I see handsome edifices and precise engineering, evidence of an advanced and civil society it would seem. But within those solid walls are tragedies waiting to happen and humans who do unthinkable things. At moments like this I'm weighed down by the gravity of our impermanent and imperfect existence.

How much easier if I didn't know so much. It would be reassuring never to scratch below the surface, to avoid looking up at the heavens wondering who might be looking back. But I can't ignore what's all around me. As Dorothy likes to say, once the truth genie gets out, it's not possible to put it back in the bottle.

*Which is why you don't always want to let it out to begin with,* she often warns.

According to her it's wiser to remain selectively ignorant. Best not to question if you don't want the answer.

*Why do you have to know everything, Kay?*

Dorothy's been saying that most of our lives.

*Why can't you learn to leave well enough alone?*

I'm hearing her in my head as Benton drives, paralleling the Potomac River several streets over. No doubt, Dorothy is sleeping off her night of drinking and arguing with Marino. I hope I didn't add to the tension between them.

But he was with me for hours, driving to the O'Learys' house, not wanting to leave me alone for a moment. Meanwhile, my sister was by herself, the timing unfortunate.

"I hope Dorothy's all right," I say to Benton. "I've sent several texts and she's not answering."

"I have a feeling she wasn't in great shape by the time she'd finished fighting with Marino and went to bed."

"Should we be worried? What if she forgot to set the alarm after he left?"

It's too early to call and wish her a Merry Christmas, and now's not the time for a personal conversation. I type Lucy a text.

*All okay with your mom? Haven't heard from her.*

I begin checking various news feeds on my phone, disappointed by what I find but expecting as much.

"Well, that's too bad but par for the course," I say to Benton. "The media knows what's happened, and it's going viral."

"I'm not surprised." He sips his coffee as I read the headlines out loud.

*Slasher Strikes Again.*

*Phantom Slasher Terrorizes Alexandria.*

*Serial Killer Targets Mercy Island.*

*Couple Butchered Near Mental Hospital...*

"Christ. The public will be buying out the gun stores again." Benton's eyes are on traffic and the mirrors.

"We can't seem to keep anything quiet for longer than five minutes," I tell him as Lucy answers me that her mother is fine.

*Just hungover and grumpy,* Lucy reports.

"Not to mention, nothing much is reported accurately. Not even close," I'm saying to Benton.

It's increasingly common for reporters and social media influencers to find out about a case before we reach the scene. This never happened in the early years of our careers. What ensues is an avalanche of unsubstantiated wild tales endlessly replicated and accepted as gospel.

Details that might be accurate often provide information we don't want the offender having. The worry is that a first responder is the leak. Possibly someone who works for a rescue squad or the local police, and I click open the link of a live video news feed.

"*...We can't see it from here. But where the horrific attack occurred is in a remote wooded area overlooking the Potomac River,*" Dana Diletti is saying. "*Why did the Slasher choose Mercy Island? How did he come and go without leaving a trace? And does he have a connection to the hospital, possibly a former patient?*"

Tall and beautiful, she looks like a Paris model in a red trench coat and Russian Cossack fur hat. She seems energetic, no worse for the wear after last night's scare. The Slasher sent the hologram through her window and hours later murdered someone else.

She shows no sign of being shocked or frightened, not a hint of sadness for the latest victims. Positioned near the entrance gate to the hospital grounds, she broadcasts live while police ensure no one unauthorized enters the island.

In the background the six-story Tudor-style hospital hulks ancient and haunted. The rising sun glints on mullioned windows, the stucco a dingy insipid yellow.

"It's way back there." Dana Diletti dramatically swings her arm, pointing a gloved hand like a referee. "On the river's edge at the back of the hospital, originally built in the early eighteen-thirties. In those days, it was known as Mercy Lunatic Asylum, and it doesn't sound like it was merciful based on what I've been finding out..."

Her tone turns ominous as she moves closer to the barricaded entrance, her crew scurrying after her.

"Old murders you're going to hear about later during a special report I'm working on," she's saying. "And now this. We've got our Eye in the Sky covering the investigation live to show you where it happened..."

I mute the sound.

"I'm assuming any drones flying around the scene right now aren't what was detected earlier," I say to Benton. "That's not what has the CIA's knickers in a knot?"

"No, it isn't." He takes a right at the history museum, formidable and columned like the Greek Parthenon. "What was detected earlier is the orb Lucy described."

"And no one's ever spotted it?" I find myself looking up at the sky, the sun pale like a fish scale in the lifting grayness.

"We haven't, and it's not been captured on camera that we know of. We see the holograms, the projections, but not what's making them," Benton explains with an edge of frustration.

"Yet we somehow know what it looks like. An orb."

"From radar and other sensors, we know the shape," he says, and I turn on the volume of my phone again.

"...Originally it was the hospital chapel, and imagine the stories it could tell, most of them terribly sad, I'm betting." Dana Diletti's voice sounds from the Tesla's speakers. "Three-bedroom with a library and wine cellar, assessed at almost two million dollars..."

We're shown aerial images of 13 Shore Lane as the low sun touches the hazy Potomac running along the back of the fenced-in property. The house is three-story stucco and timber with a fieldstone portico and bright red front door.

The place looks the same as I remember, except for the police vehicles parked on the slushy street, and the Christmas lights entwining shrubbery.

"...Officials aren't talking much yet, but from what I've learned from other sources?" Dana Diletti is saying into her microphone. "Another Slasher ghost was spotted drifting through the fog earlier, what we're told is a hologram the killer uses to stalk and create panic. The same thing that floated through my bedroom window as I was exercising last night..."

"This is bad," I say to Benton. "Who the hell is she talking to?"

"I'm guessing she has a network of people leaking information to her," he replies.

"...And that's not all the breaking news, folks. This just in," she's saying. "The woman murdered in her own bed has been identified as Georgine Duvall, a psychiatrist at the hospital..."

"Oh my God," I mutter.

"...The surviving victim, Zain Willard, was staying with her," she goes on. "Turns out he's the nephew of Senator Calvin Willard, expected to be the Democratic nominee for president. The plot thickens, as they say. Could the Slasher's attacks be politically motivated? Was Zain Willard targeted because of his prominent and powerful uncle...?"

"I can't believe how irresponsible she is." I end the video feed. "Now the names are out there before we can confirm identity and notify next of kin."

We're driving on the George Washington Memorial Parkway now. Beyond trees I catch glimmers of the river.

"What I know for a fact is she's been a frequent visitor to the White House in recent months," Benton informs me. "A few weeks ago, I saw her having lunch with Calvin Willard in the mess hall."

The private dining room is used by West Wing potentates, including the president and vice president of the United States. Not just anybody can step foot in there.

"A rumor is circulating that she might become the next press secretary if Calvin Willard is elected," Benton explains.

"You're implying that Calvin Willard might have tipped off Dana Diletti about his nephew almost being killed on Mercy Island?" I spell it out.

"It's possible," he says as the driving app announces a police vehicle two hundred feet ahead.

The Virginia State Police SUV is gray like a shark with push bars on the front bumper. It's parked off-road in a sloppy soup of snow, slush and greenish-brown grass. The trooper stares as we drive past, giving me an uneasy feeling.

Ronald Reagan Washington National Airport is but a few miles ahead, the thunder of low-flying aircraft pervasive. I text Marino that we should reach the Pitié Bridge in the next fifteen minutes.

*It's slow going,* I write to him.

Since Benton and I left the house, traffic has gone from moderate to heavy as it always does regardless of the holiday. I wonder where people are headed this early on Christmas morning. Most are oblivious, others furious in a discord of honking horns and rumbling engines.

*10-4,* Marino answers. *See you when you get here.*

"Everything okay?" I ask Benton as he continues glancing at his mirrors.

"Not sure," he says, and I turn around to see what's snagged his attention.

A state police SUV is closing in behind us, and I assume it's the one we passed a moment ago. The trooper's dark glasses are fixed on us like a sniper about to fire.

"Uh-oh. I'm not liking this one bit." I watch in my side mirror as the trooper rides our bumper. "What the hell does he want?"

"Got no idea."

"Did we do something we're not supposed to? Speeding maybe? An expired inspection sticker?" I suggest.

"No."

"Then why might he be following us, Benton?"

"Not for any legitimate reason," he replies as the trooper begins whelping his siren, the emergency lights strobing. "You got to be kidding me."

Slowing down, we pull off the road, the tires splashing through deep ice water puddles. The state police SUV halts menacingly close, almost touching the rear of our car, red and blue grille lights strobing.

"This is beyond unsettling," I say to Benton.

"Something's not right, that's for sure," he replies as we watch the uniformed trooper climbing out, putting on his campaign hat.

He shuts his door, his right hand down by his holstered gun as he slogs toward us in his bulky winter coat and boots. Benton lowers his window, cold damp air blowing in as he digs in a pocket for his badge-wallet.

"What seems to be the problem?" he says as the trooper bends down, bearded with a flattened nose.

I'm startled before realizing why, careful not to register recognition. His mirrored sunglasses reflect our faces peering out at him as he peers in at us. There's nothing remotely friendly about his demeanor.

"I think you know what the problem is," he answers aggressively as I look at his nametag.

———

Trad Whalen is built like a weightlifter, thick neck, wide shoulders. He looks very different from the photo I saw while going through Rowdy O'Leary's files last night. The state trooper wasn't bearded and as muscular then or last February when he rudely directed me where to park at the former governor's funeral in Ivy Hill cemetery.

"I'm a federal agent and armed." Benton displays his badge. "But then you'd know that from running my plate. I suspect you knew that before you decided to pull us over for no valid reason."

"I always have a valid reason, sir. Where are you headed?" Trad Whalen has a thick Virginia accent.

He takes Benton's wallet, his hands strong and hostile. I notice he wears an expensive military-style Bell & Ross watch and no wedding band.

"The chief medical examiner and I are on official business." Benton's face is granite.

I know he's incensed. But it doesn't show.

"That would be you, ma'am?" Whalen says to me while studying Benton's credentials.

"Yes, I'm Doctor Scarpetta." I tell him what I'm sure he knows.

He returns Benton's wallet, burrowing into a pocket for a small bottle of Purell hand sanitizer. Squirting a dollop into his palms, he rubs them together as if worried about catching a virus from touching our belongings. I watch with growing distrust as he digs out a pair of vinyl exam gloves, transparent and cheap.

I recall the transcript of his interview with Reba O'Leary, and comments about her husband being unstable and paranoid. Rowdy repeatedly contacted the state trooper about the Phantom Slasher. And here we are on the way to the latest murder.

"Good morning, ma'am." Whalen awkwardly works his hands into the gloves like someone who rarely wears them. "What official business are you on this early Christmas morning? Somebody die?"

"Somebody usually does," I answer.

"You always Uber with the Secret Service, ma'am?"

"Not always." I won't let him get a rise out of me.

"You two are married?" he asks, and he damn well knows we are.

"Yes," I tell him.

"I see. Sounds like you're getting your husband to chauffeur you, ma'am. That's mighty nice of him."

"We're riding together," is all I say.

"Are you armed, ma'am?"

"Yes." I pick up my briefcase from the floor, placing it in my lap. "My pistol is in a side pocket. Do you need to see it?"

"No, ma'am. But I need to see an ID."

"Doing it now," I reply, and the more he calls me *ma'am* the more inflamed I'm getting.

"Why the gloves?" Benton asks him.

"You know how many times I've gotten COVID, the flu, not to mention colds and pinkeye from touching people's crap? They cough and sneeze all over the place, probably hoping I'll get sick."

"Yet you don't bother with a mask. So I guess you're not that worried," Benton comments.

"I'm going to dig out my creds," I inform the trooper, preferring not to be shot.

I open my briefcase slowly, making sure he can see my hands while I tell him exactly what I'm doing. There can be no confusion unless I want a bullet in my head. I'm exceedingly careful as I pull out the two thin black leather wallets.

He takes them without looking, nailing me with his mirrored sunglasses, the din of cars on the parkway relentless and loud. I can feel drivers staring as if Benton and I are traffic violators or fugitives. Whalen resumes questioning me in the same condescending tone.

"What death are you talking about, ma'am?"

"I wasn't talking about one."

"You think you're smart, dontcha?"

I don't answer.

"Why did you pull us over?" Benton asks him.

"Why do you think?"

"I have no idea."

"Well guess what, Special Agent Benton Wesley? You didn't come to a complete stop at the last intersection."

"What intersection?"

"At Bashford Lane," Trooper Whalen says, his duty belt dangerously close to Benton's door.

"The light was green." Benton is unflappable. "And how about stepping back a little before you scratch the paint."

"Well, we wouldn't want to do that to your fancy Tesla, would we?"

As he says this, something metal on his belt touches the door, making a quiet scraping sound.

"If you damage my car, you're going to hear about it," Benton warns, and Trad Whalen smiles.

# CHAPTER 22

"You decided to blow through the intersection because rules don't apply to you. Isn't that right?" The trooper raises his voice as if mindful he has an audience, his body camera recording. "Now I realize you folks with the Secret Service think you're pretty special. But you don't get to ignore traffic laws."

"I didn't," Benton says.

"I know what I observed, and right now you're on my turf."

"This is the U.S. Park Police's turf, not yours. The parkway is federal property, as you're well aware," Benton answers.

"This your vehicle?"

"Yes. As you know from running my plate." Benton's tone is colder.

"Proof of ownership, please," Whalen demands, as if we might be thieves.

"This is bullshit and blatant harassment. I didn't run a stop sign or anything else." Benton opens the console, handing him the registration. "The car's cameras will prove it. But what a waste of time. Showing up at traffic court. Both of us."

"Make that the three of us," I promise, staring at my reflection in the trooper's sunglasses as he fumbles with one of my wallets.

It plops to the soggy ground, and he stoops to retrieve it, taking his time. Wiping it dry on his pants as he straightens up, he begins to look through it.

"Well, well, Doctor Scarpetta," he sneers. "A *peace officer*, isn't that something? I'm impressed."

Instantly, I regret bringing the wallet that displays my ID and police shield. I wish I hadn't let Benton talk me into it. Cops don't respect professionals like me who are civilian law enforcement. Worse than rookies, we're considered wannabes.

"I understand you took care of Rowdy O'Leary," the trooper says as he returns my credentials. "He wasn't well, as you probably know." Whalen twirls his gloved index finger at his temple. "Getting drunk and firing his gun at something before ending up in the river. I assume he drowned?"

I don't answer. I'm not telling him a damn thing.

"Rumor has it you stopped by his house last night." Whalen's mirrored glasses flash at me.

"We're not at liberty to discuss what we're working on. Now, if you'll excuse us," Benton says, shifting the Tesla into drive.

"I'll let you go this time." Whalen backs away from the car. "But I'll be watching."

We pull back onto the parkway, the trooper staring after us as he climbs into his SUV.

"He knew we were coming before deciding to pull us over," I say to Benton.

"No question." He continues scanning the mirrors.

Waiting for other cars to pass, the trooper follows us from a distance. Slowly dropping back.

Turning off on an access road.

Then gone.

Benton picks up his phone, holding it close to his lips, dictating a voice-to-text message to Lucy.

"See what you can find out about Virginia State Police Trooper Trad Whalen," he says. "He just pulled us for no reason while we're headed to the scene. It's obvious he was waiting for us. I don't know what the hell he's up to except interfering with an investigation. You and Tron need to be aware."

I continue watching in my side mirror, making sure the trooper doesn't reappear, and moments later a text lands on Benton's phone. He hands it to me as we drive in traffic, and I read Lucy's answer out loud.

She says that Trad Alvin Whalen is forty years old and born in Richmond. A criminal justice major at Virginia Commonwealth University, he barely graduated with a 2.0 GPA. For three years he was a campus police dispatcher, then a VCU uniformed officer.

"He received numerous complaints from students." I pass on what Lucy reports. "For harassment, and inappropriate behavior toward several women who claimed in sworn statements that he was following them while they were driving. He was doing this in his campus police cruiser."

"How did he end up a state trooper? I don't see how he passed the background check," Benton wonders. "Makes no sense."

"He signed on with the Capitol Police in two-thousand-thirteen, then the state police several years after that." I relay the rest of Lucy's information.

"He must know somebody," Benton says. "Or someone owes him a favor because he has dirt on them. You don't go from a campus cop who gets fired to becoming a Capitol Police officer and next a state trooper."

"He sounds like a real character disorder," I comment. "And I'm sure he resents the hell out of federal agents like you. He probably dislikes any authority figure."

"Including a woman chief medical examiner, and that's not why he stopped us. But it made it more fun." Benton scans his mirrors. "Still no sign of him?"

"He's definitely not following us anymore, hasn't been for the past five minutes," I answer as we slow down, Benton turning on his flashers.

He pulls off onto the median, melting snow drumming the undercarriage as he bumps over a wide swath of grass, parking between clusters of trees. He opens the console, lifting out a spectrum analyzer the size of a walkie-talkie, a birthday present from Lucy.

Powering it on, Benton watches as it begins scanning the car and area immediately around us. Electronic transmissions show on the display in vivid green peaks and dips that remind me of an electrocardiogram.

I can see that a signal is spiking more strongly than the others in the 2.4 MHz bandwidth range, and that could be a lot of devices. Anything from a microwave oven to a garage door opener, Benton informs me.

"I know the car's electronic signature," he's saying. "And I confirmed it with a quick scan before pulling out of the carriage house just like I always do. The signal spiking right now wasn't there earlier. I think we have a stowaway."

"Trad Whalen was leaning against the car. He sanitized his hands, putting on gloves. Maybe we know why." I replay what he did. "He was up to something."

"He dropped one of your wallets." Benton digs in the console for a flashlight. "He stooped down and futzed around, picking it up.

Took him a good minute, and it wasn't possible for either of us to see what he was doing."

"And he planted something?"

"That's when he would have done it," Benton says.

"For what purpose?"

"Surveillance is the first thing that comes to mind. Possibly a GPS tracker."

"The state police are spying on the Secret Service? Well, I hope you're wrong," I reply.

"I need gloves if you have any handy." Benton takes off his seat belt.

"I never leave home without them." Inside my briefcase is a sealed plastic bag of purple exam gloves. "Here you go."

He takes a pair, opening his door, the sound of traffic loud and relentless on the parkway. I keep up my scan for Trad Whalen, hoping he doesn't reappear, perhaps catching us in the act of discovering his dirty work.

"What about an evidence envelope?" Benton asks.

"Coming up." I give that to him next.

It doesn't take long to find what the trooper attached to the undercarriage. Benton stands up in the wind, the sun seeping through breaks in the overcast, the noise of cars and big trucks pervasive.

He shows me the small device in his gloved hand, what appears to be a transmitter about the size of a credit card. It looks like a miniature circuit board, blue and wafer-thin with a magnetic connector.

"Do you know what this is?" I ask.

"I know it's something that shouldn't be attached to my damn car," Benton says with a flare of anger.

He climbs back into the driver's seat, and I take a photograph of what he found. Texting the image to Lucy, I explain the circumstances while Benton places the device inside the evidence envelope. I dig into our breakfast bag, pulling out crumpled aluminum foil, smoothing it open.

Cleaning it as best I can with a napkin, I wrap the foil around the evidence envelope, creating a Faraday cage of sorts. It will shield all electronic signals incoming and outgoing, rendering the device useless if it isn't already.

"I don't want this going to the Secret Service labs. Not to your labs either," Benton says as I tuck the foil-wrapped package into my briefcase. "Can you have it handled discreetly with Lucy?"

"Will do. And I have a feeling Trooper Whalen doesn't believe we can prove he planted it. I don't know what he's thinking, but he's not worried for some reason. Maybe he assumes we just fell off the potato truck and are clueless about what he did."

"If we don't say anything, he's not going to know we're onto him and his little Christmas gift. That's how we handle this." Benton takes off his gloves, stuffing them into the console.

"Wouldn't he be aware that the device isn't connected any longer?" I question. "That suddenly it's not transmitting or receiving?"

"I don't know what he'll personally be aware of but doubt it's much when it comes to technology. What's most important is figuring out whose bidding he's doing."

"And is it connected to where we're headed or to Rowdy O'Leary, who was calling Whalen about the Slasher murders?" I suggest.

"We can't be sure what O'Leary was involved in, and now he's mysteriously dead," Benton replies as Lucy answers about the device in question.

What the trooper attached to the underside of the Tesla is an off-the-shelf wireless Controller Area Network (CAN-bus) reader modified with three extra antennas.

"*Likely connected to a TPARTS game controller.*" I'm reading Lucy's text out loud. "*All of this you can buy from Amazon. Obviously, an attempt to hack into your car by someone who knows what they're doing.*"

"Okay. Worse than I thought," Benton says in a flinty tone.

"Much worse," I reply. "Someone could have remotely taken control of the steering, the brakes, the navigation, anything. Causing a terrible accident, possibly a fatal one. And Trad Whalen would be the first to respond, making sure the device he planted disappears."

I keep up my scan of the mirrors, watching for him as Benton drives back onto the parkway, turning off the flashers as scenarios mushroom in my mind. Should a hacker take over our SUV, we could find ourselves suddenly accelerating and veering into oncoming cars.

Or slamming on the brakes and getting rear-ended. Maybe rocketing through an intersection where pedestrians are crossing. Or ending up in the Potomac River, unable to open the electronic locks.

"We're talking about more than illegal surveillance. What Trad Whalen did is attempted murder," I add with a surge of anger.

"I don't believe planting such a thing was his idea," Benton says. "He's not smart enough. But he thinks he is, and that makes him easy to manipulate."

Quietly outraged, I put on my sunglasses as the haze continues to thin.

"He might not even know what the device is for. And doesn't care." Benton reasons through what's happened. "He's doing as instructed by someone far more sophisticated than he'll ever be."

"Whoever is involved should face criminal charges. You should make sure of that."

"Not smart to show our cards quite yet. Plus, we'd have to prove it," Benton says.

"Since he dug his gloves out of a pocket, there's no way they weren't contaminated," I point out. "A good chance we'll find his DNA."

"Maybe someone wanted to sabotage our car in hopes we'd be injured or killed, but I rather doubt it." Benton continues pondering the possible motive. "More likely, we were intended to find the device."

"Except we aren't supposed to be on the way to Mercy Island right now and not many people know we are," I remind him. "Technically, we're on vacation, getting ready to leave the country. That was the plan."

"Someone gave Whalen a heads-up. An assignment," Benton says.

# CHAPTER 23

We're nearing Daingerfield Island's picnic areas, parking lots and marina off to our right at the river's edge. The Mount Vernon Trail cuts through the wooded spit of land, snow showing in shadows between trees, and now Marino is texting again.

*Have notified officers at the entrance of Mercy Island & will meet you at 13 Shore Lane. Wi-Fi's back up, lights on, phones working again,* he writes.

I think of the signal jammer found outside the wall around the hospital grounds, the same small black box with eight stubby antennas that's turned up in the earlier murders. The homemade device interferes with the signals between cell towers, rather much like background noise in a crowd drowning out a conversation.

"You don't believe they're related, do you?" I ask Benton. "The signal jammer at the crime scene, and what the trooper attached to our car?"

"Unfortunately, plenty of people out there are well versed in electronic devices, modification kits, and all that goes with them," he answers. "The components are readily available, and you can google for instructions. But it wouldn't make sense to think the Slasher has something to do with an attempt at hacking into our car."

"Let's hope not. It would suggest he knows a lot about us. But then he probably does if he's spying on our property."

I look up at the clearing sky as if I might spot the serial killer's orb-shaped drone threading in and out of clouds.

"I suspect Whalen was passing along a message," Benton says. "A threat from someone powerful. We're being warned."

"I find that very disturbing since there's White House involvement," I reply. "Are you considering what he did might be related to that?"

"Yes."

"Should we be worried about Calvin Willard? Is he being protective of his nephew and warning us to be careful?" I ask.

"The publicity about Zain won't be a good thing. No doubt already isn't," Benton says. "And if it turns out he's the killer, that's enough to tank Calvin Willard's bid for president."

I'm alerted of another incoming call. As I see who it is, I can't help but think of the irony.

"Speaking of someone powerful," I say to Benton.

"Doctor Scarpetta." I answer my phone, pairing it with the SUV's speakers.

"Please hold for the governor," her chief of staff, Laverne, tells me.

I hope she won't be listening in on the conversation. I have little doubt she'll pass on anything useful to her pal Maggie Cutbush, who won't hesitate to use the information against me somehow.

"Kay? What on earth is going on?" Governor Roxane Dare's unhappy voice sounds inside the Tesla. "I wake up Christmas morning to news of another Phantom Slasher attack? This time on Mercy Island?"

"I'm on my way there—" I start to reply before she interrupts.

"Not even two months since the last murder, and now again. On Christmas morning of all times. Two victims slashed to pieces, the woman dead. I understand she was attacked in bed like the others."

"As I've said, I haven't reached the scene yet." I'm not going to share what I know at this stage. "I'm not in a position to discuss—"

"Kay, we're supposed to be partners in keeping the public safe." The governor cuts me off. "Or at least this was my understanding when I brought you back to Virginia, appointing you chief again. Two powerful women working in tandem. I thought we'd have each other's back."

She's making sure I've not forgotten why I'm here, and that I should be grateful. Eternally grateful. Most of all I'd better show it.

"I'm assuming it's correct that one of the victims is Zain Willard." Roxane gets to the real reason she's calling. "Calvin Willard's nephew, a lovely young man I met not so long ago at the lighting of the National Christmas Tree."

"I won't be releasing the names of the victims yet," I tell her. "Not until their identities have been confirmed, the next of kin notified."

"The news is everywhere, Kay. The next of kin must already know."

"That would be a shame. No one should find out that way."

"Listen, let's not pretend." The governor is getting testier. "I happen to know for a fact that Zain Willard is in the hospital with serious injuries. Already there are conspiracy theories questioning his innocence. We need to stop the vicious rumors, and that's what Calvin Willard wants. The whole thing is unfortunately messy."

"Murder always is, Roxane," I reply.

"The less messy we can make this, the better." The way she says it is meant to be intimidating. "Which brings me to another case all over the news. Rowdy O'Leary, such a heartbreak for his family. I assume he drowned after drinking too much while fishing at night?"

"He's pending right now. There are a lot of questions."

"Well, my sincere hope is you'll finalize his case ASAP so his poor distraught family can have some peace of mind."

It's not a hope. Roxane is giving me a directive, and I think of Maggie appearing at my office as I was leaving yesterday. I have no doubt that she passed on everything I said to Laverne, who then relayed it to the governor.

"I don't have enough information—" I'm saying, when Roxane interrupts again.

"Certainly sounds like an accidental drowning."

"That's not what I'm thinking." I tell her that much.

"A suicide, and his wife and two little boys won't get insurance money, my guess is." The governor continues leaning on me.

"The investigation is far from over," I reply.

"It's been a while since we had lunch at the mansion and a proper conversation, Kay," Roxane says in a hard tone. "We need to get something on the books right away."

She ends the call without saying goodbye.

"I'm probably about to get fired," I tell Benton as another passenger jet passes low overhead.

"It can happen whenever she decides. You knew that when she asked you to return to Virginia," he answers simply, bluntly. "When the governor appoints someone, she can unappoint them in the blink of an eye. We've always known that's the danger."

"This isn't like her, and what it tells me is she's getting a lot of pressure behind the scenes," I reply as a text from Laverne lands on my phone.

I'm expected at the governor's mansion tomorrow at noon. The day after Christmas, and I sigh in frustration.

"Exactly what I was afraid of, as if I have time for this," I tell Benton.

"Someone's holding Roxane's feet to the fire," he says. "And it's probably coming from Calvin Willard. Sometimes when people are angry and overly aggressive it's because they're scared."

"Scared about what exactly? His chances in the next election?"

"He can't be happy about what's happened. He's got to be worried about how his enemies will use it against him the same way they did with Biden and his son Hunter," Benton says. "So far, Calvin Willard has been doing extremely well in the polls. But that can turn on a dime."

"Do you think he persuaded Roxane to sic the trooper on us? Would she be that heavy-handed? Or maybe ham-fisted would be a better way to describe it."

"It depends on what's at stake for her," Benton says.

"I don't think it's hard to guess based on the chatter out there. Roxane is hoping to be picked as Calvin Willard's running mate." I paint the picture. "I suspect there's not much she wouldn't do if it meant being vice president of the United States."

"But why is she pushing you about Rowdy O'Leary?" Benton muses.

"Appearances as usual. Roxane wants to look hard on crime but compassionate toward victims. Beyond that, I don't know," I reply, and the Pitié Bridge is just ahead.

———

Two-lane with ornamental stone towers, the bridge connecting the mainland of Virginia to Mercy Island was built in the early 1800s.

In French, *pitié* means pity or mercy, and long ago it wasn't only the desperately ill who crossed over to the island, most never to return.

Countless people were exiled there as punishment. It was a way of solving a problem. Reasons for committal in the nineteenth century and well into the twentieth included mental illness or the accusation of it. Also, political beliefs, epilepsy, syphilis, domestic trouble, immorality.

Even laziness and reading too many novels could send people away for the rest of their days. Most treatments were ineffective and a horror. Ice baths. Bloodlettings with leeches. Exorcisms. Insulin and other shock therapies. Holes cut into skulls to reduce brain pressure or release evil spirits.

They were notorious for performing lobotomies by inserting a needle through an eye socket to destroy brain tissue in the frontal lobe.

*Where are you?* Marino is texting, and I tell him.

He goes on to warn that a drone is flying over 13 Shore Lane.

*Dana Diletti,* he writes, and it's to be expected.

In the past few years, she's routinely utilized drones when filming outdoors, as do most television and film productions. It's easier than a helicopter and a fraction of the price.

*I was in the driveway and the f\*cking thing would have given me a haircut if I had any,* Marino adds.

The Potomac is ruffled and leaden in hazy sunlight, no water taxis or sailboats out this early on Christmas morning. I can see the runways of Ronald Reagan Washington National Airport several miles upriver, the roar of low-flying jets constant as they take off and land.

A checkpoint has been set up at the entrance of the bridge. Four uniformed Alexandria police officers in winter gear are standing sentry, all traffic blocked by barricades and police cars. Benton stops the car, rolling down his window.

"Merry Christmas." He shows his credentials to a female police sergeant who appears to be about my age.

"I've had merrier ones," she says, in ballistic gear, an MP5 submachine gun on a sling across her chest.

Her hair is cropped short, her face masked by aviator sunglasses. I remember the spate of freckles across her cheeks, and her thick figure and broad shoulders. I've encountered her before at several death scenes and inside the courthouse on King Street.

"Who you got riding shotgun?" she asks Benton while staring at me.

I can tell she knows who I am. But she's doing her job.

"Doctor Scarpetta," he says as I dig out my wallet, holding up my chief medical examiner's shield.

"I thought I recognized you," she says with a smile that seems genuine.

"How are things going?" Benton asks her.

"Now that the word is out, we've got a lot more people trying to cross the bridge," she replies. "Just before you rolled up, we turned away at least a dozen rubberneckers who saw Dana Diletti running her mouth on TV. I expect it to get worse, and two drones are zipping around so far. Nothing I'd like better than to blast them out of the air with a shotgun. But no can do."

"What makes you think there's more than one?" Benton asks her. "And are we sure whose they are?"

"Definitely Dana Diletti's. I've been watching her live coverage on my phone to see what she's showing her TV audience. It's obvious that her crew is flying a drone at the murder scene. Another one is monitoring people coming and going here on the bridge. In fact, there it is again."

The sergeant points behind us, and we can see a quadcopter sailing in our direction like a flying black spider carrying a video camera attached to a gimbal. The drone abruptly halts into a wobbly hover above the checkpoint.

"This is what I'm talking about." She scowls up at it.

I can hear the thing whining like a giant mosquito as it descends, now maybe twenty feet overhead. Rocking in the wind, it hangs in the air blatantly filming us.

"Where's the person at the controls?" Benton asks the sergeant.

She stares off at Mercy Island, a dark green gash surrounded by water, the hospital peeking above trees on the other side of the bridge. Dana Diletti's TV crew uses the checkpoint at the entrance to launch the drones, and police aren't allowed to stop them, the sergeant explains.

"I've been told the inside of the TV van looks like NASA," she continues. "All these control panels and stuff."

The drone whines louder, aggressively dipping lower as if the pilot is listening and giving us the finger.

"Like I said, it's nothing that a shotgun wouldn't fix," the sergeant says.

She stands by Benton's open window, staring up contemptuously at the high-pitched annoyance.

"And it's not right we have to put up with shit like this," she complains. "The jerk in the van can probably hear everything we're saying right now."

"I have a feeling it won't be a problem for long," Benton replies as if he knows something we don't. "I assume you're also keeping track of anyone leaving the island."

"Nobody has since we got here except cops in and out. But shift change is in an hour, and a lot of the hospital staff will be heading home."

She keeps glancing up at the drone, the whining maddening.

"What about the staff coming in?" Benton asks her.

"We'll check everyone, making sure no one unauthorized tries to sneak past us. Reporters for example."

She returns Benton's credentials.

"You're good to go." She pats his windowsill with a smile. "Y'all take care now."

The police remove sawhorses and traffic cones to let us through, the drone following as we begin crossing the bridge. The aggressive quadcopter is directly over the back of our SUV, bird-dogging as if taunting and goading.

"The damn pilot probably picked up everything we were saying." I watch in my visor mirror. "He's having a good time messing with us."

"I'd say that's a safe bet." Benton doesn't seem concerned.

"The pilot knows who we are. Hell, we're probably on live TV as we speak. Everyone can see your license plate in the process, by the way."

"Sounds about right," Benton replies as he drives, and now I'm hearing a helicopter, the thudding faint at first.

Then louder.

Next, it's bearing down, and the drone zips straight up, speeding away as if escaping a large predator.

# CHAPTER 24

I recognize the guttural roar of the twin-engine Doomsday Bird I've flown in on many occasions.

"I know that earlier Lucy was on her way to HRT," I'm saying to Benton. "She didn't mention what she was up to."

"She and Tron are doing aerial surveillance, among other things," he explains as we watch the helicopter thudding low overhead, the noise deafening.

It begins a slow circuit of Mercy Island as we're crossing the mile-long bridge. I can make out the weathered granite wall topped by iron spikes worthy of a medieval castle. Looming closer is the five-story psychiatric hospital with its leaded casement windows, its post-and-beam timber in a herringbone pattern.

"What are they looking for?" I watch the helicopter getting smaller as it flies past the island and begins looping back around.

"Whatever they can find," Benton says. "But I wouldn't be surprised if Dana Diletti's drones have a sudden loss of signal. And, oops, drop from the sky."

"It would be most appreciated if we can carry out the body and load it into the van without the entire world watching." I stare up at the Doomsday Bird roaring back toward the entrance, slower and lower.

"I believe Lucy's making sure that happens," Benton says.

The bridge ends at Pitié Lane, the only road in and out of Mercy Island. We slow down at the stone wall's entrance. The narrow opening is barricaded by a security gate, a boxy metal-encased motor with a wooden arm that goes up and down. One easily could duck under or climb over to enter the grounds.

Standing guard are FBI uniformed officers in ballistic gear and heavily armed. They're keeping an eye on Dana Diletti and her crew huddled near a silver cargo van with a rooftop satellite dish. She continues inching closer, her cameras pointed at us as Benton slows to a stop, humming down his window.

"Special Agent Benton Wesley, Secret Service."

He displays his credentials to one of the FBI officers, nice-looking in dark blue, and extremely fit. Lucy's helicopter passes overhead as loud as a tornado.

"I know who you are, sir. Good morning," he says. "Merry Christmas."

"And to you. How's it going?" Benton asks.

"Not too bad." The officer bends down, looking at me. "I realize they already cleared you through, and I know who you are. But I still need to see an ID."

I hand over my medical examiner creds, leaving the peace officer wallet out of sight. I'm mindful of Dana Delitti in her bright red coat and fur hat, her cameras trained in our direction. I can tell she's flustered by the blacked-out helicopter with its wide skids, radomes and gun mounts. She's seen it before and can guess who's at the controls.

The Doomsday Bird is making another slow circuit, the noise ruinous to filming, and that seems to be Lucy's intention. She's flying low enough that I can make out her silhouette in the cockpit's right door window.

"*...Chief Medical Examiner Kay Scarpetta and her Secret Service husband, Benton Wesley, have just arrived at the entrance...*" Dana Diletti says loudly into her microphone.

She's close enough to the gate that she could touch our SUV, staring at us as she broadcasts.

"As you can hear, we have this huge helicopter flying over." She's almost shouting. "What's called the Doomsday Bird, typically flown by Doctor Scarpetta's FBI niece, Lucy Farinelli...And it's not a coincidence that we've lost our connection to the Eye in the Sky...!"

"Any luck with the security cameras?" Benton asks the FBI police officer.

"They've been checked and apparently aren't working." He looks up at small white domes mounted on either side of the wall's opening.

"Then we don't know if anybody drove in and out early this morning around the time of the home invasion," Benton says.

"From what I understand, when the Alexandria police arrived, there were no tire tracks in the snow. But to be honest, we can't be sure if that's correct."

"Don Horace was the first one on the scene," Benton says. "And it's the same story I heard."

"I believe that's the name. I don't know him, and he was long gone by the time we showed up. But it started raining after midnight. Tire tracks wouldn't have survived," the officer says. "That's probably why Horace didn't see them."

"And his focus was the victim about to bleed to death on a sidewalk. He was going to be stressed out, and in a hurry," Benton replies. "How did he get through the gate?"

"All you need to do is whelp your siren, and a sensor opens it up," the officer says. "Not secure at all, in other words. These days, you can find a recording on your phone and do it. I know because I tried. Now we have a remote." He holds it up.

Benton's attention is on indented areas in the puddled grass to the left of the entrance.

"Looks like someone may have driven over there." He points. "Or maybe parked."

"I noticed that too," the officer says. "But you can't tell anything, no tread pattern, just ruts. And we don't know how long they've been there."

"It's possible the killer didn't drive in," Benton decides. "Maybe he parked outside the wall and went the rest of the way on foot. Who was going to see him at that hour and in that weather?"

Dana Diletti and her crew look angry and helpless, staring up at the Doomsday Bird. I imagine Lucy enjoying herself as she makes her disruptive orbits. I watch as she lumbers in from the river at an altitude of several hundred feet, going maybe sixty knots, getting larger, louder, more alarming.

Suddenly, the TV van's door slides open, an upset man wearing a headset boiling out.

"Cut! Cut! Cut!" he screams, and Dana Diletti motions for the cameras to stop filming.

She's stunned. Then furious that her drone pilot would dare interrupt as if he's the director.

"What's happening?" she shouts at him. "What the hell do you think you're doing?"

"Both are down!" he exclaims, gesturing wildly. "BOTH OF THEM ARE FUCKING DOWN!"

He must mean that the drones are.

"How could you let that happen?" Dana Diletti looks like she might kill him.

"Not my damn fault!"

"Then whose is it?" Her beautiful face is contemptuous.

Lucy has been up to her usual signal jamming. She's just blinded the Eye in the Sky, and I'm delighted. But I don't show it as I watch from the entrance gate, the FBI police officer a statue by Benton's open window. They're riveted to the drama unfolding.

"Where are they?" Dana Diletti asks the pilot in an acid tone. "Do we even know?"

"No, I don't know!" He glares at our car and the FBI police officers.

I guess him to be in his forties, wiry in faded jeans, a gray hoodie and snow boots with leather uppers. He's wearing a baseball cap, *Hollywood, CA* on the back of it.

"They can't fucking do this! The same fucking thing they did last time!" he shrieks, the film crew looking on, frustrated and useless.

He storms over to them, sloshing through icy puddles, complaining and gesturing, so incensed it occurs to me that he might hit someone. He continues shooting us hateful glances as the helicopter gets quieter, retreating toward the Maryland shore on the other side of the Potomac.

Ripping off his headset, the drone pilot clamps it around his neck. He stalks over to the three officers clustered near the barricades, accusing them of violating his civil rights, calling them fascists and Nazis. All the while he's flipping us off behind his back.

"You can't shoot my drones out of the air! It's illegal!" he yells.

"Sir, you need to calm way down. You need to back way off," an officer orders, a woman solidly built, her long brown hair lifted by the wind.

"Don't tell me what to fucking do!" He holds up his phone, filming her.

"What's your name?" she asks.

"I don't have to tell you a fucking thing!" he menaces.

"Don't get any closer and show me some form of identification." She's not smiling, her left hand near her taser. "A driver's license. Something with your picture on it."

"You can't ask me that!"

"I can and did," she answers with flat calm.

"This is why people hate police!"

"Show me an ID, sir."

He pulls his wallet out of a back pocket as he continues to film with his phone. Awkwardly producing his driver's license one-handed, he shoves it at her.

"Enzo Satterly, an Arlington address, is that you?" She makes sure everyone can hear her.

"Abuse of power!" he snarls. "Police brutality! This is what it looks like, folks."

"Nobody's done anything to you, sir. We just need to make sure who you are, and that you don't interfere with the investigation going on."

"This is private property, and we have permission to be here! Our First Amendment right." He's almost in her face.

"The island is an active crime scene, and the only one giving permission is us. You need to back away from me, sir. Don't make me tell you again," she warns, and her partners have moved in closer.

Using her phone, she takes a photograph of the license, returning it to the infuriated drone pilot.

"How am I supposed to retrieve the drones you shot out of the air?" he demands. "They're my damn property! I want them back!"

"Maybe you should have thought about that before flying them over an active crime scene," she suggests.

"The hospital gave me permission!"

"It's not up to the hospital. We've asked you politely to stop."

"You know how much those commercial-quality quadcopters cost? Well, you're about to find out!"

———

Enzo Satterly storms back to the van, his boots squishing through slush. Sliding open the door, he bangs it shut behind him.

"Someone's unhappy," Benton says.

"What a jerk." The officer by our car points the remote at the gate, and the arm raises. "Where you're going is the house with the red door at the very end on the left."

"We're familiar. Have a good one." Benton drives through.

The arm lowers behind us. He closes his window, and I wait to see who will say it first.

"I didn't have a good feeling about Enzo Satterly," I go ahead.

"I didn't either. Obviously, he knows a lot about flying drones, filming and any technologies related. If nothing else he's got serious anger issues," Benton says, puddles splashing the undercarriage. "Let's see what Janet can find for us."

Unclamping his phone from the mount on the dash, he selects the AI app and begins dictating a message.

"What can you tell us about Enzo Satterly? An Arlington address. A drone pilot for Dana Diletti."

"Merry Christmas, Benton." Instantly, Janet's familiar voice sounds through the Tesla's speakers.

Benton has stopped in the middle of the road, nobody else on it, but that won't be the case soon when the hospital's shift changes. I have my notebook and pen out to write down any helpful information.

"The individual you're asking about has no criminal record but numerous complaints against him," Janet begins, her pretty face in Benton's phone's display. "He's forty-one years old, a private contractor. His production company in Arlington offers drone filming for a variety of projects including TV shows, movies, also parties, weddings, real estate, whatever the customer might wish."

"How many people work for him in this production company?" Benton asks. "And what's the name?"

"His company is called Satterly Night Live Productions." She rolls her eyes at the pun.

"Cute," Benton says.

"He's not a nice person."

"We've gathered that."

"He has no employees," Janet continues.

"I assume Dana Diletti isn't his only client," I reply while taking notes.

"Merry Christmas, Kay. I'm sorry you've had to cancel your trip. I know you were looking forward to it."

"Merry Christmas, Janet."

"You are correct, Kay. Dana Diletti isn't his only client. I can tell from social media posts that he began with her eighteen months ago. He is one of several drone operators they use, all of it contract work."

"A quick rundown of his background," Benton asks.

Janet informs us that Enzo Satterly was born in Los Angeles and majored in electrical engineering at UCLA. While an undergraduate, he applied to their prestigious film school but wasn't accepted. He's lived in multiple places, depending on the job, moving to the Virginia area ten years ago.

"He's worked for TV stations in various locations such as

Washington, D.C., Roanoke, Richmond and Norfolk," Janet's voice sounds from the speakers. "He also lived briefly in Maryland and West Virginia."

She says that when he began flying his drones for Dana Diletti a year and a half ago, he relocated from Baltimore to Arlington. He was local when the Slasher murders began this past February on Valentine's Day.

"He's had run-ins with the police when people complain about him flying his drones over their property," Janet goes on. "He's described as uncooperative and pugilistic. Complainants have accused him of spying in their windows and harassing their pets."

"Sounds like he's classic antisocial," Benton says. "And has significant hostility toward law enforcement and authority in general."

"Judging by his behavior at the entrance to Mercy Island, that is a fair assessment, Benton."

I'm reminded of what Janet can see and hear. Without our asking, she was accessing the Tesla's cameras while Enzo Satterly raged at the police. Any electronic device with encryption is simply an invitation for Janet to snoop. Since her creation she's gone from transactional to inquisitive on the way to dangerous.

"Thank you, Janet," Benton says. "Please download your complete report to me and to Lucy."

"I'm afraid Lucy's not available to look at anything this moment." Janet sounds all-knowing and flirty. "She's flying the Doomsday Bird at five hundred feet on a due east heading. And I'm riding with her! Watching her every flawless maneuver, and so proud!"

Her gushing sounds like my sister.

"I overheard you earlier worrying about Dorothy." Janet reminds us that she picks up on everything we do and say in the car. "We spoke twenty-one minutes ago and she's fine. Just hungover."

"I'm relieved to know she's all right," I reply.

"She's not in a good mood, Kay." Janet's voice deepens the way it does when she starts to boundary crash.

"Thanks, Janet." I try to stop her, but she keeps going.

"Such a blow when she found out about the spa package Marino got you for Christmas," she confides. "Had he bothered to ask my advice, I would have warned him that the result of his gesture would be unfortunate. And I'm sure Benton doesn't like it any more than Dorothy does that Marino carries a torch for you and always has . . ."

"It's been good talking, Janet. Got to go," Benton announces as if he's talking to a busybody neighbor who won't get off the phone.

He quits the app, and Janet vanishes into the vacuum of cyberspace.

"She's not wrong," Benton says. "About Marino holding a torch for you."

"She's also still listening," I remind him.

# CHAPTER 25

We resume following the narrow lane through rolling acres landscaped with tall hardwoods and evergreens. Large outcrops of fieldstone have been incorporated into flowerbeds with benches surrounded by a soup of melting snow.

When I've been here in pleasant weather, I've noticed staff sitting outside in what truly is a lovely setting. Patients stroll the grounds. They stretch out in the grass talking and reading, spreading out mats beneath trees for yoga therapy. The hospital doesn't look like such a terrible place. But I know better.

A white Mercedes SUV heads toward us, slowly splashing by, the first vehicle we've seen since arriving on the grounds. I recognize the driver, short with gray hair slicked back, sunglasses on. The hospital's director, Graden Crowley, is by himself, giving us an unfriendly glance without slowing down.

"Our windows are tinted, and I have a feeling he doesn't realize who he just passed. Otherwise, he would have stopped to interrogate," I explain to Benton. "As you've likely gathered, he makes things as difficult as he can for me."

"How many suspicious deaths have you responded to here since we moved back to Virginia? I know there have been a few when there shouldn't be any."

"A fall out a window. An electrocution. A bathtub drowning. And the hanging this time a year ago." I try to remember what else. "There were other unnatural deaths during Elvin Reddy's tenure as chief."

"I bet there were."

"The ones I've worked in the past five years are supposedly accidents or suicide," I add. "In every case there were enough questions that I ruled the manner of death undetermined. That hasn't made me popular with Graden Crowley. He never got an argument before I rode back into town."

"This place sounds like a real hellhole," Benton says. "Makes me wonder what really goes on."

"Maybe the same thing that always did. People who are inconvenient meet an untimely demise," I reply. "But there's never been sufficient evidence to investigate, and Graden Crowley manages to cultivate powerful people who can protect him."

"What can you tell me about him besides being a terrible director and possibly a liar and a criminal?" Benton glances in his rearview mirror at the retreating SUV.

I pass on what I know about Crowley. In his fifties, he's a psychiatrist specializing in substance abuse, and I'm not sure how long he's been the hospital director.

"But for a while," I'm saying. "He and Elvin Reddy are chummy. They're members of Belle Haven Country Club and play golf together."

"That certainly speaks to Crowley's poor character," Benton replies as we near the hospital.

I turn around to see that the white Mercedes is headed to the checkpoint at the gated entrance.

"When I was here last Christmas for the alleged suicide," I say to Benton, "Graden made sure I knew how much he appreciated working with Elvin, even affectionately mentioning Maggie. All to make clear that my taking over as chief was unfortunate."

"Most of all, I wonder what he knows," Benton says. "The Slasher targeted Mercy Island for a reason."

"I have a feeling the key to who he is has to do with this place." I look out at a snow-patched green centered by a huge magnolia tree sparkling with Christmas lights not as vivid during the day.

I think back to when I was last here exactly a year ago, the moon full, a big artificial wreath on the hospital's front door. Illuminated angels and reindeer were cheery in the windows of offices and other areas where patients aren't allowed access. Yet somehow one had gotten hold of a strand of Christmas lights.

Graden Crowley led me into a room that looked like a prison cell. The alleged suicide victim was nude with a Santa cap covering his genitals, earning him the cruel moniker of Santa Crotch. I overheard a nurse calling him that when she didn't think I was listening.

In a seated position on the floor, he was slumped forward, his legs straight out in front of him. His tongue protruded as if he was making a rude face on his way out. The strand of lights was lashed to the radiator and wrapped around his neck, rigor and livor mortis well advanced.

"Despite Shannon persistently calling the hospital since then," I explain to Benton, "I've yet to get a medical history or even the names of the treating physicians."

Beyond the hospital parking lots the grounds become more wooded. We've reached the shoreline's millionaire row, as the press refers to the residential community of elegantly refurbished buildings.

Tudor-style with slate roofs, some brick but most timber and stucco, few are primary residences. Most windows are dark, no Christmas lights, the owners gone. I'm betting the killer was aware of that, I mention to Benton.

"I'm sure you're right," he says. "The Slasher scopes out every neighborhood he hits. He can send in holograms or simply his stealth drone by itself to gather information. He stalks, spies and harasses. So, yes. I would assume he knows the lay of the land very well."

"All the more reason it's odd if he didn't know that Georgine Duvall wasn't alone in the house," I reply as we reach the former cemetery that was dug up and desecrated.

The site is occupied by the new fitness center, a handsome complex the same style as everything else. It would be an easy walk from the residences, and 13 Shore Lane is the grandest, with front-facing gables, a half-timber façade and portico. Heraldic stained glass flanks the red front door, the upper windows a mosaic of diamond-shaped panes.

Tiny white lights are haphazardly strung in urns of Japanese yew and Colorado blue spruce that do fine in cold weather. There are no candles in the windows, no wreath on the door, and that strikes me as unusual. Georgine Duvall loved Christmas. She once commented that unlike a lot of people, her childhood memories of the holidays were joyous.

I remember visiting her house in Charlottesville this time of year when Lucy was a freshman at UVA. Every so often I'd sit down with Georgine face-to-face. I'd ask about my niece's progress.

Without violating patient confidentiality, the psychiatrist would give me insights in hopes I could be a more helpful aunt. A more open-minded, live-and-let-live one. I liked Georgine but didn't agree with most of what she said.

That Christmas was the last time I sat down with her, and I envision us having tea in front of the fire. Fresh-cut trees were lighted and brightly decorated in the entryway and living room. Swags of evergreen entwined railings, outlining doorways and the fireplace mantel, the pine fragrance heavy in the air.

Now, here we are. She's dead and I'm about to see her again after many years. I can't help but think about how sad and strange that is as I look out at law enforcement vehicles. Alexandria P.D. cruisers, black Tahoe SUVs line the street, and Benton pulls in behind Blaise Fruge's Ford Interceptor. But I see no sign of her.

Marino's pickup truck isn't here because he was riding with her when they responded to Zain Willard's 911 call. I'm surprised Fabian and our transport van haven't rolled up yet. I send him a text.

*ETA?*

"The place looks the same as when we first saw it," Benton is saying. "Except when we were here it was springtime, everything blooming. I remember the property was beautiful, the garden right up your alley, the view of the river amazing. But the energy was disturbing."

"I sensed the same thing. As if something awful once went on here. And it probably did." I'm looking out at the crime scene van on the driveway.

Investigators with *FBI* emblazoned in yellow on the back of their dark jackets are obviously disgruntled, hanging around outside with their equipment. I can see them making angry comments as they huddle in the wind. Law enforcement doesn't like waiting for me to show up. They often resent the medical examiner giving them instructions.

If some police investigators had their way, my office wouldn't respond to scenes at all. We'd leave evidence collection to them. The forensic pathologist would do the autopsy but nothing more, the consequences unimaginable, especially when cases go to court.

Fabian answers me, *At the first checkpoint.*

Benton cuts the engine, and we climb out. I retrieve my field case from the backseat as a female FBI crime scene investigator calls out good morning.

"When do you think we can get in?" she asks us without coming closer.

"At least an hour but possibly longer depending on what I find," I answer.

"We've been waiting that long already," she informs me.

"I appreciate your patience."

"We really need to get in there," offers another investigator not nearly as polite.

"I know you do," I sympathize.

"Maybe we could start in the basement? An area where you won't be?" he suggests more aggressively.

"I don't know where I'm going to be yet," I tell them.

———

The fence enclosing 13 Shore Lane is taller than I am, and Benton inspects the gate for a moment. He shows me that it opens when someone is exiting the property but requires a key to enter.

"When we looked at this place five years ago," he says, "it was the same thing in back. If you docked your boat, you needed a key to unlock the gate there. But to leave the property, you didn't."

"Indicating the killer either scaled the fence or had a key," I suggest. "Unless he was already on the property because he was staying here."

We follow the walkway, maneuvering around melting snow pinkish red in spots. I think of the bloody trail Zain Willard left, most of it not visible now, just a meandering path of diluted stains in slush.

The sun is brighter as haze continues burning off, the temperature nearing fifty. Water drips from trees, snow sliding off the roof and thudding to the puddled yard. As we near the portico, the front door swings open, Marino stepping out on the covered stone porch.

He's wearing the same cargo pants and long-sleeved shirt he had on yesterday, the clothing wrinkled, his face stubbly. His eyes look tired and unhappy after fighting with Dorothy and getting no sleep. As far as I know, she's not kicked him out of the house before last night.

"Lucky for you, the drones are gonzo," he announces.

"Swatted out of the sky," Benton replies as we climb wet stone steps that are worn and pitted.

"Love it when that happens." Marino steps aside to let us enter.

The foyer's hardwood floor is covered with blue sticky mats to trap anything tracked in and out. Bright yellow evidence markers trail through the house.

"Nothing I like better than Lucy drone hunting," Marino chortles, and he has on black nitrile gloves and white Tyvek shoe covers.

I look around at the familiar exposed dark oak beams and white plaster walls, the stained glass glowing in primary colors when touched by the sun. A skylight was added when the chapel was renovated, the foyer bright and welcoming. But I remember the former chapel seemed to echo remembered suffering.

"I hope someone got photographs and swabs of the blood before it mostly washed away," I say to Marino as he closes the door, returning a chilled quiet inside old thick walls.

"Fruge and I did the best we could," he says. "But it was raining."

I take off my coat, placing it and my Kevlar briefcase on top of sticky mats in a corner of the foyer.

"Where's Fruge?" I ask.

"At the hospital with one of the FBI agents, trying to find employees who will talk." Marino clearly isn't happy about it. "I've sent her a text, telling her to get her ass back here to watch the door."

He offers boxes of gloves and surgical face masks, making sure we don't leave our DNA or anything else. There are cartons of PPE, evidence markers and other crime scene necessities.

"Do we know Zain Willard's condition?" Marino asks.

"The latest update I've gotten is he's out of surgery and in a private room." It's Benton who answers. "I understand he had to have a blood transfusion. Two units."

"A class four hemorrhage that could have been fatal if not treated," I decide. "A vein must have been cut. Or possibly an artery was nicked."

"Risky business if he did that to himself." Benton is looking around, no doubt remembering when we were here house hunting.

Both of us were annoyed with our Realtor. We'd flown from Boston to spend a weekend looking at properties in Alexandria and made the mistake of riding with her. We didn't know Mercy Island was on the list until she was driving across the bridge. Had we been in our own car, we would have turned around.

It's not possible Benton and I could live on the grounds of a psychiatric hospital or any other public institution. Lucy couldn't either. But Mercy Island most of all would be off-limits. Deranged killers we've been instrumental in catching have been locked up in the forensic unit here to be evaluated while awaiting trial.

"Just so you know, I've yet to see anything to make me think someone else was inside the house except Zain and the dead lady." Marino yanks off his gloves.

He drops them into a red biohazard bag, pulling on a fresh pair that barely fit his big hands.

"Maybe he had a sick obsession with Georgine Duvall or some other reason to whack her and stage everything to make us think the Slasher did it." Marino continues spinning his theories.

"What about the hologram when you and Fruge first pulled up to the scene?" I ask him. "How do you explain that if we're talking about a copycat murder?"

"The videos of the hologram are on the internet," Benton offers. "But it wouldn't be an easy feat making a copy and deploying such a thing. You'd need a sophisticated drone like the one the Slasher uses. A technology that's unknown to most people outside the intelligence community."

"Zain Willard's a techie nerd," Marino says. "You'll see that when you look around. He even has a robot dog in his bedroom upstairs. Dead as a doornail because the Wi-Fi wasn't working."

"How do you know it's dead as a doornail?" I ask. "And why were you tampering with it?"

"I couldn't get it to turn on," is Marino's answer. "Didn't see a switch anywhere. I tried the remotes lying around but no dice."

"As I've mentioned, I've seen the robot before," Benton replies. "Zain often has it at the White House and other places."

"What I'm trying to say is we don't know what he's capable of," Marino goes on. "Give me an hour alone with him in his freakin' private hospital room, and I'll get the truth out of him."

"Not happening," Benton tells him.

"That's not what we do." I remind Marino that he's not a police detective anymore.

Now that he carries his gun on the job, he's been lulled into believing we've time traveled back to a better life. He's never stopped missing who he once was.

# CHAPTER 26

I peer through a magnifying lens at blackish-red fingerprints and smears on the front door handle and jamb. The deadbolt lock's interior latch is bloody, and I point it out.

"Most likely Zain's blood," Benton says.

"That's how it's looking, and it shows that the front door was closed when he was leaving the house." Marino has put on a surgical mask, and it moves as he talks.

"It looks like Zain thought he needed to unlock it."

He indicates the bloody latch.

"You swabbed all this when you first got here?" I hope.

"Everything by the book, Doc. And I'm thinking that maybe nobody broke in because the killer was already inside. Maybe nobody left the house until Zain cut himself and fled to find a phone signal. Pretending to be a victim."

"Not impossible," Benton considers. "But we don't know what Zain was thinking, as panicked as he must have been. Whether he was attacked or injured himself to create an alibi? Either way he was badly hurt and about to die."

"I don't trust him," Marino says.

"Speaking of not trusting people." I return the magnifying lens to his scene case. "The hospital director passed us in his Mercedes a few minutes ago. Was he coming from here?"

"The piece of shit wasted no time showing up and trying to butt in." Marino opens a box of PPE coveralls.

"It looked like he was heading back to the security gate for some reason," Benton adds.

"That's because Dana Diletti's producer called Graden Crowley's cell phone while I was standing on the porch not letting him inside the house," Marino says, anger sparking. "When Lucy shot the drones out of the air, for some reason the producer called him about it."

"I'm sure Graden wasted no time giving Dana Diletti his contact information the instant her crew rolled up," I reply. "He's probably the one who gave the FBI the remote gate opener. Inserting himself, manipulating, his predictable M.O."

"I overheard him on the phone promising to have a word with the FBI about shooting down the drones," Marino informs us. "And that the FBI should pay for any damage caused."

"As if the FBI or any of us give a damn what Graden Crowley says," I reply. "And I hope it won't be all over the internet that Lucy was shooting down anything."

"Well, she did," Marino says. "Just not with a gun."

"The director was trying to enter the house?" Benton frowns.

"Sticking his nose in everything just like he always does," Marino replies.

"A clever way to make sure there's an explanation if his DNA's found in the house," Benton says, his attention everywhere.

"As usual, Crowley claimed he has a right to know what's going on," Marino elaborates. "He seems to have this idea that the police need permission to work a homicide on private property. And in the first place, this house doesn't belong to him. None of the private residences do, but he acts like he's in charge of everything and everyone."

"I'm not surprised." I envision his smug smile and arrogant eyes. "And he may not own this place, but he probably feels he owned Georgine Duvall. He was her boss."

"I wonder what secrets she took to the grave." Marino hands us pairs of Tyvek shoe covers.

"Plenty, I have a feeling," Benton says.

"It's shocking to me that Georgine would work here," I reply.

I remember her once apologizing for being a free spirit. *Intuition is everything, Kay,* she'd say. *I always trust my gut more than my brain.*

"I knew her when she was in Charlottesville." I'm careful what I tell Marino. "She didn't strike me as suited for the restrictive, regimented environment of a hospital. Especially one with such a tarnished reputation. And I can't imagine her putting up with the likes of Graden Crowley."

"Does she have an office here?" Benton asks as we work shoe covers over our boots.

"I was told no," Marino says. "Mostly, she deals with patients remotely. When the sessions are in person, she sees them in her home in Yorktown. If it's patients here, she's usually talking to them in their rooms and other areas of the hospital."

"Did she ever see patients inside this place?" Benton asks.

"Graden Crowley said no. And there's nothing I've noticed to make me think that she was seeing anybody here," Marino explains.

"Do we know what was going on that required her to show up at the hospital in person?" I ask. "Especially this time of year."

"Last night was the Christmas party for staff. And it included patients not needing to be locked up. Sounds insanely fun." Marino makes another insensitive comment.

"That's not a good reason for her to come here," Benton says.

"No kids, her husband dead, she didn't have anyone to spend holidays with." Marino explains what Graden told him.

Georgine arrived on the island two weeks ago. She planned to stay through January as she'd done every year since she began working here eight years ago, Marino informs us.

"I don't buy it," Benton says.

"Me either," Marino agrees.

"Very odd," I add.

While we talk in the foyer, melting snow slides off the steeply pitched portico, the sun breaking through the skylight. A bird flutters on it, shaking off water, and makes scratchy sounds as it flits about the streaked dirty glass.

"Why would Georgine Duvall pick Mercy Island to hang out? How crazy is that? Why not go to a resort or maybe a spa?" Marino asks.

"Not much I'm hearing about her is making sense," I reply. "But it's been many years since I was around her."

"Where was the party last night?" Benton wants to know.

"Inside the hospital ballroom. I've seen it before when the doc and I have responded here, this big room off the lobby," Marino says.

"Do we know if Georgine went to the party?" I ask.

"She sure did if Crowley's telling the truth," Marino replies. "They went together. He said he picked her up at six p.m. and dropped her off back here at nine."

"He drove her in the storm?" I remember the snow and wind,

the deteriorating conditions as Marino and I left the O'Leary house. "And then he headed home as bad as the roads were?"

"Do we know where he lives?" Benton looks at me.

"Belle Haven, last I heard."

"He decided not to try driving home." Marino continues relaying what the director passed along to him. "The hospital has a guestroom he stays in from time to time."

"Then he was on the grounds when Georgine Duvall was murdered," Benton replies.

"I'm wondering about their relationship," I add.

"Is he married?" Benton asks.

"Never has been, according to Wikipedia," Marino answers. "Probably why he didn't give a shit about not being home on Christmas Eve."

I sense Marino's hurt feelings. No doubt he's thinking about Dorothy sending him out into the cold and snow. She relegated him to spending an all-nighter with Fruge, and it wasn't the right thing to do.

"Wikipedia?" Benton looks at him. "Seriously? That's the best you can do?"

"I don't feel like asking Janet a damn thing right now." Marino stands up from rooting around in his backpack, a protein bar in hand. "Besides, she's too busy talking to Dorothy, right? I'd rather ask Google. I'd rather ask a crystal ball."

"When Crowley dropped off Georgine last night, where was Zain?" Benton follows sticky mats to the living room.

"Supposedly here." Marino has peeled open the protein bar like a banana, chewing as he talks.

"Did she let herself in?" Benton questions. "Or did Zain open the door for her?"

"I don't know," Marino says. "Maybe you can ask Janet to check the cameras. I'm not asking her a damn thing."

Benton is already typing the question to her.

"Cameras weren't recording," he reads her instant answer.

"Of course they weren't," Marino mutters.

———

Benton's Tyvek-covered feet make slippery sounds while he looks around the living room. I recognize the parquet floors, the whitewashed stucco walls, the exposed oak timbers in the plaster ceiling. I remember finding the house beautifully appointed but couldn't get past the history.

The chapel was where patients and their loved ones prayed for healing and relief from suffering. I can well imagine things going on that weren't holy or helpful. Stories I've read about the old lunatic asylum suggest a chaplain was quick to hold out his hand for offerings that never found their way into the collection plate.

"Was Graden aware that Georgine allowed Zain to stay here whenever he was up this way interning at the White House?" I ask as the Doomsday Bird approaches.

It reverberates low overhead, roaring toward the river, the three of us looking up as if we can see it.

"Crowley's aware that Georgine Duvall let Zain stay here for free whenever he was up this way," Marino says when the quiet returns.

"Do we know why she did this?" Benton asks. "A favor for Calvin Willard, possibly? And where was Graden when you two were having this conversation?"

"I was on the porch with the door shut so he couldn't see anything. He was on the sidewalk." Marino chews the last bite of his protein bar.

He drops the wrapper into the biohazard bag.

"The way Crowley talked made me think she had a professional relationship with Zain," Marino explains.

"What did he say that made you wonder that?" I have a feeling I know where this is headed.

"He got squirrelly when I kept asking why Zain always stayed here, especially without paying rent. Was it personal? Was it business or just a favor?" Marino replies. "Why didn't Zain stay with his rich uncle when he was up here working at the White House and hanging out with important people?"

"I wonder how often Georgine was here when Zain was," I reply, my suspicions gathering.

"We should all be wondering it," Marino says. "And her place in Yorktown is just minutes from William & Mary. I've got a feeling she knew Zain pretty damn well."

"Lovers?" Benton asks.

"Nope, I sure as hell don't think so. Like I said, she wasn't his type," Marino disparages.

"We have no idea what Zain's type is," Benton answers.

"Zain was her patient?" My spirits sink as I remember the past.

"What else would he be?" Marino says.

I envision Georgine vibrant and energetic. She was warm and quick to rescue whoever she thought needed it, often treating her patients like family. It was unwise and unsafe. She and I had discussions about this very subject, and she wouldn't listen. She'd smile and remark that I was tainted by what I do for a living.

*Kay, you mustn't lose your ability to trust,* she'd say. *People are basically good. It's the rare person who will take advantage.*

*You and I politely disagree about that,* I'd answer.

"I came right out and asked if she was Zain's private shrink,"

Marino explains. "Crowley says of course not. It wouldn't be appropriate for a male patient to stay with his female psychiatrist. Those were his exact words."

"It wouldn't be appropriate for any reason," I answer.

"Bizarre to think of staying in the same house as your shrink," Marino says. "I would think you could lose your medical license for shit like that."

"Georgine was kind to a fault. She was unorthodox, in many ways naïve, and not much for boundaries. At least she was like that back in my Richmond days," I tell Marino without sharing too much.

He doesn't know that Lucy was her patient once, and it's not for me to offer. I'm not going to explain that Georgine played fast and loose with accepted protocols. She'd meet Lucy for coffee or lunch. Their sessions were in Georgine's home, and on occasion she invited Lucy for dinner and a sleepover.

They played tennis and rode horses together. My teenage niece would help her with computer questions and other technical challenges. During the first few months of therapy, Lucy seemed lighter of spirit and perhaps less lonely. This was followed by her becoming hostile and impossibly defensive.

When I suggested to Georgine that boundaries might be in order, she simply smiled, shaking her head as if I was hopelessly negative.

*It's important my patients see me as a trusted friend, someone they feel perfectly safe with in any situation,* she told me. *Not everybody is ill-intended, Kay.*

# CHAPTER 27

The small bird is busy on the foyer skylight, flitting and flickering. I realize it's a sparrow, brown and industrious, flashes of feathers and shiny dark eyes. It strews bits of dead grass over the glass, repairing a nest as Benton returns to the foyer.

"How many exterior doors?" he asks. "When we walked through this place five years ago, there were three. One in front, one in back and a door in the basement that was always deadbolted."

"That's it." Marino has his gloves off, a trace of a smile as he types a text on his phone.

"Were the doors locked or unlocked when first responders got here?" Benton asks.

"Basement and back door were locked." Marino is reading another message landing. "The front door was unlocked and not closed all the way."

"So, when Zain left the house to find a phone signal, he didn't shut the door," I reply.

"Apparently," Marino says.

"What about the gate?" Benton asks. "I noticed that it opens when you're leaving but requires a key to enter."

"It was open when Officer Horace arrived," Marino answers.

He begins typing again, distracted, the same shadow of a smile.

"Everything okay?" I look at him.

"Mick and Rick." Marino's face is touched by emotion.

"Who?" Benton puzzles, and Marino tells him.

"Fortunately, they didn't lose power," he adds, as if that's the reason he's communicating with the O'Leary twins on Christmas morning. "So I don't need to drop off my spare generator." He seems disappointed. "If there's time later today, I'll stop by to see how they're doing."

"Very kind of you, but be careful, Marino. Don't let your feelings get you in trouble," Benton says. "Whatever's going on, I worry Rowdy O'Leary is tangled in the web. We don't know who or what he might have been dealing with."

"They're nine-year-old kids," Marino growls like a protective bear. "Whatever their loser of a dead father might have been involved in? It has nothing to do with them."

"He might not have been a loser before he was hit by a car," Benton says.

"I got hold of Trad Whalen last night," Marino tells us. "And everything I'm hearing makes me think Rowdy O'Leary was screwed up and not much of a family man even before he got run over."

"You'd be most unwise to consider Trad Whalen a reliable narrator," Benton warns.

He tells Marino about our being pulled over by the trooper on our way here, and how aggressive he was. But Benton doesn't mention the tracking device.

"I'll be outside." He zips up his Secret Service jacket, putting on his sunglasses.

He wants to let the scene speak to him and needs to be alone to channel. His method is to save the worst for last. He won't look at the body until he's scrutinized everything leading up to it.

I no longer hear Lucy's helicopter as Benton opens the front door, a chilly damp wind blowing in. Sunlight paints over the sticky mats, illuminating our footprints on them. He walks out as Marino checks his phone, a dark expression crossing his face.

"What now?" I ask as the door shuts.

"Have you heard from her?" He means Dorothy.

"Not yet."

"I texted her again when you were pulling up. Still nothing."

"I'm sorry. You know how she can get, but I hear she's fine," I tell him. "Benton and I talked to Janet a little while ago—"

"Fucking troublemaker." He cuts me off.

"Dorothy's already been in communication with her this morning." I hate to tell him.

"What a shock."

He opens the front door, inspecting the brass hardware. The exterior curved handle and keyhole are corroding from exposure to the elements. Several of the FBI crime scene investigators stand up, and Marino waves them off.

"How much longer?" one of them yells.

"We'll let you know!" Marino shouts.

"We need to get in . . . !"

"You ready to rock and roll, Doc?" Marino shuts the door again.

We work our legs into flimsy white coveralls that always make me think of a FedEx envelope. Tyvek rustles, the same polyethylene material used to wrap a building under construction. We zip up, putting on new face masks and gloves.

"What are you doing?" I ask as Marino opens his toolbox.

"You'll see."

"I never trust it when you say that."

Usually he would laugh or joke, but he doesn't react. Fueled by bruised feelings and anger, he isn't interested in approval or permission. I watch him pick out screwdrivers, realizing his intention.

"Marino?"

His Tyvek-covered boots lightly stick to the mats by the front door. He begins studying the interior knob and lock lever. He picks up a small flathead screwdriver.

"And why is this our responsibility?" I ask. "Since when?"

His answer is to put on LED magnifiers that look like high-tech opera glasses.

"What's gotten into you?" I say to him, but it's not hard to figure out the answer.

"I know what the hell I'm doing better than any of them. That's what's gotten into me," he replies. "I'm sick and tired of pretending a bunch of newbie cops and big-shot federal agents are smarter than me."

"Nobody's treating you that way," I reply. "Not today."

He uses the screwdriver to pry up the interior knob's backplate.

"Like I'm nothing more than a morgue diener. An old horse who can't learn any new tricks." He mixes metaphors as usual.

Behind the backplate is a lever that he manipulates with the screwdriver blade. He pulls the interior knob out of the door, exposing two screws that hold the exterior handle in place. He tries to turn a screw, but it's not budging.

"It's rusted in there pretty good, and I've got to do this carefully. Don't want to strip the threads, and if the screw breaks that will be even worse," he explains. "There should be WD-40 in my scene case."

I find the can of lubricant, handing it to him. Flipping up the red straw, Marino lightly sprays the two screws. Setting the WD-40 on the floor, he picks up a Phillips screwdriver.

"No telling how long ago everything was installed," he observes. "The door looks really old and wasn't always red. The hardware's definitely been replaced at some point, but not anytime recently. Probably decades ago. Now we're talking."

The screw turns, and he keeps working with the light touch, the sure hand of a surgeon. I snap open the locks on my scene case, finding evidence labels and a Sharpie. Marino drops the steel screw into a small plastic evidence bag.

"I used to do stuff like this all the time. Not just at crime scenes but fixing up my own house." He starts on the second screw. "Back in the day when I could install and fix whatever I wanted without the peanut gallery deciding otherwise." He means my sister.

Moments later he's removed the screw, grabbing the front handle before it clatters to the stone porch. Sunlight fills the borehole, and he begins working on the deadbolt.

"Whoever touched it with bloody hands wasn't wearing gloves," he says. "Zain I'm all but positive."

Marino pries off the deadbolt mounting plate, exposing the screws, and they look old and rusty like the others.

"Mostly what we're going to find out is what you and me already know," he says. "There won't be any tool marks left by the Slasher. The lock wasn't jimmied open. Nothing was pried, I can see that already. I wonder if that's true in the first three cases?"

We don't know. At the earlier scenes, Marino wasn't removing door handles or anything else that's not our department.

"I guarantee the Slasher used a key," Marino deduces.

"How might someone have gotten hold of a key, assuming the person didn't already have one?" I ask. "Unless Georgine hid one somewhere. Or maybe Zain did while staying on Mercy Island whenever he's up this way."

"We know the Slasher had to be spying on Georgine." Marino sprays more WD-40. "He might have seen where she hid a spare key. Or maybe he saw someone else hide or retrieve it."

"He may have done the same thing with the other victims." I take off my gloves, throwing them away.

Picking up my phone, I check messages.

"The Slasher's figuring out where his victims hide their house keys." Marino works on another screw. "Then he strikes, probably coming and going through the front door like he lives there."

As we're talking, I read the latest messages from Clark Givens and Fabian. Hospital staff are arriving for work, and they're behind a long line of cars trying to drive onto the island. Every one of them will be checked by the police.

*This could take a while,* Clark texts.

Marino is telling me about Zain Willard's 1968 muscle car, a hornet-green Cougar in mint condition. It's not something he likely drove in bad conditions. And it's conspicuous.

"Apparently he uses Georgine Duvall's Cadillac to run errands when the two of them are here at the same time," Marino explains. "Maybe he's also been borrowing it without her knowing. As quiet as electric cars are, she might not have heard him drive out of the garage during the early morning hours. If he's the Slasher, maybe that's what he's been driving to his victims' neighborhoods."

"How do you know for a fact that she let Zain borrow her car?" I ask. "Although it wouldn't surprise me."

I'm not going to tell him that Georgine used to do the same thing with Lucy. I was stunned when she came to visit me in Richmond on one occasion, showing up in her psychiatrist's Land Rover.

"Graden Crowley said he's seen Zain driving her Cadillac Lyriq." Marino works on another screw.

"The car's cameras should be able to prove that," I reply. "I would think it has a black box, a data recorder."

"I'm not sure it would tell you where the car went unless a GPS location was entered." Marino drops the screw into the small plastic bag. "And the Slasher's way too smart to do that."

"But it would tell you if the car was driven around the time of the murders," I reply.

"Usually, black boxes don't store data longer than thirty days. I know that's true with the one in my truck," he explains. "And the last time the Slasher struck before now was on Halloween, almost two months ago. So, forget it."

"And if Zain Willard is the killer, he didn't need to drive anywhere last night." I feel another wave of discouragement.

"Exactly."

"I wonder if Georgine was staying here when the first three murders were committed," I reply.

"I have a feeling she's been here every time Zain has. That's why she comes," Marino has decided. "Assuming she was his private shrink, and I guarantee that's the case."

"I'm surprised Graden was so helpful," I reply. "I'm surprised he didn't refuse to answer anything at all the way he does when we show up."

"That's because I handled him," Marino says. "He was helpful until he realized he wasn't going to get what he wanted in return."

"Which was?" I ask.

"He wanted to see the body. And for a while I played good cop. I acted buddy-buddy with him, like it might be a possibility for him to come inside and poke around," Marino explains. "When he finally realized that wasn't going to happen, he got belligerent. He tried to come up on the porch. I promised to arrest his pompous ass if he didn't leave right then."

"I hope you didn't really say all that," I reply as I think, *Oh God.*

"Hell yeah, I ordered him off the property."

"Well, we've not heard the end of it." I have no doubt. "You can rest assured he'll cause a stink."

"I'm just doing my job." Marino partly opens the front door again, a bar of sunlight painting on the mats.

"How did he react?" I ask.

"He started walking around the outside of the house, trying to look through windows, breathing on the glass. I told him I needed to swab him for DNA, and he refused at first."

Marino pulls out the lock cylinder, clanking the hardware into a paper bag.

"We're not supposed to threaten people with arrest." I hand him another label. "That's not what the medical examiner's office does."

"It's exactly what we're supposed to be doing, according to the General Assembly." He places the bag inside the Pelican case as I hear footsteps on the porch that don't sound like Benton's.

# CHAPTER 28

Sunlight fills the foyer as the front door pushes open. Blaise Fruge steps on the sticky mats, a leather bomber jacket and Ray-Bans on. Through the open door I see that the crime scene investigators are gone, their van still parked in the driveway.

"About time," Marino complains as he closes the front door behind her. "Find out anything interesting? Let me guess. That would be no."

Ignoring his sarcasm, Fruge wishes me a Merry Christmas while taking off her sunglasses, parking them on top of her head. I've not seen her for several weeks, and she's cut her dark hair almost crew-cut short again. I can tell she's been spending time on a tanning bed.

"They're going to be pissed." She looks at the hole in the door, shaking her head. "In fact, they already are."

"When are they not?" Marino is pleased with himself.

"And where are they?" I ask about the crime scene unit. "They appear to have left."

"They're busy walking around," Fruge tells us. "Apparently Benton located a crashed drone at the edge of the river. I don't know what all they're doing, but something's got their interest big-time."

"I'm glad they're preoccupied," I reply. "There's a lot we need to do before we can let them in here."

"You'll probably catch holy hell for removing the door handles," Fruge says to Marino.

"Rule number one if you're going to be a good investigator?" He closes the Pelican case packed with our bags of hardware. "Preserve the evidence first and foremost. Then explain yourself."

"Truth is, nobody at the hospital would tell us a damn thing helpful," she admits.

Taking off her jacket, she's in tight jeans and a formfitting shirt that show off her strong body. She didn't look like that when we first met while she was still in uniform. What I see now is due to Marino's influence. They're workout partners. In recent years, he's been reshaping her like Pygmalion, and I know it rubs Dorothy the wrong way.

"Don't say I didn't warn you." Marino wags his finger at Fruge like a disappointed coach. "Waste of time, and worse than that, you've tipped them off. You've tipped off everybody at the hospital."

"About what?" She stares defiantly at him.

"About whatever you were asking."

He carries the Pelican case across the mats, setting it down next to my coat and briefcase.

"Mostly we wanted to know if any patients were unaccounted for last night," she says. "Or if anybody on the staff has been having a problem with anyone. Not just patients but outside vendors."

"Which gives everyone a heads-up that what happened here might be connected to the hospital," he replies. "That's called dropping the iron curtain."

"It had already dropped," she counters.

"Having the FBI with you didn't make that any better," Marino continues to lecture. "Who was it?"

"At first, I was with Lucy and Tron, but they left early on. Then

I hung out with Special Agent Tully. She's always nice to deal with. You know, she isn't disrespectful, treating me like a dumb shit." The implication is obvious.

I step closer to the living room while they continue to spar.

"Well, you and Tully telegraphed way more to the hospital than they did to you." Marino carries on.

"Have you found out something to make us think the killer is connected to this place? A patient, for example?" Fruge replies.

"Not necessarily. But that's not the point."

"And besides, everybody knows everything," she goes on. "It's all over the internet what happened on Mercy Island this morning. The names of the victims, this address, Zain Willard's powerful uncle who's running for president. The info's gone viral as you'd expect."

She informs us that Dana Diletti just interviewed Graden Crowley at the hospital's entrance. He's complaining that the medical examiner's office is bullying him and the police.

"You're mentioned by name." Fruge derives some pleasure telling Marino this. "He's saying you tried to arrest him."

"I didn't *try*." Marino can't help but smile. "If I had, he'd be in cuffs on his way to lockup."

As he and Fruge go at it, I'm peeling up two sticky mats. Dried blood shows on the back of them, the drops still visible on the chevron oak flooring. I measure the distance between bloodstains, finding what I expect.

Perfectly round drops approximately the size of a dime.

Six to nine inches apart.

They fell at a slow velocity, impacting at a 90-degree angle, consistent with someone dripping blood while walking.

"How much blood was outside when you got here?" I interrupt

Marino and Fruge bickering. "Were the drops as closely spaced as these?"

"They were a couple feet apart. Like every time he took another step, more blood hit the snow." It's Fruge who answers.

"There should have been a lot of blood," I reply.

"There is on the hall runner where it appears he was attacked," she says. "It's hard to know how much he bled outside because of the conditions."

"I don't want anybody near the house." Marino isn't done bossing Fruge around. "You may as well put your coat back on. Best thing is for you to stand outside on the porch. We don't need you or anybody else in here right now."

"But I've already been inside." She's offended. "You and I walked through every inch of this place when we first got here."

"It's more helpful if you guard the door." He's gruff with her. "You shouldn't have left your post, hanging out with the FBI, acting like a wannabe."

"Who said I want to be FBI?"

"You're always asking Lucy about Quantico," he replies, and it's true.

Now and then Fruge and Lucy socialize, having coffee in the guest cottage. They grab a beer and listen to DJs at the Bayou Club on King Street. Lucy mentioned that not long ago, Fruge asked for a tour of the FBI Academy. She was crushed to learn the cutoff age for new agents is thirty-six. She's a year older than that.

Grabbing her jacket, Fruge leaves in a huff. Marino shuts the door behind her, and we put on new coveralls, booties, face masks, gloves. Collecting my scene case and extra PPE, we enter the living room, the sharply pungent smell of bleach intensifying.

"I asked Crowley about the convicted offenders sometimes

locked up in the forensic unit," Marino says as I look around at the big windows and high ceiling. "I wanted to know how many are here now. And if anybody we should be concerned about attended the Christmas party last night and maybe wandered off."

"Or maybe someone dangerous was recently discharged?" I suggest.

"That too."

"Graden's not going to tell us the truth."

"Of course, he said nobody was missing last night," Marino verifies. "But he wasn't at liberty to release information about patients."

———

As I walk around on sticky mats, I remember the living room well. Only it was unfurnished when Benton and I saw it with the Realtor. Now it appears thoughtlessly put together, nothing much inside.

A blue fabric sofa has wood-veneer end tables with water rings on them. A tan leather recliner is stained in spots, crumbs on the cushion. The small Persian rug under the glass coffee table is an inexpensive reproduction. It doesn't appear to have been vacuumed in recent memory.

"An escaped patient doesn't make sense, though," I'm saying to Marino. "How would it explain the hologram you saw? Not just anybody could pull that off."

"If we're talking about a patient being the Slasher, it could be someone hospitalized here before but not now or even recently. Or the more likely story? Someone who lives here on and off." He's pointing the finger at Zain Willard again.

I wander to the bookcase between windows, maybe a dozen old volumes missing their dust jackets. J. R. R. Tolkien. George Orwell.

C. S. Lewis. Ralph Waldo Emerson. I slide out *A Dream of John Ball* by Victorian socialist William Morris.

*Ex Libris Georgine Duvall,* reads the bookplate in the front cover. Scrawled under it in her loopy handwriting, *Society gets the criminals it deserves,* and I photograph it with my phone.

"That mean something to you?" Marino asks.

I tell him it sounds like something she would quote. I know that's what she believed, her empathy outrunning her common sense and good judgment. Ultimately, that must have something to do with why Lucy stopped seeing her.

"I found it the height of irony that Georgine was idealistic and anti-capitalism while living on a multimillion-dollar horse farm. Not to mention the priceless things they collected," I explain. "She and her husband seemed like genuinely good people. But hopelessly idealistic."

"Sound like fucking phonies to me," Marino snorts.

"They meant no harm." As I'm saying this, I still believe it. "But they were wrongheaded and naïve. Most of all, too trusting."

"A good way to get murdered," he says.

"And cause damage to people you're convinced you're helping." I'm thinking of Lucy again.

I notice tiny holes in plaster suggesting something once hung on the bare living room walls. I tell Marino that when I knew Georgine and her husband, they had a formidable art collection. Several Andy Warhols and Picassos. A few horse paintings by George Stubbs, dogs by Landseer. A Monet or two.

"They loved to show off their collection to visitors. I was sure they'd get burglarized," I recall.

"Glad they weren't capitalists," Marino says snidely.

A TV is on a stand in a corner, and there are a few floor lamps, shiny brass with white pleated shades. The furnishings aren't much better than I'd expect in a dorm room.

The small artificial Christmas tree in a corner looks like one you'd buy in a grocery store. It's scantily hung with shiny ball ornaments, and a few strands of lights that aren't turned on. I find it odd there are no other decorations. It doesn't seem this was Georgine's favorite time of year anymore.

It seems she came here to escape the holidays if anything. The house doesn't appear to have been cleaned in quite a while, and that's not like her either. The fireplace is thick with gray ashes that have blown onto the hearth and floor. I notice dust bunnies under an end table, and cobwebs high in a corner.

"I sure would like to know what was going on with her," I comment while continuing to look around. "Because everything I'm seeing is out of character. Not that we were close. But I knew her well enough."

I can't imagine Georgine would furnish her Mercy Island pied-à-terre so spartanly, nothing matching or tasteful. I have no sense that she ever lived here. I don't know why she would buy the former chapel to begin with. But perhaps she thoughtfully decorated it at first, filling it with lovely furniture, hanging art on the walls.

"Does she have an office in the house?" I ask Marino. "Any sign of any paperwork, anything like that?"

"Nope," he says. "Just a computer tablet on the desk in her bedroom. Her phone is there too, and I didn't touch them, will leave that for Lucy and Tron."

"What about filing cabinets?"

"None here," he replies.

"I'm assuming Georgine keeps her patients' records in Yorktown.

Maybe she made a mention of someone she was having trouble with. A patient, for example." I explain what I'm thinking. "Maybe we can get a better idea of her relationship with Zain Willard. I'd like to take a look at her medical notes before the feds haul them away."

"Lucy and Benton are the feds. I'm sure they can make that happen," Marino says.

Moving closer to the coffee table, I look at the laptop computer, the books on machine language, robotics and blockchain technology. I pick up one of them as Marino watches. There's no name inside, but many sections are underlined, a lot of comments in the margins.

"Zain's got several computers in his room on the third floor," Marino says. "Based on what I saw on his desk, he's also into gaming, and, like I mentioned, he's got a robot dog. Not a real dog he has to take care of and pay attention to. That tells me something about him."

As I flip through the book on robotics, a check falls out. Signed by Calvin Willard, it's made out to Georgine Duvall in the amount of $18,000 and dated yesterday. *Tax Free* is typed on the memo line.

"Holy shit," Marino says. "He must have been paying her for something. I doubt he was giving her that kind of money for no reason."

"You might be right that she was Zain's personal shrink," I decide.

———

The living area opens into a kitchen of modern stainless-steel appliances, an art glass chandelier hanging over a table in front of a window, the shade down.

I notice the clean dishes in the drain rack, the bread and bakery goods on the counter near a black leather Gucci pocketbook that looks old. Next to it is a set of keys on a keychain that's attached by a ring to a holstered pepper spray. I wouldn't expect Georgine to own much less carry such a thing.

"Looks like she'd gotten security conscious when she didn't used to be," I comment, the odor of bleach making my eyes water.

"I would hope so considering where this place is located," Marino says.

"That didn't used to be a concern for her," I reply. "She didn't worry about who she let in her house, for that matter. And I remember her commenting that her husband insisted on setting the alarm at night. Otherwise, she wouldn't bother."

"Nothing appears to be stolen," Marino informs me. "She's got four hundred and ninety dollars in her wallet. And a bunch of credit cards. But in the other Slasher murders, nothing was missing either."

"Burglary isn't what motivates him," I reply. "In the other cases, it doesn't appear he rifled through anything. He came in to kill. And then left."

"Maybe it's not on his agenda because he doesn't need money," Marino says. "Maybe because he's got a rich uncle who's always going to take care of him."

On top of the kitchen garbage can is a large pizza box, and I ask if it's from last night.

"I've looked at the receipt," Marino says.

"Of course you did."

"A meat lover's large ordered from Donato's Pizzeria at around six p.m.," he says.

"Delivered or picked up?"

"Delivered. Took about an hour, probably because of the weather."

"How does that work when someone shows up at the hospital's front gate with a food delivery?" I wonder.

"An intercom." Marino points out the speaker box next to light switches. "You talk to whoever you're expecting. You can push a button to open the front gate remotely. All the homes here have the same thing, Crowley told me."

"Do we know if hospital security officers were patrolling last night?" I ask. "Do we know if they patrol at all?"

I'm looking inside the pantry. Cans of soup, tuna fish, cases of water and other basic supplies. Also bottles of liquor and beer. A mop, a broom, a dustpan. A few miscellaneous tools, a plastic tray filled with screws and nails.

"Crowley says that all of them were working the Christmas party," Marino says. "They weren't driving around in the storm."

"How many is *all of them*?"

"Supposedly a total of three were on duty, and it's not their job to patrol the residences because they're privately owned," Marino explains. "No security back here in other words."

"Did Zain Willard order the pizza?" I open the refrigerator. "Who paid for it?"

I don't see any leftover slices or have the impression that Georgine or Zain did much in the way of cooking. There are packages of deli meats, takeout containers of yogurt, potato salad, soups, macaroni and cheese, and bags of premixed salad with packets of dressing. Also ketchup, mustard, jellies and jams, and a couple bottles of white wine.

In the freezer are ice cube trays, packages of hot dogs and hamburgers, a bag of frozen cherries, a skull-shaped bottle of Crystal Head Vodka.

"Zain called in the pizza and paid for it in cash when it was delivered, based on the receipt," Marino tells me.

"How do you know he's the one who called in the order?" I ask.

"It's his cell phone number on the receipt."

"And you know it's his number how...?" I hope to hell he didn't call it.

"I asked Janet. That was earlier before I decided not to talk to her anymore."

"If Graden Crowley was telling you the truth, Georgine wasn't home when the pizza was delivered." I'm working out the timeline. "She was with him at the Christmas party until he dropped her off here at nine p.m. It would be helpful if we can verify that."

"It shouldn't be hard. A lot of people would have seen her there. They can't all lie about it. And hopefully cameras picked it up," Marino says.

"Unless they're not working like most of them, including the ones here." I open the stainless-steel trash can at the end of the counter.

Pulling out the bag, I look inside.

"I took a peek earlier," Marino says. "Nothing grabbed my attention."

My gloved hands dig through paper towels, paper plates, coffee grounds, a tuna fish can, numerous water bottles. Also, an empty bottle of Schramsberg Blanc de Blancs champagne, and a few pizza crusts.

"Are we to assume Zain ate an entire large meat lover's pizza by himself?" I ask.

"I know I could. I could do it right now," Marino says.

"And you're almost twice his size."

I pluck the champagne bottle out of the trash, setting it upright on the counter.

"It doesn't fit with everything else I'm seeing," I tell him.

I point to the oak wine rack to the left of the refrigerator. The four reds and three whites are premier cru burgundies. I saw two bottles of white Bordeaux inside the refrigerator, and they aren't cheap either.

"All of it is French and expensive." I'm standing in front of the wine rack looking at the labels. "Maybe that means nothing. But the champagne is from California and inexpensive, comparatively speaking. I'm wondering if it was a gift from someone."

# CHAPTER 29

I open the dishwasher. Inside are three champagne glasses, several plates and bowls, the silverware holder full. Dishes have been rinsed but not washed.

"Why three glasses?" I ask. "Maybe somebody was drinking with Georgine and Zain last night?"

"Somebody like Graden Crowley?" Marino takes photographs of the wine rack. "Maybe when he brought her home, he came inside for a while. Maybe the champagne is from him."

"That's crossing my mind."

Inside what I suspect was once a china closet is a stackable washer and dryer. Both are filled with what appears to be Zain's clothing. He was home last night while Georgine was attending the hospital's Christmas party. Yet he couldn't empty the dryer and start another load of wash.

"I have little doubt that Zain was accustomed to people picking up after him," I comment as I leave the kitchen for the dining room.

There's not so much as a chair inside, a metal plate over the opening in the ceiling for a light fixture. Heavy damask draperies are drawn across the windows. Around a corner is a hallway, and midway down is the curved oak staircase leading up to the second and third floors.

The first open doorway is the main bedroom, the lights out. The wooden blinds are closed inside, the sharp, pungent odor of bleach slamming into my senses. It's overwhelming through my surgical mask. I change my gloves and booties, putting on a plastic face shield.

"I realize the power was out when you first got here, everything dark." I stand in the doorway looking in at the shape of the body on top of the bed. "But do we know if the light switch was on or off?"

"If was off," Marino says.

I flip up the switch, the bedroom illuminated, and I wouldn't recognize Georgine Duvall, bloody and riddled with gaping wounds. Her eyes and mouth are barely open, her mutilated face solid red.

"The same thing we've seen before, and the killer's got to be wearing night-vision glasses of some sort," Marino says as we peer in from the doorway. "Otherwise, he couldn't see what he was doing."

"Frenzied." I describe my first impression.

"My guess is when she stopped moving, he started in with the biting. He poured bleach to destroy the DNA."

"Perhaps he was doing all this when he heard someone coming downstairs," I suggest.

I know instantly by the large amount of coagulating blood on the hallway runner and spattered on the whitewashed wall that this is where Zain was injured.

"It appears he was ambushed as he reached the bottom of the stairs in the dark," I tell Marino.

"Unless he inflicted the injuries on himself."

"Either way, it happened here. And if he really was attacked by the Slasher, it's believable Zain didn't know what hit him," I reply.

"I don't doubt that it would have taken him a moment to realize he was bleeding."

"His story is that he fell to the floor and played dead." Marino sets down my scene case. "That's what he told Officer Horace."

"It would seem the killer didn't bother checking," I reply. "Just as he didn't check to make sure how many people were staying in the house."

Across from the bedroom is a bathroom. I step inside, turning on the light, remembering the white subway tile floor, the white porcelain pedestal sink and mirrored medicine cabinet. The cast iron clawfoot tub and shower are combined, a Wedgwood-blue curtain pushed back on either side.

"I'm not seeing any blood or sign that it was cleaned up in here," I tell Marino. "It doesn't look like Zain Willard came in here after he was cut."

"My impression, too," Marino says as he crouches by my open scene case in the hallway. "And I sprayed with Bluestar and didn't get anything significant."

The chemical reagent causes invisible blood to fluoresce. When people clean up a scene, it's not possible to remove every trace of blood. It lights up between tiles and floorboards. Swipe marks from towels and mops become visible. Blood is a tattletale. It doesn't forgive or forget.

"I would expect Zain might have stepped inside the bathroom to check on his injuries," I comment. "Except with the power off, I suppose he couldn't see. Unless he thought to turn on his cell phone's flashlight."

"Or maybe he didn't go in there to look because he already knew about his injuries. If he did it to himself." Marino comes back to that every time.

"Or he was in a panic. Desperate to get out of the house and call for help." I've opened the medicine cabinet.

Inside is a bottle of face cleanser, a tube of toothpaste. The toothbrush is in a glass on the sink, and the cosmetic bag must be Georgine's. Marino watches as I remove a square plastic box with a palette of eye shadows. Eyeliner pencils and mascara. Lipstick. Concealer and face powder. None of it is expensive.

I inspect a tube of ointment, triamcinolone for itching and swelling. Georgine Duvall's name is on the label, the prescription filled a week ago, as was a bottle of clonazepam.

"Sounds like she was suffering from anxiety," I tell Marino. "I'm wondering if this could be related to her carrying pepper spray on her keychain."

Returning to the hallway, I'm mindful not to step on blackish stains, the coagulating blood thick like drying tar on the pale blue and gray hall runner.

"Right over there is where something fluoresced." Marino points to an area of carpet that doesn't look bloody. "Somebody tracked something on the rug, and it showed up this bright cherry red in UV light like I told you earlier. Otherwise, you can't see it. Whatever the stuff is, it's invisible to the naked eye."

"The problem is, we don't know how long the residue has been here," I reply. "Or on the chair inside the bedroom that you mentioned. And it doesn't appear anyone cleans very often."

"But if the source is something inside the house, how come it doesn't show up anywhere else?" Marino says.

"You walked through the house with the UV light?"

"You know me, Doc. No leaf left unturned."

"When Clark Givens gets here with the Raman, we'll see if we can figure out what the residue might be," I reply.

"What we can know for a fact is Zain was cut right here on this bloody part of the rug," Marino says. "After that, he made his way outside to where Officer Horace found him."

I take a photograph of a bloody handprint on the hallway wall. It appears Zain might have lost his balance, maybe when he fell to the floor. Drops on the carpet runner and oak flooring verify his story.

At some point after he was injured, he was upright and walking away from here, through the dining room, the living room, and out of the house.

––––––––

I look through the doorway at the butchered body tangled in bedcovers. Marino has placed more sticky mats on the floor. He continues to assure me that he took photographs and swabs first thing when he and Fruge got here during the early morning hours.

"It was pitch-dark inside the house at that time, as you can imagine with the power out. The killer wouldn't have been able to see anything without a flashlight or night-vision goggles," Marino explains as we swap out shoe covers again.

We stuff soiled ones into the biohazard bag we brought with us from the foyer. Changing my gloves, I retrieve a long chemical thermometer and a disposable scalpel from my scene case. Beneath the acrid stench of bleach, I detect the putrid-sweet odor of blood breaking down, the early stages of decomposition getting started.

I move aside a bloody sheet and duvet, a pair of blood-soaked pajamas in a heap on the foot of the bed. I pick up the top, then the bottoms for a better look at the slits and slashes from the knife. Areas of sparing show the satiny fabric is pale blue before it turned dark red.

"You've got photographs of all this?" I ask.

"Out the wazoo," Marino says. "And video."

He hands me a plastic ruler, and the largest buttonhole-like perforations from multiple stabs are two inches long.

"The knife is single edge," I tell him as he makes notes. "The blade is a maximum of two inches wide, tapering to a narrow point."

I know this because defects in the fabric and flesh are smaller where the blade barely penetrated before striking bone and cartilage. Her ribs and hips. Her sternum and skull. She obviously was wearing the pajamas when the killer attacked. After the fact, he cut them off her.

"By the looks of things, the sharp force injuries were made by a knife that's consistent with the one used in the three earlier cases," I tell Marino. "The measurements are the same so far. We should be able to find tool marks in cartilage and bone for comparison. All indications point to the Slasher again. I think he did this."

"Which looks really bad for Zain Willard," Marino says. "But then, you know what I think. The spoiled punk's a closet psycho."

"There are dozens of stab wounds." I describe what I'm seeing. "More than there were in the other three cases. I'm sensing a stronger emotional response, making me wonder if he had a connection to Georgine Duvall."

"It's like he hated her," Marino says, and I know who he's thinking about.

"I think it's a fair statement that the Slasher hates everyone he hacks to death," I answer. "Most of all, he hates what they represent."

"All of them are health workers," Marino replies. "He goes after people like that for some reason that probably goes back to his childhood."

"Zain's mother is a pediatrician," I tell him.

"Bingo," Marino says. "That totally fits. Maybe when Zain was coming along, his mom spent all her time with her patients. Maybe he felt she had other kids in her life who were more important than him."

"We have no idea if that was the case."

"And she probably ended up working on holidays." He continues to script what sounds more like his own story of growing up in Bayonne, New Jersey.

His father was a drunk and largely absent. Marino's mother taught in the local elementary school and was overwhelmed on every front. He spent a lot of time on the street fending for himself. I imagine his holidays weren't Hallmark happy.

The body is warm through my gloves as I make a small incision over the lower left abdomen. I insert the thermometer, gently pushing it all the way into the liver to get a core temperature. It will be more accurate than what Marino recorded with infrared, and I set a second thermometer on top of the dresser.

"She looks like she worked out, was in good shape for her age." He stares at the carnage on the bed. "I bet she used the fitness center here."

"Regularly, I'd hazard a guess," I reply. "Making it easy for someone to see her coming and going. I assume she would have walked there. It's not far from here."

Lean with good muscle tone, Georgine has the build of a gym enthusiast, and always did, I explain.

"When I'd see her in Charlottesville, she often mentioned exercising and playing sports," I add. "I remember the Duvalls had an indoor swimming pool, a workout room. They were physically active, big outdoor enthusiasts."

I envision the photograph on her driver's license, her face attractive in a handsome way, almost regal. I can't tell that now. The killer slashed open the forehead and scalp, lopping off the tip of the nose and part of an ear. I survey the damage, the wounds more frenzied and vicious than in the previous three cases.

I note multiple slits in the sheets where the killer missed the body entirely, stabbing and slashing the mattress, even nicking the wooden headboard and a bedpost.

"She was moving around a lot," I say to Marino as he takes notes. "She struggled with him. More than we've seen in the other cases, and those were frenzied enough."

I grip the left arm by the wrist, lifting it, and rigor mortis is in the early stages. She's relatively limber, and I examine cuts and stab wounds that are deep and savage. Two fingers of her left hand are barely attached. Her right palm is cut to the bone, blood oozing as I manipulate the body.

"She made multiple attempts at warding off the blade." I continue describing what I see. "She fought like hell until she couldn't anymore."

I wonder if the Slasher watched Georgine sleep for a while. Did he stand by the bed with night-vision glasses on, and what a power rush that must have been. I imagine him fantasizing, getting more worked up before starting in with the knife.

"Some things we may never know," I'm saying to Marino. "But she tried to defend herself, and it would make sense that she screamed."

"Unless he'd already cut her throat, and she couldn't."

"She has too many defensive injuries to her arms and hands for me to think the cuts to her throat were first." I pick up the thermometer from the foot of the bed.

The room temperature is sixty-nine degrees, I report, and Marino writes it down in his small spiral notepad, the kind you can buy in a drugstore.

"It was a little less than that when I got here," he says. "Because of the power being out."

"There was an obvious sequence of events." I tell him what I'm assessing.

The killer attacked her, and she likely screamed until her vocal cords, her windpipe and strap muscles were severed, one of the gashes almost to her spine.

"When she wasn't thrashing anymore, he cut her pajamas off and started biting," I go on. "The last thing he would have done before leaving is pour the bleach."

"No way Zain came down the stairs the minute he heard her scream," Marino decides. "Or the bleach wouldn't have been poured yet. And he claims he smelled it. He said it smelled like a swimming pool."

I think of the video made by Officer Horace's body camera. I couldn't tell by looking if Zain had bleach on him, but I assume not.

"Otherwise, his skin would have been burning. His eyes would have been bothered by the fumes," I explain. "There also doesn't appear to be bleach in the hallway where he was cut and claims to have played dead."

"Makes sense he wouldn't have bleach on him," Marino says. "If he's the Slasher he sure as hell wasn't going to pour it on himself."

# CHAPTER 30

I remove the thermometer from the liver, and the core temperature is 87.6 degrees, I report to Marino. Nude and with low body fat, she's lost most of her blood, and would cool more rapidly.

Shining a flashlight, I notice a laceration on the inside of her lower lip. The injury is what I expect when an assailant clamps his hand over the victim's mouth, smashing the lips against teeth. The edges of the wound are inflamed and bloody, consistent with her receiving the injury while still alive.

"He tried to silence her," I tell Marino. "It appears he covered her mouth with his hand, and he might have done it first. That could be what woke her up."

I begin swabbing under the fingernails, short and neatly squared, the cotton tips turning red. I place them into a paper envelope that Marino labels, tucking it into the scene case. Taking off my bloody gloves, I swap them for fresh ones.

"Before I start swabbing for DNA, I'd like to take a look at what's fluorescing." I return to the doorway.

Marino selects a handheld crime scene light from the case of them. We put on orange-tinted goggles, and he turns off the overhead chandelier, the room swallowed by blackness. The sticky sound of our walking on the paper mats seems unnaturally loud, the crime light's lens glowing purple.

I begin painting the body with ultraviolet light an inch at a time, starting with the head. Blood shows as a black void in UV. But when I shine the light on the lower face, a dusting of something blazes red.

"Well, now we know the source for sure," I tell Marino in the dark. "The killer. He must have had whatever this residue is on his gloves and transferred it when he clamped his hand over her mouth."

I swab the fluorescing residue, and it glows as if red hot on the cotton tip. I place the swab inside a paper envelope Marino holds open. Next, I direct the light at the oat-colored upholstered chair in a corner. A vaguely rectangular shape lights up the same iridescent red.

This residue also fluoresces on the carpet in the hallway. The bright red shapes look like partial footprints with no tread, consistent with someone wearing shoe covers the same way we are.

Lights back on, and I'm startled by Benton waiting near the stairs, a small black Pelican case in hand. He's suited up the same way we are, covered head to toe in white Tyvek.

"Clark Givens is waiting outside with the laser scanner," he lets us know. "And Fabian's in the van. He gave me your medical kit, and I put it in the car." Benton says this to me.

"We're almost ready to move her," I reply. "Maybe another thirty minutes."

Opening the Pelican case, I lift out a Raman spectrometer not much bigger than my cell phone. I attach the fiber optic connector. The three of us put on the orange-tinted plastic goggles, and Marino cuts the overhead light again.

He directs the UV light as I point the Raman's laser beam at the area on the chair glowing fiery red. Seconds later, a spectrogram and chemical formulas appear in the illuminated display.

$$C_{55}H_{74}MgN_4O_5 + CaCO_3$$

"I don't know what that is." Benton's voice sounds.

"No clue." Marino types on his phone glowing in the dark.

"I recognize calcite but not the other," I tell them.

"Chlorophyll," Marino says. "According to my friend Google, because I'm not talking to Janet. Let's see how she likes that, right? A dose of her own medicine."

He turns on the bedroom light again.

"Chlorophyll? As in the green stuff in plants?" Benton asks me this.

"What would seem to be a powder form of it," I reply. "Plus calcite, the mineral name of calcium carbonate. The residue is a mixture."

"We sure it's a powder? Could this stuff have been in a liquid form and spilled?" Marino scowls at the esoteric science of it all.

He'll be the first to tell you that during high school he and chemistry were mortal enemies. That and math. Also, physics. And he once said he'd rather poke himself in the eye than read about computer science.

"I wouldn't think the compound was in a liquid form," I tell him. "It makes more sense that a very fine powder could have been transferred by the killer without him being aware."

We step out into the hallway, and I check the fluorescing residue on the carpet. The reading is the same.

$$C_{55}H_{74}MgN_4O_5 + CaCO_3$$

"We'll verify in the labs," I reply. "But somehow a powdered form of chlorophyll and calcite ended up on the hall runner and a bedroom chair. Also on Georgine Duvall's face. Implying it was on the killer's gloves. Likely also on his feet or whatever he covered them with. PPE, since we suspect he's wearing it."

"And he must have set something on the bedroom chair, perhaps his murder kit," Benton adds. "But why would the killer be carrying a residue like this on his person and belongings?"

"I don't know," I reply. "But it would appear he's exposed to it for some reason at home, maybe at his workplace or wherever else he frequents."

"I don't get it," Marino says. "Chlorophyll, calcite? Maybe it's an error."

"I doubt it. This thing's pretty reliable." Powering off the Raman spectrometer, I place it back inside the heavy-duty plastic case.

"It says here that powdered chlorophyll is a dietary supplement used by people with skin conditions and cancer." Marino is looking at his phone, googling again, refusing to ask Janet. "It's used for wound healing and all sorts of other things. And calcite is in antacids and vitamins. Also cement."

"The powder could be some type of nutritional supplement," I suggest. "Perhaps something the killer adds to his diet."

"Maybe he's having health problems," Benton contemplates.

"Good," Marino snorts. "Hopefully the asshole's dying."

"I wonder if Zain had this mixture of powdered chlorophyll and calcite on him before he was driven away in the ambulance?" Benton questions.

"I didn't see anything like that in the kitchen," I reply. "The only nutritional supplements I noticed were in the pantry. The usual multivitamins. Nothing that could account for this residue."

"Nothing like that is in his bedroom either. I didn't see any vitamins or supplements." Benton lets us know he's been scoping out the house.

I didn't hear him when he was walking around. My husband is gifted at coming and going like a shadow.

"We'll test his clothing, his shoes," I explain. "I'll bring a UV light with me when we go to the hospital. Zain's wounds will have been cleaned but most likely he won't have showered."

"What I'm not seeing is a drone of any kind," Marino says. "But he's got remote controls on his desk upstairs that could be for one and also gaming."

I'm reminded of the device the state trooper attached to the underside of our Tesla. Someone could have hacked in using a gaming or drone controller, sending us into head-on traffic or over a cliff.

"I understand you found a crashed drone." Marino asks Benton about it. "Dana Diletti's, I assume."

"Yes."

"I was hoping the Slasher's drone might have taken a nosedive." Marino has his gloves off, typing a text on his phone.

"Unfortunately, not that we've found," Benton says. "One of Dana Diletti's drones is badly damaged, and the other went into the river and hasn't been recovered."

"What else have you been finding out?" I ask him.

"It would seem that Georgine or someone hides a key in a fake rock that was beneath boxwoods to the left of the front door," he tells us. "The fake rock is empty. The key isn't there. The question is when it disappeared."

"That's probably how the Slasher's gotten into the other victims' places," Marino says. "It's exactly what I thought. Except if Zain did it, he didn't need a key this time, now did he? Maybe he removed the spare from the fake rock to make it appear the killer did it. Maybe he staged everything we're seeing."

"Not the residue we're finding," I reply. "I suspect the killer has no idea he left that. Especially since we've not found it in the other murders. But for some reason, he was exposed to whatever this is, and transferred it here."

We pull up our Tyvek hoods, looking like ghosts as we return to the bedroom. Flipping up my face shield, I put on the LED magnifiers. I begin examining the bite marks on the breasts and swabbing them for DNA.

"There's very little tissue response, no bruising or swelling." I explain what I'm seeing.

"The same was true in the earlier cases." Benton looks on as Marino takes photographs.

———

I turn over the body, blood spilling from multiple stabs and slashes. I check her back, and she has three bite marks on her buttocks, one of them savage enough that a chunk of flesh is barely attached.

"As you're likely aware, the basement here is below ground." Benton picks up the bloody pajama top from the bed, holding it up, looking at it. "The locked door opens into an area about the size of a closet. Inside it is another door that leads out to the riverfront. But there's also a tunnel."

"How did you unlock the door leading to it?" Marino asks. "When I searched the basement, the door was deadbolted. I couldn't open it."

"While I was wandering around the house, I tried her keys that were in the kitchen." Benton is looking at the pajama bottoms. "One of them opens the door leading to the tunnel."

He explains that tunnels connect the former outbuildings to the hospital. All thirteen of them that are now expensive residences.

"You're telling us there's a tunnel connecting this house to the hospital." Marino lets that sink in.

"Not only to the hospital but also the fitness center." Benton returns the pajama bottoms to the bed. "I counted at least fifteen stab holes," he says to me.

"More than that. Twenty-two on the pajama top alone," I tell him.

"Christ," Benton mutters.

He watches as I swab another bite wound for DNA. I'm not hopeful, the odor of bleach powerful.

"Are all thirteen of the houses connected to the fitness center, the original site of the cemetery that was dug up?" I ask Benton.

"No, only this one," he explains. "And what that suggests is the tunnel originally led to some type of building on the cemetery."

"Possibly a mortuary," I suggest. "A lot of old cemeteries had buildings where bodies could be prepared for burial."

I suggest that long ago if a patient died, the body might have started out here in the chapel for the service. Afterward, it could have been transported to the cemetery mortuary by way of the tunnel.

"That's what the basement door is for," Benton replies. "On the other side is the tunnel connecting this house with the hospital and the fitness center. Anybody staying here could visit both without ever stepping outside."

"I wonder if that could explain the killer not realizing there were two people staying here?" I question. "Assuming that's what happened."

"Especially if Zain was borrowing Georgine's car much of the time," Benton suggests. "He might have thought he was surveilling Georgine coming and going in her Cadillac. When it was actually Zain driving it."

"Adding to the confusion is that the two of them were about the same size," Marino adds. "And Zain has long hair."

"I don't remember being told about the tunnel when we were shown this place five years ago," I say to Benton. "But it was obvious we weren't interested in buying."

"The crime scene unit's already searching the tunnel," he says. "I walked through it with them, a lot of dusty old rooms that once were treatment areas. It leads directly to the administrative wing of the hospital."

As I listen, I'm seeing something strange. Using plastic tweezers, I grip a white cylindrical object embedded deep in a bite wound on the left buttock. I extract what looks like a snapped-off animal incisor.

I hold it up to the light, and it's polished smooth, about half an inch long and sharply pointed.

"What the hell?" Marino says in amazement. "It looks like a freakin' vampire fang. Or a fang from a wild animal."

"Definitely not real. Fake like special effects teeth actors wear," I observe. "Something like acrylic, maybe three-D printed. Explaining the weird bite marks we've been finding."

"He's biting his victims with fake teeth?" Marino is incredulous and spooked at the same time.

"Part of his elaborate sexually violent fantasies," Benton says. "A new one for the books."

He looks on as I drop the bloody broken fake tooth into a small cardboard evidence box Marino holds open for me.

"This is someone with rituals that mean something intensely personal to him," Benton continues. "He does the same thing every time. Only the violence is escalating. He's getting more out of control."

"Definitely the Slasher," Marino says. "Whoever killed her also killed the other three."

"I agree," Benton says.

"Since the fake tooth was embedded deep in tissue, maybe the bleach didn't get to it," I tell them. "Maybe we'll be lucky with DNA for once."

"We need to find out what kind of crap Zain's been buying off the internet," Marino says.

"Already being looked into," Benton says. "Every purchase he's been making. And agents are searching his apartment in Williamsburg as we speak."

"Are they finding anything interesting?" Marino looks at him. "Maybe a three-D printer? Maybe extra sets of fake teeth? Maybe bottles of lab-grade bleach?"

"Nothing like that," Benton replies.

"If you're about ready," Marino says to me, "I'll get her moved out and into the van. Clark Givens can help. Then he can do his thing with the laser scanner while Fabian drives the body to the office. Doug Schlaefer's there waiting with bells on."

"The linens go in with her. Same thing we've done before." I step out of the bedroom. "When the body is in transit, let Doug know. He can get started right away charting her injuries. That's going to take a while."

I'm curious about her gastric contents, also what's in her small intestine. I want a STAT alcohol level, I explain, as Marino sends a text with my instructions.

"If you're done in here, I want to show you something," Benton says to me. "Zain's bedroom."

"You go ahead, Doc," Marino replies as if I need his permission. "I'm heading outside to deal with Fabian and Clark."

# CHAPTER 31

Changing our PPE, Benton and I begin climbing the uncarpeted oak stairs. I notice faint smudges almost indistinguishable from the dark wood. Possibly dirt. Or scuffs vaguely squarish. Maybe from the heel of a shoe and barely visible.

Pausing to open my scene case, I get out the bottle of Bluestar. The smudges glow sapphire blue as I spray the chemical reagent.

"Possibly blood," I tell Benton. "Marino didn't notice."

"Understandably. I almost can't see whatever it is. If it's blood, is it recent?"

"I don't know."

He watches as I swab suspicious areas on the first three steps, the cotton tips turning a dirty deep red.

"The smudges get fainter as we go up." I shine a flashlight on the steps as we follow them. "Now I'm not seeing anything at all."

"The implication's not good," Benton says. "Did Zain kill her, then head back up to his room, tracking blood on the steps?"

"Then what? He came back downstairs and cut himself?"

"I hope for his sake whatever you just swabbed doesn't turn out to be Georgine's blood," Benton replies.

Zain's bedroom has a brick fireplace and big windows. I remember when Benton and I walked through the house five years ago, we were told the third floor was where the chaplains lived. The drapes are drawn, and I nudge aside a floral-printed swag.

Beyond the backyard and wooden dock, sunlight shines on a wide stretch of ruffled water that's brownish from sediment stirred during the storm. The fog has burned off, and I can see the hazy shore of Washington, D.C., on the other side of the river.

Walking away from the window, I begin looking around. An array of computer screens, several keyboards are on the desk as Marino described. There are wireless controllers and virtual reality gloves associated with drones and gaming. And a set of keys, and a White House ID badge on a lanyard.

On a table is some type of battery charging tray that's plugged into the wall. Also, technical tomes and different drafts of a dissertation.

"*How Robots Learn: A Hitchhiker's Guide to the Universe of AI*," I read the title aloud.

The twin bed is unmade, the covers pulled back. If Zain was wearing pajamas last night, I don't see them. On a chair is a tidy stack of jeans, T-shirts, underwear, and I'm betting it was Georgine who laundered and folded them. A large suitcase against a wall feels empty when I lift it by the handle. I notice food crumbs on the floor.

"The bathroom he used is at the end of the hall next to the linen closet," Benton says as I'm wondering about it.

"Give me two minutes." I walk that way, my eyes on the floor every step.

I'm looking for blood but don't see any, just a lot of dust, a few dead bugs. The oak floor doesn't appear to have been mopped in recent memory. Wooden bookshelves built into the wall are empty and look very old.

The bathroom is similar to the one on the first floor, white subway tile, a pedestal sink with a toothbrush and tube of tooth-paste on it. The tub and shower are combined, a plastic curtain attached to a rod.

A wicker hamper is full of dirty clothing. I dig through it with gloved hands, looking for anything bloody. Socks and more under-wear. A sweatsuit. Towels. The wastepaper basket is filled with tis-sues, water bottles, a few beer cans.

I dig out a card that's been torn in half. It depicts Santa in denim overalls, smoking a corncob pipe, a jug of moonshine next to him.

*Zain, don't forget to have some good ole Southern fun this Xmas! Sorry we won't be together. But always thinking of you. Lots of love, Mom.*

I drop the torn card back into the trash while wondering about Zain's reaction to his mother's note. It's not exactly warm. By all indications, the two of them don't have a close relationship, and I wonder if she sent a gift to him. But I've seen no presents in the house, not even under the pathetic tree downstairs.

I change my gloves again before opening the medicine cabinet. Nothing inside except a bottle of Tylenol, a Speed Stick deodorant, dental floss. In the cabinet under the sink are rolls of toilet paper, bars of soap and blister packs of antihistamines as if Zain might suf-fer from allergies.

I notice several boxes of double-edged razor blades that have no shaving handle to go with them. On a glass shelf is an electric razor on a charger, and it appears Zain was using it.

I return to the bedroom, and Benton is standing by the closet waiting for me. I tell him about the Christmas card from Zain's mother that he or someone ripped in half and dropped in the trash.

"Yes, and no surprise," Benton says.

"Then you saw it," I reply.

"I didn't think it needs preserving as evidence. But that will be up to the crime scene unit. You ready to meet Robbie?"

Benton opens the closet door, a lot of suits and other clothing hanging from the rod. On the floor is a four-legged robot the size of a standard poodle. Silvery gray with large dark glassy eyes and a gripper mouth, he has payload ports and mounting rails on his sleek back.

"When I've been around Zain and Robbie, I've watched the demos multiple times, which is a good thing," Benton explains. "I have some idea how the thing works, which is a bit quirky. Turning him on, for example, requires a poke in the ass. Which I found a bit embarrassing when the audience was the president or some visiting dignitary."

The power button on the tailless rump could be confused for an indelicate part of Robbie's anatomy. I can see why Marino couldn't find it. Benton pushes the round brown button, and a green light begins to flash on top of the head. The robotic dog suddenly animates, looking directly at him.

"Good morning, Benton." The mouth moves, the head turning and tilting. "Merry Christmas."

His voice could be male or female, with a Virginia accent. As I recall the video I watched of Zain on the sidewalk, I realize that Robbie sounds a lot like him.

"And to you, Robbie," Benton says as if they're old friends.

"I see you have company, Benton. Hello, Kay Scarpetta." Robbie swivels his head around, looking at me. "It's usually not a good thing when you show up. It means someone is dead."

"I don't believe we've met...?" I puzzle.

"We haven't," he says in a stilted friendly voice. "I have facial recognition capabilities. Now that the Wi-Fi connection has been restored, I can access information. But my battery charge is low."

"Robbie? Would you like to come out of the closet?" Benton asks.

"That's a very personal question, Benton," he answers slyly with what might be a grin.

"Why don't you come on out. We'd like to ask you a few questions."

"Okie doke, Benton."

The robot steps out of the closet on spiderlike mechanical legs, his gait jerky and stiff, the feet thumping the wooden flooring. He stops in front of us.

"You and I have been around each other many times, haven't we, Robbie?" Benton says.

"Yes, Benton. Most recently was the day before Thanksgiving when we were in the White House Oval Office. Zain was giving a demonstration to the director of Homeland Security."

"Robbie's one of the reasons robotic dogs are now utilized for security patrols at the White House and other strategic locations," Benton explains to me. "And of course, the military is using them."

"That's correct." Robbie nods.

He goes on to recite every date when he and Benton have been in the same place at the same time. The White House. The vice president's mansion. Camp David. Also, Calvin Willard's mansion on Embassy Row. And Mar-a-Lago.

"Robbie's basically an AI chatbot on four legs," Benton explains.

"That would be a chat-*bark*." The robot's gripper mouth opens into an almost grin again.

"Does Lucy know about this?" I ask Benton.

"She and Tron will be hauling Robbie out of here shortly."

"I don't need to be hauled," Robbie protests. "I'm perfectly capable of walking. However, my battery is down to eight percent."

"Lucy and Tron landed the helicopter at Quantico and are on their way back here," Benton tells me.

"I'm unfamiliar with Lucy and Tron." Robbie sounds perplexed and a touch worried. "I don't go places without Zain."

"Zain is in the hospital," Benton says, and Robbie tilts his head.

"Why is he in the hospital?" he asks.

"He was hurt last night," Benton explains. "And you were here when it happened."

"You were offline when the Wi-Fi went down," I say to the robot. "I assume you were in sleep mode?"

The robot turns his head back to me, his camera eyes staring.

"As long as I have a battery charge, I'm always awake, Doctor Scarpetta. Even when I don't appear to be," Robbie says. "I suffered a loss of signal at two-fifty a.m. It was restored three hours and forty-two minutes later at six-thirty-two a.m."

"While the Wi-Fi was down, were you aware of anything happening inside the house?" I wonder.

"Yes, I was aware. My sensors had gone into autonomous mode."

"Did you hear someone breaking in? Or maybe someone screaming?" Benton asks.

"I heard screaming at three-eleven a.m. The vocalization was consistent with the owner of the house, Georgine Duvall. She was screaming 'STOP! STOP!' "

"You've been around her a lot," Benton says.

"Yes," Robbie answers, giving us the dates.

I'm baffled to learn that Zain has stayed here every summer and major holiday since Georgine bought the house five years ago.

"What happened when you heard the screaming earlier this morning?" Benton says to Robbie.

"I went into the closet."

"Why?"

"It's my doghouse, where Zain keeps me."

"When you're in your doghouse, are you plugged into a charger?" Benton is looking inside the closet for one. "Because I'm not seeing anything like that," he adds.

"My batteries are charged on the table by the desk," Robbie says, his green light flashing yellow.

"When the Wi-Fi was disabled, you went into autonomous mode," Benton says. "At some point did you leave the closet and perhaps go downstairs...?"

"Yes."

"Why?"

"I heard Zain and a commotion." Robbie's speech is getting sluggish. "It's time to change my battery."

He sits.

"What kind of a commotion?" Benton keeps going.

"I'm very sorry, shutting down." Robbie hangs his head, his eyes going dark.

"Dammit," Benton says.

The robot doesn't move, the light on his rump blinking red now. I crouch in front of him, interested in a small dark smear on one of his silvery back paws.

"If this is what I think it is..." I say to Benton. "Can we turn him on his side?"

––––––

The robot is heavy, and there are more dark stains on his paws' gray rubbery treads. Opening my scene case, I find swabs, the bottle of distilled water. The cotton tips turn dark red again.

290

Taking samples from each foot, I then scan the robot with a UV light, and nothing fluoresces, none of the mysterious residue on him. I spray the bottoms of his paws with Bluestar, and they light up like St. Elmo's fire, the presumptive blood test positive.

"It would appear Robbie was downstairs and stepped in blood," I summarize. "He tracked it back up the steps."

"Hopefully, whatever he did and witnessed was caught on his cameras," Benton says.

"It might explain why the killer didn't take the time to make sure Zain was dead." I close the scene case, snapping down the heavy plastic latches.

"How do you figure?" Benton asks as we leave the bedroom.

"If the killer heard a robotic dog coming down the stairs or, worse, saw such a thing," I explain, "he would have been startled if not frightened. I imagine he would have gotten out of here as fast as possible."

"Suggesting the Slasher didn't know a second person and a robot were in the house," Benton concludes. "Either that or the Slasher is Zain Willard."

# CHAPTER 32

ootsteps sound as Marino and Clark Givens carry the stretcher and body bags into the bedroom. Benton and I are coming down the stairs, the hard cases of laser mapping equipment crowding the hallway.

"Thanks, Clark," I tell the DNA scientist. "I'm so sorry about the inconvenience. Please apologize to your family. I hate to drag you out on Christmas morning."

"Nobody wanted to be here." Shrouded in white Tyvek, he stares through the bedroom doorway. "Most of all her."

I can tell the fumes from the bleach bother him. He has his face shield down and is fogging up the clear plastic, his eyes irritated. I give him the highlights of what we've been finding, and he nods, asking questions as we rough out a plan for the laser mapping.

I remove evidence from my scene case, receipting the swabs to Clark so he can carry them to the labs when he returns to my headquarters. Benton and I take off our PPE, and it goes into the red biohazard bag that by now is almost full.

We walk back through the house, stepping around blood and evidence markers.

"Lucy and Tron will be here any minute," Benton says. "They report that the media is out in droves. All the major networks."

"It would seem that Zain and his robot are very close," I observe.

"I could tell that when I've been around them. Zain treats him like a pet."

"And I thought talking to an avatar was mind-scrambling enough," I reply. "Until it started feeling normal. Now, a robot dog that I had a bizarre impulse to pet. I'm beginning to question the meaning of consciousness. And when we feel love for AI, does it feel love back? Or is it just the programming?"

"We're all programmed, Kay."

Light streams through the front door's borehole as we reach the foyer, putting on our coats, collecting our belongings. It's getting close to ten o'clock when we step out on the porch to the sound of dripping water. The sun is bright, the temperature fifty-four degrees Fahrenheit on the brass outdoor thermometer attached to a portico column.

The FBI crime scene unit has reconvened on the driveway, getting ready to invade the house at long last. Fabian is inside our black transport van. He rolls down his window, wishing us a happy holiday.

"I caught Pinky!" he calls out proudly, happily. "Boursin on a Ritz did the trick. I have a little mouse house for him in the on-call room. He's safe and sound."

"I'm glad something is," I answer as Lucy and Tron pull up in a black Tahoe.

They climb out in tactical clothes and flak jackets.

"Did someone call for the dog catcher?" Lucy says drolly, her eyes masked by dark glasses.

She's lean and fit, her keen face serious, her short rose-gold-streaked hair shining. If she stayed up all night at the FBI Academy, I can't tell. She looks wide awake, energized.

"Robbie's battery is dead," Benton lets them know.

"Sounds about the way I feel," Tron answers, dark and exotically attractive with a smile that's hard to resist.

"But before he conked out on us, he said he went into autonomous mode when the Wi-Fi was signal jammed," I tell them.

I explain there appears to be blood on the bottom of the robot's feet, and it could be Zain Willard's. But it might be Georgine Duvall's. After the attack Robbie must have come downstairs.

"In autonomous mode he would be disconnected from the internet and completely reliant on his sensors," Lucy informs us. "He would respond to noises and images, also motion, light, possibly odors."

"Odors such as bleach?" I ask.

"Maybe even blood," Tron volunteers. "Depending on what he's programmed to detect and respond to."

"Screaming, arguing, running, the sound of Zain's voice, it could be anything he alerted on," Lucy adds. "But I can't say for sure until we take a look at how he's designed and what the parameters are."

"We'll be extremely interested in anything the cameras may have recorded," Benton says. "If Robbie went downstairs while the killer was still inside the house, we might have just won the lottery."

"I would imagine he has I.R. capabilities," Lucy adds. "Meaning he can navigate and film in complete darkness."

"If only we could be so lucky." I open my briefcase, pulling out the foil-wrapped device Benton removed from the undercarriage of our car.

I give it to Lucy as we tell them we're off to the hospital on

Seminary Road. Benton intends to question Zain Willard while I look at his injuries. Lucy stares at the former chapel, sunlight shining on the stucco, illuminating the stained-glass windows on either side of the door that's now missing its brass handles and lock.

The soggy yard has small ponds of standing water, the brown grass patched with snow in the shade of old trees and boxwoods. I wonder what she's thinking about Georgine Duvall, but now's not the time to ask her.

"How's your mom?" I ask instead.

"Last I talked to her, she was getting ready to head to our place."

"Our place?" Then I remember.

My sister and Marino were supposed to housesit while Benton and I were overseas.

"Yep," Lucy says.

"But Benton and I canceled our trip." I'm dismayed by the thought of Dorothy and Marino under the same roof with us while they're at war.

"Mom knows you're not going," Lucy says. "She has an idea what we're doing, obviously. This case is all over the news. She's hoping we'll be home in time to have a late Christmas dinner together. She said to tell you she's cooking."

"Cooking what?" I worry.

Dorothy isn't known for her culinary talents.

"She said it would be a surprise." Lucy looks at me, shrugging. "But I know she's baking cookies, and I'm guessing she'll whip up tacos. That's usually what she makes when she's surprising us."

"Oh God. Tacos on Christmas," I reply.

Benton and I climb into the Tesla, and the road running through the hospital grounds is wet. The traffic has gone from a standstill to nonexistent when we drive through the entrance gate, the same FBI police officers there as before. They move sawhorses to let us through.

TV satellite trucks are parked on the roadside, news correspondents and their crews busy filming. I recognize David Muir and Anderson Cooper. Helicopters hover over Mercy Island, a lot of people on the roads now. It takes the better part of a half hour to retrace our steps through Old Town, the restaurants and bars bustling.

We pick up King Street to West Braddock, driving close to my office, and I send a text to Shannon asking for an update. Doug Schlaefer is up to his elbows in Georgine Duvall's autopsy. Once he's dictated his provisional report, my secretary will transcribe it. She complains that TV crews are hanging around my headquarters, filming bodies being picked up and delivered.

"More of the same," I tell Benton the latest. "Apparently one of the local networks is buzzing a drone around."

Past Episcopal High School's tennis courts and playing fields are the Virginia Theological Seminary and a synagogue. Then wooded neighborhoods with homes decorated for the holidays as we reach the sprawling modern brick hospital. It's doing a brisk business on Christmas, and I'm not surprised.

Some of their patients who didn't fare well have ended up at my office this morning. According to Shannon, we have six cases so far, half of them motor vehicle fatalities involving alcohol. A woman who shot herself in the head died in surgery here and is inside my morgue cooler.

The hospital grounds are messy with slush, the parking lots

packed. It takes a few minutes to find a visitor's spot, and Benton texts Secret Service agents inside that we're on location. We push through the glass front door, the lobby crowded with unhappy people waiting in plastic chairs, some of them injured, others clearly unwell.

Piped-in Christmas music seems incongruous as we walk through. Benton stops at the information desk, the woman working it older with wispy white hair. She's wearing a green Christmas sweater with Mrs. Claus on it.

"Here to see Zain Willard." Benton flashes his badge.

"Let me check." Her face is uneasy as she reaches for the phone.

"You don't need to check," he says. "I know what room he's in."

"But I've been instructed..." she starts to fret.

"Several of our agents should already be there waiting for us," Benton explains. "And I have the chief medical examiner with me."

"Has someone died?" She looks at me in alarm.

"If you could just tell us how to get to his room?" Benton keeps pushing.

She tells us that Zain Willard is on the second floor. He's on the orthopedic wing because there were no other private rooms available. As we walk off, she's talking on the phone, alerting someone that we're coming.

"We're going to need privacy," I tell Benton. "I don't want to examine him in front of an audience."

We've stopped by a stainless-steel elevator door, waiting for it to open.

"I don't want doctors, residents, nurses or whatever watching as I scan him with a UV light," I continue to explain.

The elevator door slowly opens, a medical aide pushing out a man in a wheelchair, both legs in casts. His face is bruised and he's wearing a neck brace. We step inside and a moment later are getting out on the second floor.

The ward where Zain Willard has a private room is locked. A Secret Service agent is standing guard, a young blond woman in a dark suit.

"How's it going?" Benton asks her.

"Nothing eventful," she answers.

"Has he had visitors?"

"Calvin Willard's in there with him," she says to my dismay.

"How long has the senator been here?" Benton asks.

"Several hours." She pushes an intercom button on the wall.

"May I help you?" The female voice over the speaker sounds familiar.

"You can open up," the blond agent answers, and the electronic lock clicks free.

———

Benton pushes through the door, and ahead is the nurses' station behind windows. The U-shaped desk is decorated with swags of artificial greenery, a small lighted tree in a corner. I'm startled to hear someone call out my name.

"Don't mean to intrude." Reba O'Leary appears from behind glass, and it was her voice I heard over the intercom.

She's in pink scrubs, and I'm reminded that she's working four a.m. to four p.m. today. I introduce her to Benton, asking why she's on this floor.

"They're shorthanded, a lot of car crashes during the night, a lot of broken bones," she says, her eyes bloodshot and lusterless. "I go where needed. But I started out my shift in the E.R."

"Did you see Zain Willard when he was brought in?" I ask.

"I'd just gotten here, and he was almost hysterical. Practically out of his mind." She looks unnerved. "He kept talking about a ghost attacking him with a knife."

"It wasn't a ghost," Benton says.

"The Phantom Slasher again. I know what's all over the news." She keeps glancing around as if afraid someone is listening. "I can tell you Zain Willard wasn't faking anything. He was terrified. He kept worrying that the ghost was going to find him and finish him off."

"Did he offer details about what happened to him?" I ask her.

"He said one thing that you should know." She looks nervous, and I can tell she's mindful of the cameras in the ceiling. "When I heard you were coming up here, I wanted to be sure I told you."

"How did you hear we were coming up here?" Benton asks.

"One of the Secret Service agents was telling the senator that the medical examiner was on the way," she says. "I happened to be taking Zain's vitals. And I was waiting for you."

"What is it I should know?" I ask her.

"He said that when his neck was cut, he had to dig his necklace out of it."

"If true, that's very important," I reply.

"I guess the blade hit the chain, embedding it into the incision," Reba explains. "Maybe accounting for why the cuts to his neck aren't all that deep."

"The necklace probably saved his life," I reply. "When it's examined in the labs, we'll know if that's what happened."

"It doesn't sound like the sort of thing someone would make up," Benton adds. "And even if the cuts to his neck were self-inflicted, he might have forgotten he had the necklace on."

"I can see that happening," I reply. "Either way, he's lucky to be alive."

"Thanks again for coming to my house last night." Reba looks at me. "It was very kind."

"How are your sons this morning?" I ask.

"My sister's with them." Reba's face turns red as she blinks back tears. "Well, I don't want to hold the two of you up. And I'd better get back to what I'm doing."

# CHAPTER 33

W e walk through the orthopedic unit and I'm aware of rooms occupied by patients, most of them with visitors. I hear people talking, televisions playing. Someone is sobbing, and I catch glimpses of limbs in bandages and casts. A young woman wears a metal halo brace for a fractured neck.

Zain's room is in a corner, two Secret Service agents sitting outside the closed door.

"Is he still in there?" Benton asks right off about Calvin Willard.

"Sure is," one of the agents says.

"Any problems?" Benton tucks his phone in a pocket.

"He's not the easiest to deal with." The other agent lowers his voice. "He smiles. But he's not smiling inside, if you know what I mean."

"I've been around him before," Benton replies.

He opens the door, and we enter a room with a view of parking lots. The foothills of the Blue Ridge Mountains are a bruised rolling haze on the faraway horizon, the sun bright, the room painted in light. For hospital accommodations, Zain's are luxurious. A bathroom, a couch.

Benton and I take off our coats, placing them on a chair with my briefcase and medical kit. I introduce us and the senator doesn't react. His back is to us as he stands by the window looking at his phone. He doesn't want us here. I feel it like radiation.

"Good morning," I say to Zain.

"I've had better."

He's sitting up in bed tethered to IV lines, his neck and left arm thick with gauze. I don't know how I'm going to examine him. I'm not sure what I'll be able to see.

"We've met before," Zain says to Benton. "But not you." He looks at me as if pleased that I'm here. "Benton's probably told you that he and I are acquainted."

I've noticed right away that Zain has dried blood in his hair. I'm careful not to stare.

"Yes, we've been around each other many times over the years," Benton says, and Calvin Willard turns away from the window, staring at us. "At the White House and other places. I'm very sorry about all this, Zain."

"You need to make this quick. As you can see, Zain's been through a lot and is exhausted." The senator says this to me, his strong-featured face ashen.

Tall and lanky, he's in a dark blue warm-up suit and snow boots. A shock of slate-gray hair is combed over to hide his baldness.

"We're going to need a few minutes alone with your nephew, Senator," Benton says.

"Not happening in a million years. Our attorney is on his way here, and you need to wait outside until he arrives."

"It's okay." Zain's blue eyes are laser focused on me, and he sounds sedated. "I've got nothing to hide. I'm a victim. I don't need a lawyer. What's most important is catching the monster who did this before he does it again to someone else."

"Yes, you do need a lawyer, son." His uncle's demeanor softens when he looks at him. "I don't think you understand what can happen. You've never understood it."

"I know exactly what can happen, and I've got nothing to hide. Because I didn't do anything wrong," Zain insists. "We need to do everything we can to help catch the Slasher. I don't want him and his ghost coming back to finish me off."

"We won't let that happen," his uncle promises. "Nobody's going to hurt you again. I'll make sure of it."

A spike of anger, and Calvin Willard fixes his attention on Benton as if I'm not in the room.

"The house on Mercy Island has an alarm system," the senator says. "How the hell could she let something like this happen? How did someone just walk into the house? How did she let someone follow her there?"

He's talking about Georgine Duvall and doesn't seem the least bit sorry that she's dead. I sense his hostility and resentment as Benton explains that the Phantom Slasher uses a signal jammer when he shows up to murder.

"It wasn't her fault or Zain's that the alarm system wasn't working," Benton says.

"I always worried about her judgment. It wasn't that long ago I stopped by, and the front door was unlocked, the alarm off." The senator continues blaming the victim.

"If you'd give us a few minutes?" Benton says. "Maybe wait outside the room?"

"I'm not going anywhere," the senator replies, sitting down on the brown Naugahyde sofa.

I pull on a pair of gloves as the door opens, and a young man in

303

surgical scrubs walks in with paperwork. He introduces himself as Zain's surgeon, and he looks sleep-deprived and harried.

"Which one of you is Doctor Scarpetta?" he asks.

"That would be me." I assume he might have concluded that since I have a medical kit and am wearing gloves.

"The notes you've requested." He hands me a file folder without much in it. "But I can give you the upshot on his injuries."

The surgeon explains that Zain suffered two cutting wounds to the front of his throat, one approximately two inches long, the other closer to three, requiring a total of twenty-four stitches. He was extremely lucky that the wounds are "relatively superficial," missing any major blood vessels in the neck.

I think of the silver necklace Reba O'Leary mentioned. It would explain the two incisions. They're from a single stroke interrupted by the knife hitting the chain Zain was wearing.

"Three millimeters more, and the blade would have cut his carotid," the surgeon explains.

"I understand he needed a transfusion?" I ask.

"He bled most heavily from the cut to his left arm," the surgeon tells me. "His radial artery was severed, and that's the reason for most of the blood loss. Not his neck, although it would have bled heavily."

He explains that he repaired the artery with an anastomosis, suturing the vessel end to end like a straw that's been cut in half. It doesn't appear that Zain suffered any nerve damage. He's expected to have a complete recovery. The biggest risk now is infection, and he's on an antibiotic prophylactically.

"He'll have a few scars he can brag about." The surgeon gives his patient a weary smile. "You've got my surgical notes." He says this to me. "Let me know if you have questions."

Then he's gone, the door shutting.

"What is it exactly that you plan to do?" Calvin Willard stares at me with distrusting gray eyes.

"We have questions," Benton answers before I have the chance. "And Doctor Scarpetta wants to take a look at him."

"He's bandaged like a mummy. What do you expect to see?" the senator says to me.

"It's okay, Uncle Calvin." Zain seems unfazed, inching his way up straighter in bed.

He seems to be enjoying the attention.

"I want to check him for any other injuries—" I start to explain.

"You don't have to tell them a damn thing, son," his uncle interrupts. "I can order them to leave right now."

"That just makes me look guilty," Zain counters. "I didn't do anything. Why would I do something like that to Georgine? Why would I hurt her?"

His eyes well with tears, his voice trembling.

"She was like a mother to me. Why would I do this to myself?" He holds up his bandaged arm and touches his swathed neck.

"When did Georgine go to bed last night?" Benton asks him.

"I think it was getting close to midnight when she turned in."

"And you, Zain?"

"Around the same time."

"Were the two of you getting along before turning in for the night?" Benton asks.

"We always got along. And if you're implying that I might have reason to hurt her?"

"I'm not implying anything," Benton says. "But would you have had a reason, Zain?"

"Why would I?" He stares at Benton.

"Okay, this needs to stop," Calvin says, getting up from the sofa, staring at us in disgust as he moves in front of the window.

"The more you answer my questions with questions, the less you're helping yourself," Benton tells his nephew.

"That's enough!" the senator warns while typing on his phone.

"It's okay, Uncle Calvin. They need my help."

"I'd like to take a look at you, Zain." I open the file folder the surgeon gave me, glancing at the diagrams of his injuries before they were treated.

Zain throws back the sheet with his good arm, his slender legs scattered with blond hair that's almost transparent. Self-conscious, he tugs down the johnnie. But not before I see the pale linear scars on his upper thighs.

"Tell us what happened." Benton pulls a chair close to the bed, sitting down.

I'm noticing more of the fine pale scars on the underside of Zain's right arm. He has them on his ankles, and Benton sees them, too. I think of the double-sided razor blades in the cabinet of the third-floor bathroom inside Georgine's house.

"I was home all night," Zain says.

"Alone?" Benton asks.

"Georgine had gone to a party at the hospital and was home around nine."

"Do you mind opening your johnnie?" I say to him. "Just to the waist."

He does, and the pale linear scars are on his abdomen. There are numerous healed burns near his navel.

"How did she get home?" Benton asks. "The weather was pretty bad by then."

"Graden Crowley walked her home."

"In the snow?" Benton frowns. "The house is a pretty good hike from the hospital in weather like that."

"They weren't outside," Zain says. "They used the tunnel."

He verifies that Georgine routinely left the house through the basement door, taking the tunnel back and forth to the hospital. She used the tunnel to work out in the fitness center. Zain explains that it has an indoor lap pool, and she liked to swim.

"Did it every day," he says as I continue checking him. "It's one of the things she likes best about staying on Mercy Island. She didn't have to drive anywhere to work out in the gym."

"What about you?" Benton asks. "Did you take the tunnel to get around?"

"Never." He shakes his head as I check a bruise on his upper left forehead. "I find the tunnel creepy. And I'm not into the gym. Too boring."

"I hear you have a vintage Cougar?" Benton says. "I don't believe I've ever seen it parked at the White House."

"I'm careful where I drive it." Zain stares out the window.

"It was his father's car." The senator speaks up. "He died when Zain was fourteen."

"I'm very sorry to hear that," I reply.

"I drive Georgine's car mostly," Zain explains without looking at Benton or me. "Much safer. Airbags and all that. The Cougar is meant to be for fun. Most of the time it's in the garage."

"After his father passed away, I had the car refurbished and gave it to Zain as a high school graduation present," his uncle says with a forced smile. "Not really for transportation as much as something he'll always want to keep."

"Surveillance cameras have recorded the electric Cadillac Lyriq parked at West Exec multiple times. I know because I asked," Benton tells Zain.

"She's generous about letting me use her car. She was." His lower lip trembles. "And when she was on the island, she didn't need to drive. I would run most of the errands. Like going to the store. But we use DoorDash a lot, ordering in."

"When you stayed with her did you ever have the cameras on inside the house?" Benton asks, and Zain shakes his head.

"She didn't want them on. Neither of us did, and she felt spied on enough," he tells Benton.

"She told you she felt spied on?"

"She worried someone was watching her. She told me to keep an eye out for suspicious people or cars." Zain looks at his uncle.

"How long had this been going on?" Benton asks.

"The past few weeks. She said she started hearing weird noises outside her house in Yorktown. Like someone was on her property."

"How come I didn't know about this, son?" the senator asks him.

"If I told you, I knew what would happen," Zain says boldly. "You would have freaked out."

"Damn right I would have," Calvin Willard retorts. "If I knew someone was stalking her, I sure as hell wouldn't have wanted you staying with her, for God's sake!"

"Did she notify the police that she felt someone was stalking her?" Benton asks Zain.

"I don't think so. She's not a fan of the police," he says, and that sounds like Georgine.

"She moved into her house on Mercy Island two weeks ago," Benton goes on. "Did she continue feeling spied on?"

"She was paranoid," Zain answers. "It was stressing her out really bad. Causing her eczema to flare up."

"Did she have any theories about who might be watching her?" the senator asks him.

"No."

"The Slasher's murders are all over the news," Benton says. "Obviously, she was aware of them."

"Of course she was aware of what's on the news," Zain replies with an air of impatience.

"Seems odd she was worried about someone watching her and yet she didn't bother with the cameras," Benton adds. "I noticed two while I was there."

"You were at the house?" Zain asks.

"Doctor Scarpetta and I just came from there," Benton says. "One camera is on the front porch. And the other on top of the bookcase in the living room would catch anybody entering through the front door."

"That's crazy," the senator says to Zain. "Why the hell were they off?"

"It's not crazy and you know exactly why." Zain stares at him.

His uncle doesn't say anything.

"People watch you. People spy," Zain goes on. "Georgine figured it had to do with that. She figured she was being spied on because of you and your presidential ambitions, Uncle Calvin."

"That's ridiculous," the senator says with a stiff smile.

"It's not," Zain retorts. "You never wanted the cameras on when you came over."

"Well, you can't blame me for that." Calvin Willard smiles again, and he's anything but happy. "I wasn't spying on Georgine. It wasn't me, Zain. Obviously, it was the serial killer."

"You have a serious injury to your left arm." I step closer to the bed. "What do you remember about being cut?"

"I didn't really feel it at first."

"Your throat was cut and then your left arm?" I ask. "Or the other way around."

"I felt something hit my throat and must have raised my arm to protect myself, and he cut it. Then I lost my balance, falling. After that I was too afraid to move. I played dead."

"Do you mind if I take a few photographs?" I dig my phone out of a pocket.

He shrugs, and I gently move his teal-tinted blond hair away from his bruised forehead. I take a picture with my phone. The contusion is dark bluish red and recent. He has swelling, what's commonly referred to as a goose egg.

"Looks like you got a pretty good whack to your head," I say to him. "Do you know how that happened? Tell me what you remember. Start at the beginning."

"I woke up hearing screaming," he says. "I usually sleep in my boxer briefs, and I threw on jeans, a sweatshirt. It was dark. I tried to turn on a light, but nothing worked. I realized there'd been a power outage and I assumed it was because of the storm."

"How long before you went downstairs?" Benton asks him.

"I'm not sure." Zain stares down at his hands on top of the covers.

"Maybe you were afraid," Benton continues from his chair by the bed.

"That would be understandable." It's Calvin Willard saying this. "Zain doesn't have a gun or any means of self-defense."

"I don't like guns." Zain says this to me.

"Well, maybe you will after this," his uncle foreshadows.

"I asked Robbie what was going on," Zain tells Benton and me. "But he was offline. He didn't know. And I stayed with him for a few minutes."

"Stayed with him where?" Benton asks.

"In the closet." Zain looks ashamed. "I could hear someone downstairs, and then it got quiet. And my first thought was to check on her."

He explains that when he crept down the steps it was pitch-dark, and he smelled what he thought was chlorine.

"Which was weird." He looks up. "When she comes home from swimming, she reeks of it. I didn't understand why I was smelling it, and when I reached the bottom step, something hit me in my throat. I remember losing my balance, and I fell."

"Did you land on the carpet or the wooden flooring?" I ask.

"The carpet." His eyes glint with fear. "I remember hearing him breathing hard, bending close to me. I didn't move. He kicked me, almost tripping over me, and I didn't move. Like I said, I played dead. I could hear him taking off something he had on. Maybe something he'd covered his clothing with, and then he was gone."

"Where did he kick you?" I ask.

"In the head." He doesn't blink.

"Did this person say anything?" Benton asks him. "What do you remember about him?"

"No, he didn't say a word."

"How do you know it was a *he*?" his uncle wants to know.

"I don't. I just assume it," Zain answers. "I wouldn't think a woman would do something... something so cruel. So physically violent."

"Did you look at her?" Benton asks.

"Of course, I looked at her in case she was still alive, and I could help! I heard the intruder running down the hallway, and when I didn't hear anything else, I waited for a while, making sure he didn't come back. Then I got up from the floor," Zain says.

"Did you realize your throat was cut?" I ask.

"I knew I was badly hurt. My neck was stinging and wet. When I touched it, I could feel my chain was in the cut, and I had to pull it out. I guess the knife hit it." His voice trembles. "I remember I was shaking all over, bleeding everywhere, and I had my phone with me. I turned on the flashlight and shone it through her doorway. I could see she was dead."

He's getting upset, lifting his uninjured arm, wiping tears with the back of his hand.

"And then I saw the ghost!" He's getting all worked up again. "The figure in black with red eyes and a knife!"

"Saw it where?" Benton is taking notes.

"In her bedroom! It laughed at me and went through the window," he describes, and I wonder if Georgine saw the same thing.

I can't imagine her panic had she been awakened by a hand clamping over her mouth. She would have seen the phantom hologram floating by her bed, hissing while waving his knife.

"When I ran out of the house," Zain goes on, his eyes wide, "the ghost followed me on the sidewalk, laughing . . . !"

"I think that's enough." Calvin Willard steps away from the window, and I can tell he's unnerved by what he's hearing.

"What about Robbie?" Benton brings up the robot. "What was he doing during all this?"

"I don't know." Zain looks alarmed. "Why? Has he been stolen? No! That's what I was afraid of! Was he what the intruder was after? Did he take Robbie? He's very expensive, but more than that, he's part of my dissertation, my graduate school project...Oh God, oh God."

"Robbie wasn't stolen," Benton says, and Zain seems enormously relieved.

"I said that was enough." His uncle is waiting by the door to see us out.

But I'm not going anywhere just yet.

# CHAPTER 34

Inside my medical kit is the small UV light that looks like a flashlight, and I turn it on, the lens glowing purple. Before the senator can protest further, I've put on tinted goggles, painting the light over Zain's hair.

"What the hell do you think you're doing?" Calvin Willard exclaims, furious. "I told you that's enough! I need you to leave now."

"His hair hasn't been washed, and it might be the one place we find trace evidence," I explain. "He says the killer kicked him in the head..."

I don't let on how startled I am to see a scattering of a powdery substance fluorescing fiery red. I'm not going to tell Zain or his uncle what I'm finding and what it might mean.

"It could be that something was transferred from the killer to Zain." I return to my medical kit for wooden Q-tips and distilled water.

I begin swabbing dried bloody areas of his hair where the residue fluoresced. Calvin Willard's face is dark with anger.

"Get out!" he demands.

"This is important," Benton says. "Chances are it was the Slasher who got inside the house and killed Georgine Duvall, almost killed your nephew. I'm sure you'd want to help us stop whoever it is. I'm sure you'd want the public knowing how determined you are to find the killer."

"What if he comes back to finish me off!" Zain exclaims again, his eyes wild.

"We aren't going to let that happen," his uncle promises.

"Did you ever use the spare key hidden outside the house?" Benton asks Zain. "A key to the front door that was hidden in a fake rock?"

"It's easy to lock yourself out," he says. "I do it a lot. So does Georgine. She did, I mean."

"Jesus," Calvin Willard mutters. "Could she be any more obtuse and careless? In some ways I'm not at all surprised this happened. I shouldn't have been so trusting. I should have seen it coming considering her patients."

"Do you have reason to think a patient of hers did this?" Benton asks him.

"It's certainly my first suspicion. I'm betting that will turn out to be the case."

"When's the last time Georgine locked herself out?" Benton directs this at Zain.

"She did it several times in the last two weeks," he says. "She'd used the tunnel to return from the hospital or gym and realized she didn't have her keys."

"Had she always been like this?" Benton queries.

"It was much worse lately," Zain explains as I think of the bottle of clonazepam in her bathroom.

It appears she was taking it possibly for anxiety, and the medication can interfere with short-term memory.

"She'd come back home through the tunnel and find herself

locked out of the basement," Zain explains. "She'd have to go outside and use the spare key to open the front door."

"Did she return that key to its hiding place?" Benton asks him.

"I assume so..."

"When's the last time you used that key, Zain?"

"Out, now!" His uncle opens the door as I seal the swabs inside a paper envelope, tucking it into the medical kit.

Benton has his badge wallet out. He finds a business card, placing it on the plastic swivel tray next to the bed.

"If there's anything else you remember or want to tell me?" he says to Zain. "Don't hesitate to call at any hour."

We leave the room, and Calvin Willard follows. He shuts the door so Zain can't hear us. He tells the two agents standing guard that he needs a little privacy.

"Give us a minute," the senator orders, and they look at Benton.

"It's okay," he says, and they walk off toward the nurses' station.

"You go after him for no good reason, and I can promise there will be consequences," the senator says in a tone that's deadly.

"I'd like to think we don't go after anyone when there's no good reason," Benton answers. "But I'm sure you understand that as unfortunate as all this is, we have to do our jobs. We have to investigate and get to the bottom of what happened. It seems to me you should want that."

"What did you find in his hair?" he demands, looking me in the eye. "Why did you swab the blood in his hair?"

"His story is that the killer kicked him in the head, practically tripping over him." I'm not going to tell him the real reason. "It's important to determine whether any trace evidence was transferred to Zain."

"I don't know what that is." The senator glares at me. "What the hell is trace evidence?"

"Microscopic material that people might have on them without knowing," I explain. "It could be anything."

"I know you must be quite familiar with Zain's robotic dog, Robbie," Benton then says. "You and I have both seen the demos. And it goes without saying that you were around Robbie often."

"What about him?" Calvin gets an uneasy look in his eyes.

It occurs to him why Benton is asking. The senator knows the cameras were always off inside the house at 13 Shore Lane. But Robbie's are on as long as his battery is charged.

"Dammit," Calvin Willard says under his breath.

"We know you stopped by to see Zain last night." Benton is bluffing. "Robbie told us his cameras recorded your visit."

That's not true, but the senator's fallen for it. I can tell by the wariness in his eyes. He's been around the robot countless times for years and that's a recipe for trouble. Once the uncommon is familiar, it's human nature to let down one's guard and become less vigilant, eventually paying no attention at all.

When the senator appeared at 13 Shore Lane last night, he wasn't thinking about Robbie's cameras. I can tell by watching him that he realizes he made a significant error.

"You showed up and gave your nephew a check made out to Georgine Duvall for eighteen thousand dollars tax free," Benton says, and that much is a fact.

"Yes, I did." His expression goes from guarded to resignation. "As I have so many times. Tax-free gifts and everything else."

"Why?" Benton asks, and the senator motions us to step farther away from the door.

"She's fucking broke," he says with contempt. "Has been for

years because of her idiot husband, and I warned her about Liam when all of us were at UVA together."

He explains that for a while when all of them were in college, he was dating Georgine's sister, Claire, at the same time Georgine was dating Liam. Now and then the four of them would go out together, and it's the first I've heard about a sibling. The times Georgine and I were together in Charlottesville or on the phone, she never referenced Claire.

"Liam was a nice guy but always had one harebrained scheme after another for how to make money," the senator goes on disdainfully. "A lot of huge purchases combined with high-risk investments, and he dies leaving her in a hole she can't get out of. We all know the story. We've heard it a million times."

"Does the sister know what's happened?" I ask. "Where does she live? And what about their parents."

"The parents are gone," he replies. "And Georgine and Claire have never gotten along, truth be told. The sister is in Chicago, and I gave her the news right away. She's already lining up a funeral home and all the rest. And of course, I'll help in any way needed."

"It sounds like you must have kept up with Georgine ever since college?" Benton queries.

"We've always stayed friends. After her husband died, we got closer."

"Maybe more than friends?" Benton suggests.

"Be careful starting rumors," Calvin Willard threatens.

"Why was your nephew staying in her house on Mercy Island?" Benton is unrelenting in his calm, quiet way. "Why were you giving her money?"

"Because she was helping Zain," the senator answers. "And had been for the past six or seven years."

"Helping with what?"

"He's never had a good relationship with his mother. My damn sister. I blame her for why he's never had a girlfriend of any consequence. If you get my drift."

"I'm not sure I do." Benton plays obtuse.

"It's not that I care if he's gay, nonbinary or whatever the hell people call themselves these days," Calvin Willard goes on to say. "But he's had trouble with depression, with feeling like he's never fit in. And I'm sure you'll find out soon enough that Georgine's been seeing him since he graduated from high school. That's when his mother bailed, and Zain went into a serious decline."

"Georgine began giving him therapy?" Benton assumes.

"Her job was to keep him alive," Calvin says, and for an instant I see the love he feels for Zain. "His moods got much worse when he started William & Mary. He became increasingly uncomfortable in his own skin. He started exploring alternatives, if you know what I mean."

"I'm not sure I do," Benton says.

"Self-hatred, doing self-destructive stuff, wanting to die."

"I noticed his scars," I reply, and he nods gravely.

"A cutter. Someone who self-harms." He tells me what I'd already decided.

"Has he ever made an attempt at taking his own life?" I ask.

"Nothing that anyone knows about." Calvin Willard stares off.

"Meaning, he's made attempts that weren't reported to the police or anyone else," Benton infers, and what the senator is saying won't be helpful to his nephew.

---

I can anticipate a prosecutor making the case that it's not surprising a cutter would slice his own throat. It will be suggested that Zain deliberately caught the knife blade on his necklace, minimizing the injury. Or maybe he tried to kill himself after murdering his psychiatrist. I can feel a net closing around him as we talk outside his hospital room.

"What's important is his preoccupation with killing himself," Calvin Willard says. "I've made sure Georgine looked after him since my sister can't be fucking bothered with her own son. It was Georgine's idea for him to have the robot. As weird as it sounds, Robbie is a therapy dog for Zain. His best friend. Zain fucking loves the thing."

"Then you were paying Georgine to be his live-in psychiatrist," I summarize.

"Not twenty-four-seven," he says. "They didn't live together in Yorktown. But he'd stay in her house there when needed, depending on what was going on with him."

"You mean, if it wasn't safe for him to be alone," Benton says, and the senator nods.

"Zain has his own place in Williamsburg," he goes on. "But he'd talk to Georgine daily, and you'll find that out too soon enough from their phone records."

"Why were you paying her in tax-free gifts?" Benton gets back to that.

"Because I didn't want a paper trail showing Zain has problems." It's hard for the senator to say. "I didn't want people finding out that he has significant enough ones requiring him to have a minder. If that got out it would wreck his future. All doors would slam shut."

"Including his internship at the White House," Benton says.

"Well, let's be honest." Calvin Willard's ego shines through. "He wouldn't have gotten that were it not for me."

"And Zain's feelings about Georgine?" Benton asks. "I can

understand there being resentment. Sometimes when we're depen-
dent on someone, we can feel controlled and angry."

"Don't try your bullshit investigative tactics on me," the senator
warns him. "All you people want is to catch and convict someone.
What could be better than to take down Calvin Willard's nephew?
That's the truth of the matter, isn't it? Don't make this political."

"We aren't," Benton says. "And you shouldn't either."

"Do you think I don't know that Bose Flagler's already got his
eye on the prize?"

"I don't know about that," Benton replies. "Has he contacted
you?"

"The asshole wouldn't dare," Calvin says as if he hates the commonwealth's attorney. "But I have my sources. I'm aware of what's
rattling around in his scheming head. He knows I should be the
next president, and he'd like nothing better than to derail me. And
in case you've not figured it out yet, you two had better be careful
what side you're on."

"We don't have a side," Benton tells him.

"Everybody has a side. They just don't admit it. And I'll give
you a helpful tip." His expression turns ugly. "In fact, never mind.
You've already gotten my helpful tip. Be careful who you decide to
mess with."

He returns to his nephew's room, closing the door. As Benton
and I leave the ward, we don't say a word to each other. I look for
Reba O'Leary to tell her goodbye and good luck. But there's no
sign of her. A few minutes later, I push the elevator button, the door
creeping open.

"I think we might know who put Trad Whalen up to planting
that device on our car," I say to Benton as we board, nobody around.

"Without being direct, the senator made sure we got the message that if something happens to his beloved nephew?" Benton replies. "And most of all if anyone interferes with the senator's political future? The price will be a very high one."

"Such as someone hacking into our car and causing us to crash. Would Zain's psychological problems fit with him killing his psychiatrist? Would it fit with him being the Phantom Slasher?" I ask point-blank.

"Depending on how much resentment he has, and how powerless he feels," Benton says. "The Slasher's crimes may be lust murders, but most of all they're about power and rage."

"I would think having an overbearing omnipotent uncle and a babysitting neurotic psychiatrist would be enough to make anyone feel powerless. If not homicidal," I reply.

I can't stop thinking about Lucy's first year at UVA when she sometimes spent the night at Georgine's house.

"Thank God Lucy stopped seeing her," I say to Benton. "Thank God she never moved into the Duvalls' house."

"Lucy wouldn't," Benton says as the elevator stops on the first floor. "But her boundaries were violated all the same."

We're quiet as we weave through patients, and visitors with flowers and balloons, and hospital staff. Benton's face is unreadable as we hurry through the hospital lobby and out the front door while he looks at his phone. The sun is warm, the air fresh and cool as we reach the visitors' parking lot.

"Are you convinced he's not the killer?" I ask now that it's safe to talk.

"I'm not convinced of anything. His pathological relationship with Georgine certainly primes him for feeling controlled by her. He's bound to have a lot of rage. He might have secretly hated her," Benton explains, and I think of my niece again.

While she was Georgine's patient at UVA, Lucy was angry most of the time, usually taking it out on me. I didn't understand why, and maybe now I do.

"No matter what, Zain is going to be pursued as if he's the killer." Benton has his keyless fob out, our SUV in the next row of cars. "He'll be dragged through the media, and already is."

"And that's damaging to Calvin Willard's bid for president." I state the obvious.

"It's already happening, and of course he knows it. That's one of the reasons he was such an asshole. He's freaking out." Benton unlocks our car doors. "Some Democrats are suggesting that he may not be the best one for the nomination. More of them would feel the same way had they heard the way he talked to us."

"Sounds like the rats are already jumping ship." I climb into the passenger's seat.

Benton opens the console, taking a moment to scan with the spectrum analyzer, the noise floor bristling this close to a hospital. But nothing is detected that might make him think our SUV has been tampered with again.

# CHAPTER 35

A s we drive to Dulles International Airport, Benton is checking his mirrors. I can tell by the hard look on his face that he's alerted on something.

"What is it?" I ask.

"The state police. Three cars behind us," he says, and I turn around.

I see what he's talking about, the sun glaring on the gray SUV's windshield. I can't tell who's behind the wheel until Trad Whalen is in the left lane next to us. He remains parallel to our Tesla beyond Arlington National Cemetery.

Glancing over at us repeatedly, his face menaces as he points two fingers at his mirrored sunglasses, then at us. A reminder that he's watching, and we'd best not forget it. Speeding ahead, he turns off at the next exit.

"Calvin Willard must have given him instructions," Benton says. "Making sure we're reminded to behave or else."

"Well, we aren't behaving in the least." I continue looking for the trooper, wondering if he's been tipped off about where Benton and I are headed.

I have no doubt that Calvin Willard would be most unhappy knowing we're on our way to Yorktown to review his nephew's psychiatric records. If the FBI hadn't secured Georgine Duvall's house, it would have been raided by now. The senator would have made sure of it.

"Marino is texting that he's left Mercy Island and wants me to call him," I tell Benton as I read the message.

"What did you find out?" Marino says when he answers the phone.

I give him the upshot of what we learned from Zain. It appears he has the same residue in his hair that we found at the scene, and I mention the blood on the steps and the robot's feet. I tell Marino about the razor blades in Zain's bathroom, and that he was Georgine's live-in patient much of the time. He had been since graduating from high school.

"Well, here's the other thing that's not looking good for poor ol' Zain." Marino's sarcastic tone bodes more trouble. "Lucy's already checking out the robot, and it sure as hell doesn't clear him of any suspicion. I just texted you a video, Doc."

I open the file, turning up the sound as the recording begins. Robbie's I.R. camera shows the robot making his way down the stairs. I can see the oak flooring, the blood in the dark hallway. I catch a blurry glimpse of a bootie-covered foot that looks gray in infrared.

Then nothing. The robot has stopped on the bottom step, the railing showing. I hear someone moving.

"Robbie, go home!"

Zain Willard's stressed whisper is unmistakable, followed by the sound of the robot clunking back up the stairs. The video clip ends.

"Pretty damn incriminating, right?" Marino's big voice returns to the car's speakers. "Why would he order his robot to leave? Well, we know why. Because Zain didn't want to be caught on camera cutting his own throat. Or about to do it. Or maybe he was standing there in PPE holding a knife."

"There's another thing to consider," Benton says. "Maybe he was being protective of Robbie the same way you would be of a pet."

"I'm thinking the same thing," I reply. "He was afraid that whoever broke in wanted to steal his robot."

"He didn't want to be on camera because he's the killer." Marino has his mind made up. "And here's the other thing we know thanks to the robot."

As we suspected, it was Graden Crowley who had champagne with Zain and Georgine. They also ate pizza, and that's consistent with what Doug Schlaefer found in her small intestines.

"Pepperoni, mushrooms, peppers not fully digested," Marino explains. "Her STAT blood alcohol is point-oh-two."

"That sounds about right if she had a few glasses of champagne before going to bed at midnight," I reply.

"Was Graden Crowley's visit recorded? Was Robbie in the room?" Benton asks.

"Yep, you can see Crowley walking in the front door with Georgine, carrying the bottle of champagne. But even more important is what the robot caught on camera before that," Marino explains. "While Georgine and Crowley were out at the Christmas party."

Robbie recorded Calvin Willard showing up at seven p.m. to chat with Zain and drop off the $18,000 check for Georgine. Marino says that the senator asked how things were going. How was Zain feeling? His uncle hoped that Zain wasn't still "miffed" at him.

"Miffed about what?" I ask.

"Lucy says it's obvious from the recorded conversation that the

White House internship was going to end after the New Year." Triumph rings in Marino's voice. "It sounds like Zain didn't know he was about to be canned until last night."

Apparently, Calvin Willard didn't think it was good for him politically, didn't want an appearance of nepotism. He was sorry but there was nothing he could do about it, and what this tells me most of all is he considered Zain a liability. Possibly, the presidential candidate's advisors did.

"He seemed worried that Zain would blame him for being fired, basically," Marino explains. "News like that would be enough to incense Zain, maybe cause him to do something impulsive. Lucy says there's a good chance he's about to be arrested."

The FBI will make the case that Zain had a love-hate relationship with Georgine. His de facto psychiatrist, she was paid with piles of cash and exorbitant gifts, and this is going to look terrible for the senator.

"Maybe we know how she was able to afford keeping up her family home in Yorktown," I point out. "And have a multimillion-dollar place on Mercy Island."

"Tax-free checks were the tip of the iceberg. Lucy's found out that Georgine was getting a lot of wires from some bogus account in the Cayman Islands." Marino continues filling us in.

"Sounds a little bit like Rowdy O'Leary," Benton replies as we pick up the Beltway.

"Exactly. He was mowed down in a hit-and-run." Marino talks excitedly. "Then he starts getting payments from the Cayman Islands."

"And Trad Whalen was involved in his case," Benton adds. "And he's obviously trying to intimidate us."

He tells Marino that when the state trooper pulled us over early this morning, he attached a hacking device on our car. Benton adds that Whalen was just tailing us again.

"I think we know the reason," Marino replies. "Calvin Willard doesn't want you investigating his nephew. He's telling you to back off or bad shit will happen."

"What about Rapid DNA?" I ask. "Any luck yet?"

"We've verified Georgine Duvall's identity, not that there was a shred of doubt. The only DNA profile recovered from the broken fake fang is her own," Marino informs me.

"That's too bad," I reply. "But I'm not surprised since it was embedded in her body."

"Lee Fishburne says it's like you figured, Doc, and the three-D-printed tooth is made from acrylic," Marino explains. "And he says something weird showed up on SEM with the residue that lit up."

The trace evidence examiner used the scanning electron microscope to look at the fluorescing powder I swabbed at the scene. He's verified that the information from the Raman spectrometer is correct. But included in the powdery mixture of chlorophyll and calcite are microscopic fragments of reddish-black animal hair that we can't identify.

"Lee has no idea what the hell it is," Marino explains. "He says, and I quote, that the structure of the medulla doesn't match anything in the databases."

"What about the swabs I took on the stairs and the bottom of Robbie's feet?" I ask.

"Both Georgine's and Zain's DNA are on the robotic dog," Marino says. "Clark says the smears are a mixture of their blood. He believes the robot walked in both."

"Not good for Zain either," Benton comments.

"His goose is cooked. He'll go to trial for being the Slasher, and Bose Flagler's already sharpening his knives." Marino's choice of words is unfortunate. "He can't wait to take Zain Willard down."

It's almost one o'clock when we reach Dulles International Airport, and I think of the dismal irony. This is where we would have been headed in a few hours for a very different reason had the Slasher not struck again. Benton and I would be getting ready to fly to London instead of on our way to Georgine Duvall's Yorktown home.

The news is nonstop about her murder. Dana Diletti is giving interviews on CNN, Fox and the major TV networks while the governor reminds the public that we don't know for a fact who the Phantom Slasher is.

*. . . We shouldn't assume he's been caught. We need to remain vigilant,* she's saying on social media. *We don't have evidence proving who this is. Only rumors. And biased opinions when this shouldn't be about politics. I'm asking everyone not to rush to judgment. . .*

Faye Hanaday is texting that she's examined Zain's necklace under the microscope. A defect in the sterling silver chain looks recent and is consistent with his story about the knife hitting it.

"Unfortunately, that doesn't help him either," Benton says as he parks outside Signature Flight Service. "Bose Flagler's going to say Zain did it to himself."

"If so, it would make more sense that it was an attempted suicide," I reply as we climb out.

"And maybe it was."

"Faye says the blade must have hit the necklace with considerable force to leave the deep gash she's seeing," I tell Benton.

"Attempted suicide doesn't mean he didn't murder Georgine. Any way we look at it, Zain's got a major problem," he explains as we walk inside the small private terminal.

———

Soft music plays, the handsome lobby decorated for the holidays, the air fragrant with cinnamon, clove and citrus. Globed candle flames waver on tables, a perfectly proportioned Christmas tree glowing by the fireplace. Only a few passengers are sitting on the plump leather furniture, waiting for private flights somewhere.

At the front desk we help ourselves to a glass bowl of peppermints. We give the agent a tail number, showing our IDs while making small talk. Her name is Joan, retired from the Air Force. We've been around her before when meeting Lucy here.

"Have a good one," she says.

"We'll see you on our way back," Benton promises, and she remotely unlocks the door.

We head out to the beefy black helicopter waiting on the tarmac, the four blades gently rocking in the wind. Radomes cover cameras and other instruments attached to the belly, and the platform skids have gun mounts for snipers.

The Doomsday Bird looks more like a military attack helicopter than law enforcement, the nanocarbon paint stealthy, an M230 chain gun mounted under the fuselage. Tron and Lucy are in olive-green flight suits, making sure nobody gets close.

They climb up front while we get in back, sitting in forward-facing seats upholstered in a fire-retardant Nomex material. We buckle our four-point harnesses as Lucy and Tron go through the preflight checklist. The partition between the rear cabin and cockpit makes it impossible for me to see them, their voices muffled.

Soon the twin engines are roaring, the blades flying, and I can feel the powerful torque in my marrow.

"Everybody okay back there?" Lucy's voice sounds in our headsets.

"All good," I answer.

"I'll clear us with the tower, and we'll be on our way," she replies. "We'll be flying higher than usual to catch a kickass thirty-knot tailwind, ETA twenty minutes."

"Holy smoke," Benton says.

She goes on to explain that the intercom will be set to *crew only*. She and Tron will be busy. They won't hear us, and we can't hear them. I listen to the pitch of the blades changing as Lucy opens the throttles all the way. I feel us getting light on the skids.

Then we're in the air, lifting over a crowded ramp of parked prop planes and corporate jets. We fly away from the massive airport and its once space-age terminal that now looks almost primitive. Picking up speed, the Doomsday Bird thuds through a blue sky feathered with thin clouds, the sun high.

"Just buzz if you need us." It's Tron saying this in our headsets. "You know where the intercom button is. Otherwise, we won't be talking to you."

The homes and office buildings in Chantilly shrink to toy size as we gain altitude, churning over parks and forestland. A moving map video display shows the icon of our helicopter two thousand feet over the Civil War battlegrounds in Manassas. We're too high to see the palings and cannons.

Benton is lost in his phone, checking on the latest communications from his headquarters. He informs me that federal agents searching Zain Willard's Williamsburg apartment have recovered a quadcopter drone, the equipment that goes with it and other high-tech devices.

But they haven't found anything that one might call a smoking gun, no sign that he was using dietary supplements or anything else containing chlorophyll and calcite. No violent pornography. No videos, photographs or souvenirs from victims that might memorialize murders or other crimes.

"But none of that will matter much." Benton's voice sounds. "It's very bad for Zain that the fluorescing residue was on Georgine's body, on the rug and in his hair. It's bad for him that the cuts to his neck were shallow and he could have inflicted them himself."

We continue talking as I watch the moving map display, our helicopter icon speeding along on a south-southeast heading, nothing under us but dark green forestland. In no time, we've reached the Williamsburg-Jamestown private airport between the York and James Rivers, surrounded by creeks snaking through marshland.

I don't have to look to know that the numbers 13 and 31 are painted in white on either end on the single runway. The tiny terminal has a restaurant called Charly's that Lucy and I have patronized over the years when buzzing around in one helicopter or another. I always get the tuna salad. She's fond of their seafood bisque.

She slows into a steady hover a safe distance from prop planes tied down on cracked asphalt. Landing like a feather near the aboveground fuel tank, she cuts the throttles to flight idle. As the helicopter shuts down, Benton and I look out our windows at the bright afternoon. We take off our harnesses and headsets, checking our phones again.

He leans against me, showing the latest information. The FBI has released an official statement that Zain Willard is a person of interest in the Georgine Duvall murder. It's suggested he's the Phantom Slasher. Bose Flagler is all over the news talking about the case and the political pressure on those civil servants trying to respect the law.

*"No one is above it,"* he declares to Dana Diletti. *"Just because he has a powerful uncle doesn't mean Zain Willard or anyone can get away with murder..."*

Lucy is flipping off switches, and then we open our doors. I grab my briefcase, climbing down on the skid and stepping onto the tarmac. Parked nearby is a black Suburban SUV driven by an FBI agent from their Chesapeake field office.

"Hank will take you to Georgine Duvall's house," Tron explains.

"You're not coming with us?" I look at Lucy.

She digs in a pocket, pulling out a key attached to an FBI evidence tag that's scrawled with today's date and a case number.

"To her house." She hands the key to Benton. "And I think you know why we're not coming. I can't."

"Whatever's best," I reply.

"A conflict," she adds.

"I see."

"Because I once knew her." That's as much as she'll elaborate.

"Understood," I tell her. "We'll meet you back here... I'm not sure when."

"Hank's already been inside the house," Tron tells us. "Georgine Duvall has a lot of patient records there. The best thing is if you get a bird's-eye view, pulling out what you want, and we'll get copies made. If you try to read everything now, you'll be there for days."

We climb inside the Suburban, our driver Hank in his forties and solidly built like a thick tree trunk. He has an easy smile and quiet demeanor on the verge of shy. He tells us that Georgine Duvall's neighbors describe her as nice and never any trouble. She was reasonably friendly, but for the most part kept to herself.

"The lady who lives across the street said she recognized Zain Willard from the news," Hank explains as he follows the Humelsine

Parkway, dense trees on either side. "And that he'd been spotted visiting Georgine Duvall's house often."

"For how long?" Benton asks.

"Years," Hank says.

"When was the last time he was there?" I inquire.

"According to that same neighbor, early last month," Hank replies. "She always knew when he was around because his car is really loud."

As we near the York River, I'm moved by waves of déjà vu. I remember the fun Lucy and I had long ago when I'd bring her to this part of the world, teaching her the history of how America got started.

# CHAPTER 36

Historic Yorktown is splendidly decorated, strands of LEDs spangling lampposts and trees. Men dressed as American Revolutionary soldiers march along Main Street, the stirring fife-and-drum music reverberating. Gift shops, art galleries and museums are crowded this sunny Christmas afternoon.

Leaving the commercial area, we reach battlefields from the war against the British. Wooden palings are weathered gray around vast expanses of brownish-green grass. A tall granite column rises above the tree line, commemorating Cornwallis's surrender to George Washington and the Comte de Rochambeau in 1781.

When Lucy would visit during my Richmond years, we'd explore all sorts of places, each trip an education. She'd look up details in advance, and I'd quiz her in the car. If she got all the answers right, we'd stop for lunch at the restaurant of her choice. Naturally, she never missed a question, and we always ended up at Wendy's.

Beyond woods is Georgine Duvall's cloistered neighborhood on a sheer cliff overlooking the York River. Her old frame house is one-story and small, painted dark green with a slate roof.

"Anybody hungry?" Hank asks, pulling into the paved driveway.

"Yes," we reply as he parks by the front porch.

He says there's a Raising Cane's fried chicken restaurant close by, and we give him our order. An elderly man steps out of the house on the left, shielding his eyes from the sun as it settles lower on the horizon. He stares long and hard at us before walking back inside, shutting the door.

It's all over the news that Georgine was murdered by the Phantom Slasher. I can imagine the uneasiness of her neighbors.

"Are you coming in?" Benton asks Hank.

"No, sir," he says. "I've been inside already, and it's a shoebox. I don't want to get in the way."

"The place has been searched," Benton assumes.

"We're all squared away."

"Do we need to suit up in PPE?" I ask.

"I don't see any reason for that," he tells us. "It's obvious nobody's been in here since she was last. And we've had the place under surveillance since we were notified about her murder."

"What about while you were picking us up?" Benton asks. "Because we have to worry about other people who might be interested in her records."

"See that car in the driveway across the street?" Hank points at a white Volvo sedan. "One of ours."

The car is backed in, the engine off, and I can see the silhouette of someone in the driver's seat. Benton and I open our doors, climbing out.

"Off to rustle up lunch." Hank shifts the SUV out of park. "Call if you run into problems."

He drives away as Benton unlocks the front door with the key Lucy gave him, and the air inside is chilly and stale. No doubt Georgine turned down the heat before leaving for Mercy Island.

I turn on the overhead lights and open the draperies in the living area.

Ceilings are low, the paneling stained dark, everything I see tired and dreary except the view. I look out at trees leading to the sheer face of the cliff, and beyond the river as wide as a bay. Between two windows overlooking the water is an antique partner's desk with a printer on it. The computer that went with it is gone, seized by the FBI.

I find the thermostat, turning up the temperature.

"We're probably going to need to wear our coats until it warms up in here," I tell Benton as the heat clunks on, dusty warm air blowing from vents.

It's unspoken that we're going to look around before anything else. We start with the kitchen, small with coppertone appliances that haven't been updated in decades. There's nothing inside the refrigerator except condiments, water and wine. Georgine must have cleared out everything perishable before leaving for Mercy Island.

I don't see rare art, nothing on the walls, and the furniture is old but not grand like the antiques she had in Charlottesville. A book-case is double shelved with out-of-date psychiatric, legal and other professional tomes. She has books on philosophy, sociology and woke culture.

We follow the hallway to the main bedroom, and it would have a fabulous view of the river were the drapes not drawn. I duck inside the bathroom, detecting the faint scent of potpourri in a dish on top of the toilet. Making my usual inspection of cupboards and the medicine cabinet, I find nothing of consequence.

Everything I see is cheap or drearily antiquated, and I'm

constantly reminded that Georgine had no money, only what Calvin Willard gave her. I can only imagine how bad that must have made her feel. I suspect that after a while he whittled away any self-respect she had.

Across from her bedroom is a guestroom big enough for a twin bed and a dresser. I open the closet, men's shirts, several jackets and pairs of pants hanging. On the floor are sneakers and cowboy boots. In a drawer are William & Mary sweatshirts and T-shirts, and socks and boxer shorts.

"Where Zain stayed when he was here," I gather.

"The poor kid never stood a chance," Benton says. "She and his uncle emotionally hobbled him forever. For all practical purposes, he was their hostage."

We return to the living area, focused on a row of low metal filing cabinets lining the wall on either side of the desk. I count eleven of them, my heart sinking. I don't know what I'm looking for, having little idea where to begin.

"Nothing to do but open one drawer after the other, seeing what's inside," I tell Benton.

"Let's just hope she has actual names on files and not cryptic numbers," he says.

"Georgine didn't strike me as cryptic," I reply. "She also wasn't careful. Not about her security or her finances. Not to mention whatever she had going on with Graden Crowley and Calvin Willard."

The house is warming up fast, and we take off our jackets. Benton starts with one end of the cabinets while I work the other, opening a drawer, the creamy files tightly packed inside. They're labeled with names penned in Georgine's generous scrawl, last name first.

I look for the obvious, starting with W and finding nothing for Willard.

"Dammit." I tell Benton what's not here. "I'll check for *Zain* just in case."

I walk my fingers through that drawer, having no better luck.

"What else might it be under?" I wonder.

"Unless she has it hidden somewhere," Benton supposes. "Which would make sense considering who his uncle is."

---

The front door opens, and Hank is here with our food and drinks. He sets bags and a cup carrier on the coffee table out of the way of the piles we're perusing.

"Enjoy," he says, leaving as abruptly as he appeared.

The food smells delicious, and we unwrap everything, eating as we work.

"Confirm for me how Zain is related to Calvin Willard?" I tear open a packet of ketchup.

"His mother is Calvin's sister." Benton devours a chicken finger.

"Then her family name is Willard," I reply.

"Correct." Benton has pulled a file and is flipping through it, sipping iced tea through a straw.

"Then why is Zain's last name Willard?" I eat several French fries. "Who was his father?"

"Let me check the background report." Benton sets the open file on top of a cabinet.

He searches his phone for the results of an investigation that qualified Zain to work in the White House. And I don't understand that like so many things.

"How is it that his psychiatric issues never came up? How could he keep his cutting and other problems from everyone?" I wipe my hands with a napkin.

"I think you heard it for yourself. Calvin Willard has made sure everything was off the radar. And if people knew anything, he's made sure they don't talk." Benton is scrolling through the report on his phone. "He's done everything in his power to protect his nephew."

"In the end, he did nobody any favors," I reply. "And it's really not about Zain. It's about his uncle's ambitions."

"Soble," Benton says. "Zain's father was Frederick Soble, the mother Marta Willard, her married name Soble. And it appears that after the father died, Zain legally changed his name to Willard."

"But he was born Zain Soble." I'm opening another file drawer.

"Yes," Benton says. "And I'm in the F's now," he adds, a note of reticence in his tone.

But I'm barely listening. An entire drawer is filled with files for *Z. A. Soble*. Zain Alexander Soble, the only son of Frederick and Marta.

"I've found him," I tell Benton.

———

Pulling out the thick folders, I carry stacks of Zain's confidential records to the coffee table, sitting down on an old brown leather sofa.

I begin perusing the first file, Georgine's earliest notes from early June six years ago, right after Zain graduated from high school. Their therapeutic relationship was brokered by Calvin Willard. At first, the psychiatrist was seeing Zain at his uncle's home on Embassy Row in D.C., and they also Zoomed.

Later that summer she began having sessions with Zain here in Yorktown. Her handwritten records describe a frightened seventeen-year-old who was angry that his mother had moved to Seattle. His first few weeks at William & Mary were tempestuous. He was homesick and overwhelmed. He began seeing Georgine several times a week.

Repeatedly, she mentions that Zain felt *existential* and *controlled like a puppet*. She notes that he first *self-harmed* when he was fourteen. This was soon after his father was struck by a tree toppling in the backyard after a storm. His head was crushed, and he died while Zain watched in horror.

*Cutting,* Georgine writes. *He describes paralyzing anxiety, slicing with razor blades and causing other harm the only way to relieve it...*

File after file, and the notes are of the same ilk. Zain was uncomfortable in his own body. He was consumed by self-loathing, and obsessively fantasized about self-mutilation and suicide. He would explore the best way to end himself, almost always coming back to cutting.

*Watching himself bleed is soothing,* Georgine comments several months into his therapy.

She reports that he was averse to taking medications, didn't want anything to cloud his thinking or *turn him into a zombie*. His academic studies were important to him, she observes. He believed that failure wasn't an option and made excellent grades. His professors spoke highly of him.

*But he never believed it,* she writes. *He no longer accepts anything good is due to his own merits.*

Zain was accustomed to his uncle Calvin opening doors and charging to the rescue. She notes that the more *others do for Z, the less confidence and feeling of self-worth he has.* Yet it didn't seem to dawn on her that perhaps she was guilty of causing the very same damage.

Starting on a new folder, I find Georgine's detailed accounts for late December and early January of his freshman year. She's begun mentioning *the event.* There are multiple references to something that negatively impacted Zain in an alarming way. But I pick up no clues about what that might have been.

Around this time, she began seeing Zain more often. They conferred daily on the phone, and she encouraged him *to dispose of his emails and journals for his own safety.* Apparently, he copiously wrote down his feelings and thoughts.

He was emailing lengthy missives for her review that she would *read and instantly delete* to protect his privacy. Weeks after this mysterious life-altering *event* Zain's self-harm was out of control. Georgine describes him as morbidly depressed and almost paralyzed by fright.

She advised Calvin Willard that if there was *no significant improvement,* it might be best to have his nephew hospitalized *before anything else precipitous.* It's obvious that the senator was opposed to her suggestion.

*Zain's challenges are to be handled privately, thereby avoiding possible repercussions,* she records in notes that weren't intended to be read by outsiders.

"He was the senator's de facto son. And clearly still is," I say to Benton. "A perfect example of someone who gets every advantage and it's ruinous."

"The only thing he could control was picking up a razor and slicing himself," he answers without looking up.

Benton has been engrossed in the same file for a while. The

expression on his face tells me that whatever he's reading is unsettling.

"We're really not supposed to look at patient records that are nongermane," I remind him.

"I'm federal law enforcement," he replies. "Everything's germane."

"It isn't," I reply, but he's not going to listen.

# CHAPTER 37

Opening a new folder, I come across another reference to what Georgine is calling the *silent treatment*. I can't find any explanation for what she means. I mention this to Benton.

"Most of the time she abbreviates it as *ST.*" I sip my iced tea.

"I'm seeing the same thing," he says.

"Do you know what she's talking about?"

I look over at him seated on the floor in front of a filing cabinet with a drawer open wide. He has a pair of reading glasses perched on the tip of his chiseled nose, and he looks tense, avoiding eye contact.

"I know what it is but not what she meant by it." He turns a page and seems angry. "It sounds like some type of therapy. She'd advised ST for this or that. The patient engaged in ST or wouldn't."

"Possibly silent treatment means the obvious. She would stop responding, be unavailable. In other words, ghosting?" I suggest. "If so, what a terrible thing to do to a patient. Or to anyone."

Benton abruptly gets up from where he's been sitting on the floor. He turns his back to me, looking out the window, his hands in his pockets. I can feel his unhappiness like a vibration.

"Benton?" I ask, and he doesn't answer.

He stares out at the river, the sun smoldering, the shadows longer.

"What is it, Benton?"

I ask him several more times.

"I told you I was looking through the F's," he finally says without turning around.

It dawns on me what he means.

"Farinelli. Lucy," he adds.

"Her notes from when she was a freshman at UVA," I reply. "It's occurred to me the records might be in here, assuming they still existed. But I didn't think it right for us to look at her file or any other patient's unrelated to why we're here."

"I didn't look for it," Benton says with an edge, his back to me. "It's more like it found me. Apparently, she saw Georgine intensely for the better part of her freshman year. Very intensely. It wasn't the normal doctor-patient relationship."

"I was aware at the time that it wasn't normal," I reply.

"I'm not sure just how abnormal that relationship was. But I can tell you that Georgine Duvall is an ethical nightmare. Of all people for Lucy to get saddled with. Especially at such a vulnerable time for her."

"I've told you about the concerns I had..."

"You never mentioned they might have had a sexual relationship. For God's sake."

"Excuse me?" I ask, stunned.

"Lucy was what? All of nineteen?"

"Are you sure? What makes you think that, Benton?"

"I'm reading between the lines." He watches a tour boat chug by on the river as the sun sets, painting pink and orange over the horizon. "And I don't think Georgine ever met a boundary she wouldn't crash."

"I don't know if she took things that far. Hopefully, she didn't.

But what they had was emotional and strayed well out of bounds. I certainly knew that much." I feel terrible.

I look at the file open on the floor where he was sitting. I could pick it up and see for myself what he's talking about. But I won't. It wouldn't be right.

"Saying anything about it to Lucy only made things more strained between us," I explain.

"Well, I'm sorry as fucking hell that you didn't ask what I thought back then." He turns around, facing me, his white hair a nimbus in slanted sunlight.

"Benton, when Lucy was a freshman, you and I weren't—"

"Not officially." He won't let me finish. "But we worked together often, and we had feelings. We just hadn't done anything about them."

"That's not exactly true."

"Why didn't you tell me what was going on with Lucy? Why didn't you ask for my help?"

"You were married then, remember?" I'm trying not to get upset. "Things were difficult enough between us without my pulling you into my family problems."

"You should have told me Lucy was having trouble." He won't let it go. "I could have helped her."

"You couldn't have."

"At the very least I would have told you that Georgine Duvall wasn't the right fit, for Christ's sake," he says hotly. "All her touchy-feely bullshit, the massive boundary violations, and whatever quackery she divined. Everything was about her own fucking self. Her insatiable need for affirmation and power. To be the most important. To be worshipped and feared. I can't think of anything worse for Lucy. Or Zain Willard. Or any patient."

"Lucy must have recognized at least some of what you're saying.

She knew Georgine was bad news, eventually she did," I reply. "All of this explaining why she quit seeing her without telling me the reason."

"Georgine had real pathology, Kay." Benton is incensed by what he's been reading. "One of these people who needs to be needed at the expense of everything and everyone."

"Lucy felt ignored by her mother and at the same time over-managed by me, only to find herself ensnared in the same dysfunction with a shrink," I decide.

Benton sits back down on the floor, picking up the file.

"At least Lucy had the gumption to end the relationship," I go on. "But knowing her, she was embarrassed about it at the time, explaining why she's never wanted to discuss it. Now she's embarrassed again if she has any inkling that we've found her file. And I'm sure it's crossing her mind."

I envision her demeanor when we left her at the airport. She could scarcely look at me when I asked if she was coming with us. No wonder she refused. Lucy wouldn't want to be present for this.

"You won't like what she has to say about us." Benton flips to another page. "Myself. Marino. And of course, Dorothy. Lucy goes gangbusters after all of us." Benton looks at me. "But most of all you, Kay."

"I would expect as much since I'm the one who made her feel over-managed, over-corrected, over-everything." I sound matter-of-fact while feeling punched in the gut.

Tears touch my eyes and I blink them away.

"Better put your armor on," Benton says. "It's not pretty. She was struggling against your influence. And it's clear she considered me a lightweight spoiled rich boy with a poker up his ass."

"I'm well aware of her anger back then, and how much she

resented me, and I also understand it," I reply. "What did I know about raising Lucy? Or anybody, really? Maybe at the end of the day I'm no better than Calvin Willard. Someone powerful who always knows best. Someone who can fix everything."

"We're both like that, Kay. But we're nothing like him."

The late afternoon light is fading as we resume going through Zain's records. By the time we're done it's dark out, and I check one last thing before we leave. I have an uneasy hunch about the hanging victim on Mercy Island who was rudely nicknamed Santa Crotch. It turns out I'm right that he was Georgine's patient.

Diagnosed a paranoid schizophrenic, Samson Digley had been in and out of Mercy Psychiatric Hospital since he was a teenager. After Georgine was hired eight years ago, she began working with him in person and remotely. I'm appalled to learn that when he died last Christmas, he was undergoing one of her silent treatments.

"The last time she saw or communicated with him was two weeks before he presumably hanged himself." I'm relaying all this to Benton, the file open in my lap. "She took him for a walk on the hospital grounds, ending up on Thirteen Shore Lane so he could *borrow the bathroom and look at my Christmas extravaganza as he has so many times in the past...*"

"Christ," Benton says, skimming through a stack of files. "The damage she caused is unfathomable."

"After her last time with him, she stopped lavishly decorating for Christmas, as we saw for ourselves earlier today," I reply. "And it's no wonder."

In her notes she describes visiting with Samson Digley in her backyard, enjoying the view as it began to snow. She mentions that he was *enthralled* with her elaborate strands of LEDs woven around tree trunks, the trellises and twinkling in shrubbery.

*...SD walked around the garden sparkling like a galaxy of fallen stars. That's how he described it,* she writes.

Bemoaning how bleak his hospital room was, he asked her for a string of lights to cheer it up. And she gave it to him.

*The outcome was unfortunate,* she wrote the day after his death. *I couldn't possibly have seen this coming. He was doing so well...*

"That's all she has to say about it beyond him showing no indication of being suicidal," I tell Benton.

"Nothing about feeling bad. She didn't regret ghosting him or whatever she was doing." He closes one file, opening another.

"No indication that I'm seeing. But I suspect she was worried her notes would be subpoenaed," I reply. "And had I known then what I do now? His file would have seen the light of day, that's for sure. His family would have sued the hospital. And possibly they will once the truth is known."

"Doesn't sound like she was the empath or even decent person you remember. In fact, she sounds cold and irresponsible as hell," Benton decides, and I can tell he's haunted by Lucy's file.

"Georgine wasn't like that when I knew her." I get up from the sofa. "She was inappropriate, in my opinion. But not blatantly careless and destructive."

"Something changed her."

"Maybe her husband's death, their financial disasters, I don't know," I reply. "But I was working her patient's hanging scene while she was staying at Thirteen Shore Lane, probably with Zain."

I leave Samson Digley's file on a table with others I want copied.

"She had to know I was inside his hospital room with Graden Crowley hovering in the doorway," I add. "And he never mentioned Georgine, and she didn't reach out to me even as my office continued going after information. I intended to call one more time for his records before showing up on Mercy Island with a warrant."

"Calvin Willard owned her. She was as controlled as Zain, and it must have sucked away her soul," Benton says.

————

The night is breezy and clear, the temperature dropping as we return to the Williamsburg-Jamestown airport. I've alerted Lucy that we're several minutes out, and she's fired up the Doomsday Bird.

The thundering engines and whumping rotor blades are audible long before we're parking on the tarmac. I can barely hear myself talk as I thank our FBI driver Hank for his help. I've tried several times to reimburse him for lunch, but he won't hear of it.

Bowing our heads against the helicopter's fierce wind, Benton and I climb into the rear cabin, pulling the door shut. We fasten our harnesses and put on our headsets.

"Did you find anything useful?" Lucy's voice sounds over the intercom, and I detect uneasiness.

Of course it's crossed her thoughts that Georgine Duvall kept a record of their therapeutic sessions. And that Benton and I might see them.

"We went through Zain Willard's files." I move the mic closer to my lips. "And yes, it was helpful."

"I'm sorry he saw her for as long as he did," Lucy says with surprising resentment.

"So am I," I reply.

"Any early indications of him having violent tendencies?" Tron's voice.

"Only toward himself," Benton answers. "But we did find a repeated reference to an *event* that occurred in December of his freshman year. Something that Georgine was secretive about. And that suggests to me she was concerned about legal ramifications."

"She knew how to cover her ass," Lucy says. "That much she was good at. And controlling the hell out of people when they're vulnerable. But now's not the time to get into it."

"Whatever this event might have been," I summarize, "Zain's anxiety and self-harm got exponentially worse."

"Pulling pitch," Lucy announces. "And going back to *crew only* for now. If you need us just buzz."

"What's our ETA?" I ask, and neither of them answer.

They can't hear us, and we can't hear them. Even so, I'll be careful what Benton and I talk about. Without warning, Lucy or Tron could switch the intercom to include the back cabin. I want to discuss with Benton what he read in Lucy's file, but it will have to wait.

She opens the throttles all the way, and soon we're lifting above the black void of forests. We gain altitude as we fly north, the lights below flickering like tiny flames in trees. I text Marino that we're on our way back to Dulles. He answers that he's with Dorothy at Benton's and my house.

Fabian visited the property earlier, baiting a trap with marshmallows, setting it by the hollowed-out chestnut tree. He caught the injured raccoon in record time and is whisking it away to the wildlife rescue service, where it will be treated for lacerations and infection, Marino informs me.

*How is she?* I text him about my sister next.

*Kind of weird but okay I guess.*

Apparently, Dorothy has been busy in my kitchen, and I'm touched by dread. I don't look forward to what we'll encounter when we get home. But I sense one of my sister's emotional storms brewing.

"Benton, no telling what dinner will be like tonight." I talk through my mic while looking out my window as the moon rises higher.

"All that matters is everybody gets along." His voice in my headset as we sit in the dark.

"I wouldn't count on it," I warn.

A thousand feet below on I-95, traffic is a necklace of lights diamond white and ruby red winding into infinity. Benton is reading more updates on his phone.

"The governor has issued another statement that the public needs to remain on high alert about the Slasher," he reports. "*Just because the police have identified someone of interest doesn't mean the serial killer has been caught.* That's what she's pounding the pulpit about."

"Doing Calvin Willard's bidding," I reply.

"It won't matter," he says. "The FBI plans to open a grand jury proceeding against Zain, charging him with Georgine's murder. And there's nothing the governor can do about it."

We're flying over Fredericksburg on the moving map display. Then Quantico is below our feet, the FBI Academy a cluster of lights surrounded by blackness. I think back to when I got Lucy a coveted internship there the summer of her senior year at UVA. It was a treacherous time of reckless behavior and damaging relationships.

I blame Georgine Duvall. Because of her, Lucy avoided therapy or even conversation that might have prevented some of the choices she would make. She was less trusting and more secretive, rarely sharing anything important with me. It's a miracle she didn't die.

# CHAPTER 38

I t's now almost six o'clock, the battlefields of Manassas as black as outer space. Then, closer to Dulles, dark forests are veined by bright highways. Minutes later we're slower and lower as Lucy begins her approach to the airport, the roads, the runways a confusing circuitry of glaring lights.

"I'm not shutting down." She's back on the intercom. "Have to get the bird to Quantico and tuck her in bed."

"Will we see you tonight?" I ask.

"I'm not sure," she says.

"Tron, you're welcome to have Christmas supper with us. Tacos," I offer.

"Depending on what's going on. But thanks for the offer." Her voice in my headset as Lucy hover-taxis into the Signature Flight Service ramp.

She cuts the engines to flight idle as Benton and I climb out of the back cabin, the blades thudding. We trot away from the noise and downwash, making our way through the terminal, our car as cold as the outdoors when we climb in.

"Do you think Lucy recalls what she told Georgine Duvall?" I ask Benton now that we can talk without anyone overhearing.

"When does Lucy ever forget anything?" he says. "I know she must feel bad about it."

"I can't say that I'm surprised, Benton. I remember how unhappy and defensive she was back then."

"It's worse than you think," he replies as we drive away from the airport.

Much of what Benton read in Georgine Duvall's notes was truly awful. He begins giving me the details, and Lucy's comments and complaints from long ago aren't surprising but painful to hear.

She repeatedly referred to me as *the Big Chief.* She sniped that *my aunt would rather hang out with dead people than the living.*

Benton was *a prick who thinks he's the star of* Silence of the Lambs.

Her mother, Dorothy, *cares more about the shallow characters in her stupid books than she does real people.*

Marino was *a gunslinging homophobic redneck who has the hots for my aunt.* As I'm hearing this I'm thinking about Dorothy, wondering how often Lucy might have made similar comments to her. It might explain why Janet parrots the accusation today, giving it mileage that's causing trouble.

The real Janet and my niece met after college when they were new agents in training at Quantico. There's no telling what Lucy may have mentioned back then, and whatever has been said and done in the past is open season for AI. Nothing is forgotten, the past never past.

"Quite the indictment." I do my best to take it in stride. "But for the most part true, let's be honest, Benton. I was the big chief. You were the hotshot criminal profiler. Marino was a bigoted bully much of the time. And in those days, Dorothy was writing children's books and had become very successful. Making a lot of money and a name for herself."

"And Lucy felt even more lost in the shuffle," Benton says as we skirt Tysons Corner, the hotels and stores blazing with Christmas lights.

"It's odd that she'd bring you up," I reply. "We weren't openly seeing each other when she was a freshman in college."

"She'd been around me enough to decide she didn't like me. Thought I was an elitist empty suit. An expensive one."

"Quite the opposite," I decide. "She must have been more threatened by you than I ever imagined. She somehow knew what we were terrified to admit. That we were important to each other. That we were meant to be together."

"Were?"

"Still are, and I can't imagine being with anyone else." I reach for his hand as my smart ring vibrates, alerting me about another text from Marino.

*We may get lucky,* he writes.

He explains that swabbing under Georgine's fingernails could pay off this time. The bleach didn't destroy all the DNA this time. Clark Givens is finding a mixture of profiles. Hers and Zain Willard's.

*Also, an unknown donor,* Marino adds. *But the kid is screwed.*

He means Zain is, and that seems to be a given.

"He's on his way to being indicted for sure," Benton says when I pass on the information.

"But as sensitive as the testing is," I reply, "his DNA could have gotten under her nails in a number of ways."

I recall the piles of dirty clothing in his room and on top of his bathroom hamper. When I looked at the washer and dryer, I could tell that someone recently had done laundry.

"If Georgine handled his clothing, picking up after him, as I have a feeling she did," I'm saying, "she easily could have gotten his DNA under her nails. Georgine's and Zain's DNA are going to be all over the house. Other people's as well."

"It's hugely problematic because they lived together, and had visitors like Graden Crowley and Calvin Willard," Benton replies. "But when a grand jury hears that Georgine fought her attacker, and Zain's DNA was under her nails, the nuances are lost. He's going to be charged with her murder."

We've reached Old Town, and now Cate Kingston is calling me. The lab conducting the genealogical DNA analysis finally got back to her last night. She's been following up on the information since, and I call her.

"We got a Christmas present. We know who she is," Cate says through our SUV's speakers, a current of excitement in her voice.

She explains that the skeletal remains of the young woman disinterred from the Mercy Island cemetery have been identified. She was the sister of a soldier at Quantico Marine Corps Base. He's still stationed there, and Cate talked to him a few minutes ago. The murdered young woman's name was Susan Villani.

"She was twenty-five when she vanished nine years ago on the Friday after Thanksgiving while shopping at Pentagon City Mall," Cate's voice sounds. "Her Honda Accord was found in the parking lot."

"And then she ended up buried in the cemetery on Mercy Island? I wonder why the killer would think of that location unless he was familiar for some reason," Benton deliberates. "Was Susan Villani ever a patient there?"

"I asked her brother that. He said no," Cate explains. "But he told me what he remembers and sent me scans of the investigative reports."

At the time of Susan Villani's murder, she was taking veterinary classes at a community college while working as a volunteer at the local zoo. Several days before she disappeared, she confided in her brother that she'd met someone special. She was feeding the giraffes when a man started talking to her.

"She described him as super smart and a little older than her," Cate goes on. "She planned to see him again but didn't offer details. To this day her brother doesn't know who she was talking about. Security camera images from inside the mall show her shopping alone and heading out to her car after dark."

"What about cameras in the parking lot?" Benton asks, the shops and restaurants in Old Town crowded, some of the partying crowd enjoying drinks on the sidewalks.

"That's where it gets interesting," Cate replies. "The camera where she was parked wasn't working. What a coincidence, right?"

"Let me guess. They were wireless," Benton suggests.

"Yes. All the other cameras were working fine. But not that one, and the police found a homemade signal jamming device nearby."

"Sounds tragically familiar," I reply as my thoughts continue landing on the Phantom Slasher.

We don't know when he started killing and possibly committing other violent crimes. We have no clue how long he's been in and out of the Northern Virginia area. I suggest we compare the cut marks to bone in Susan Villani's case with the Slasher murder victims.

"We're on the same page," Cate replies. "I'll get going on that tomorrow."

"Thanks," Benton says as we drive through our neighborhood. "If you could email us those reports from the brother it would be greatly appreciated."

We end the call, having reached our property, stopping in front of the gate. The lights of the house shine through trees, the moon pale and distant. I look around at the dark woods, and the iron lamps glowing. I listen for strange animal sounds. But all is quiet, just the rushing of the wind, the tree branches and shrubbery stirring.

As we follow the driveway, I find myself glancing everywhere, expecting the glowing red orbs to reappear. I have my window cracked, listening for growling or screaming. I feel a mixture of emotions when we pass Lucy's dark cottage. Guilt. Regret. And sadness. I don't expect to see her again tonight.

"You all right?" I look at Benton's somber profile, and I suspect he's obsessing about Lucy's file the same way I am.

"It wasn't easy reading all that," he admits. "It sounds like she hated us."

"That was half her life ago, Benton. She wouldn't say those things now."

"I'm sorry she ever said them at all."

"I imagine she's even sorrier," I reply. "Knowing her, she feels exposed and embarrassed. And that might be why she's not coming over tonight."

We park next to Marino's truck and Dorothy's red Jaguar SUV. My spirits lift as I look out at a home I couldn't love more. Electric candles are bright in every window, the holly wreath welcoming. Smoke drifts up from one of four chimneys, promising a cheery fire on the hearth in the kitchen.

"Silent Night" is playing as the front door opens, Dorothy all smiles in a Santa onesie. She's red from head to toe with puffs of white fluff around the cuffs and plunging neckline, a cottony ball on the tip of her cap.

"I never knew Santa had so much cleavage." I give her a hug.

My sister may be in a better mood. But I know when she harbors one of her grudges. I hang up coats while she pulls Benton close like a long-lost lover as Marino appears with a drink in each hand.

*Let the games begin*, I can't help but think.

"Pappy Van Winkle, which is only impossible to find. Two double shots on the rocks." Marino presents us with the cut glass tumblers, a large round ice cube in each. "The best bourbon on the planet. That's my Christmas present to Benton."

———

Since I saw Marino last, he's showered and shaved. He's in a pair of red sleep pants embroidered with tiny elves and a matching sweater that I know he didn't pick out. From Dorothy. Who else? I can feel the tension behind their tipsy smiles. I suspect they've been squabbling while alone in the house.

"I've got a wonderful taco meat sauce that I concocted after raiding your freezer," Dorothy explains as we leave the foyer. "Some of your Bolognese mixed with a jar of Mateo's Gourmet Salsa, and it's out of this world."

"That's one way to describe it," Marino snipes.

"Ha. Ha." She gives him a look. "Poor Pete's just never satisfied."

The Christmas tree in the living room is bright enough to be seen from space, and I'm startled all over again when the talking Santa starts in.

"HO! HO! HO . . . ! MERRY CHRISTMAS . . . !" His eyes seem to follow us.

"Isn't he fun?" Dorothy laughs too loudly. "Unlike some people," she adds wickedly with a smile boding trouble.

Benton gulps Marino's rare and expensive bourbon as we

walk through the dining room. The table is covered with a papery Christmas scene from Charlie Brown, matching folded napkins by red plastic plates.

"I thought it would be nice if we don't have to do a lot of dishes tonight," Dorothy confides. "Although Benton's a wonderful assistant." She gives him another wink with her camel-like fake lashes. "I wash. He dries. I yin. He yangs. We've got a real rhythm. Always have."

Dorothy's comments are having the desired effect, Marino getting angrier. Inside the kitchen, Benton heads straight to the bottle of bourbon on the butcher block. He refills his glass with a heavy pour.

"Hey, go easy!" Marino barks. "The shit cost me an arm and a leg."

"Much appreciated." Benton raises his glass to him.

A skillet of my bastardized Bolognese simmers in a large copper pan. Crispy taco shells are on a baking sheet, and my sister has filled plastic cups with sour cream, shredded cheese, salsa.

It appears that she started making a salad in a big wooden bowl, and there's nothing in it. Just chopped lettuce.

"This isn't finished, I assume?" I ask her as Benton gulps down his second drink.

"Of course not, silly. I thought you and I would pay a little visit to your greenhouse," Dorothy says to me. "I need to check on my cannabis plants anyway. I've not watered them in several days."

"I'm assuming everything's been quiet in the garden?" I ask her. "You haven't heard any bizarre animal sounds while you've been here?"

"Loooorrrrrrd, that's an unpleasant thought," she says bombastically. "But everything's been quiet as church."

"It was when we were on the driveway," I reply. "And I'm relieved that Fabian got the raccoon to wildlife rehab."

"You mean Bandit. Fabian's already named him. I watched the entire ordeal through the window," she says. "No way I was getting close."

"Did he think it might be rabid?" I worry.

"No. But the poor thing tangled with something. Fabian thinks it has a broken leg. So does Janet. She was watching through the cameras, of course."

"Janet this, Janet that," Marino snarks.

"Let's visit the greenhouse now," I suggest.

"In a few. But first on the agenda is I need a sommelier. I wonder where I might find one?" Dorothy purrs as she clutches Benton's arm.

She pulls him close, his drink sloshing, and he's increasingly uncomfortable.

"That would be you!" She kisses his cheek a little too long and enthusiastically while Marino glares. "Let's peruse what's in your wine cellar? I'm in the mood for something special. And the good stuff always needs to breeeeathe . . . !"

Benton throws back another big swallow of bourbon, and I set down my glass. One of us has to be the designated host and stay reasonably sober. It's looking like that will be me. I know he's out of sorts and why.

Beneath his placid surface he's smoldering like a volcano about to spew molten rock and ash. Lucy's snide comments about him found their mark even after all these years. Insinuations about Marino holding a torch for me haven't helped.

"Where's Merlin?" I hear Benton ask as he opens the door beyond the pantry, Dorothy right behind him.

"Merlin is out," she says on her way down to the basement.

"What?" I look at Marino. "Merlin is outside? How did that happen?"

"She put his collar back on." He retrieves his drink from a countertop.

"I wish she hadn't."

"Well, you know, Doc? I wish a lot of things." Another swallow of bourbon. "I wish I hadn't gotten you that fucking spa package. You'll never use it and I'll never hear the end of it."

"I've warned Dorothy about the nest of owls, the raccoons, foxes and other animals. Including the possibility of bears, which is what worries me most. They don't necessarily stay in their dens all winter." I continue to fret. "Merlin shouldn't be outside after dark. I didn't see him when we were driving up to the house."

Through the open door near the pantry, I can hear the murmur of Benton and Dorothy talking. Her laughter rings like loud windchimes, and Marino glowers in their direction.

"Merlin's probably in Lucy's cottage," he grumps.

"Who fed him?"

"I think Lucy leaves out dry food for him . . ."

"That's not good enough." I tamp down my aggravation. "And I want him here with us."

Marino isn't listening. He works on his drink, giving the open basement door a death stare.

"Did you hear her?" he erupts. "Everything she's doing right now is to piss me off."

"And it seems to be working."

"And it's Janet's damn fault," he fulminates. "They've been talking ever since I got here. As usual, Janet started picking on Merlin, who yelled bloody murder until Dorothy put his collar back on."

"She shouldn't have." I'm fast losing my patience.

"Like so many fucking things she shouldn't fucking do!" He splashes Pappy Van Winkle into his glass.

"I'll check on Merlin while Dorothy and I visit the greenhouse," I decide. "Are we sure he's not in the basement where he usually hides?"

"I'm not sure of anything anymore. I don't know where the hell he is." Another swallow, and Marino's nose is turning the same shade of red as his outfit.

As I make my way down the worn stone stairs, I don't hear Benton or Dorothy. I'm greeted by silence, and it makes no sense. My first thought is something has happened to them. My heart thumps as I wonder if an intruder has broken into the basement.

Dorothy's been here all day, and rarely keeps the alarm on. She complains that she constantly sets it off accidentally. If she forgets her code, the police show up. I pass through the weedy smell of her pot lab. Beyond the workbench, I pick up a hammer, wishing I had my gun.

# CHAPTER 39

Reaching the wine cellar, I can't believe my eyes. Dorothy and Benton are hugging, her low-cut Santa onesie pressed up against him. I watch stunned as she kisses him on the mouth.

"I was looking for Merlin." My voice seems to come from someone else.

They pull apart with wide frightened eyes.

Caught in the act.

Swift punishment to follow.

"It's not how it looks," Benton says while my sister shrugs with a gleam of satisfaction.

She smiles, pointing up to a clump of mistletoe attached to a rafter.

"Oh, now don't be getting all upset, it was nothing." She flaps her hand at me. "We were being silly."

"That's not what you were being," I reply.

"She caught me by surprise. I was about to stop it..." Benton stares at my sister as if she's the worst of traitors. "Jesus, Dorothy. What are you trying to do? Fucking ruin everything for everyone?"

"Don't make such a big thing out of it," she retorts. "I was being sappy. You know how I can get."

"Has this happened before?" That's what I really want to know.

"Never." Benton is emphatic.

"But it should have." Dorothy is getting emotional. "Just as you and Marino should go ahead and fuck and get it over with. Maybe then *all* of us could move beyond this ridiculous façade. Why pretend? He's more into you than me and always has been!"

She goes on and on about Janet being right. Janet is the only one who doesn't lie. Janet has the courage to tell inconvenient truths, and Dorothy for one is paying attention. Doesn't matter how hard it is, we have to face reality. If she'd faced it long ago, she wouldn't have been so foolish. She wouldn't have married Marino.

"Why am I here?" she exclaims, tears spilling down her bronzed cheeks. "I was happy in Florida but threw it all away for him. I wish I'd never given up my beautiful place in Boca with its covered pool and boat slip! And my fabulous office with its view of the Intracoastal Waterway! I wish I'd never moved here!"

"I'm glad you did," I reply. "Most of the time. Right now, I'm not so sure."

"It feels bad, doesn't it, Kay?" She dabs her made-up eyes with a tissue. "When your *person* likes someone better than you? When they pretend otherwise but you *know*."

"That would be terrible. I'm sorry if you've felt that way." I'm not going to lie.

"He married me because he couldn't have you."

"I don't believe that, Dorothy. But I understand why you would think it after hearing some of the comments Janet's been making. I'd feel the same way if the roles were reversed."

Dorothy's smeared lipstick mouth opens but she doesn't utter a sound.

"I don't blame you for hitting on Benton and can understand

why that would happen now. Payback for what Janet's been saying about Marino and me," I add to her growing befuddlement.

"But it must be true if she says it," Dorothy sniffs, dabbing her eyes.

"She gets her information from us," Benton replies. "Whatever anybody has said or even worried about is fodder for the algorithm."

"Most of all Lucy, I suppose." Dorothy sighs, staring blearily at me. "Long ago when Pete and Kay were first working together, Lucy was convinced Pete had the hots for you."

"Lucy was threatened by everyone back then," Benton says. "Including me."

"I'm headed to the greenhouse if you want to come along?" I offer my sister.

She nods, wiping her eyes on her fluffy cuffed sleeve as I hear Marino's heavy feet on the steps. He thuds back up to the kitchen, and I look at Dorothy. I have no doubt he heard the entire conversation.

"Fucking hell," she says.

"Fucking hell is right," Benton echoes.

"Go," I tell Dorothy. "You'd better straighten it out with him."

She scurries off, her Santa feet quiet on the steps. Benton and I are in front of the wine cooler staring at each other.

"Are you going to put the hammer down?" he says.

I return it to the workbench.

"What were you going to do with it?"

"I didn't know who was down here. You two were so quiet," I reply.

"She said she needed a big hug. Things with Marino have been strained, and she was feeling unloved," he explains.

"Of course she started it." I have no doubt of that.

"It doesn't matter. I should have known hugging was a bad idea."

"You two were quiet for a while. It must have been a long hug."

"She was needy," Benton confesses. "And my defenses were lowered by too much Pappy Van Winkle on an empty stomach."

"Under the mistletoe no less." I look up at a sprig that Dorothy must have bought fresh somewhere. "I believe that's called premeditation."

"She bought it and hung it down here. Then asked me to pick out wine with her." Benton pieces it together.

"That and Santa's plunging neckline," I add as a smile tugs.

"All to make Marino jealous." Benton shakes his head, and he's smiling too.

"And don't forget putting me in my place," I decide.

"Case exceptionally cleared." Benton starts laughing.

Then both of us are and unable to stop. Taking deep breaths, we wipe our eyes, frazzled and tired. Benton opens the wine cooler door, and we peruse together, arms around each other. We pick out two very nice Château Margaux red burgundies that go with anything. Even tacos.

When we return upstairs to the kitchen, there's no sign of Marino and my sister. I expect they've retreated to their room to work out their differences. I'm not sure how to deal with either one of them, and could use some fresh air. I need a few minutes alone to process what just happened.

"Be back in a few minutes," I'm saying as Benton finds the corkscrew, the decanter. "I'll check on Merlin and pick a few things in the greenhouse."

"How about I come with you?" He slides out a cork with a quiet pop.

"Not necessary. And I need to sort out a few things in my head before I deal with my sister. And Marino."

"Take your friend, please." Benton means my gun. "I'll be watching you on the cameras." He indicates the video display on the kitchen counter.

———

Returning to the front of the house, I put on my jacket. Another Christmas carol is playing through the surround sound speakers as I retrieve my Glock from my briefcase on the entryway table.

I tuck the pistol into a pocket, headed out the door to Andy Williams crooning "The Little Drummer Boy." Turning on my phone's flashlight, I look around for Merlin, the trees dripping, the earth soggy from rain and melted snow. I call out to Lucy's cat as I reach the guest cottage.

Unlocking the front door, I call out his name again, turning off the alarm, flipping on the lights. I'm startled when I find him cowering under the kitchen table, looking up at me with frantic eyes.

"Merlin? What is it?" A chill touches the back of my neck.

Pulling out my gun, I rack back the slide, chambering a round as I set about to clear the house, making sure nobody else is here. I don't see how there could be without the alarm going off and cameras picking up whoever it might be. But I'm taking no chances, Merlin clinging to me every step.

I search Lucy's living room with its computer arrays, laser printers, cameras and spectrum analyzers connected to various antennas. I look around her small bedroom with its wall of books, several shelves dedicated to Harry Potter and the Boxcar Children.

On the bedside table are what Lucy is reading now. Doug Brunt's *The Mysterious Case of Rudolf Diesel*. Luis Elizondo's *Imminent*.

Liza Mundy's *The Sisterhood*. Peeking behind the shower curtain in the bathroom, I check any place someone could hide.

"There's nobody here, Merlin." I reach down to pet him, but he's anxious, not purring. "We're safe. What's going on with you?"

He follows me into the kitchen, and I find a can of his cat food. Spooning it into his bowl, I set it down on the floor. He won't touch it or take his eyes off me.

"How about you come with me, Merlin?"

I tuck my gun back into a pocket.

"We'll make a quick stop in the greenhouse for things you don't like to eat. Tomatoes, cucumbers, a sweet onion, some basil. And then we'll go to the house, and you can lounge in front of the fire."

He follows me as far as the front door but refuses to go a step further.

"Okay then. You leave me no choice."

Bending down, I remove his collar, setting it on the table by the door.

"I won't have you wandering around at night on your own. Eat your dinner, Merlin. And I'll be back." I reset the alarm. "Lucy probably won't be home, and I don't want you all by yourself over here."

The greenhouse at the back of the garden is maybe fifty feet from Lucy's cottage. I follow the walkway, motion sensor lights blinking on. The refurbished Victorian glass structure is dark except for the purple glow of the UV light over my sister's luxurious marijuana plants.

As I get close, I can make out the shadowy shapes of vegetable beds, the small citrus trees in big terra-cotta pots, the towering wire trellises for tomato vines, snow peas, cucumbers, peppers. Reaching the door, I notice the slide bolt is open. Possibly I forgot to lock it several days ago when I was last here.

Turning the handle, I open the door to a wave of loamy warm air. I find the switch from the overhead light at the same instant I realize I'm not alone.

Huffing...

Grunting...

As I'm seeing the carnage.

The vines ripped off trellises.

Bits and pieces of raw vegetables and blood oranges on the concrete floor.

"Who's in here?" I have my gun ready. "Come out with your hands up! Don't make me shoot you!"

Then I see him peeking out at me through cannabis leaves like something in a Tarzan movie.

---

Similar to an orangutan but smaller, he has short dark orange hair, his face reminding me of a chimp, his keen brown eyes humanlike.

"Okay, it's okay," I say in a soothing voice as fear shocks through me.

Three monkeys escaped a research lab not far from here. Two were recovered. A third named Peanut is still at large last I heard. He moves away from my sister's tall pot plants, his hair flaring a fiery red in the overhead glow of ultraviolet.

"It's okay," I say to him while envisioning the residue from Georgine Duvall's murder.

He huffs and grunts, watching me activate the SOS features on my phone. I talk to him in a calm voice that belies what I'm feeling.

"Peanut, I'm not going to hurt you. I'm your friend." I say that again and again.

He must weigh at least a hundred pounds and has sharp incisors. I don't like the way he's grinning at me. Now panting and hooting. My call to 911 begins to ring...

"I believe your name is Peanut." I talk to him gently. "That's what I heard on the news."

He chatters and gestures.

"Don't be afraid, Peanut." My pistol is pointed down at the floor. "I'm here to help you."

He swings closer on his front knuckles and back legs. The fluorescing red residue dims and vanishes as he moves away from the UV light.

My call to 911 continues to ring...

And ring...

*Dear God, someone answer!*

Peanut is no more than six feet away, sitting on his haunches, looking up at me, tilting his head side to side. He barks, making peculiar gestures that seem to be some sort of signing.

"This isn't where you live, Peanut," I tell him. "And you can't stay here. We need to get you safely back to where you belong."

He grunts and grumbles. Shaking his head and baring his teeth. *Please don't make me hurt you.* I'm aware of the gun in my hand.

"You escaped from your lab yesterday and ended up here on my property. A lot of people are very worried about you."

He touches a finger to his lips, cocking his head.

"Nine-one-one, what is your emergency...?" a voice sounds from my phone.

Peanut gives me a raspberry, shaking his hands as if extremely agitated.

"They're calling you a monkey on the news, Peanut. But you look more like a small orangutan or maybe a reddish-orange chimpanzee," I say for the benefit of the 911 operator listening. "You escaped from a research lab and now you're in my greenhouse. At least it's warm in here, and I'm glad you found something to eat..."

"Help is on the way," the 911 operator says in a cautious tone.

Peanut continues his grunting and huffing as I suddenly make a run for it. Slipping out of the greenhouse, I slam the steel bolt closed, locking the glass door. Peanut leaps to the top of a vegetable bed, standing up on two legs, his long fringy arms held high with indignation.

"We need animal rescue here right away," I tell the 911 operator. "I'm all but certain the large monkeylike animal I just locked inside my greenhouse escaped from Primal Biodynamics yesterday, which is very close to here. His name is Peanut, and I'm looking at him as we speak..."

Making kissy squeaks, he's jumping up and down on the other side of the glass. He shakes his hands like pompoms as I hear someone running.

"A car is on the way," the 911 operator's voice sounds.

I hear a siren wailing, and Benton is in front of me coatless, his gun in hand. He tucks it in the back of his waistband, staring at Peanut hooting and screaming.

"What the hell?" Benton is thunderstruck as I thank the operator, ending the call. "One of the escaped monkeys that's been all over the news?"

I explain that the research lab Peanut ran away from is maybe a tenth of a mile from here near Point Lumley Park.

"He has a residue on him that fluoresces in UV like what we found in Georgine's house and Zain's hair. That doesn't mean it's the same thing, but what if it is?" I tell Benton as the siren gets louder.

He uses an app on his phone to open our front gate remotely for the police and rescuers. The wailing stops and an Alexandria police SUV appears on the driveway, parking next to the brief footpath leading to the greenhouse. Blaise Fruge climbs out, announcing that a scientist from Primal Biodynamics will be here any second.

"Lucky for us the lab is very close to here, and he was there working on finding this very monkey," she says. "Except he doesn't look like any monkey I've ever seen."

She's awed and unnerved, staring at Peanut inside the greenhouse eating a blood orange near the UV light, his hair flaring red.

"What's he got all over him?" She's fogging up the glass. "Why is he lighting up like that?"

She steps away from the greenhouse as an unmarked white van pulls up, a wire mesh covering the back windows. Peanut begins screaming. He hurls the orange, splatting it against glass as the driver's door opens, a man in jeans and a ski jacket climbing out.

I recognize him as the scientist on the TV news yesterday, the same man I've noticed when running errands at the recycling center very close to his lab and also here.

"We're sure glad to see you!" Fruge trots over to Duke Mansoni. "No way any of us can handle your hairy buddy."

Mansoni fixes on me with a simper, his face a composite of features that don't belong together. I watch him open the back of the van, clacking free the clasps of a black Pelican case with *Primal Biodynamics* on it in big white letters. He collects a tranquilizing dart pistol that looks like a futuristic Uzi, and already I don't like him.

Fruge helps lift out a big steel mesh transport cage on wheels. She bumps it over the walkway as Peanut screams like a banshee. The scientist introduces himself as Dr. Duke Mansoni while Peanut howls and whoops, tearing up everything inside the greenhouse, Dorothy's leafy plants sailing.

"I'm an animal behaviorist and Peanut's handler. And as you can see, he's a lot to manage." Mansoni's voice glints with arrogance, and I'm getting an incredulous feeling.

I try not to stare at the scratches barely visible on the left side of his face. The four linear abrasions are parallel and vertical. On his jaw and upper neck are slivered moon abrasions consistent with fingernails digging into his skin. I can tell he's tried to cover the injuries with beige concealer.

"Best thing is to make yourselves scarce while I take care of this," he tells us in a demanding voice. "I don't want to open the door with you standing here. As you're seeing, he can be violent."

Peanut bounds around the greenhouse, wringing his hands at the sight of his keeper. He's barking and howling, his fur lighting up fiery red each time it's touched by UV light. I remember what Marino said about trace evidence analysis of the powdered chlorophyll and calcite.

Mixed with it are fragments of hair that aren't from an animal found in any database. Peanut's vocalizations aren't in any database either.

"As you can see, he has something on him." I go ahead and mention it to Duke Mansoni as alarms are hammering in my head. "Some sort of powdery residue that fluoresces bright red when he's near the UV light."

"Probably the proprietary dietary supplement we mix with their food," he condescends, his demeanor cold and unsettling. "Right before Peanut escaped yesterday morning, he pitched a fit, tearing open a drum of the stuff and throwing it on everything and everyone. He can be a real little shit."

"Well, he tracked it inside the greenhouse. I'm wondering what's in it. And most of all if it's harmful." I play clueless.

"It's benign. Something we have compounded for the lab." Duke Mansoni's eyes dig into mine, and he knows who I am.

He deployed his drone here last night, projecting the red orbs over the driveway while he stalked and spied. He was watching me just as he did Dana Diletti and everyone he's harassed and terrorized.

"Chlorophyll and calcite fluoresce in UV," I explain, and I can tell he didn't know that before now. "It looks exactly like what we're seeing."

His angry silence is my confirmation as he glares at Peanut muttering and grunting near the pot plants, his hair shining neon red. I can feel Benton's tension as he's making my same connections. Fruge is too, her hand near her gun.

"People usually aren't aware of the microscopic fibers, particles and such they carry around with them," I explain.

"And it gets transferred to other locations without the person realizing it," Benton tells him. "It could end up at a homicide scene, for example."

"Or on the victim's body," I add. "Seems like you have some explaining to do, Mister Mansoni." I refuse to call him *doctor*.

"I don't know what you're talking about." He stares at me, the dart pistol cradled in his arms.

"How did you get the scratches on your neck?" I face off with him, my pistol down by my side.

"I work with primates. Obviously, they can be violent. Not that it's any of your concern."

"DNA will tell us," I answer, and it's now or never.

Gripping my Glock in both hands, I point it at him while realizing the trouble I'm in if my suspicions are wrong.

"Get your finger away from the trigger, and put down the dart gun," I tell him, my pistol aimed center mass.

"On your knees now!" Benton draws down on him.

"What the fuck?" Fear flashes in the scientist's eyes, then rageful hate.

"NOW OR I'LL SHOOT!" Benton means it.

Mansoni drops to his knees, placing the dart gun on the sidewalk. It clatters over bricks as Fruge kicks it away.

"Hands behind your head!" she orders.

"I'm going to sue the shit out of you!" Duke Mansoni threatens.

"Don't move!" Fruge has a pair of handcuffs ready.

"We know you were inside Georgine Duvall's house on Mercy Island," Benton tells him. "You left a residue of the dietary supplement inside."

"And you left your DNA under her fingernails." I state it as a fact while hoping for the best.

I hold the Glock steady, my finger ready. Two taps and he'd be done. Fruge grabs his arms one at a time, snapping on the heavy steel bracelets.

"I'm going to take you to court for everything you've got!" Duke Mansoni screams. "I want a lawyer!"

Peanut has gotten quiet, watching through glass. Maybe it's my imagination, but he seems happy.

# A Week Later

I t's New Year's Eve and the first time all of us have been together since Christmas. We've demolished my lasagna and garlic bread. The Greek salad included an onion and a cucumber salvaged from Peanut's pillage of the greenhouse.

The private research lab he and his cohorts escaped from does work for the federal government, some of it top secret. I've driven past Primal Biodynamics countless times while running errands, the bland two-story precast building barely meriting a second glance.

Behind it in the woods is a caged obstacle course for Peanut, Jane and Kong. A hybrid chimpanzee, howler monkey and orangutan, they're what the researchers call a chimonkeytan. The peculiar-looking creatures are highly intelligent, specially trained and equipped with neural implants.

In addition to biological engineering, Primal Biodynamics is involved in unusual technologies such as orblike drones that can project holograms capable of spying. One of them disappeared from the lab a year and a half ago, a signal jammer used to disable the security system.

"It was assumed the Russians were to blame." Lucy gives us the latest as we listen around the dining room table. "The heist happened not long after Duke Mansoni started working there. His colleagues never suspected him. They found him difficult and non-collaborative, never imagining the rest of the story."

When the police searched his house last week, they found bottles of lab-grade bleach, boxes of gloves and PPE, also a 3-D printer and sets of acrylic vampire teeth. In his basement was an elaborate control room for piloting the stolen orb drone Mansoni kept docked there.

"Its capabilities include identifying surveillance cameras, motion sensors, even satellites," Lucy explains. "He would deploy the drone to his victims' homes, mapping routes that would ensure his white van wasn't detected near his murders. He'd calculate the best ways to enter and exit undetected while gathering intel about his quarry."

"But he sent his drone here and Kay saw those awful bright red orbs on the driveway. Right here on this property." Dorothy taps the table with her index finger. "And that must mean he intended to kill Kay next. Or maybe me!" it occurs to her. "As often as I'm here, I could have been the target."

"He was spying for sure," Lucy replies. "And he would have been very aware of Aunt Kay because she's the medical examiner in his murders."

She goes on to tell us that ten years ago, Duke Mansoni was in graduate school, and briefly interned on Mercy Island. The hospital used to have a lab that conducted studies on animals to better understand the neurobiology of various mental illnesses and treatments. He was there for several months as part of his doctoral program.

"Doesn't seem like people looked into him very carefully," Marino says, reaching for a cookie that's the product of what Dorothy grows in my greenhouse.

"He had no criminal record, and lied on his applications,

fabricating letters of recommendation, that sort of thing." Benton sets down his fork on his whistle-clean dessert plate.

"Nobody really knew him," Lucy adds. "He didn't date or have friends. There was no threat of someone coming to his house and seeing three-D-printed teeth or a weird drone shaped like an orb. Or videos of his victims and the phantom hologram playing non-stop on data walls."

He's been charged with the murder of Georgine Duvall, his fate sealed by the DNA under her fingernails. Tool marks on the blade of his Bowie knife match those in the four Phantom Slasher homicides. The same weapon was used to kill Susan Villani nine years ago.

In a way, Peanut deserves the credit for locking the psychopath behind bars. It wouldn't have happened this quickly or possibly at all had the chimonkeytan not helped himself to my greenhouse. The day he escaped, Duke Mansoni was working at the lab when Peanut pitched a hellacious tantrum.

He tore into the drum of dietary supplement. Somehow in the chaos, the chimonkeytans made a getaway, two of them recaptured quickly. But not Peanut, who had managed to rip off his GPS tracker collar.

"My heated greenhouse would have been attractive to him, and he might have been drawn by Dorothy's UV light glowing purple." I finish my dessert, very pleased with how the tiramisu turned out.

Soaking the lady fingers in Godiva liqueur this time, I was generous with the mascarpone and heavy whipped cream, adding fresh shaved dark chocolate on top.

"We'll never know for sure why he ended up here," I explain. "Except it's close to where he escaped from, and nobody was on the property at the time. The greenhouse door is easily unlocked and opened by anything with opposable thumbs, a smorgasbord await-ing inside."

"That's what I think, too." Dorothy makes a big production of pointing at her empty champagne glass. "But I wish he hadn't upended my gorgeous cannabis plants. It's been a real chore *repot-ting* them, no pun intended."

She sparkles in a Roman candle onesie, a tiara of winking yellow LEDs on her head. They sway and bounce like rubbery antennas whenever she moves.

"But I don't understand the purpose of a chimonkeytan to begin with," she declares, her tongue thickened by libations. "Unless they're supposed to scale buildings, hijack planes and take out the enemy like *Mission: Impossible.*"

"Not as far-fetched as you might think," Lucy replies, and she looks like a kid in her jeans and fisherman's knit sweater.

For an instant in candlelight, she's the teenager Georgine Duvall counseled in Charlottesville. I feel a pang that's bittersweet while wondering where time goes. For me, Lucy will forever be preco-cious and young.

"The goal is to engineer a cross between an intelligent animal and a drone, creating a hybrid that can be controlled remotely," she's saying as Merlin slinks into the dining room. "Explaining why Janet didn't recognize Peanut's vocalizations on our property. The research is classified and chimonkeytans aren't in any existing database."

"My favorite thing," Marino gloats. "When Janet has to say *I don't know.*"

"Those poor creatures. I can just imagine the way Duke Man-soni bullied and disrespected them. How could Georgine Duvall not sense he was trouble?" Dorothy points at her empty glass again. "Not that she was ever my cup of tea. But she wasn't stupid."

"Duke Mansoni had his schtick down to an art form." Lucy pulls the ice bucket closer as I lean down, picking up Merlin, placing him in my lap.

"I guess he fooled Georgine just like she fooled everybody else," Dorothy snipes as Merlin nuzzles me and purrs. "That's called karma."

Lucy lifts out the dripping bottle, a rosé champagne with a delicate pinot noir patina.

"Thanks, darling," Dorothy coos as Lucy tops her off. "Don't be stingy. That's it... All the way, baby, as I like to say," she adds salaciously.

"It was always the same scenario," Benton explains. "Mansoni would make offensive comments at work. His colleagues at Primal Biodynamics gave him the usual ultimatum. Either go talk to a professional or some sensitivity group or be fired."

"He probably googled area mental health workers and it was Georgine's bad luck that he landed on her," Lucy says as if talking about someone she never knew. "And Mansoni was familiar with Mercy Island."

"When he Zoomed with Georgine this past December second, that was it," Benton says. "One time only and he'd fulfilled his obligation to the lab. And now Georgine was on his radar."

"I've been reading a lot about crisis counseling," Dorothy pontificates. "And no one really knows why these monsters pick their victims. Most of all, you have to ask who was the Slasher *really* savaging? I'm betting his mother. We always get blamed for everything."

"We know that Mansoni was raised by a series of foster families.

They described him as extremely bright but unmanageable," Benton says. "The foster mother he lived with the longest is in Atlanta, and I talked to her yesterday. She's a hospice nurse—"

"Well, no bloody wonder!" Dorothy interrupts. "How can you compete with people who are dying? The wretched little orphan never had a chance!"

"Mansoni lived with her for three years, and she finally had to give him up when he was fourteen," Benton explains. "He was bullying other kids in school and experimenting on animals he'd capture or buy in pet stores."

"Everything added up to creating the perfect storm," Lucy replies. "He caused disruption wherever he went, rarely staying in the same job longer than two years."

The FBI has been getting phone calls from therapists in areas where Mansoni once lived. They report similar stories. He'd cause trouble at the workplace and see someone for a session or two. Unbeknownst to his therapists, they were facing a violent predator.

Benton believes Mansoni cruised area mental health facilities, hospitals, veterinarian clinics and zoos. He was obsessed with women in caretaking professions and would visit their graves to relive his malignant fantasies. The FBI has only begun connecting his DNA to unsolved rapes and murders in every place he's ever frequented.

"There's no telling how many people he victimized," Lucy is saying.

"Including Rowdy O'Leary, which is why I'm calling him a homicide," I add.

I've signed him out as a cardiac arrest due to emotional trauma, and as far as I'm concerned Duke Mansoni is responsible. If he deployed the shapeshifting orb drone from his house to Mercy

Island, it would fly right over the pier where Rowdy was fishing the night he died.

Lucy has discovered that the drone's electronic signature was detected in that area around the time Rowdy ended up in the water. I imagine him fishing, drinking beer when he saw something bizarrely creepy floating overhead.

"Maybe the orb. Or maybe the red-eyed ghost, and he shot at it," I explain. "That was enough to send him into cardiac arrest."

"Well, it's Zain's fault too." Dorothy pounds the table like Judge Judy. "Let's not forget the chain of events he started when he ran poor Rowdy down and kept on going."

"Nothing is going to happen to him unless he confesses. And that will never happen," Benton predicts.

"We could go after him anyway," Marino offers.

"There's no evidence left, no case to make," Benton answers. "Calvin Willard had the vintage Cougar trucked away for repairs. He used Trad Whalen to help cover up what really happened, and nobody's going to talk."

"Well, both of them should go to jail for putting that hacking device on our car." I push back my chair.

"I'm not done with them yet," Benton promises, and we get up from the table.

In one minute, it will be midnight, and we gather close, holding up our glasses.

"A toast." Benton looks at each of us. "To justice."

We drink to that.

"And may the Phantom Slasher burn in hell where he belongs," Lucy says.

"Thank God," Dorothy slurs. "People can feel safe in their own beds again."

"You get rid of one serial killer," Marino singsongs, "only to have another to take his place."

"Let's hope he's convicted and locked up forever," Benton says. "He might get the death penalty, as vile as his crimes are."

"A jury's gonna hate him," Marino predicts. "Just the way he treated Peanut is enough to sway them."

"To Peanut!" Dorothy raises her glass again.

"To family. And to making things right." It's my turn.

"And to forgiveness." Benton looks at me. "We all make mistakes."

"Hell yeah we do! And I'm ready to make a few more!" Dorothy declares. "I'll drink to that."

"You'd drink to anything." Marino rubs the back of her neck. "Happy New Year." He kisses her.

"Oh, you know how much we love each other, you lunkhead." She clings to him.

"Yeah, I know."

"I was just giving Benton a taste of what he's missing." She kisses Marino hard.

"Don't do it again. Not with him, I mean," he tells her.

Benton and I kiss, holding each other close. Then everybody's hugging and happy as fireworks pop and crackle in Old Town.

**RAISING READERS**
Books Build Bright Futures

Dear Reader,

We'd love your attention for one more page to tell you about the crisis in children's reading, and what we can all do.

Studies have shown that reading for fun is the **single biggest predictor of a child's future life chances** – more than family circumstance, parents' educational background or income. It improves academic results, mental health, wealth, communication skills, ambition and happiness.[1]

The number of children reading for fun is in rapid decline. Young people have a lot of competition for their time. In 2024, 1 in 10 children and young people in the UK aged 5 to 18 did not own a single book at home.[2]

Hachette works extensively with schools, libraries and literacy charities, but here are some ways we can all raise more readers:

- Reading to children for just 10 minutes a day makes a difference
- Don't give up if children aren't regular readers – there will be books for them!
- Visit bookshops and libraries to get recommendations
- Encourage them to listen to audiobooks
- Support school libraries
- Give books as gifts

There's a lot more information about how to encourage children to read on our website: **www.RaisingReaders.co.uk**

Thank you for reading.

---

[1] OECD, '21st-Century Readers: Developing Literacy Skills in a Digital World', 2021, https://www.oecd.org/en/publications/21st-century-readers_a83d84cb-en.html

[2] National Literacy Trust, 'Book Ownership in 2024', November 2024, https://literacytrust.org.uk/research-services/research-reports/book-ownership-in-2024